THE CUCKOO'S BOYS

ROBERT REED

GOLDEN GRYPHON PRESS • 2005

"Abducted Souls," copyright © 2005 by Robert Reed. Previously un-published.

"The Children's Crusade," first published online on SCIFICTION, April 24, 2002.

"Coelacanths," first published in *The Magazine of Fantasy & Science Fiction*, March 2002.

"The Cuckoo's Boys," first published in *Science Fiction Age*, September 1998.

"First Tuesday," first published in *The Magazine of Fantasy & Science Fiction*, February 1996.

"Night of Time," first published in *The Silver Gryphon*, edited by Gary Turner and Marty Halpern, Golden Gryphon Press, 2003.

"On the Brink of That Bright New World," first published in *Asimov's Science Fiction*, January 1993.

"One Last Game," first published in *The Magazine of Fantasy & Science Fiction*, August 2001.

"River of the Queen," first published in *The Magazine of Fantasy & Science Fiction*, February 2004.

"Savior," first published in *Asimov's Science Fiction*, August 1998.

"She Sees My Monsters Now," first published in *Asimov's Science Fiction*, June 2002.

"Winemaster," first published in *The Magazine of Fantasy & Science Fiction*, July 1999.

"Afterword," copyright © 2005 by Robert Reed.

The Cuckoo's Boys copyright © 2005 by Robert Reed

Edited by Marty Halpern

LIBRARY OF CONGRESS CATALOGUING–IN–PUBLICATION DATA
Reed, Robert.
　　The Cuckoo's Boys / by Robert Reed. – 1st ed.
　　　　p.　　cm.
　　ISBN 1-930846-37-1 (hardcover : alk. paper)
　　　　1. Science fiction, American.　　I. Title.
PS3568.E369　C83　2005
813'.54—dc22　　　　　　　　2005008247

Printed in the United States of America.

First Edition

Contents

For Bill Kloefkorn

Acknowledgments

For help in the life of these stories and, inevitably, the life of this book, I must thank editors Ellen Datlow, Gardner Dozois, Scott Edelman, Ed Ferman, Gordon Van Gelder, and Marty Halpern and Gary Turner. And for their assistance in providing electronic files of some of these stories, special thanks to Ellen Datlow, Gordon Van Gelder, Brian Bieniowski at *Asimov's SF*, and Scott Pendergrast and Daniel Jorissen at Fictionwise.com.

The Cuckoo's Boys

On the Brink of That Bright New World

I KNOW HIM. HE'S THIS LITTLE OLD GUY SITTING alone, watching the countryside sliding past, and I keep thinking that I know his face. But from where? Soft white hair and soft hands, his suit meaning money. Not a fortune maybe, but enough. He's riding in first class because he paid. Not like me. He didn't slip in from the cattle cars, I'm thinking. And how the hell do I know him?

The weird thing is, every now and then I can practically hear his voice talking to me. *To me.*

And that's when it hits. I look past him, focusing on his window. It's thick and square and glass, sealed tight because we'll be passing through poisons soon, moving 200 miles an hour on magnet juice. And I start thinking how his window looks like an old-fashioned TV screen. Sort of. Which makes me think: Oh, sure. Sure! I remember the little guy. It's got to be him, and think of the odds! He used to be famous. For a little while. A scientist, some kind of astronomer. And a lucky shit for being in the right place, saying all the smart things, with everyone in the world watching him. That's the face all right. Not a doubt in my mind.

This is a huge chance, a huge risk, and it takes me a couple, three minutes to think things through. To get myself ready. Then I stand and go over to him, sitting beside him, saying, "Aren't you the one? The guy who said, 'We're on the edge of a bright new world'? I can't remember your name—"

"On the brink," he says. Then he says, "Cummings. Dr. Leonard Cummings."

"Oh, Cummings. Sure!" What'd he mean about "brink"? Then I remember. "On the *brink* of a bright new world." That's how he said it, and it seems like a million years ago.

He sort of fidgets, watching me and acting worried.

Which is fine.

I tell him, "My name's Steve," which it isn't. I make him shake my hand, acting like I'm glad to meet a famous guy. Then I tell him something out of left field. Something he'd never expect from a stranger in a train that's going to cross over radioactive lands. "I've got to give you a big thanks," I tell him. "You helped me out once, you and the other astronomers. You did me a whole bunch of favors that night."

That night.

He knows which night I mean. He can't really trust me—who am I?—but nobody turns away a compliment. It's something his mother probably taught him. He sits up straighter, eyes showing some light, and he says, "Well, I'm glad to hear it. A favor? It's good to know—"

"Some crazy night," I interrupt.

"Yes. Yes, it was interesting." The voice is the same one I remember. Smooth and soft. Cummings seems like the sort of guy who's never had to scream in his life. Who wouldn't know how if he had to. "It was quite a spectacular evening," he's saying. "Yes, sir."

"Crazy," I repeat.

"Thrilling," he says.

And I say, "Isn't that the truth?" while laughing hard. Enjoying myself.

Laughing and shaking my head until I worry him, then cutting it off. Boom. I turn dead silent, staring out his window. Then I tell him, "Do you want to hear about it."

Telling, not asking.

Cummings doesn't want to say, "No, I'd rather you didn't." He's not that sort. But he can't seem to tell me, "I want to hear it," either.

"It's a quick story," I promise. "All true."

He gives a little nod.

"Listen," I tell him.

And he does. I make sure he's looking at my eyes, listening because there's no choice. Because he's curious. Because I've got him scared. And while I'm talking the sun comes out from behind fat clouds, yellow light feeling warm and the air around us swimming with bits of dust. They're like tiny, tiny worlds, those bits. Twisting and twisting. Every time I speak, and every time one of us decides to breathe.

I was working in a factory back then. Back when we got to the brink of the new world. It was mostly an ordinary day. At the end of the first shift I called up my wife and said, "Listen. A couple guys from the next shift called in sick. Brown-bottle flu, I guess. And the foreman wants me to stay late tonight. Otherwise he's short bodies, he won't be able to run shit."

My wife said, "Yeah?"

"It's all time and a half," I told her.

She said, "Okay," with her voice flat. Dead. Then she said, "We could use the money all right."

What a bitch. That's what I was thinking then.

"So what are you doing tonight?" I asked. "Anything special?"

"I don't know," she said. "Talk on the phone, I suppose. Watch some TV or something."

"Just asking," I said.

And she said, "Hey, I know what you're thinking."

"That's good," I warned her. "So you remember it." Then I hung up on her. I slammed down the phone and walked over to the line. I was running the line that night, making the big money. Because we sure did need it. Meaning *she* needed it, the bitch. Always wanting more, just like all of them. Only more so with her. I was so busy thinking of her, talking to her in my head, that I didn't see the foreman come up. "Let's get going," he told me. As if pissed. Then he stood watching me, making sure that I started. The prick.

It was stupid work, running that line. Stupid but easy, and there was time to think. I started remembering how it was when I first married the girl. How I'd thought I was so goddamn lucky. We used to do it every night—I tell this to Cummings—and I wouldn't wash one of my hands afterward, smelling her on it the whole next day.

Everything started perfect. Everything always does, doesn't it?

Then I warn Cummings, "Never marry a beauty. Particularly if she's been spoiled sick since she was a kid." I tell him how a beauty fools you with her ass and her little tricks. A beauty makes you nuts and squeezes your nuts, laughing at you all the time and you not even knowing it.

Cummings sort of nods, hearing all of this.

The guys at the plant used to tease me. The assholes. They'd tell me that I had a fine, fine wife. They'd tell me they were jealous, and how'd it feel to be so lucky? So I'd tell them to fuck themselves. "Shut the fuck up," I'd say, "or we'll go a few rounds. Get me? Understand?"

She and me used to have fights. Pushing and shoving, and what could I do? Humans can't take more than so much. But you hit that sort of woman, and you're in trouble. You know? All you do is teach her that a little pop to the jaw doesn't kill, that she can wash herself clean and go to her mom's and plan new shit before she comes back home again. Then she's got you where she wants you. All over again, and what can you do?

It was like that that night. I couldn't stop thinking about how much she pissed me off.

And all the sudden the big red warning lights were flashing. It was dark outside by then. I saw their reflections in the window beside me. Machines were roaring, so I couldn't hear anything. I shut down the line, figuring that I must have fucked up. That I didn't watch what I was doing. *Her fault for distracting me.* Only when I walked up the line I didn't see anything broken or backed up. All I saw was the foreman and the other guys bunched around someone's ghetto blaster, listening with the sound cranked high. Of all the crazy shit, the news was playing. The news. And I asked what was what.

The foreman went, "Shush," with a finger on his mouth. "Shush."

The asshole.

Some woman was talking, her voice big and booming. Sounding real excited about something. She was saying something about pictures and how they started coming during the day, and they were coming from a long, long distance. Nobody knew from where, she said. A couple times. "Nobody knows their origin."

I asked someone, "What's happening?"

The guy said, "Aliens," and gave this big grin. "From outer space? They're beaming us messages, Steve."

"Aliens?" I said. Not believing it.

"Yeah," he swore. "Martians, or whatever."

How could I believe it? I said, "What do you mean, messages?"

The foreman said, "Photographs," and gave me a look. "The news is on every station. Astronomers just announced it." He shook his head and pushed the hair out of his eyes, then he was laughing. To himself.

I still didn't get it, and I said so.

So everyone jumped on me.

"ETs?" they said. "Little green men? From other fucking worlds?"

"They're sending us pictures?" I said.

"Like postcards," said one guy. "Like pretty postcards from Yellowstone, only they're from a lot farther away."

Everyone had a good laugh, then they went back to listening. And I was thinking: Screw you! Some new reporter was talking about alien landscapes, pretty but weird, and no, the scientists didn't know this world. It was circling a different sun, only there weren't any right-colored stars in the right place. The signals were coming from the middle of nothing, maybe light-years away. Then the reporter was talking about the new photos. Scientists were handing out big colored ones. Just as soon as they got them decoded.

It was some wild night, I was thinking.

First I'm doing a double shift, and then it's aliens. Slime monsters from space, and they're talking to us with pictures. As if we're kids too young and stupid to understand words.

The foreman was smiling, shaking his head and happy as a pig in shit. It took him forever to send us back to work. I could tell he'd rather be home, sitting in front of the TV. This was big stuff for him. But finally he sent me up front to start things up again, and we worked straight to the supper break. No interruptions. Then we stopped for our usual long half-hour. I bought pop and some candy bars, and I watched the foreman sitting by the radio, eyes big and round, someone describing some kind of foamy lake with critters swimming on top. Big fins and white spouts, and the voice was saying how this was history in the making, and lovely, our first look at another world and that sort of noise.

The foreman couldn't take it anymore. He turned and swallowed, making a show of things. Getting up his courage. "I'm feeling sick," he told us. Then he halfway coughed. "I must have gotten that flu bug." He looked straight at us, saying, "You can't run without everyone, so I guess we're done. All right?"

Everyone nodded, glad to hear it.

"Clean up," he told us, "and get out of here. I'm going home and throw up." And then he grabbed his stomach, trying to fool somebody. As if anyone gave a good hard shit.

Leaving was great, I tell Cummings. The way I figured it, I was tired enough and rich enough for one night. Besides, nobody was going to chew *my* ass come morning. I wasn't the one who'd have to explain orders left undone, so what did I care?

Outside it was cool and dark. And clear. I remember the drive home in my pickup, the radio off, the roads almost empty. It felt like late, late Sunday night. No bars open. Everyone indoors. Everyone in the world was watching TV, except me. And my wife. She was home because her car was in the driveway, but when I pulled in behind her I heard the stereo playing. Screaming. The stereo I'd bought her with my time and a half, and she was trying to blow the speakers or some such shit.

Lights were blazing away in the living room. I came in and shut the door, halfway looking around. She was down in the basement or in the back somewhere. Not watching the big news, that's for sure. I pulled off my boots and hit the remote, thinking: Would it be something if she didn't know? I could spring the news on her, painting it up real good. Aliens? She'd call me nuts. A liar, and worse. She'd wonder if I got kicked out of work for fighting. Was that it? And me watching her face when she saw it was true. All true. I'd know something she didn't, and screw you, lady. Screw you!

They were showing one of the alien pictures just then. On TV. A bunch of buildings on a wooded hillside, the sky full of sunset colors and thin clouds and some kind of faraway airplane or space-ship gleaming up high. Then the buildings got larger. Closer. I couldn't hear shit for the music, but I could see fine. I still remember all of it. The buildings had steep roofs and star-shaped windows. Five-pointed stars. And there was a fat old tree in the middle of them. The tree trunk looked like a mess of heavy-duty ropes twisted around each other, and there weren't any leaves on the branches. Just wads of blue-green spongelike crap. Except even knowing it was a different world didn't help. Aliens? I kept thinking of China or somewhere. Maybe someplace somebody had invented, the whole thing someone's fancy big-time joke.

Then the stereo quit. It was between songs, the house all quiet, and I could hear people. They were talking on TV, then some-where else too. More than one. Just for a second, I could hear them.

I sort of froze.

I could hear talking, movements, and I got a weird feeling that made me hold my breath and do nothing. I froze up inside, waiting, and finally I made myself start thinking again. I tried to decide what to do.

When the next song was hammering, I slipped into the hallway and next to the big bedroom. The door was mostly open. I could see the mirror over her chest of drawers. My wife's back was in the mirror, long and brown except where her tiny swimsuit needed straps. Her back was moving up and down, up and down. Then I saw a big hand and a hairy forearm sliding up her back, and the hand pulled around to the front. Enjoying a tit, I suppose. But then again, she had beauties. And when that happened someone made a noise. Her. Him. Maybe me. Which was when I backed into the living room again, my heart trying to fill up my chest with its pounding blood.

I wasn't thinking anymore.

Maybe I wasn't even surprised. I don't know. All I remember is wanting to be outside, putting distance between her and me. I pulled on my boots before the song finished, getting out without being heard. Then I remembered the TV being on, and what if they noticed? Fuck them, I thought. So what? I got as far as climbing partway into my pickup, and that's when I got an idea. I stopped where I was. Looking up at the stars, I was breathing hard, feeling the sweat soaking my clothes. Then I started walking, not fast, going around back and through the gate and the patio door, into the little bedroom where I kept my hunting gear. Where I had some pistols.

One gun was this little thing I used on squirrels, on targets. A .22, that's all. I wanted to scare them. I'd wave it at them and make them crazy. Maybe I'd put a shot over their heads, I was thinking. But that was it. Whatever it took to be heard.

I walked down the hallway feeling nothing. Just nothing. It was like floating, all dreamy, not really touching the floor and my legs moving out of habit. Going easy and slow. And I came through the doorway with the lovers still banging. Right with the music, I tell Cummings. And me floating above the floor, just watching. I was there maybe a week before my wife noticed, looking back over her shoulder and halfway surprised, halfway smiling. Her pretty face was sweaty, and what she did was the biggest mistake possible. Smiling with her pretty mouth. Opening that pretty mouth. Saying with it, "Home early, huh dear? Or'd they fire your stupid ass?"

✳   ✳   ✳

I stop talking, and Cummings keeps very quiet.

He's scared and maybe a little confused. We've gotten out of what he knows, all right. This isn't stars and gravity, and none of this comes to him naturally.

I don't tell him what happened.

All I say is, "Afterward," and then wait. Then I start again, telling him, "I went back in the living room afterward and turned off the stereo, and I sat down and watched TV. Sort of. That's probably where I saw you first. I remember you, I'm pretty sure, sitting with a couple other science types, plus this old broad, everyone talking about the pictures. Fighting about what they meant and why. I can't remember what you said, but you understand. I was feeling kind of wrung out." I give him a little smile. "Go figure."

Cummings nods a little, then says, "I happened to be near the studio. They wanted an astronomer with exobiology interests, and they caught me at my hotel. I was visiting town. Pure chance."

"Oh, sure," I say.

"Anyone could have been called. It was my luck, that's all."

"Hey, don't apologize to me!"

"But we weren't fighting," he says. It's a big deal to him. "I remember that round-table discussion. We weren't fighting. It was a creative debate—"

"Hey," I warn him, "who's telling what?"

And he shuts up. I've got him more scared than anything, and it's fun. A lot more fun than I'd ever guessed it would be.

I tell him about the mountain pictures, a string of them being shown while I sat there. They were my favorites, I claim. Big green mountains, real rough, looking like great deer country. The sort of place you could hide in for years. One scientist talked about that world having more gravity than Earth, him judging by the mountain shapes and the thick trees. Then the woman said it was warmer, judging by the sun angles and whatnot.

Clues were everywhere. That's what the four of them kept saying, over and over again. The pictures were full of clues about the aliens and their world, and it was just a matter of finding them and knowing what they were.

"It was like you were warning me," I tell him.

He looks at me.

"Thanks."

He stays quiet, eyes dropping now.

I had a couple big-ass clues in my bedroom, dead and bleeding, and I started telling myself to get up and do something. To start hiding the clues before someone began missing someone.

And all the time there were new pictures. Rivers and beaches and strange birds and bugs up close. Then came the first pictures of the aliens themselves—

"I'll never forget that moment," Cummings mutters.

—with their four legs each, like big dogs, and each of them raising four arms at the cameras. All very weird. The hands seemed awfully human. And their faces were halfway normal too. They looked like sick people with sky-blue hair and funny yellow eyes. Lab dog eyes. Friendly and happy, and always watching you. That's how they've always seemed to me.

My stomach started hurting, but finally I made myself stand and get to work. I found some old tarps in the basement, plus clothesline ropes with wire cores. Then I went around the house pulling drapes closed and collecting shit. "Clues are everywhere," I kept telling myself. I got the bodies and the bloody bedding, sure. Plus cigarettes and any strange clothes. Everything went inside the tarps. I didn't know loverboy, but I went through his wallet a couple times. He lived on the other side of town. There wasn't any strange car parked nearby, so I figured my wife must have brought him. Or he'd walked partway. I decided what I needed was to make it look as if she'd run away. That's why I loaded up a suitcase with her clothes, plus her best purse and most of her jewelry. Stuff she'd always taken when she ran off to her mom's. Then I threw in my pistol and wrapped the tarps up like Christmas presents. Four tarps altogether. Everything tied and tied again and then tied a third time too.

The loading was a bitch. I pulled my pickup into the back yard, every light off, then tried not to make noise. Which was tough. I nearly shit my pants when I carried loverboy. I knew where I'd take them—I had this perfect place all planned—and after them I loaded up a bunch of concrete blocks. *She* had wanted me to build a grill with those blocks. Which is funny. Then I shut the back end —*wham*—and drove back around her little car, out onto the street and down the block before turning my headlights on.

Being careful didn't matter.

Nobody was out. Nobody noticed. The world was too busy, leaving me alone, and it was pretty much perfect. I couldn't have asked for a better night. Not ever.

There were some gravel pits near the river. I knew one pit was just abandoned, and I tell Cummings about my plan. I'm hoping that he's impressed with what I did. Those fresh pits slough off their sandy sides, getting shallower and wider and burying their floors. I drove up next to the one pit and dropped the tarps in one at a time: the bedding and other shit. Then loverboy. Then my wife last. I stood there on the brink of a deep hole, watching the sand fall in after her. Listening to it move, that dry living sound that sand makes. Thinking how this was the easiest thing she'd ever done for me, dropping fast into the cold dead water. No fuss at all. And afterward I drove home, going nice and easy. Just out for a drive, I'd tell any cops. And wasn't it some day? Some day! If they stopped me I'd ask if they had heard about the aliens calling to us, and wasn't that something? Pretty neat, I'd tell them. Pretty god-damn neat!

"This is real," says Cummings. Softly. Almost without talking out loud. "You're confessing it to me, aren't you?"

"I guess so," I say. "Only you don't know me. You don't know where this happened. I get off this train, and there's no way you can find me again. What can you do? Wrestle me down? You?"

He sits still, looking smaller and older. He has a hurt face, sad for a lot of reasons. Sad to be here now. Sad to know what he knows. Sad for my dead wife, I suppose, and her boyfriend too. And probably a bigger sadness. He starts looking out the thick window, the country getting wilder, full of weeds nobody cuts and empty houses falling down on themselves. Poisoned country and the ninth year of the Depression. There's a new war starting in the Far East, and the old one in Russia is heating up again. Cummings seems ready to die from all his sadness, but he doesn't. Instead he looks back at me, asking, "Don't you ever regret doing what you did?"

"Regret what? Being patient with the bitch? Waiting that long to take care of business?" I laugh out loud, telling him, "I had a few bad dreams, but those were years ago. No, I'm fine. I'm happy. Almost perfect, if you want to know."

He almost looks at my eyes, asking, "What did the police do?"

"To me?"

"I'm assuming they didn't convict you."

"They didn't even try." I laugh again. "Sure they suspected me. Her mom suspected me. Anyone could put together the basics for themselves. But they couldn't find evidence. Not one good clue. You see, it was days before the police started checking. By then I'd cleaned the bedroom fifty times. By then—maybe you remember this—a whole lot of people were missing, what with the craziness. Pure craziness. It was like a big party everywhere after those pictures came. There were all kinds of runaways and divorces, everyone sure that the aliens were about to land and make everything right. Just by snapping their fingers."

"But they weren't coming," he tells me. He talks louder, saying, "The aliens made it clear they weren't—"

"I know, I know."

"They were transmitting from light-years away. Their only message was fixed to the last photograph. Their only words. 'We wish you good fortune. We wish you peace.' "

"I know how it goes."

"In fifty-two languages," he tells me. "They must have eavesdropped on our television broadcasts, learning about us. They were very forthright in telling us that they weren't going to intrude on our lives. 'We do not wish to distort the precious patterns of your societies.' They sent photographs and that one brief message, and people were foolish to expect spaceships. They wouldn't listen to us. . . !"

I say, "Sure."

"The aliens knew better than to come and change things."

And I say, "Except they did. Distort things, I mean."

"Not intentionally," he says real soft. But with anger too. It's as if he's defending the yellow-eyed critters, telling me, "The craziness, as you termed it, was short-lived."

"Oh, sure."

"Nothing major was altered," he says.

"Unless you ask my wife," I tell him.

He looks at me, then at his knees. Angrier now.

"Anyway," I say, "that's what happened. A few days later the police came and asked about my wife. Her mom was worried about her. I told them we had a fight and I left, and when I got back she was gone. I didn't know where to. 'Not her mom's house, huh? Well, that's odd. You don't suppose something bad has happened to her?' "

He's listening but pretending not to hear. He's taking everything to heart, even better than I'd hoped. I know it because he starts dropping tears now. Runny little tears on the white old face.

"They came back eventually and searched my house. My truck. Talked to my neighbors, but what could they know? My little pistol couldn't be heard over the stereo, and anyone awake had been watching TV that night. There wasn't time to snoop on neighbors, and thank you." I'm talking to Cummings now. "I mean it. Thanks for distracting everybody. Thanks for all your help!"

The man bends lower, almost crumbling.

"They never found the bodies. There were ties between my wife and loverboy, but he'd vanished too. And what could they prove? No clues for them, just guesses."

Cummings makes a low sound, then nothing.

"So I just wanted to come over and say, 'Hi!' You gave me my big chance. You and the other scientists got me home early in the first place. If it wasn't for you, I'd have finished my shift and gone home and slept in that bed without guessing any of it."

He shuts his eyes and holds them shut.

"I saw you," I say. "When you said the famous words? It was morning. I was getting ready to go back to work, trying to keep everything normal. And you told the cameras, 'We're on the brink of a bright new world.' "

He gives a little nod.

"All because some aliens were sending us postcards from space." I wait a second, then I say, "You know what postcards are, don't you? They're things you send when you don't want to spend much time. You write a couple nice words on them, and people think good things about you."

He looks at me, his eyes big and strange.

"Anyway," I say, "thanks again for everything. I mean it."

And he tells me, "You're welcome," and takes a huge breath, holding tight to it. Not wanting to let it go, not for anything.

The Children's Crusade

If one tallies weekly allowances, part-time employment, birthday and holiday gifts, as well as limited trusts, the children of the world wield an annual income approaching one trillion NA dollars. Because parents and an assortment of social service organizations supply most of their basic needs, that income can be considered discretionary. Discretionary income always possesses an impact far beyond its apparent value. And even more important, children are more open than adults when it comes to radical changes in spending habits, and in their view of the greater world.

Please note: We have ignored all income generated through gambling, prostitution, the sale of drugs and stolen merchandise, or currency pilfered from a parent's misplaced wallet.

We need to conspicuously avoid all questionable sources of revenue . . . at least for the present . . .

—Crusade memo, confidential

THE PREGNANCY COULDN'T HAVE BEEN EASIER, and then suddenly, it couldn't have been worse.

We were still a couple weeks away from Hanna's due date. By chance, I didn't have an afternoon class, which was why I drove her to the doctor's office. The checkup was supposed to be entirely routine. Her OB was a little gray-haired woman with an easy smile and an autodoc aide. The doctor's eyes were flying down a list of numbers—the nearly instantaneous test results derived from a drop of blood and a sip of amniotic fluid. It was the autodoc who actually touched Hanna, probing her belly with pressure and sound, an elaborate and beautiful and utterly confusing three-dimensional image blooming in the room's web-window. I've never been sure which professional found the abnormality. Doctors and their aides have always used hidden signals. Even when both of them were human, one would glance at the other in a certain way, giving the warning, and the parents would see none of it, blissfully unaware that their lives were about to collapse.

Some things never change.

It was our doctor who said, "Hanna," with the mildest of voices. Then showing the barest smile, she asked, "By any chance, did you have a cold last week?"

My wife was in her late forties. A career woman and single for much of her life, she delayed menopause so that we could attempt a child. This girl. Our spare bedroom was already set up as a nursery, and two baby showers had produced a mountain of gifts. That's one of the merits of waiting to procreate to the last possible moment; you have plenty of friends and grateful relatives with money to spend on your unborn child. And as I mentioned, it had been a wondrously easy pregnancy. Hanna has never been a person who suffers pain well or relishes watching her body deformed beyond all recognition. But save for some minor aches and the persistent heartburn, it had been a golden eight-plus months, and that's probably why Hanna didn't hear anything alarming in that very simple question.

"A cold?" she said. Then she glanced in my direction, shrugging. "Just a little one. There and gone in a couple days. Wasn't it, Wes?"

I looked at our doctor.

I said, "Just a few sniffles."

"Well," our doctor replied. Then she glanced at her aide, the two of them conversing on some private channel.

Finally, almost grudgingly, Hanna grew worried, taking a deep breath and staring down at her enormously swollen belly.

Seeing her concern, I felt a little more at ease.

Someone had to be.

Then our doctor put on a confident face, and a lifetime of experience was brought to bear. "Well," she said again, her voice acquiring a motherly poise. "There is a chance, just a chance, that this bug wasn't a cold virus. And since the baby could be in some danger—"

"Oh, God," Hanna whimpered.

"I think we need to consider a C-section. Just to be very much on the safe side."

"God," my wife moaned.

My temporary sense of well-being was obliterated. With a gasp, I asked, "What virus? What chance?"

"A C-section?" Hanna blurted. "God, when?"

The doctor looked only at her. "Now," she answered. And then with an authoritarian nod of the head, she added, "And we really should do it here."

"Not at the hospital?" Hanna muttered.

"Time is critical," the doctor cautioned. "If this happens to be a strain of the Irrawaddy—"

"Oh, shit—"

"I know. It sounds bad. But even if that bug is the culprit, you're so far along in the pregnancy, and you have a girl, and the girls seem to weather this disease better than the boys—"

"What chance?" I blurted. "What are we talking about here?"

The autodoc supplied my answer. With a smooth voice and a wet nurse's software, it told me, "The odds of infection are approximately one in two. And if it was the Irrawaddy virus, the odds of damage to a thirty-nine-week fetus are less than three in eleven."

Our doctor would have preferred to deliver that news. Even in my panic, I noticed the bristling in her body language. But she kept her poise. Without faltering, she set her hand on my wife's hand. I think that was the first time during the visit that she actually touched Hanna. And with a reassuring music, she said, "We're going to do our best. For you and for your daughter."

About that next thirty minutes, I remember everything.

There was a purposeful sprint by nurses and autodocs as well as by our doctor and her two human partners. The largest examination room was transformed into a surgical suite, every surface sterilized with bursts of ionized radiation and withering desiccants. Hanna was plied with tubes and fed cocktails of medicines and microsensors. Needing something to do, I sent a web-flash to family and friends, carefully downplaying my worsening fears. And then I was wrapped inside a newly made gown and cap and led into the suite, finding Hanna already laid out on a table with her arms spread wide and tied down at the wrists. Some kind of medical crucifixion was in progress. She was sliced open, a tidy hole at her waist rimmed with burnt blood and bright white fat. I could smell the blood. I overheard the doctor warning Hanna about some impending pressure. And all the while, the autodoc worked over her, those clean sleek limbs moving with an astonishing speed and a perfect, seamless grace.

Thirty seconds later, my daughter was born.

With a nod to custom, our doctor was allowed to cut the cord.

Then both professionals worked with my daughter, stealing bits of skin and blood for tests, and in another few moments—a few hours, it felt like—they decided that Hanna's cold had been a cold and nothing more.

The autodoc began gluing my wife back together, and with a congratulatory smile, the doctor handed my baby to me. Veronica, named after her mother's mother. I had just enough time to show the screaming baby to Hanna, and then the ambulance arrived, flying the three of us to a hospital room where we could start coming to terms with the changes in our lives.

Veronica slept hard for hours, swaddled tight in a little blanket infused with helpful bacteria and proven antibodies. Hanna drifted into a shallow sleep, leaving me alone. I was holding my child, and the room's web-window was wandering on its own, searching for items that might interest me, and there was this odd little news item about a fifteen-year-old boy in France—a bright and handsome young man blessed with rich parents and a flair for public speaking. Standing in a mostly empty auditorium, Philippe Rule was announcing the launch of some kind of private space program.

It involved Mars, I halfway heard.

But honestly, I wasn't paying attention. I was too busy holding my happy, healthy daughter, watching her eyes twitch as she dreamed her secret dreams.

Three times in the last twenty years, the great dream of humanity has been attempted:

A manned mission to Mars.

The Americans were first, and by some measures, they had the greatest success. Seven astronauts completed the voyage, only to discover that their lander was inoperative. Repairs were attempted while in Martian orbit, but with the launch window closing and limited supplies on hand, the mission had to be canceled. An American flag was dropped on Olympus Mons, pledges were made to return soon, and, after several months in deep space and a string of catastrophic mechanical failures, three of the original crew returned home alive.

Four years later, the European Union sent nineteen astronauts inside a pair of elaborate motherships. One of the mission's twin landers exploded during its descent, but the other lander managed to reach the surface. Photographs made from orbit show a squat, buglike machine tilted at an unnatural angle, its landing gear mired in an unmapped briny seepage. At least one of its crew managed to climb out of the airlock, crossing a hundred meters of the Martian surface. Then she sat on a windswept boulder and opened the faceplate, letting her life boil away.

The Chinese mission was the most expensive, and ambitious, and, in the end, it was the most frustrating. The nuclear-powered rocket was intended to solve the difficulties of past missions. The voyage to Mars would consume only two weeks. With the added thrust, a wealth of supplies and spare parts could be carried along, and the inevitable problems of muscle and bone atrophy would be avoided.

Depending on circumstances, the crew would stay on Mars for as long or as briefly as needed, exploring various sites while building the first structures in a permanent settlement.

Unfortunately, the ship that held so much promise survived only sixty-five minutes. A flaw in the reaction chamber triggered a catastrophic series of accidents, culminating in that brief, awful flash that lit up our night sky.

Since that tragedy, no nation or group of nations has found the courage, much less the money, to attempt a fourth mission.

This is wrong.

These countries, and the adults who lead them, are cowards.

Mars is out there. Mars is waiting, and we know it. It is a new world, and it is wonderfully empty, and you want to go there. I know that's what you want. You dream about walking in its red dust, and exploring its dry riverbeds, and building castles out of its red rock, and hunting for alien fossils. Or better still, you want to find living Martians hiding in some deep canyon or under the floor of an old sea . . .

I know you.

You want to do what your parents couldn't do.

Help me! Together, let's do this one great thing! If you give me just a little money . . . a week's allowance, or what the tooth fairy leaves under your pillow tonight . . . then maybe you will be one of the lucky ones chosen for the next mission!

The mission that succeeds!

—Philippe Rule, from the announcement

I love my little sister, but it's hard to imagine us as sharing parents. We don't look alike—she is a wispy blonde while I am stocky and dark. Our interests and temperaments have always been different. And in most ways, we don't think alike. Both of us married for love, but it was a foregone conclusion that Iris's spouse would have money. Where Hanna and I have a comfortable little home, Iris needs two enormous houses, plus a brigade of AI servants to keep both homes pretty and clean. Instead of having one child late in life, Iris started early, producing five of the rascals. Being a parent is everything to my sister: She hovers over her babies and babies her children as they grow older. Every birthday is a daylong celebration, and every holiday is a golden opportunity to spoil her children while flaunting her husband's wealth. By contrast, I've always forgotten birthdays, and Christmas is an insufferable burden. I don't approve of outrageous gifts. Yet with a distinct and embarrassing selfishness, I wish she would send some of her wealth my way.

She is my only sister, and how can anything be easy between us?

I love my nephews and nieces, but according to Iris, I have never shown the proper interest in them.

Tom was her middle-born—an undersized kid with a bright, overly serious manner and a real talent for getting whatever he wanted. When he was eight years old, he decided that he wanted money for Christmas. Nothing but. He pushed hard for months, pleading and arguing, and begging, and generally making his parents miserable. And even when they surrendered, his demands didn't stop.

"He won't accept even one present," his mother complained to me. "Not from anyone. He says he'll throw any package into the fire."

"Give him fireworks," was my snappy advice.

Iris put her arms around herself, and shuddered.

Then with a more serious tone, I offered, "Cash is good. I always liked getting it when we were kids."

"I didn't," my sister snarled.

In secret, I was admiring the boy's good sense. His mother's gifts tended toward the fancy and the lame, and after a day of fitful abuse, the new toys usually ended up inside some cavernous closet, forgotten.

"This is our deal," Iris continued. "Every relative puts money into a common account, and Tom buys himself something. A real gift."

It was Christmas Eve. Hanna and I had flown into town that

afternoon, bringing our baby girl. "So you want me to throw in a few dollars?"

Iris blinked, and a tension revealed itself. She looked thinner than normal, nervous and pretty in equal measures. As if in pain, she winced, and then with a stiff voice, she admitted, "He really likes you."

"Tom does?"

"He adores you, a little bit."

I always thought the kid was high-strung and spoiled. But everybody likes to hear that someone adores him.

"I told him you'd help. Help him pick a real gift."

I halfway laughed. "Okay. I don't understand any of this."

"This is part of our deal. We aren't going to let him just throw his money away on something stupid."

" 'His money,' " I quoted.

Iris missed my point.

So I told her, "You're not negotiating with the Teamsters here. This is an eight-year-old child. Your child."

Iris was four years my junior. But there were moments when she looked older than me, her youthful beauty tested by childbirth and the burdens that followed. Her face had a paleness, brown eyes rimmed with blood. I saw the cumulative wear and tear. For an instant, I almost felt sorry for her. But then she looked at Veronica sitting in her bouncy seat, purring and blabbering. And with a cold menace, my sister warned me, "You wait, Wes. Wait. You think you know things, but you'll see how hard kids can be."

I nearly said an honest word or two. But a lingering pity kept me quiet.

Iris decided to smile, using her own brand of begging. "I want your help. Would you do this one favor for me?"

Grudgingly, I shrugged my shoulders, and with a whiff of genuine pain, I muttered, "Why not?"

It was a very peculiar Christmas. Four children and an assortment of adults sat at the center of a cavernous living room, tearing open dozens of brightly colored packages, and in the midst of that relentless greed sat one little boy, nothing in his hand but a small Season's Greetings card and a piece of paper on which nothing was written but an account number and two passwords. Yet the boy was the happiest soul there. Even while his siblings built mountains out of the shredded paper and luminescent ribbons, my nephew clung to his single gift, grinning with the pure and virtuous pleasure of a genuine believer.

Once the gift-grab was finished, he approached me, whispering, "Uncle Wes? Can we go now?"

"Sure," I purred.

The family web-room was at the back of the house. With an unconscious ease, Tom took us to a popular mall. A thousand toyshops lined themselves up before us. But he hesitated. Turning abruptly, he spotted his mother watching from the hallway. "Go away!" he shouted. "You told me I could do this myself! Leave us alone!"

I will never let a child of mine talk that way to any adult. But honestly, I felt a shrill little pleasure watching my sister slink away, vanishing inside the illusion of a candy factory.

Tom turned to me and smiled. With a bottled-up joy, he admitted, "I want to go to Mars."

I didn't understand, and I said so.

"Mars," he repeated. "If I give enough, and if I'm a good enough astronaut, I can go there."

The last few months had been a blur. Between taking care of a newborn and teaching a full class load, I hadn't found the time to keep up with the affairs of the world.

"Explain this Mars business to me," I said.

"This is my money," Tom replied, clinging to his tiny piece of paper.

All at once he was this earnest and pleasantly goofy little kid, buoyed up by his relentless enthusiasm. "Pretend that I'm stupid," I suggested, feeling a sudden affection for the goof. "Explain everything to me. From the start."

With a passion that I hadn't mustered in decades, the boy told me all about Philippe Rule. He described a future mission to Mars and all the good neat stuff that would come from it. Millions of kids had already given money; he would have to hurry to catch up. And then he told me how the Rule Project would use the money to build rockets and habitats and spacesuits—all that good neat stuff you had to have if you were going to travel across millions of miles of space.

"Okay," I said. "But why do *you* get to go to Mars?"

"A lot of kids are going," he countered. "Uncle Wes, there's going to be dozens and dozens of us—"

"Out of millions and millions," I cautioned.

"I know that," he claimed.

And I explained, "A million is a lot of people, Tom. If Philippe takes just one kid out of a million, what are your odds going to be?"

Eight-year-olds don't believe in odds. Feelings matter, and this eight-year-old had the sudden feeling that I was going to fight him. "This is my money," he repeated, waving that piece of paper under my nose. "I can do what I want with my own money!"

My affections wavered.

Quietly, I asked, "How much money is it?"

He showed the account number to a scanner, and after reading both passwords aloud, an account balance appeared before us.

I was appalled. My few dollars dangled at the end of that king's ransom.

"I know Mars won't be easy," Tom offered. "But I'm going to work hard. I'm going to be one of those astronauts."

"What else happens?" I asked.

He didn't understand.

"Your mother's going to ask to see your gift," I said. "What are you going to show her?"

He had a ready answer.

"This," he said, punching in a new address. An instant later, we were standing on the surface of Mars. Beneath us was the eroded channel of an ancient river, its sediments peppered with tiny shell-fish. A towering rocket stood before us, sleek and silvery against the dusty sky. Downstream from us was a crystal-domed city, implausible and lovely, a thousand little homes gathered around a pink-face lake—some tiny portion of the ancient Martian seas reborn inside a digital dream.

"I get to come here," my nephew gleefully reported. "Because I'm giving them money, I can walk anywhere on Mars. I'll meet kids like me. While I'm here, I'll train to be an astronaut. And there's classes about the planets, and games, and I'll learn every-thing about space and science and things like that."

The illusionary Mars was astonishingly vivid, and for a middle-aged biology professor, it was a little unsettling.

"She'll think it's okay, Uncle Wes. If you like it, and tell her so . . ."

Honestly, I was curious. Even a little intrigued. I took a weak breath, halfway expecting to find the air suffocatingly thin and brutally cold. Then with a defeated laugh, I said, "Sure." I put a hand on his bony little shoulder, telling him, "I guess I don't see the harm."

Web-Mars is perched at the limits of representational technol-ogy. Millions of square kilometers have been created, using data from automated probes, telescopic observations, and Martian meteorites. But scientific accuracy cannot be our primary goal. This must be an optimistic, unlikely Mars. An elaborate fossil record waits inside the digital stone, describing a world that has been wet and warm for most of an interesting history. The dangers of hard radiation and peroxide poisoning are being ignored. Engineering problems will always be minimized. For example, terraforming will prove to be an easy trick. Over the next few years, the children will help build a shallow blue sea and a breathable atmosphere. Selected children—gifted in money or in ability—will have the opportunity to find buried tombs and other alien artifacts. Did Mars once produce intelligent life? Or did visitors from a distant sun set down beside its muddy rivers, leaving important traces of their passing?

Web-Mars will be an entertaining and gentle realm.

When children dream of Mars, this is the Mars they will see. This is the world they will believe in. This is what it will take to inspire them—for a day, or a year, or in some cases, for the rest of their lives.

—Crusade memo, confidential

"Have you seen her?"

"Very?" I asked.

"I thought she was with you," Hanna explained. Then she sighed in exasperation, and with her hands around her mouth, she called out, "Very! Where are you?"

The playroom was enormous, and it looked empty. But you could never be sure. I walked twice through the armies of toys before my sister finally drifted into view, mentioning, "She's in the web-room with Tom. Sorry, I forgot to tell you."

"Thanks," I growled.

With a hard stare, Hanna delivered my marching orders.

It had been a difficult visit. My mother was dying, and most of my sister's kids had been perfect brats. Three days of uninterrupted rain hadn't helped anyone's mood. Plus Hanna and I didn't appreciate watching our five-year-old growing accustomed to this new life of abundance and anarchy. The sole exception was Tom. We only saw him at the dinner table, and he was nothing but polite, pleasantly uninvolved with the rest of his chaotic family.

I found the web-room open but guarded by a visual fog and the image of a handsome, suspicious young man. With a thin French accent, the man asked, "May I help you, sir?"

"My daughter's here."

"Is Veronica your daughter?"

I wasn't in a patient mood. I said, "Drop the screens. I want to see her."

Philippe Rule broke into a sudden smile. "She's a very bright girl, sir. You should feel proud—"

I stepped through the doppelgänger, finding myself climbing stairs onto some kind of platform. No, it was a boat—a simple, square aerogel raft drifting in the midst of a smooth ocean. In every direction, I saw the close horizon and a patchwork of thin clouds. The air tasted of saltwater and fish. The gravity had to be Earth's, but when I took my next step, the scene moved, producing a powerful illusion that sixty kilograms of meat and fat had been stolen from me.

It was almost fun.

And then I realized that I couldn't see anyone else. Hands on hips, I screamed, "Very! Come here! Very! Where are you?"

The fictional water splashed, and my daughter burst to the surface. Giggling, she grabbed at the raft and crawled up. She was wearing both a skintight stimsuit as well as one of her girl-cousin's old swimsuits, and she looked thoroughly soaked. But when I touched her, she felt dry and cool.

For no good reason, I said, "You can't swim without an adult."

"Daddy," she snapped. "This isn't water. So I wasn't."

Ignoring her seamless logic, I asked, "What have you been doing?"

"Watching."

"Watching what?"

"The fish!" Very was a small five-year-old with an infectious laugh and easy smile. Tugging on my arm, she told me, "You should see them, Daddy! They're pretty, and funny, and neat-strange!"

Curiosity licked at me.

But then Tom broke the surface, arms and legs pretending to swim as he came closer to the illusionary boat. I understood most of the trickery. But I barely saw the stimsuits, and the smart-wires were almost invisible. I had no idea how the AIs could so perfectly anticipate his every flail and kick, moving his thirteen-year-old body over to the ladder.

"Here it comes!" he cried out.

What was coming?

With a coarseness born from youth and excitement, he screamed, "Damn, it's a monster . . . shit. . . !"

A scaly head broke the surface. I saw jaws longer than I was tall, and great fishy eyes, and then a ropy body twisted, propelling the apparition past the raft, the long head dipping for an instant, bringing up a rainbow-colored fish with three eyes and a peculiar ventral gill.

For an instant, I was a biologist studying these marvels.

But then fatherhood reclaimed me. I kneeled and looked at my daughter, touching her again on that wet-looking, perfectly dry shoulder. "You know," I growled. "When you go somewhere, you have to tell us first."

"I'm still in the house, Daddy."

Here was the heart of it. To her old father, web-Mars was a separate place—a peculiar and potentially dangerous realm that happened to be a whole lot closer than the real Mars.

Ignoring my daughter's argument, I looked at her cousin. "Don't," I warned Tom. "Very's mother and I don't want her involved with this project. So I'm telling you: Don't bring her here again."

"Why not?" Thirteen and full of opinions, Tom grinned in an aggravating way. "All these things," he said. "These fish and plesiosaur and everything . . . they all come from fossil DNA—"

"No," I interrupted.

But he couldn't hear me. Dancing to the edge of the raft, the boy shook his dry leg, scattering slow drops. "I know this place, Uncle Wes. Better than anyone. You'd like it here. There's an old starship on the beach over there, and it's full of neat games and puzzles . . . I could take you, as my guest . . . if you want . . ."

With a quiet fury, I told my nephew, "Mars is nothing like this."

He stared at me. He seemed appalled, and then in the next instant, he was laughing at me.

"On its warmest day," I explained, "Mars was a very cold place. The old seas were covered with ice. Life was scarce, and it was single-celled, and there's absolutely no reason to think we could find starships there."

He laughed again, dismissing me with a sturdy shake of his head. "How do you know, Uncle Wes? Have you ever gone to Mars?"

I took my daughter by the hand.

"I'll be going there," he reported, nothing about his voice or manner betraying the slightest doubt.

"Good for you," I told him.

Then I hauled Very and myself out of the room.

Philippe Rule waved good-bye to both of us. "It was nice meeting you, Veronica," he called out. "And I hope to see you again."

Truthfully, it never occurred to me that so many people would take offense with my work, and myself . . . these malicious ideas that my intentions are impure, or selfish . . . that all I want is to steal money from their children, or enslave them in some vague fashion . . .

   But of course, I was a boy when this great adventure began.

   Boys don't know much about anything, except for their own hearts . . .

—Philippe Rule, interview

"This is the first year," I mentioned.

"The first for what?" Hanna asked.

"I'm actually noticing them," I told her. "At school. In my classes."

"Okay, I'll bite. Who are you talking about?"

"Rule's kids." I blanked my reader and set it on the nightstand. "This year's freshmen had to be twelve, maybe thirteen, when Rule got rolling. Older kids were too skeptical, or too something, to buy into this business."

Hanna let her reader fall to her lap, saying nothing.

"If they were fourteen and older . . . I guess there were too many hormones raging inside them, keeping them safe . . ."

"Safe," she echoed.

That wasn't the best word, but I was in no mood to correct myself. "Anyway, I've got at least seven believers sitting in my intro class."

"How do you know? Do they wear uniforms?" She gave a laugh. "I know. Inverted fishbowls set over their heads."

I laughed, but without much heart.

"No, they just sit together," I explained. "Down in front, and from day one. Very chummy. I asked if they came from the same high school. But they aren't even from the same state. They met on web-Mars."

"Understandable," said Hanna.

Which irritated me. For a lot of vague and silly reasons, I growled, "Sure, it's understandable. We all know people that we've never seen in person."

"Seven," she remarked, "is not a lot of students."

I said nothing.

"How many are in that class?"

"Two hundred and six."

"A little more than three percent," she said.

And I gave her a hard smile, reminding her, "I'm also teaching that advanced placement class."

She saw my trap closing.

"Forty students," I said. "The best of the best."

"And how many believers?" Hanna asked.

"Half," I replied.

"Twenty?"

"Nearly." I shook my head, admitting, "They're wonderful students. In most ways, I can't complain."

"It sounds like complaining to me."

"I'm a cranky middle-aged man. Grumbling is my business."

Hanna just shook her head.

"No, these kids have a good working knowledge about genetics and evolution, and metabolisms, and how ecological systems operate."

"They sound perfectly horrible."

I let her have her fun.

"Okay," she finally said. "Where's the tragedy in having so many smart, wonderful students?"

"I wish I knew," I muttered.

"You know what bothers you," Hanna growled. Then she picked up her reader again, telling me, "You didn't teach these children any of those great lessons. Which means their allegiances lie elsewhere, and that's what has you pissed."

I gave a snort and a half-laugh.

"God," I said. "We can hope that's all!"

Whenever we are sued, and each time some nation's anti-cult laws are unleashed . . . my organization and I are forced to defend ourselves, in court as well as the public eye. Time and again, we have opened our books and our facilities. Outside auditors have scoured every aspect of the Project, and there has never been any hint that money has been misplaced or misused. Nobody is growing rich on the backs of children. Believe me. And as for these allegations that I'm enslaving impressionable young minds . . . well, we can debate the meanings of "enslave" until we are breathless. Or I can gracefully accept responsibility for having a role, maybe an important role, in the development of millions of young and promising lives . . .

— Philippe Rule, interview

"Of course it's mostly bullshit," my student remarked. "I mean, when I was a kid, the whole thing seemed awfully compelling. I believed everything. Everything. But if you're even halfway smart, you eventually realize it's just a fictional world, and a learning tool, and beautiful in its own right. That's what the web-Mars is, you know. Beautiful. In a lot of ways, it's a genuine work of art."

We were sitting inside my tiny office—a professor and his best student trading profundities and gossip. It's the old college tradition, honorable and occasionally useful.

"I can agree about the bullshit," I mentioned. "But really, I don't have too many strong feelings about Rule's project. As long as it obeys the law and leaves my family alone—"

"You've got a nephew, don't you? A kid named Tom?"

I tried not to appear surprised.

"Yeah, I ran into him this summer. Working at the Omega Site."

Professors don't like to confess to gaps in their encyclopedic minds. But my confusion must have shown.

"The Omega Site," the young man repeated, relishing his advantage. "It's the biggest artifact on web-Mars. A mountain-sized starship. Some billion years old, nearly." Then he seemed to hear his own words, and with a dismissive laugh, he added, "I know. The whole bastard's just eight years old, and it's nothing but someone's tangle of digital codes and puzzles and shit."

"So what do you do there?" I inquired.

The student was tall and leggy—a gifted junior on track to graduate a full year early. With a wide grin, he admitted, "We gather there. We talk. And, of course, there's teams that you can work on, trying to piece together the mystery of that artifact."

Again, he was shifting back into the language of a believing child.

"And you met my nephew?" I asked.

"Yeah, he's what? Sixteen?" With a long-limbed shrug, he admitted, "The software put me on his team. By chance, maybe. But more likely, the AIs noticed I was at this school, and they assumed Tom and I would have common ground. Because of you, I mean."

"I don't see my nephew much," I confessed.

And I never have, I could have added.

"How is Tom?" I inquired.

"Doing great," he sang out. "Yeah, in fact, he was my team leader." The young man giggled, pleased to report, "The kid's way,

way up the chain of command. From what I hear, he's barely a couple, three rungs away from Philippe's inner circle."

"He's been at this for years—"

"And he's generous," my student interrupted. "His folks must have some impressive money. Judging by his gifts."

I didn't make a sound.

"Anyway," my student continued. "He warned me. Tom did. He said you aren't all that in love with our work."

"I just think it's a waste, in a lot of ways."

The young face absorbed the news without blinking. In fact, he seemed pleased to hear my harsh assessment.

"Billions of dollars have been poured into Rule's scheme," I continued. "And what do you have to show for it?"

"The launch pad in the Pacific," he offered. "Factories and test facilities in twenty countries. Millions of devoted supporters, and millions more who give a few dollars to be able to play on web-Mars."

"What exactly have you launched from your Pacific base?"

"A shitload of automated probes—"

"Half of which didn't even make it to Mars." I shook my head, reminding him, "Three landers lost contact with the Earth. And that was just this year."

"Space is a tough neighborhood," he admitted. "But we're learning. We've had some successful launches with our heavy boosters. And our orbiting habitat has kept its monkeys alive for nearly three years."

"All those billions spent—" I began.

"Eight years ago, we had nothing," he countered, beginning to bristle. "We've gotten less than no help from every government. Every piece of machinery has to be built from scratch, by us. And since nobody lets us have nuclear rockets—"

"Do you blame us?"

"Not that much. No." He laughed with a forced amiability. "It's just that we're forced to make some fat concessions. Chemical fuels only, and payload limits, and once we get into space, there's all sorts of orbital restrictions. We're going to have to be clever to get around your stumbling blocks."

"I haven't put anything in your way."

He looked at me for a long moment, and then remembered to smile. "You know what I mean."

"Mars is going to throw up its own barriers," I reminded him.

My student seemed to recall where his grades came from. "I

can appreciate your perspective," he said. "I really do. And I'm not like your nephew. Not much. The Project is just one possible route to Mars. Someday, with us or without us, someone is going to walk on its surface and return home again."

I hesitated, and then asked, "What does Tom do exactly? As a team leader, I mean."

"He oversees the puzzle solvers."

"What's the puzzle?"

"I can't give you details," he told me with a sharp, virtuous smile.

"Just the basics, then."

"We're trying to learn everything we can about the pilots and the crew of that ancient starship."

"You're talking about fictional aliens," I reminded him.

Shrugging his shoulders, my student said, "Point taken." But he was still flashing the incandescent smile of a true believer.

> *Every reporter asks about our timetable. How soon, and how many? Well, let me just say this: I don't know exactly when we will leave for Mars, but it will not be tomorrow. And I don't know how many will be going on this great mission. But everyone will be invited, and that's all that I can say about that . . .*
>
> —Philippe Rule, interview

"You look beautiful," I offered.

Very gave me a disapproving frown. Then she turned to her mother, asking, "How do I look? Really."

"Don't you believe your father?" Hanna inquired.

"He always says, 'Beautiful.' "

"You think I'm dishonest?" I teased.

"Mom? Just tell me!"

"We have arrived," our car announced with a soft little voice.

The park lay far below the surrounding land. This had once been the basement of some great old building, but my sister and her husband had bought the ground for the simple purpose of building a sunken garden—a wealth of color and fishponds meant to bring good fortune to those about to be married within its borders. My sister was standing in the parking lot. She saw us roll up and greeted us with one arm waving, demanding our immediate attention. My oldest niece stood before her, dressed in a shimmering, almost metallic white gown. The girl looked tired and happy, and nervous enough to puke, and spoiled in that deeply intoxicating way that only brides can be spoiled.

"You look fine," Hanna finally told our daughter. "I think you're even lovely."

With a musical chirp, our daughter said, "I know," and laughed, leaping from the car. "Thanks, Mom."

Veronica was twelve and absolutely in love with life. She sprinted past her distracted aunt and down a set of limestone stairs —a pretty tomboy forced to wear a pretty girl's frilly dress—and watching her, I felt the old aches and worries, and a sturdy, clean pride that took too much credit for my daughter's happiness.

Very was going to trip and fall down those stairs.

I knew it. With every careless stride, that horrific image presented itself to me. But somehow she survived to the bottom, bolting across the grassy glade toward a pair of cousins, and my consuming fear simply changed its face now. I breathed, and breathed, and with an old man's gait, I started after her.

"You're late," my sister observed, not quite looking at me.

And before I could reply, Iris barked, "Flatten, dress. Get the crease out, under my hand. Here!"

The dress complied.

My little sister rose to her feet, satisfied for this very brief moment. She looked exhausted but focused. "I can't find Tom," she began. "He's going to be an usher. He's supposed to fly in this morning. From Paris, I think. But I haven't seen him. Would you go look for him, Wes?"

I must have hesitated.

"Or you can baby-sit Dad," she offered. Then with a malicious grin, she added, "He's been smoking his favorite weed again. By the way."

"I'll find Tom," I replied.

"Hurry," she called. And then with a distinctly more patient tone, she began talking to the wedding dress again.

The garden was filled with newborn flowers—enormous and colorful and oftentimes impossible species born from biology and electrochemical metabolisms. In the natural world, nothing could be so brilliant, so gloriously wasteful. But this foliage was tied into the city's power grid, feeding on raw electricity. Sunshine was little more than a convenient museum light helping each plant display its majesty and wild colors. Perfumes and more subtle pheromones gave the air a rich wondrous stink. On this business of modern horticulture, I have always been of ten minds. Nine minds are against it, but there is always this other voice whispering, "Stop now, and look. Isn't it incredible?"

Rows of white chairs and a simple white archway had been erected on the biggest patch of an emerald-green moss. A few guests had already arrived, standing at the edges, impatiently waiting for someone to tell them where to sit.

Under my breath, I whispered, "Tom."

Louder, but not loud, I called out, "Tom."

His brothers stood beside a rectangular fishpond, girls on their arms. Everyone looked happy and distracted. Then I came up behind them, and the younger brother told me, "Very just flew through here. Then she flew off. I don't know where."

"I'm not looking for her," I confessed. "Where's Tom?"

"I don't know," he replied.

His girlfriend brightened. "I really want to meet him," she sang out.

"You will," he muttered.

Then she had to ask, probably for the umpteenth time, "Does Tom really know Philippe Rule?"

"Oh, yeah," he replied, rolling his eyes. "Yeah, those two are always hanging out together. Rule's got Tom sitting inside his wallet."

The brothers enjoyed a harsh laugh at Tom's expense.

The girl smiled nervously, trying to understand the meaning.

I grinned and moved on. Wasted stares at strangers taught me a lesson. I hadn't seen my nephew since last Christmas, and then only when the families met in our respective web-rooms. He was a twenty-year-old man now. He could have grown a beard, or he could have put his hair to sleep. I wasn't entirely sure what face I was looking for. And with that revelation, I temporarily quit my search, standing in the shadow of an odd little tree—a synthetic species that might not exist anywhere else in the universe.

My distractions ended with the sturdy thump of a car door.

A second set of stairs rose out of the sunken garden. Maybe there was a second parking lot, and maybe Tom had just arrived. Pushed by a tattered sense of duty, I climbed. But halfway up, an ornate peacock-like bird strode out of the flowerbed, stubby wings rising as its tail spread wide. A marveling wash of colors startled me. How did it change its colors so quickly? The scientist in me needed to solve that little puzzle, and that delayed me for another few moments. Mirrors. Its tail feathers were covered with flexible organic mirrors, and, with an expert's grace, it moved each feather, borrowing the glories from the surrounding flowers.

"Neat," I said.

Then I shooed the bird aside, finishing my climb.

Three vehicles were parked in the tiny lot. The first car was obviously empty. The second car had darkened windows, and, with a boldness that surprised me, I tapped on the glass. There was motion inside, and then the window dropped with a slick hum. A young woman held her shirt against her chest, while the man beside her, using a cutting voice, said to me, "Move along, old man."

I took his advice.

The last vehicle was a blister-van. It didn't look like anything my nephew would drive. But I walked up and called out, "Tom?"

"There is no Tom here," the van answered.

"Do you know him?" I inquired, giving his full name.

With a mysterious tone, the van said, "Yes, I do. But I can't help you find him."

Back to the garden, I decided.

Walking past the first car, a notion took hold of me. It was a little ladybug car, rusty red in color, and its windows were dialed to clear, showing an interior that looked clean and new. Showroom cars don't look any better, I realized. Standing in front of it, I said, "Tom. Your mom's hunting you, and guess what. She's getting pissed."

Very slightly, the car shivered.

Then the left front window dropped, and my nephew stuck his head out. "Uncle Wes!" he cried out. "How are you?"

I came around. "Fine, Tom."

The car was a rolling web-room. With a glance, I knew where he was. The view inside stretched for miles. Some kind of robot, elaborate and contrived, stood guard beside a glittering archway. I had no idea what anything meant, but there was a blue sky wrapped around a shrunken sun. I gave web-Mars a quick look. And then Very leaned forward, emerging from the back end of the car, grinning broadly as she said, "Hi, Dad!"

I said, "Shit."

With about the worst possible tone, I said, "Get out."

If anything, Tom seemed pleased. He opened his door and climbed out, and my daughter followed. He smiled, and she smiled, and the combination of those two faces made me crazy.

Again, with feeling, I said, "Shit."

Veronica laughed at my anger.

"You know our rules," I began. "Until you're grown and living on your own, you have to ask for our permission before you go anywhere!"

For a moment, she said nothing.

Then her smile brightened, while her slate-blue eyes grew a little sorry. With an amazing indifference, she confessed, "I did ask you."

"When?"

"Years and years ago," she told me. "'Can I go to Mars with Tom?' I asked. You and Mom, both."

"And what did we say?"

" 'No. Never.' "

I discovered that my voice had been stolen away.

"But then I went anyway," my daughter told me, absolutely unconcerned by this breach of the law. Standing high on her tip-toes, she kissed my nose, and once again she said, "I asked. Didn't I? And you said, 'Never.' Which was silly. So I decided to do what I wanted anyway."

A long moment passed, and then I said, "Shit," once again.

But nobody was with me. Except for the web-car, which shut its door and closed its window, offering me not even one polite little word.

Under the watchful gaze of various government agencies and the press, we designed and constructed seven scientific probes —fossil hunters and water hunters and deep-boring machines. And then with the simplest sleight of hand, those probes were removed from their rockets and dissolved in liquid steel baths. Machine assemblages built in secret replaced each probe. Each machine was designed entirely by mathematical models. Untested technologies were married to forty flavors of theory. The rockets were launched over a period of three years. One of the boosters failed, but that left six redundant packages streaking toward Mars. Each one of those payloads failed to enter Martian orbit, a different malfunction blamed for each loss. Misleading telemetry data helped keep any suspicious minds confused. The only true question was whether these machines, once reaching their target, would work properly in the alien environment.

But then again, these were the second-finest machines ever created by living minds.

—Crusade memo, confidential

I thought I was the first one up that morning. My watch roused me with an adrenalin cocktail, and I sat up and rubbed at my eyes for a long moment. It was a little before six o'clock. My advanced placement class started early, at seven thirty, and what with breakfast and my morning rituals, I didn't have time to spare.

Shuffling toward the bathroom, I noticed the light beneath my daughter's door.

While the toilet was flushing, I knocked on her door—lightly, fondly—and she instantly said, "Come on in, Dad," as if I was expected.

Very was sitting at her grandmother's old rolltop desk. She was dressed for school, which was exceptionally strange at that hour, and she was reading, which was perfectly ordinary. I found myself staring at that composed and handsome young woman. She had her mother's features and my dark hair, plus a watchful, perpetually amused expression that was entirely her own. One of her little hands hovered above the reader, prepared to blank it. But then she decided to leave it on. The hand dropped into her lap, and she smiled at me, and watched me, and I thought she was waiting for me to say, "Happy birthday."

So I said, "Happy birthday, darling."

With a genuine astonishment, I said, "Eighteen years old."

How could she have gotten to this moment so quickly? It was a marvel and a tragedy, and I felt like crying.

"Thank you, Dad."

Her web-wall was dialed to Mars—the real Mars, bleak and dry and brutally cold. The image was a live feed from a Rule-owned weather station. It was a favorite of hers. Jagged rocks and alluvial sands filled a wide, dead riverbed. I found myself staring at the scene, and with a distracted voice, I asked, "Have you decided yet?"

She knew what I meant.

Quietly, she said, "I have. Yes."

I smiled and looked at her. "Which college wins?"

Her smile turned a little sorry, a little sad. But then with a positive voice, she told me, "Later. I'll talk to you and Mom together. Later."

"Fair enough," I replied.

A dozen schools were chasing her. All were better schools than the college where I taught, but part of me—a selfish, paternal heart —hoped that Veronica would live at home for another four years, and, before I retired, she would sit in a class or two of mine.

"You're up awfully early," I observed.

"I couldn't sleep."

Nothing made me suspicious. I nodded and glanced at the reader on her desk, seeing nothing. The reader was blank to begin with, or some other hand had wiped it clean.

"Dad," she said.

I looked at her mother's eyes.

"You're going to be late for school, Dad."

"Happy birthday," I said again.

"Thanks," she told me. And then with her hand, with a motion almost too quick to be seen, she rubbed at her bright, watery eyes.

Our little house sits a few blocks from campus. It makes for a pleasant walk, particularly on warm mornings. Ten minutes from home to office, usually. Which is more than enough time for the world to change.

Students were waiting at my office door.

I started to say, "Good morning." But something in their communal expression made me uneasy. With an uneven voice, I asked, "What's wrong?"

"Something's going on," a young woman warned me.

"It's huge," a boy purred. "Just huge."

"What is?" I sputtered.

"The ship," he told me, amazement swirled with a dose of fear. "They spotted it last week, coming in from somewhere . . . I don't know where . . . and the president just made the announcement—"

"What ship?" I asked.

Then a third student blurted, "It's a goddamn alien ship. It's huge! And guess where it's heading. . . !"

We headed for the classroom. I dialed the web-wall to a news-feed, and we found ourselves staring at the image of a tiny, tiny bullet. The ship was gray and smooth-faced and spinning slowly as it plunged through space, moving past the orbit of the moon. A tiny bullet in the depths of space, but, according to radar, it was nearly ten miles long and half again as broad.

The droning voice of a commentator reported that the ship was silent, unresponsive to every hail from Earth.

"Aliens," a dozen voices muttered behind me.

I turned and looked at my class.

"No," I whispered.

"Look who's missing," I urged them.

Half of my students were somewhere else.

"Where's the Rulers?" someone muttered—the current short-hand for the Martian believers. "What do you think it means?"

I didn't answer the question.

On old legs, I was already running, fighting to get home again.

My sister finally answered our calls. Iris appeared sitting on one of several sofas in the middle of her enormous living room. With a glance, I knew she had been crying. Her face was stern and cold, and the red eyes had a fire. Her voice failed when she tried to speak. Then she swallowed and straightened her back, and she looked past me, asking, "What?" with a disgusted tone.

Tom was missing, I assumed.

I didn't mention her son. Instead, I confessed, "We're looking for Veronica. Hanna and I are. Would you know—?"

"God, no." My sister flinched, and shook. She brought her hands up to her face and held them against her mouth, wrapping fingers together before dropping them into her lap. "Well," she muttered, "this makes it even worse."

Hanna was sitting beside me. She grabbed my knee and squeezed.

"Of all the stupid things," Iris muttered. "The injustice of it all . . . !" She shook her head, dropping her eyes. "You put your hopes into something. Something important. Something great. All that time invested. The energy. All the money that you've just pissed away . . ."

Hanna interrupted. "Is there any way that you can reach Tom? Very left here with some other kids, and she didn't show up at school—"

"I heard you before," my sister growled.

She looked up, her fierce eyes fixed squarely on me. "He's only invested his entire life trying to reach this day. Tens of thousands of dollars. Our money, and his. And shit, they didn't even select my own son—!"

I felt myself falling.

"Did you know? You didn't, did you? Not even Philippe was picked! He's going to watch this mission with the rest of us!"

"What. . . ?" I sputtered.

"Which is even worse," she said, laughing harshly. "It's a thousand times worse than Tom's situation. I mean, it always looked like his project, his baby, and it never was . . ."

Hanna and I held each other, falling together now.

"You want to talk to Tom?" my sister asked. "He's upstairs somewhere. Crying. I've got the house watching him. In case." Then she shook her head, crying for herself. "Those bastards," she wailed. "Those damned machine bastards. . . !"

If humans haven't the will to journey to Mars, then it remains for someone else to do the impossible and glorious, for themselves. . . !
                                    —from the Crusade's mission statement

The mountain was no mountain, and its red flanks weren't made of anything as simple as stone. A billion years of thin winds and the occasional rain had cut into the ship's sides, revealing a ceramic exoskeleton. Tiny gray machines poked out here and there. A simple diamond arch served as a doorway. Tom stood before the arch, waiting for us. With a soft, almost matter-of-fact voice, he explained, "Most of the ship is underground. When it landed, mass and momentum carried it into the crust. Then the alluvial soils were washed in around its sides." He paused for a moment, and then added, "That's what the puzzle told us. Of course, it's all just a made-up story. Someone's little game."

Tom looked tired. Otherwise, he seemed very much the same: A boyish man in his middle twenties, with an astronaut's clipped hair and a small, exceptionally fit body.

Hanna told him, "Thank you."

He nodded, glancing into the darkness inside the Omega ship.

"I know this is difficult," she added. "You've got to be disappointed, and we can only imagine—"

"I don't know if I can take you inside," he interrupted. "I mean, I'm not all that sure about my clearance status anymore."

"But Very's in there somewhere," I said. "You're sure of that much, right?"

He nodded again, bit his lip, and breathed. Then with a fearful slowness, he stepped through the archway, a faint pleasure showing when he reached the other side.

We followed after him, the tunnel brightening around us. I noticed very little. Somewhere during the long illusion of a walk, the ship's ceramic skeleton became something else. The walls were composed of densely packed horizontal beds, paper-thin and varying in color but not in texture. Tom touched the walls with an habitual fondness, and then quietly, angrily, he said, "This is them."

"Who?" Hanna asked.

"We didn't realize," he offered. Then he glanced back at us, eyes forlorn and lost. "For years, every team missed the obvious. What this ship was saying to us. What this puzzle really meant."

I didn't care about meanings; I wanted to see my daughter.

"The dead aliens," he said. "There were thousands of bones. Thousands of old skulls. This ship is big enough to house a small city. But when we sat down and actually worked out the numbers . . . well, most of the ship is this. These bands of doped ceramics and such. It took us forever to see what was simple. But then, of course, they knew it would surprise us. They know us. Better than we know ourselves, I bet."

I touched the wall, my stimsuit feeding me a cool, slick sensation.

"'Everyone will be invited,'" Tom quoted. "That's what Philippe Rule promised. And I think the poor bastard actually believed those words."

The tunnel twisted to the left and widened.

"The bastard had this crazy idea about flying to Mars, and he had rich, indulgent parents." Tom glanced back at us, admitting, "That sounds a little too familiar." Then he laughed for a moment, with a gentle bitterness. "Philippe told his parents about his dream for Mars, and they rented an auditorium and hired media help. AI web-managers, mostly. What nobody knew then was that the AIs were already shopping for someone like Philippe. A figurehead. A face. Some innocent to help raise the money and make their work look legal."

I quickened my pace, moving up beside Tom. Ahead of us, with a smear of bright yellowish light, the tunnel came to an abrupt end.

"These aliens," he muttered. "The Omegas. We studied them in teams. Each team was supposed to work independently. There was this race going on. Each team wanted to be first to figure out this alien society. We studied their bones and homes and how they lived, and we explored the starship, and for years we tried to understand something very basic: How did the Omegas pilot this ship? There were no obvious controls. No physical access to the engines or the reactors. Every team proposed a telepathic answer, and the AI game-shepherds would tell us flat-out, 'No.' So we went back to the evidence again, and again. We were kids working at something beyond us. And then, we weren't kids anymore. We were adults, and experienced, and one at a time, each team figured it out for itself."

Tom hesitated.

"Cargo," he said, followed by a long painful sigh.

"There was this quiet guy on my team," he said. "He hadn't said five sentences to me in all those years. Then last year, while I was presiding over one of our endless bull sessions, he made a bizarre suggestion. The Omegas didn't have any power over the ship, he said, because they didn't have any real function. The ship was nothing more, or less, than a great hive filled with artificial intelligences. And the ship's organic entities were nothing but a kind of fancy cargo. Something carried for reasons of commerce, or, at the very best, out of respect for their long-ago creators."

Hanna joined us, laying a sympathetic hand on her nephew's shoulder.

"'Bullshit,' I said." Now Tom slowed his gait. "I told him he was crazy, and it was a stupid, ugly idea. But the guy wanted to offer his answer for judging. He called for a vote from the team, and after a lot of speeches, he won his vote. Barely. Everybody who voted against the proposal is going to remain on the Earth. Probably for the rest of their lives. But if you voted for that bullshit idea, you gave yourself almost a two percent chance of being invited. By our masters."

Tom came to a halt, leaning against the delicately bedded wall, panting as if he was exhausted.

"What about Veronica?" I asked.

He didn't seem to hear my question.

With a flickering pride, Hanna pointed out, "Very has always had a fair mind. She probably just wanted to give the idea a chance—"

"No," Tom interrupted. And he laughed at us. He shook his head and laughed with a sudden force, explaining, "She's why the vote went the way it did. Your daughter liked the idea . . . it made so much sense to her . . . which is probably why she isn't going to be with us much longer. . . !"

"I'll come home for a visit," Very promised. "Before we launch, and probably more than once. I just thought it would be best to meet with the others, and to get my head ready for what's coming."

"How soon would you leave?" Hanna blurted.

"A few months from now. At most, a full year." The image of our daughter wore a bright white spacesuit, her helmet dangling back on a hinge. Behind her, stretching on for what seemed like miles, were people similarly equipped, all listening to robots talking in professorial voices. "The ship's interior isn't quite finished," she explained. "The microchines and robots need another few weeks to make it perfect. And, of course, some governments are going to put up legal barricades, which the AI lawyers have to defeat. And even with the best com-lasers, it's going to take time to download the crew." With a respectful nod, she said, "Most of the world's AIs are planning to send copies of themselves."

Everyone will be invited, Philippe had promised.

Hanna gave a low, sorrowful moan.

"After Mars?" I asked, with a ragged hope.

Very could have lied. She must have considered kindness, telling us, "I'll come right back again." But the girl had always been honest, and she knew it would be best if she were the one to break the difficult news. "This isn't going to be a quick trip to Mars," she cautioned. "After a year or two of exploring, they plan to leave. They'll drop past Venus and then swing out toward Jupiter. They need to use its gravity well to help us accelerate. They've decided to see the worlds circling the Centauri suns."

I felt sick. Cold, and sick, and furious.

"You'll die out there," I muttered.

Hanna flinched.

"It's going to take you hundreds of years—" I began.

"More than ten thousand years," she said, correcting me. "It's going to be a very long voyage, and you're right. You are. After an adventurous life, I'll die of old age, and we'll barely have reached the comets."

I didn't know what to say.

"But Father," she purred. "Think of your descendants. Imagine them walking on all those strange, wonderful worlds."

"They'll be cargo," I snapped.

Very absorbed the insult without blinking. She almost laughed, telling us, "Our benefactors prefer to think of us as emblems. As treasures. To them, we're holy objects tying them to their first lucid thoughts."

With an easy shrillness, I said, "The Children's Crusade."

Very closed her eyes, and nodded.

"That's what the AIs dubbed this secret project. And that's just part of the mud that's coming out now," I added.

"I know—"

"And you know what that name's taken from? In the Middle Ages, the children of Europe were lured away in an awful crusade . . . cynically used by the powers of the day . . . dying for no reason, or sold into slavery—"

"But Dad," Very whispered.

Then she stepped close to me. Her image lifted on its toes, touching my image on the nose. She always kissed me that way. I felt it, the illusionary touch of her dry lips. "Daddy," she purred. "What were those children promised? For going on their crusade, what was going to be their reward?"

Hanna answered, whispering, "Salvation."

"There is no salvation!" I growled. "Not in any bullshit crusade!"

My daughter laughed at me, and stepped back. "But what if there was?" she asked. "What if a heaven was possible, and it was real, and what if that heaven was offered to us? Really, where's the sadness here? That all that talk of salvation was a lie, or that you have spent your entire life not taking that staggering, wonderful risk. . . ?"

———

Night of Time

ASH DRANK A BITTER TEA WHILE SITTING IN THE
shade outside his shop, comfortable on a little seat that he had
carved for himself in the trunk of a massive, immortal bristlecone
pine. The wind was tireless, dense and dry and pleasantly warm.
The sun was a convincing illusion—a K-class star perpetually
locked at an early-morning angle, the false sky narrow and pink, a
haze of artful dust pretending to have been blown from some faraway hell. At his feet lay a narrow and phenomenally deep canyon,
glass roads anchored to the granite walls, with hundreds of narrow
glass bridges stretched from one side to the other, making the air
below him glisten and glitter. Busier shops and markets were set
beside the important roads, and scattered between them were the
hivelike mansions and mating halls, and elaborate fractal statues,
and the vertical groves of cling-trees that lifted water from the distant river: the basics of life for the local species, the 31-3s.

For Ash, business was presently slow, and it had been for some
years. But he was a patient man and a pragmatist, and when you
had a narrow skill and a well-earned reputation, it was only a matter of time before the desperate or those with too much money
came searching for you.

"This will be the year," he said with a practiced, confident tone.
"And maybe, this will be the day."

Any coincidence was minimal. It was his little habit to say those words and then lean forward in his seat, looking ahead and to his right, watching the only road that happened to lead past his shop. If someone were coming, Ash would see him now. And as it happened, he spotted two figures ascending the long glass ribbon, one leading the other, both fighting the steep grade as well as the thick and endless wind.

The leader was large and simply shaped—a cylindrical body, black and smooth, held off the ground by six jointed limbs. Ash instantly recognized the species. While the other entity was human, he decided—a creature like himself, and at this distance, entirely familiar.

They weren't going to be his clients, of course. Most likely, they were sightseers. Perhaps they didn't even know one another. They were just two entities that happened to be marching in the same direction. But as always, Ash allowed himself a seductive premonition. He finished his tea, and listened, and after a little while, despite the heavy wind, he heard the quick dense voice of the alien —an endless blur of words and old stories and lofty abstract concepts born from one of the galaxy's great natural intellects.

When the speaker was close, Ash called out, "Wisdom passes!"

A Vozzen couldn't resist such a compliment.

The road had finally flattened out. Jointed legs turned the long body, allowing every eye to focus on the tall, rust-colored human sitting inside the craggy tree. The Vozzen continued walking sideways, but with a fatigued slowness. His only garment was a fabric tube, black like his carapace and with the same slick texture. "Wisdom shall not pass," a thin, somewhat shrill voice called out. Then the alien's translator made adjustments, and the voice softened. "If you are a man named Ash," said the Vozzen, "this Wisdom intends to linger."

"I am Ash," he replied, immediately dropping to his knees. The ground beneath the tree was rocky, but acting like a supplicant would impress the species. "May I serve your Wisdom in some tiny way, sir?"

"Ash," the creature repeated. "The name is Old English. Is that correct?"

The surprise was genuine. With a half-laugh, Ash said, "Honestly, I'm not quite sure—"

"English," it said again. The translator was extremely adept, creating a voice that was unnervingly human—male and mature, and pleasantly arrogant. "There was a tiny nation-state, and an island, and as I recall my studies, England and its confederate tribes acquired a rather considerable empire that briefly covered the face of your cradle world."

"Fascinating," said Ash, looking back down the road. The second figure was climbing the last long grade, pulling an enormous float-pack, and despite his initial verdict, Ash realized that the creature wasn't human at all.

"But you were not born on the Earth," the Vozzen continued. "In your flesh and your narrow build, I can see some very old augmentations—"

"Mars," Ash allowed. "I was born on—"

"Mars," the voice repeated. That simple word triggered a cascade of memories, facts and telling stories. From that flood, the Vozzen selected his next offering. "Old Mars was home to some fascinating political experiments. From the earliest terraforming societies to the Night of the Dust—"

"I remember," Ash interrupted, trying to gain control over the conversation. "Are you a historian, sir? Like many of your kind—?"

"I am conversant in the past, yes."

"Then perhaps I shouldn't be too impressed. You seem to have been looking for me, and for all I know, you've thoroughly researched whatever little history is wrapped around my life."

"It would be impolite not to study your existence," said the Vozzen.

"Granted." With another deep bow, Ash asked, "What can this old Martian do for a wise Vozzen?"

The alien fell silent.

For a moment, Ash studied the second creature. Its skeleton and muscle were much like a man's, and the head wore a cap of what could have been dense brown hair. There was one mouth and two eyes, but no visible nose and the mouth was full of heavy pink teeth. Of course many humans had novel genetics, and there were remoras on the Ship's hull—men and women who wore every intriguing, creative mutation. But this creature was not human. Ash sensed it, and using a private nexus, he asked his shop for a list of likely candidates.

"Ash," the Vozzen said. "Yes, I have made a comprehensive study of your considerable life."

Ash dipped his head, driving his knees into the rough ground. "I am honored, sir. Thank you."

"I understand that you possess some rather exotic machinery."

"Quite novel. Yes, sir."

"And talents. You wield talents even rarer than your machinery."

"Unique talents," Ash replied with an effortless confidence. He lifted his eyes, and smiled, and wanting the advantage in his court, he rose to his feet, brushing the grit from his slightly bloodied knees as he told his potential client, "I help those whom I can help."

"You help them for a fee," the alien remarked, a clear disdain in the voice.

Ash approached the Vozzen, remarking, "My fee is a fair wage. A wage determined by the amoral marketplace."

"I am a poor historian," the Vozzen complained.

Ash gazed into the bright black eyes. Then with a voice tinged with a careful menace, he said, "It must seem awful, I would think. Being a historian, and being Vozzen, and feeling your precious memories slowly and inexorably leaking away . . ."

The Ship was an enormous derelict—a world-sized starship discovered by humans, and repaired by humans, and sent by its new owners on a great voyage around the most thickly settled regions of the galaxy. It was Ash's good fortune to be one of the early passengers, and, for several centuries, he remained a simple tourist. But he had odd skills leftover from his former life, and as different aliens boarded the Ship, he made friends with new ideas and fresh technologies. His shop was the natural outgrowth of all that learning. "Sir," he said to the Vozzen. "Would you like to see what your money would buy?"

"Of course."

"And your companion—?"

"My aide will remain outside. Thank you."

The human-shaped creature seemed to expect that response. He walked under the bristlecone, tethering his pack to a whitened branch, and, with an unreadable expression, stood at the canyon's edge, staring into the glittering depths, watching for the invisible river, perhaps, or perhaps watching his own private thoughts.

"By what name do I call you?"

"Master is adequate."

Every Vozzen was named Master, in one fashion or another. With a nod, Ash began walking toward the shop's doorway. "And your aide—"

"Shadow."

"His name is?"

"Shadow is an adequate translation." Several jointed arms emerged from beneath his long body, complex hands tickling the edges of the door, a tiny sensor slipped from a pocket and pointed at the darkness inside. "Are you curious, Ash?"

"About what, Master?"

"My companion's identity. It is a little mystery to you, I think."

"It is. Yes."

"Have you heard of the Aabacks?"

"But I've never seen one." Then, after a silence, he mentioned, "They're a rare species. With a narrow intelligence and a fierce loyalty, as I understand these things."

"They are rather simple souls," Master replied. "But whatever their limits, or because of them, they make wonderful servants."

The tunnel grew darker, and then the walls fell away. With a silent command, Ash triggered the lights to awaken. In an instant, a great chamber was revealed, the floor tiled simply and the pine-faced ceiling arching high overhead, while the distant walls lay behind banks upon banks of machines that were barely awake, spelling themselves for those rare times when they were needed.

"Are you curious, Master?"

"Intensely and about many subjects," said the Vozzen. "What particular subject are you asking about?"

"How this magic works," Ash replied, gesturing with an ancient, comfortable pride. "Not even the Ship's captains can wield this technology. Within the confines of our galaxy, I doubt if there are three other facilities equally equipped."

"For memory retrieval," Master added. "I know the theory at play here. You manipulate the electrons inside a client's mind, increasing their various effects. And you manipulate the quantum nature of the universe, reaching into a trillion alternate but very similar realities. Then you combine these two quite subtle tricks, temporarily enlarging one mind's ability to reminisce."

Ash nodded, stepping up to the main control panel.

"I deplore that particular theory," his client professed.

"I'm not surprised."

"That many-world image of the universe is obscene. To me, it is simply grotesque and relentlessly ridiculous, and I have never approved of it."

"Many feel that way," Ash allowed.

A genuine anger surged. "This concept of each electron existing in countless realities, swimming through an endless ocean of potential, with every possible outcome achieved to what resembles an infinite number of outcomes—"

"We belong to one branch of reality," Ash interrupted. "One minor branch in a great tree standing in an endless canopy in the multiverse forest—"

"We are not," Master growled.

The controls awoke. Every glow-button and thousand-layer display had a theatrical purpose. Ash could just as easily manipulate the machinery through nexuses buried in his own body. But his clients normally appreciated this visible, traditional show of structured light and important sounds.

"We are not a lonely reality lost among endless possibility." In Vozzen fashion, the hind legs slapped each other in disgust. "I am a historian and a scholar of some well-earned notoriety. My long, long life has been spent in the acquisition of the past, and its interpretation, and I refuse to believe that what I have studied—this great pageant of time and story—is nothing more than some obscure twig shaking on the end of an impossible-to-measure shrub."

"I'm tempted to agree with you," Ash replied.

"Tempted?"

"There are moments when I believe . . ." Ash paused, as if selecting his next words. "I see us as the one true reality. The universe is exactly as it seems to be. As it should be. And what I employ here is just a trick, a means of interacting with the ghost realities. With mathematical whispers and unborn potentials. In other words, we are the trunk of a great and ancient tree, and the dreamlike branches have no purpose but to feed our magnificent souls. . . !"

The alien regarded Ash with a new respect. The respect showed in the silence, and then with the hands opening, delicate spiderweb fingers presenting themselves to what was, for at least this moment, their equal.

"Is that what you believe now?" Master asked.

"For the moment." Ash laughed quietly. Two nexuses and one display showed the same information: The historian had enough capital to hire him and his machinery. "And I'll keep believing it for a full day, if necessary."

Then he turned, bowing just enough. "What exactly is it that you wish to remember, Master?"

The alien eyes lost their brightness.

"I am not entirely sure," the voice confessed with a simple horror. "I have forgotten something very important . . . something essential, I fear . . . but I can't even recall what that something might be . . ."

Hours had passed, but the projected sun hadn't moved. The wind was unchanged, and the heat only seemed worse, as Ash stepped from the cool depths of his shop, his body momentarily forgetting to perspire. He had left his client alone, standing inside a cylindrical reader with a thousand flavors of sensors fixed to his carapace and floating free inside the ancient body and mind. Ash kept a close watch over the Vozzen. His nexuses showed him telemetry, and a mind's eye let him watch the scene. If necessary, he could offer words of encouragement or warning. But, for the moment, his client was obeying the strict instructions, standing as motionless as possible while the machines made intricate maps of his brain—a body-long array of superconducting proteins and light-baths and quantum artesians. The alien's one slight cheat was his voice, kept soft as possible, but always busy, delivering an endless lecture about an arcane, mostly forgotten epoch.

The mapping phase was essential, and quite boring.

From a tiny slot in the pink granite wall, Ash plucked free a new cup of freshly brewed, deliciously bitter tea.

"A pleasant view," a nearby voice declared.

"I like it." Ash sipped his drink. As a rule, Aabacks appreciated liquid gifts, but he made no offer, strolling under the bristlecone, out of the wind and sun. "Do you know anything about the 31-3s?"

"I know very little," Shadow confessed. The voice was his own, his larynx able to produce clear if somewhat slow human words.

"Their home is tidally locked and rather distant from its sun," Ash explained. "Their atmosphere is rich in carbon dioxide, which my Martian lungs prefer." He tapped his own chest. "Water vapor and carbon dioxide warm the day hemisphere, and the winds carry the excess heat and moisture to the cold nightside glaciers, which grow and push into the dawn, and melt, completing the cycle." With an appreciative nod, he said, "The Ship's engineers have done a magnificent job of replicating the 31-3 environment."

Shadow's eyes were large and bright, colored a bluish gray. The pink teeth were heavy and flat-headed, suitable for a diet of rough vegetation. Powerful jaw muscles ballooned outward when the mouth closed. A simple robe and rope belt were his only clothes. Four fingers and a thumb were on each hand, but nothing like a fingernail showed. Ash watched the hands, and then the bare,

almost human feet. Reading the dirt, he felt certain that Shadow
hadn't moved since he had arrived. He was standing in the sun, in
the wind, and like any scrupulously obedient servant, he seemed
ready to remain on that patch of ground for another day, or twenty.

"The 31-3s don't believe in time," Ash continued.

A meaningful expression passed across the face. Curiosity? Disdain? Then with a brief glance toward Ash, he asked, "Is it the
absence of days and nights?"

"Partly. But only partly."

Shadow leaned forward slightly. On the bright road below, a
pack of 31-3s was dancing along. Voices like brass chimes rose
through the wind. Ash recognized his neighbors. He threw a little
stone at them, to be polite. Then with a steady voice, he explained,
"The endless day is a factor, sure. But they've always been a long-
lived species. On their world, with its changeless climate and some
extremely durable genetics, every species has a nearly immortal
constitution. Where humans and Vozzens and Aabacks had to use
modern bioengineering to conquer aging, the 31-3s evolved in a
world where everything can live pretty much forever. That's why
time was never an important concept to them. And that's why their
native physics is so odd, and lovely — they formulated a vision of a
universe that is almost, almost free of time."

The alien listened carefully. Then he quietly admitted, "Master
has explained some of the same things to me, I think."

"You're a good loyal audience," Ash said.

"It is my hope to be."

"What else do you do for Master?"

"I help with all that is routine," Shadow explained. "In every
capacity, I give him aid and free his mind for great undertakings."

"But mostly, you listen to him."

"Yes."

"Vozzens are compulsive explainers."

"Aabacks are natural listeners," said Shadow, with a hint of
pride.

"Do you remember what he tells you?"

"Very little." For an instant, the face seemed human. An embarrassed smile and a shy blinking of the blue-gray eyes preceded
the quiet admission, "I do not have a Vozzen's mind. And Master is
an exceptional example of his species."

"You're right," said Ash. "On both accounts."

The alien shifted his feet, and again stared down at the 31-3s.

"Come with me."

"He wants me here," Shadow replied. Nothing in the voice was defiant, or even a little stubborn. He intended to obey the last orders given to him, and, with his gentle indifference, he warned that he couldn't be swayed.

Sternly, Ash asked, "What does the Master want from this day?"

The question brought a contemplative silence.

"More than anything," said Ash, "he wants to recover what's most precious to him. And that is—"

"His memory."

Again, Ash said, "Come with me."

"For what good?"

"He talks to you. And yes, you've likely forgotten what he can't remember." Ash finished his tea in one long sip. "But likely and surely are two different words. So if you truly wish to help your friend, come with me. Come now."

"I do not deserve solitude," the Vozzen reported. "If you intend to abandon me, warn me. You must."

"I will."

Then, "Do you feel that?"

"Do I . . . what. . . ?"

"Anything. Do you sense anything unusual?"

The alien was tethered to a new array of sensors, plus devices infinitely more intrusive. Here and in a hundred trillion alternate realities, Master stood in the same position, legs locked and arms folded against his belly, his voice slightly puzzled, admitting, "I seem to be remembering my cradle nest."

"Is that unusual?"

"It is unlikely," the Vozzen admitted. "I don't often—"

"And now?"

"My first mate," he began. "In the nest, overlooking a fungal garden—"

"What about now?"

He paused, and then admitted, "Your ship. I am seeing the Great Ship from space, our taxi making its final approach." With a warm laugh, he offered, "It is a historian's dream, riding in a vessel such as this—"

"And now?" Ash prompted.

Silence.

"Where are you—?"

"Inside a lecture hall," Master replied.

"When?"

"Eleven months in the past. I am giving a public lecture." He paused, and then explained, "I make a modest living, speaking to interested parties."

"What do you remember about that day's lecture?"

"Everything," Master began to say. But the voice faltered, and, with a doubting tone, he said, "A woman?"

"What woman?"

"A human woman."

"What about her?" Ash pressed.

"She was attending . . . sitting in a seat to my right. . . ? No, my left. How odd. I usually know where to place every face—"

"What was the topic?"

"Topic?"

"Of your lecture. The topic."

"A general history of the Great Wheel of Smoke—"

"The Milky Way," Ash interrupted.

"Your name for everyone's galaxy, yes." With a weblike hand, the alien reached in front of his own face. "I was sharing a very shallow overview of our shared history, naming the most important species of the last three billion years." The hand closed on nothing, and retreated. "For many reasons, there have been few genuinely important species. They have been modestly abundant, and some rather wealthy. But I was making the point . . . the critical line of reasoning . . . that since the metal-rich worlds began spawning intelligence, no single species, or related cluster of sentient organisms, have been able to dominate more than a small puff of the Smoke."

"Why is that?"

The simple question unleashed a flood of thoughts, recollections, and abstract ideas, filling the displays with wild flashes of color and elaborate, highly organized shapes.

"There are many reasons," Master warned.

"Name three."

"Why? Do you wish to learn?"

"I want to pass the time pleasantly," said Ash, studying the data with a blank, almost impassive face. "Three reasons why no species can dominate. Give them to me, in brief."

"Distance. Divergence. And divine wisdom."

"The distance between stars . . . is that what you mean. . . ?"

"Naturally," the historian replied. "Star-flight remains slow and expensive and potentially dangerous. Many species find those reasons compelling enough to remain at home, safe and comfortable, reengineering the spacious confines of their own solar system."

"Divergence?"

"A single species can evolve in many fashions. New organic forms. Joining with machines. Becoming machines. Sweeping cultural experiments. Even the total obliteration of physical bodies. No species can dominate any portion of space if what it becomes is many, many new and oftentimes competing species."

Ash blinked slowly. "What about divine wisdom?"

"That is the single most important factor," said Master. "Ruling the heavens is a child's desire."

"True enough."

"The galaxy is not a world, or even a hundred thousand worlds. It is too vast and chaotic to embrace, and with maturity comes the wisdom to accept that simple impossibility."

"What about the woman?"

"Which woman?" Master was surprised by his own question, as if another voice had asked it. "That human female. Yes. Frankly, I don't think she's important in the smallest way. I don't even know why I am thinking about her."

"Because I'm forcing you to think about her."

"Why? Does she interest you?"

"Not particularly." Ash looked up abruptly, staring at the oval black eyes. "She asked you a question. Didn't she?"

"I remember. Yes."

"What question?"

"She asked about human beings, of course." With a gentle disdain, the historian warned, "You are a young species. And yes, you have been fortunate. Your brief story is fat with luck as well as fortuitous decisions. The Great Ship, as an example. Large and ancient, and empty, and you happened to be the species that found it and took possession. And now you are interacting with a wealth of older, wiser species, gaining knowledge at a rate rarely if ever experienced in the last three billion years—"

"What did she ask you?"

"Pardon me. Did you just ask a question?"

"Exactly. What did this woman say?"

"I think . . . I know . . . she asked, 'Will humanity be the first species to dominate the Milky Way?' "

"What was the woman's name?"

A pause.

Ash feathered a hundred separate controls.

"She did not offer any name," the historian reported.

"What did she look like?"

Again, with a puzzled air, the great mind had to admit, "I didn't notice her appearance, or I am losing my mind."

Ash waited for a moment. "What was your reply?"

"I told her, and the rest of my audience, 'Milk is a child's food. If humans had named the galaxy after smoke, they wouldn't bother with this nonsense of trying to consume the Milky Way.' "

For a long while, Ash said nothing.

Then, quietly, the historian inquired, "Where is my assistant? Where is Shadow?"

"Waiting where you told him to wait," Ash lied. And in the next breath, "Let's talk about Shadow for a moment. Shall we?"

"What do you remember . . . now. . . ?"

"A crunch cake, and sweet water." Shadow and Ash were standing in a separate, smaller chamber. Opening his mouth, he tasted the cake again. "Then a pudding of succulents and bark from the Gi-Ti tree—"

"Now?"

"Another crunch cake. In a small restaurant beside the Alpha Sea."

With a mild amusement, Ash reported, "This is what you remember best. Meals. I can see your dinners stacked up for fifty thousand years."

"I enjoy eating," the alien replied.

"A good Aaback attitude."

Silence.

And then the alien turned, soft cords dragged along the floor. Perhaps he had felt something—a touch, a sudden chill—or maybe the expression on his face was born from his own thoughts. Either way, he suddenly asked, "How did you learn this work, Ash?"

"I was taught," he offered. "And when I was better than my teachers, I learned on my own. Through experiment and hard practice."

"Master claims you are very good, if not the best."

"I'll thank him for that assessment. But he is right: No one is better at this game than me."

The alien seemed to consider his next words. Then, "He mentioned that you are from a little world. Mars, was it? I remember something . . . something that happened in your youth. The Night of the Dust, was it?"

with a careful tone, he asked, "Should I bring your assistant to you? Would you like to see him now?"

"Please."

"Very well." Ash pretended to step outside, turning in the darkened hallway, centuries of practice telling him where to step. Then he was inside the secondary chamber, using a deceptively casual voice, mentioning to Shadow, "By the way, I think I know what you are."

"What I am?"

With a sudden fierceness, Ash asked, "Did you really believe you could fool me?"

The alien said nothing, and, by every physical means, he acted puzzled but unworried.

Ash knew better.

"Your body is mostly Aaback, but there's something else. If I hadn't suspected it, I wouldn't have found it. But what seems to be your brain is an elaborate camouflage for a quiet, nearly invisible neural network."

The alien reached with both hands, yanking one of the cables free from his forehead. Then a long tongue reached high, wiping the gray blood from the wound. A halfway choked voice asked, "What did you see inside me?"

"Dinners," Ash reported. "Dinners reaching back for billions of years."

Silence.

"Do you belong to one of the first five species?"

The alien kept yanking cables free, but he was powerless to void the drifters inside his double-mind.

"No," said Ash, "I don't think you're any of those five." With a sly smile, he reported, "I can tell. You're even older than that, aren't you?"

The tongue retreated into the mouth. A clear, sorry voice reported, "I am not sure, no."

"And that's why," said Ash.

"Why?"

"The woman asked that question about the old species, and you picked that moment because of it." He laughed, nodded. "What did you use? How did you cut a few minutes out of a Vozzen's perfect memory. . . ?"

"With a small disruptive device—"

"I want to see it."

"No."

Ash kept laughing. "Oh, yes. You are going to show it to me!"
Silence.

"Master doesn't even suspect," Ash continued. "You were the
one who wanted to visit me. You simply gave the Vozzen a good
excuse. You heard about me somewhere, and you decided that you
wanted me to peer inside his soul, and yours. You were hoping that
I would piece together the clues and tell you what I was seeing in
your mind—"

"What do you see?" Shadow blurted.

"Basically, two things." With a thought, he caused every link
with Shadow to be severed, and, with a professional poise, he
explained, "Your soul might be ten or twelve billion years old. I
don't know how that could be, but I can imagine: In the earliest
days of the universe, when the stars were young and metal-poor,
life found some other way to evolve. A completely separate route.
Structured plasmas, maybe. Maybe. Whatever the route, your
ancestors evolved and spread, and then died away as the universe
grew cold and empty. Or they adapted, on occasion. They used
organic bodies as hosts, maybe."

"I am the only survivor," Shadow muttered. "Whatever the reason, I cannot remember anyone else like me."

"You are genuinely ancient," Ash said, "and I think you're
smarter than you pretend to be. But this ghost mind of yours isn't
that sophisticated. Vozzens are smarter, and most humans, too. But
when I was watching you thinking, looking at something simple
—when I saw dinners reaching back for a billion years — well, that
kind of vista begs for an explanation."

Ash took a deep breath, and then said, "Your memory has help.
Quantum help. And this isn't on any scale that I've ever seen, or
imagined possible. I can pull in the collective conscience of a
few trillion Masters from the adjacent realities . . . but with you, I
can't even pick a number that looks sane . . ."

The alien showed his pink teeth, saying nothing.

"Are you pleased?" Ash asked.

"Pleased by what?"

"You are probably the most common entity in Creation," said
Ash. "I have never seen such a signal as yours. This clear. This
deep, and dramatic. You exist, in one form or another, in a fat,
astonishing portion of all the possible realities."

Shadow said, "Yes."

"Yes what?"

"Yes," he said with the tiniest nod, "I am pleased."

*   *   *

Always, the sun held its position in the fictional sky. And always, the same wind blew with calm relentlessness. In such a world, it was easy to believe that there was no such monster as time, and the day would never end, and a man with old and exceptionally sad memories could convince himself, on occasion, that there would never be another night.

Ash was last to leave the shop.

"Again," the historian called out, "thank you for your considerable help."

"Thank you for your generous gift." Ash found another cup of tea waiting for him, and he sipped down a full mouthful, watching as Shadow untethered the floating pack. "Where next?"

"I have more lectures to give," Master replied.

"Good."

"And I will interview the newest passengers onboard the Ship."

"As research?"

"And as a pleasure, yes."

Shadow was placing a tiny object beside one of the bristlecone's roots. "If you don't give that disruptor to me," Ash had threatened, "I'll explain a few deep secrets to the Vozzen."

Of course, Shadow had relented.

Ash sipped his tea, and quietly said, "Master. What can you tell me about the future?"

"About what is to come—?" the alien began.

"I never met a historian who didn't have opinions on that subject," Ash professed. "My species, for instance. What will happen to us in the next ten or twenty million years?"

Master launched himself into an abbreviated but dense lecture, explaining to his tiny audience what was possible about predicting the future and what was unknowable, and how every bridge between the two was an illusion.

His audience wasn't listening.

In a whisper, Ash said to Shadow, "But why live this way? With him, in this kind of role?"

In an Aaback fashion, the creature grinned. Then Shadow peered over the edge of the canyon, and speaking to no one in particular, he explained, "He needs me so much. This is why."

"As a servant?"

"And as a friend, and a confidant." With a very human shrug, he asked Ash, "How could anyone survive even a single day, if they didn't feel as if they were, in some little great way, needed?"

River of the Queen

I

EVERY VOICE SPOKE OF THE QUEEN. "WHERE IS She?" "Ascending!" "Do you see Her?" "In my dreams, yes!" "Do you smell Her?" "Absolutely, yes!" "The All ends, the new All walking in its tracks!" "Praise the Queen!" "Bring us the Queen!" "Where is She now?" "Ascending!" Stirred among the voices were animal grunts and hollers; better than any words, they captured the wild anticipation—a chorus of piercing, wordless roars that almost obscured the tumbling thunder of the great river. And behind the voices and roars were the percussive clack of nervous limbs and the extruded symphonies of pheromones, a giddy sense of celebration laid so thick across the setting that even a pair of human beings— mere tourists—could appreciate the unfolding of great, glorious things.

Quee Lee shivered beneath her robe, purring, "This is wonderful. Remarkable. And really, it hasn't even begun yet."

Her husband nodded and smiled, peering over the edge.

"Can you see Her?" she joked.

"I see some of Her entourage," Perri admitted. "Down in the mists. Can you make them out?"

The railing was made from thick old vines grown into elaborate knots, golden leaves withered, dried spore-pods ready to burst. Quee Lee leaned against the top vine. A beautiful woman in a thousand ways, she gazed into the mayhem of plunging water and endless snowstorms, her smile widening when a few wisps of black appeared for the briefest instant. Long albatross-style wings were trying to rest inside bubbles of calm air; a few of the Queen's devoted assistants were gathering themselves before resuming their long climb.

"Will the wind-masters reach us?" she inquired.

"Most won't." Perri had a young, almost pretty face, fine features amplifying a pair of clear bright eyes that could only be described as sweet. He had turned to the right, watching the main lane, watching thousands of Dawsheen wrestling for position. "The last time I was here," he allowed, "only a handful of those big flyers survived the climb."

"Is it too far?"

The cliff was more than eleven kilometers high.

"It's more the cold and snow, I think. And not just the wind-masters suffer. Most of Her entourage dies along the way." Then in the next breath, with an easy conviction, he added, "But still, this is the best place to be. This is Her final gathering point. Being here is an enormous honor."

"I know," Quee Lee sang. "I know."

Perri didn't mention costs. His wife had donated a substantial sum to the Dawsheen, and nothing would come from it but this one opportunity to endure the glacial cold, standing among the alien throngs to catch a glimpse of the fabled Queen. Their private vantage point was an ice-polished knob of black basalt. The river was to their left—a shrunken but still impressive body of water hugging the cavern wall, flowing hard and flat until it reached the neatly curled lip of the towering cliff. The city lay to their right, perched on the higher ground. Beneath the city, where the cliff was a dry black wall, a single zigzagging staircase had been etched into the stone. By custom and for every good reason, the Queen never took a step upward. Her assistants carried her beautiful bulk, using the honored old ways. On foot and with the fading strength of their limbs, they were bringing her up the final eleven kilometers of a grand parade that began centuries ago, in the warm blue surf of the Dawsheen Sea.

"She won't arrive for a little while," Perri cautioned. Then he touched Quee Lee with a fond hand, adding, "This is our ground. Nobody can take it from us. So why don't we go somewhere warm, and sit?"

"I don't want to miss—"

"'Any little thing.'" Perri winked with one of his sweet eyes. "But remember. This is a wonderful city in its own right, and in another week or two, there won't be anything left to see."

"We should walk around," she agreed.

Stepping back from the dying vines, he suggested, "And maybe we can treat ourselves . . ."

"'To a little drink or two,'" she said, doing a seamless imitation of her husband's voice.

"'To be social,'" he said, imitating his wife's voice and mannerly sense. "'To be polite.'"

Then together, inside the same moment, they thought of the city's fate. In another week or two, it will be dead and buried under the relentless blizzards; and with that thought, a sudden respectful silence fell over the two of them, accompanying them as they moved hand in hand down their own little set of carved stone stairs.

II

Perri had that young face, for, in a fashion, he was a youngster. Born on the Great Ship, he possessed an immortal's durability and memory, his body endowed with relentless good health. In ancient times, he would have looked like a man in his early twenties— adulthood just achieved, childhood still lurking in the face and manners. But time and age were different creatures today. The youngster was a few centuries more than forty thousand years old, and, in that busy long life, he had explored just a tiny fraction of the avenues and caverns, chambers and odd seas that lay inside the Great Ship.

By contrast, Quee Lee preferred an older, more mature appearance. She moved like a woman who had forever to accomplish the smallest deed—a suitable facade, since she was considerably older than her husband. Born on the ancestral Earth, she still remembered that magical day when the first alien words and images were captured by telescopes. An explosion of learning and change was unleashed, her wealthy family becoming wealthier, and her own life extended beyond all calculable measure. Humanity expanded to the stars, but without Quee Lee. She preferred home and its comfortable pleasures. Then an automated probe discovered the Great Ship—a world-sized derelict still on the fringes of the Milky Way, falling out of deepest space. Humans claimed the Ship as their own. They made it habitable and sent it on a looping cruise around the galaxy. For a muscular fee, anyone could book passage. For a fortune, a wealthy individual could travel in seamless luxury. From the time of the pharaohs, old women had been embarking on great voyages. Starships and river barges served the same function: Here was a chance for novelty and learning, and maybe a little adventure or two, which was all the reason a lovely and rather naïve woman needed to abandon one comfortable life for another, beginning a lazy stroll around the Milky Way.

Husband and wife were perfectly at ease, walking up the wide lane, hands clasped and heads tipping toward one another whenever one of them spoke. Sometimes a finger would point, some little question asked and answered, or the question was repeated to a buried nexus, dislodging a nugget of information from some data ocean, another tiny piece of the Dawsheen existence explained to the curious tourists.

The little lane was covered with hard sheets of living wood, turquoise and photosynthetic when the weather was warm, but now turning black and soggy in the cold. No one else used the lane. Heaps and ridges of hard dirty snow stood to the sides, and behind the snow were vegetable masses, dome-shaped and crenulated where they pushed through the snow, their sides punctured with doorways leading into chambers of every size. What passed for leaves had died with the first hard freeze. The masses themselves were dying, choking under the snow while their roots froze with the soil. But the hollow chambers in their wooden hearts remained inhabited. Sheets were hung across the doorways, the heated air inside making them ripple, and the sloppy, half-melted ice on the thresholds was littered with the long, faintly human prints of busy feet.

In one sense, Dawsheen biology was perfectly simple. Diversity was low, ecosystems few and trimmed to a minimum of trophic levels. One species always held prominence based on intelligence and tools. For convenience's sake, the rest of the Ship referred to them as the Dawsheen. Tripeds with a single burly arm in front and two flanking arms tipped with delicate hands, in the high country they tended toward round-bodied and short. Their skin was the color of sun-bleached straw, and their hair turned from black to gold as they aged. They were normally vegetarian. The Dawsheen home world had small continents, and feeding a mature civilization meant eating low on the food chain. But whenever the All collapsed into winter, meat became a cheap, holy indulgence. As the lovers strolled away from the edge of the cliff, the smell of burning fats and spiced vitals began to fill the air. With a hungry sigh, Perri mentioned, "There was a restaurant, last time. On that hilltop overlooking the river."

"Last time," she repeated.

That was nearly a hundred centuries ago. But with a tug on the arm, he reminded Quee Lee, "The Dawsheen don't like change."

Sure enough, another eating establishment was perched on the summit. But the hill was smaller than Perri remembered, the rock scraped down by the last glaciation. And the view wasn't quite the spectacle that he had promised Quee Lee. For that, he apologized. Snow was falling again, fed by the drenched air and the gathering cold. They sat together in one of the communal booths, on the steeply tilted bench, gazing at a gray expanse of water and the swirling white of the snow, and except for the occasional slab of ice being carried toward the falls and its death, nothing seemed to change outside.

But that was fine. There was the building itself to enjoy—a great home-tree hollowed out by worms, the flat floor and immovable furniture carved with a million relentless mouths. They could happily study the creatures sitting and walking about. There were tourists of several species, plus Dawsheens too old and feeble to stand in the cold, waiting for their Queen. The indoor air felt warm and smoky. Most of the patrons stared at an interior wall sprinkled with live images from downstream. The Queen Herself was never quite shown; She was too important to be reduced to a mere digital stream. Instead, audiences were treated to the celebrations held in distant cities. Beneath the illusion of a warm blue sky, millions of Dawsheen stood in the open and sang, wishing their Queen luck and bravery on the trails awaiting Her, and in the trials awaiting their species.

What passed for a waiter approached the two humans. Speaking through a translator, he called out, "Adore the Queen!"

"Adore the Queen!" they replied, amiable words transformed into an amiable singsong.

The alien face was narrow and stiff, the crest of hair turned a dull whitish gold. His breath smelled of broiled fish and exotic oils. Three pearl-colored eyes regarded them with no obvious emotion, but the translator made the voice sound angry. "She is a slow Queen," their waiter exclaimed. "A late Queen, at this rate."

Quee Lee glanced at her husband, waiting for advice.

With a shrug of shoulders, he told her to say nothing.

"If this weather worsens," the alien continued, "we will all be dead and frozen before She can Gather us."

A few of the elderly patrons growled in agreement.

The tourists shifted their weight against the polished wood. They had no menus, and no fees were expected. Where was the value of money when the world was dying? An enormous fire pit was dug into the middle of the room and lined with rock. Perri was ready to point at one of the platters of blackened food. But Quee Lee was a problem. As a rule, she didn't appreciate heads on her dinner—

"You've still got time," another voice called out. "The glacier isn't going to beat your little Queen!"

For an instant, Perri didn't notice what was different about the voice. Then he heard the singsong translation following in its wake, and, curious now, he turned. Four humans were sitting in a distant booth. The largest man was glowering at their waiter. Two other men were cutting at the seared flesh on their plates, eating with a famished urgency. The final man stared out at the falling snow, saying nothing and apparently paying no attention to his companion's complaints.

The waiter turned toward them, lifting one leg while standing on the other two—the standard Dawsheen insult.

The talking man didn't seem to notice the gesture. "I want a fresh plate," he called out. "And I want you to stop badmouthing your Queen."

The Dawsheen dropped his leg and faced Quee Lee, a tight little voice asking, "What would you like to eat, madam?"

"Nothing," she allowed.

"Ask me," the loud man called out. "I want something. Come here!"

"And you, sir?" the Dawsheen said to Perri. "I have a large pudding char that died of old age. For an adventurous set of stomachs, perhaps?"

Perri began to say, "Yes—"

"Hey!" the loud man shouted. "Before you're dead, old man. Why don't you pay a little attention to—"

Crack.

The sound was abrupt and astonishingly loud. No one was watching the loud man, and then everybody was. His face was beginning to bleed. His shattered nose hung limp on his face, too damaged to heal itself quickly. Two of his companions laughed quietly while they ate, enjoying his discomfort and embarrassment.

The other man continued to stare out at the relentless snow, his face and posture unchanged, while his left hand slowly and carefully set an empty iron platter back on the worm-carved table where it belonged.

III

The Dawsheen home world was a cyclic snowball.

Many worlds were. Even the young Earth passed through its own snowball phase. Watery bodies with a few small continents were most susceptible, particularly when their continents lay scattered along the equator. If its sun's energies flagged, or if the world's orbit shifted by the tiniest margin, the dark open waters at the poles would abruptly freeze over. Sea ice was a brilliant smooth white. Light and heat were suddenly hurled back into space, allowing the climate to cool further. The newborn icecaps then expanded, reaching into normally temperate regions. And with the world brightening again, it cooled again, and, again, the ice spread, and over the poles it began to thicken.

Seven hundred million years ago, the Earth's climate collapsed. A murderous cold reached to the equator. Glaciers born on the high peaks rumbled into once-tropical valleys. The ocean froze to a depth of nearly a full kilometer, and the water beneath was black and choked of oxygen. The cold was enormous, and enduring. Without evaporation, there were no clouds or fresh snows, and the glaciers began a slow retreat. Deserts of glacial till covered the barren land, frigid winds piling up towering dunes. But even in the most miserable cold, volcanoes kept rumbling and churning, spitting carbon dioxide into the sky. Without rainwater or plant life, the greenhouse gas built up to staggering levels. A tripping point was reached, and the seas began to melt, and snows fell again, the glaciers growing even while the heat continued to soar.

In a matter of decades—in a geologic blink—the glaciers burned away, and the world moved from snowball to furnace.

On the Earth, climates eventually moderated. The continents gathered together and drifted away from the equator, while the aging sun grew warmer. But with each snowball phase, earthly life was battered. Entire lines of multicellular species were pushed into extinction. The biosphere that eventually arose—the world of grass and men and jeweled beetles—owed its existence to those tiny few survivors that had clung to the deep-sea vents or swam in the hot springs on the shoulders of the great volcanoes.

But the Dawsheen world never moderated.

The largest moon of a massive gas giant, it was a blue body with tiny continents and tidal-churned tectonics. The climate continued swinging in and out of the snowball state with the precision of a pendulum clock. Predictability was a blessing. Predictability allowed the ancient Dawsheen to adapt to their suffering. Obeying the season, terrestrial plants threw spores on the wind, trusting that one in ten trillion would survive the cold drought. Animals climbed into the high mountains, building nests inside deep caves and stuffing them with thick-shelled eggs. The ocean's creatures changed their metabolisms, borrowing the slow, tiny ways of anaerobic organisms, living sluggishly in the deep darkness while the ice creaked and roared above them.

Every winter was a savage winnowing.

And every thaw left the world stripped and lifeless, defenseless and full of promise.

Surviving the winter wasn't enough. Success meant spreading quickly, breeding children to adapt to a landscape transformed by glaciers and eruptions. Success meant being first to swim into the first dark thread of ocean seawater, and breeding first, and fending off every rival to your rapidly growing empire.

Cooperation brought the greatest successes.

The early queens were ensembles: Species hiding together in the largest, most secure redoubts, existing as totipotent spores and fertilized eggs along with a dowry of mummified bodies and dried shit—organic wealth brought to feed and fertilize what was, in simple terms, an ark that was waiting for the next All.

That was a billion years ago.

Life on the Earth was a little more than a film, a gray tapestry woven of single-celled bacteria; while on Dawsheen, the Queen was gradually and inexorably becoming more interesting and more elaborate, evolving into an absolutely beautiful woman.

IV

"Bride of the world, Bride of the All!"

They could scarcely hear their own translators. At this penultimate moment, the city's entire population was standing along the main lane, every Dawsheen chanting in an eerily smooth chorus, the melded voices loud enough to shake stone and passionate enough to make humans shiver and smile at one another. Quee Lee turned to her husband, winking in a certain way, remarking, "It's as if we've wandered into—"

"What?" Perri shouted. "What did we—?"

"An orgy!" she hollered. "We've stumbled across an orgy!" Then she reconsidered, saying, "No, no! It's a salmon run. Coho spawning! Isn't it a little that way, Perri—?"

Their translators screamed:

"Accept our selves, our offerings, our souls!"

The crowd was a blur, a vivid living mass of the Dawsheen lining the parade route, plus another twenty or thirty, or perhaps forty, animal species visible from that little knob of basalt. The bulky species stood alone, clambering little bodies dancing on their shoulders and backs. Limbs rose high. Every creature was full-grown, and many were elderly. Why make children when this world was about to end? Trembling bodies shoved against their neighbors, forming two astonishingly straight lines. Nothing mattered but the Queen. Nothing else existed. The exhausted vanguard of Her entourage moved onto the wide lane. The intelligent Dawsheen led the procession, each wearing elaborate ceremonial robes and carrying relics from great, long-past Alls. Behind them, big work-grazers pulled wagons filled with a tiny sampling of Her wealth—sacks of blessed soil, and armored plates made from titanium and cultured diamond, and slabs of pasteurized fat sealed in plastic, and one long banner lit from within by electrified gases, showing the redoubt that had already been prepared for Her at the top of the cavern, at the birthplace of the Long River.

"There . . . I see Her. . . !" Quee Lee cried out.

The Queen was being lifted up the last long flight of stairs, rising over the cliff's lip at a slow pace that might have been majestic, but more likely signaled great fatigue. She was huge. Her body looked like an enormous caterpillar, turquoise and gold plates shining in the snowy light. What might be legs were wrapped securely around the trunk of a sky-holder tree. Handles and saddles had been fastened to the tree, and every possible species helped carry Her. Work-grazers and Dawsheen and bounce-maidens and three-cautions and whisper-winds; and in the middle of the tree trunk, a pair of massive hill-shakers strode along, each with six pillarlike legs, each leg stepping with practiced care, setting the pace for the others.

A centuries-long climb was nearly finished.

But the achievement wasn't quite as astonishing as it seemed. The sky-holder tree was mostly hollow, saving weight. And the Queen's body was nearly as empty. The carapace was a tough, enduring contrivance—diamond fibers woven into a structure able to endure the angry weight of entire glaciers. The Queen's true self was astonishingly small. But as Perri liked to explain, "It makes sense, being small. A little body is easier to move and protect. A little body can fall into hibernation faster, and then awaken first." Over the recent centuries, on various occasions, he had reminded his wife, "Really, you don't need much space to hold a world's genetics. A sampling of every species . . . a few million examples, each no larger than a single cell . . . well, you could hold that treasure inside one trustworthy hand . . ."

The thundering chants reached a higher, brighter pitch. It felt as if the cliff was shaking, ready to collapse. And then the enormous Queen was in view, and the mood changed, the crowd falling into a perfect, sudden silence.

Quee Lee sighed, and shivered.

Perri looked back across the city. Thousands of spore-pods began to leap high, home-trees and vines and the living lanes throwing their genetics into the damp, snowy wind. And in the next instant, the pods detonated, filling the air with talclike dust. Perri coughed, and Quee Lee sneezed. But the natives remained silent, focused on this ultimate moment. As the Queen passed, each Dawsheen stepped forward. The two lines pushed inward, bodies clambering on top of bodies. With the aliens came the rough equivalent of rats and scorpions, dogs and sparrows, and underfoot, furry worms and tiny bugs. With a quiet solemnity, every creature opened its clothes or parted its fur—in some way exposing itself—needlelike penises and distended vaginas delivering their cargo with a minimum of fuss, and just enough bliss.

Quee Lee nudged Perri with her elbow. She gestured, and he followed her gaze. Half a dozen giant wind-masters were still trying to finish their long climb. Exhausted, ancient, and nearly starved, their movements were weak but precise, using a last little updraft somewhere in the cold, dense air. Perri began to say, "Too bad." They were majestic creatures. Perri had hoped he and Quee Lee would see at least one of them glide in above the parade; that would make the spectacle complete.

Not today, he thought.

Then a new motion grabbed his gaze. Another wind-master was skimming along the edge of the cliff, just above the falls. It was black and elegantly slender, and large even at a distance. After a moment, it flapped its wings and twisted its body, and the body rose, rising up level with Perri.

He nudged her with an elbow, and nodded.

Quee Lee whispered a few words.

"What—?"

"Stronger," she whispered. "Than the others."

It was. The enormous flyer was powerful enough to flap hard, gaining velocity as it continued to ascend. Suddenly it was above them, vanishing into the snow and spores. For an instant, Perri thought he could hear air moving fast. Which was ridiculous. The deep rumbling of the waterfall wouldn't let him hear anything as subtle as wings . . . and then, inside that same instant, he heard what seemed to be a new chant, unexpected and sloppy, and not half as loud as the Gathering had managed before.

"No, no, no!" their translators cried out.

And then with a bluntly descriptive voice, the machines shouted, "PANIC. THIS IS THE SOUND OF. PANIC."

Again, there was a rush of air overhead.

Almost too late, Perri looked back at the Queen. A strange little fire had erupted along Her back, a haze of blue plasmas brightening, lifting up like a flap of iridescent flesh. There was a clean, sharp *crack*, and the Queen collapsed into three pieces. The carapace shattered and fell off its perch on the sky-holder tree, and out of the clouds came something narrow, black, and wingless. It dove hard and stopped instantly, absorbing that terrific momentum; an instant later, mechanical hands delicately reached inside the Queen, retrieving a squirming gray body not much larger than a human being.

Quee Lee moaned, calling out, "What is it—?"

The machine had lifted again, vanishing into the falling snows.

"What was that?" she asked, more puzzled than worried, more disappointed than angry.

Perri said nothing.

He was staring at the enormous panic—arms swaying in agony; voices cursing wildly; waves of tiny sparrowlike flyers struggling to chase after their stolen Queen—and then with an expression that looked a little amused, and thrilled, and focused, he turned to his wife and shook his head, telling her, "Stay with me. Stay close!"

V

The building only resembled its neighbors—a home-tree facade encompassing a set of rounded rooms that pretended to have been shaped by determined worms. But every surface was cultured diamond braced with threads of hyperfiber. The furnishings had a slick, impervious feel promising durability as well as ease of cleaning. One of the back rooms, visible at the end of a remarkably straight hallway, was enclosed with hyperfiber bars—horizontal, not vertical—and inside that cage stood half a dozen curious Dawsheen, with a single harum scarum sitting behind them, threatening to crush anyone who came near her.

Many things in the universe were not universal, Perri reflected. But police stations very nearly were.

"I have no authority," said the officer on duty.

Quee Lee halfway laughed, admitting, "And I'm not precisely sure why we're here."

The Dawsheen looked at Perri. "I have no authority," he repeated. "Do you claim special knowledge about a criminal incident?"

"Maybe," Perri said.

The alien spoke, and three separate translators asked, "Which criminal incident?" with a flat, incurious sound.

"The kidnapping."

The translators struggled to deliver that simple concept. A blur of barks and tweets ended with the station's translator taking charge of the interview. Its AI asked Perri directly, "Do you mean the Queen?"

"Yes."

"Do you know Her whereabouts?"

"No." Then he shook his head, deciding that wasn't quite true. "Or maybe I do. Maybe."

"But you have some useful knowledge?"

"I think so. Yes."

The officer sat listening to the conversation between machine and man. One leg was thrown behind his tilted bench, while the others were locked in front. Every hand lay in a pile on the little desk set before him. He wore a greenish-black uniform of densely woven yarns. His face was covered with bristly golden hairs. Every eye was open, but there was no way to determine if he was even a little interested in what was being said.

Finally, he muttered a few syllables.

"My superiors are searching for Her," he offered. "I have no authority, but I will listen to whatever you say."

"I saw some men," Perri began. "Human men. My wife and I noticed them before the Gathering."

Quee Lee glanced at him, sensing some little portion of his reasoning.

"I recognized one of those men," Perri claimed.

"What did you know?" the officer inquired.

"He's a smuggler, on occasion."

Quee Lee was not particularly surprised, nor disappointed. She knew her husband well enough to leave this matter until later. For now, it was enough to make a dismissive cluck with her tongue, smiling and staring back at the jail cell.

"You recognized this smuggler?"

"I think so," said Perri. "Yes."

"His appearance was familiar to you?"

"No."

"No?"

"His face had been modified. Disguised. Smugglers have a thousand methods—"

"But you recognized his voice," the officer pressed.

"No. It's a new voice, and that also means nothing. Every time that I've seen him, he sounds different." Perri cut the air with one hand—a Dawsheen gesture promising that he was telling the truth. "I've known this man for thousands of years. I know his manners, his methods. I know how he moves his hands, and his tongue. Lately, he's been working with a pair of brothers. The fourth man in their party was a stranger, and he seemed to be in charge."

Like any cop, the Dawsheen had to ask, "How is it, sir, that you are familiar with a notorious smuggler?"

"I know just about everybody," Perri replied without hesitation.

Quee Lee flinched. It took all of her willpower to say nothing.

"I have no authority," the Dawsheen said once more. "My superiors are searching upriver. The Queen will be recovered soon. Soon." An unreadable expression passed across the narrow, bristly face. "In a matter of moments," he promised. "But you can be sure, I have already relayed your words to every one of my superiors."

"How can you be sure?" Quee Lee blurted. "That you'll find Her, I mean."

"Every escape route is closed," Perri offered. Turning to his wife, he explained, "Up and down the Long River, every tunnel and little doorway has been closed. And sealed. No one can get inside this cavern, much less escape." Then he looked at the officer, asking, "Is that why you're confident?"

The Dawsheen replied and the translator snapped, "Yes."

"Loon Fairbanks," Perri offered. "That's the smuggler's name. And believe me, he anticipated everything. He knows all about your security systems. Your psychology. The weather, and every other factor. Loon will have a good, solid plan. That plan's unfolding now. If those men and your Queen are still inside the cavern, it won't be for long. And if he can get Her out, what chance do you have to find Her inside the Great Ship?"

The officer fell silent, his white eyes dulling slightly.

"I can help you," Perri said. "I want to help you. I don't particularly like that man, and I wish to be of service to your Queen."

The alien stood abruptly.

"I have the authority!" he shouted with an astonishing energy. A cabinet jumped open, a hyperfiber vest and two weapons flying across the room. He put on the vest and pocketed the weapons, and then one of his little hands touched a control, causing the cage in the back room to open. The horizontal bars fell into a neat triangular pile at the feet of the prisoners. In a near-scream, he told the Dawsheen, "You have been freed. Go home and wait for the glacier."

The harum scarum rose to her feet, towering above the rest. From her speaking mouth, she snarled, "What about me?"

"I do not like you. You have earned my scorn and my distrust, and if you can live with that burden, you also are welcome to leave."

VI

Slowly, slowly, the Dawsheen biosphere grew more sophisticated, intricate, and robust. The brutal winters both delayed and inspired the wheel of evolution. There were never many species, but each was highly adaptable. Native genetics were intricate and miserly. No gene, useful or otherwise, was thrown away. Who could guess when or how one of these developmental oddities might become precious?

In little steps, intelligence arose. Simple civilizations flickered into existence—in the scattered valleys, typically—and each was summarily crushed under the next river of ice. Yet there are advantages in the occasional Death. Wipe your world clean and begin again; what society wouldn't relish that chance now and again? The young Dawsheen began to educate their Queens, leaving them with instructions. Each All began with hints and advice, and clear warnings left behind by the wise departed. Each All blossomed with the help of thousands of past Alls. Every new city was superior to its forbearers. Every new society was quicker to grow and more likely to remain at peace. Gradually, the Dawsheen acquired industry and high technology. Like humanity, they cobbled together enormous telescopes—radio ears listening to alien gossip. With that burst of knowledge, they built starships and found empty worlds. But where most spacefarers embraced some flavor of immortality, the Dawsheen resisted. Their winters and the cleansing glaciers were too important, too deeply embedded in their bones. They bolstered their life spans, but only to a few thousand years. And when they learned to control their climate, they made their winters as brief as possible. But they wouldn't surrender their most powerful myth: The Dawsheen regarded themselves as creatures of endless change, born from a world of relentless reinvention. The occasional Death was a blessing, and each new All was fresh and full of potentials. In the Dawsheen's lustrous white eyes, most alien species seemed humdrum, and stodgy. And pleasantly, even deliciously, contemptible, too.

VII

Perri sat in the back of the little ship studying his own holo-map.

"You may examine our map," the Dawsheen remarked. He was sitting at the ship's controls, carefully touching nothing. The AI pilot was keeping them close to the river's face, ice piled on ice, tiny leads betraying the cold black water beneath. "My map is accurate to the millimeter, and updated by the instant."

"Thank you," Perri replied, his voice distracted. "But no, thank you."

Quee Lee glanced over her shoulder. She was sitting beside the Dawsheen, her robe pulled snug across her squared shoulders. Suspicious and a little amused, she watched her husband as he stared into that maze of colored lines and pale spaces. "My husband is very proud of his map," she mentioned. "He loves it more than he loves me, I think. There are entire months when I can't pry his nose away from it."

Perri acted oblivious, enthralled with his own narrow business. The tiny projector in one hand displayed a comprehensive view of the Long River, and with his free hand, he poked and prodded. For no obvious reason, certain points needed to be enlarged and studied in detail. He let his instincts steer him. Quietly, he explained, "You have an enormous area to search. The river starts under the ship's hull—here—and twists and turns its way back and forth, down, down, down, into your little sea. The drop is nearly three thousand kilometers. Except near its source, it's a lazy river. A couple meters down for every kilometer crossed. The river is nearly one and a half million kilometers long. The longest river in the galaxy, no doubt. And since the cavern has an average width of twelve kilometers, your living area is about equal to the lands on your home world . . ."

"It is a satisfying relationship," the officer interjected.

Passage on the Great Ship was expensive, even for a single entity. To lease an enormous habitat required frightful sums. The Dawsheen had surrendered titles to half a hundred worlds—difficult planets with climates too stable or seas too tiny to feed deep ice ages; perfect for an inventive ape that could terraform, then colonize, making homes for billions of prosperous souls.

"This is a maze," Perri cautioned. "A huge and intricate, beautiful maze. And I don't think you can search it. Not in the time left, no."

For the umpteenth time, the officer remarked, "We have sealed every exit. There is no way to escape."

"You're searching upriver," Perri continued. "But they could have taken the Queen downstream."

"No," the Dawsheen replied. "We tracked them coming this way."

Perri said, "I bet so."

He touched an approaching sector, asking for an enlargement. A thousand square miles of ice and raw stone appeared before him. And again, he fingered portions of the map, gazing into the wasteland's corners.

Quee Lee smiled gently.

"It just occurred to me," she said. "I don't know your name."

The Dawsheen uttered something quick and soft. His translator said, "Lastborn Teek."

With genuine sadness, she repeated, "Lastborn."

"A common name," the Dawsheen explained. "As Firstborn is common at the beginning of an All."

The river was entirely frozen. And the weather continued to worsen, snow falling in thick white waves, hurricane winds trying to push them out of the sky. The worst gusts made the ship tremble. But shape-shifting wings and powerful engines kept them on course. Lastborn studied his controls and listened to reports from distant search parties, empty hands closing and opening again with a palpable nervousness.

Quee Lee looked over her shoulder.

"Darling?"

Perri didn't react.

She said, "Darling," again, with a certain weight.

He noticed. A soft sigh proved it, and his eyes blinked, his poking hand held steady for a moment.

"What are you thinking, darling?"

He wasn't sure. Until the question had been asked, his thoughts were utterly invisible to him.

"Our friend deserves to know." She reached back. Her hand was small and warm, soft in every way, little fingers wrapped around his elegant young hand as she pulled gently, insistently, saying again, "Lastborn deserves to know."

"The flyer is up in the glacier," Perri guessed. "It's going to be buried, but not that deep. Camouflaged, but not that well."

Lastborn said nothing.

"And there's going to be at least three trails worth following. Heat trails, boot prints. Signs of another flyer, probably. That's how it will look."

Alien fingers tightened into knots.

"Have there been any ransom demands?"

With a touch, the Dawsheen took the controls away from the AI pilot. In a near-whisper, he spoke for a long moment. Then his translator admitted, "The flyer was discovered a little while ago. It was left empty, hiding in a rock crevice. Not in the ice."

Quee Lee smiled with a nervous little pride.

"The flyer was empty almost from the beginning," Perri explained. "If I was stealing Her . . . I think I would have slipped the Queen into a second ship. A better ship. Then I'd double back. Somewhere below the city—"

"Where?" Lastborn asked.

Then, in the next instant, he reminded Perri, "Every passageway out of our world is closed, and secured, and—"

"Here," Perri interrupted.

He pulled his view back a hundred kilometers, passing over the city and dropping with the enormous falls. "A lot of things in this universe are difficult," he explained, enlarging the map again. Beside and beneath the Dawsheen cavern were more caverns and tunnels, plus innumerable fissures too tiny to wear any name. "But cutting a new door isn't difficult," he muttered. "In fact, with the right tools, it's about the easiest job that there is."

VIII

Ten thousand years ago, Perri came home from a long wandering.

His wife greeted him in every usual way. She made love to him, and he returned the pleasure. She fed him and let him sleep, then woke him with fond hands, using his body until both of them were spent, breathless, and dehydrated. Then they staggered into Quee Lee's garden—a many-hectare room filled with jungle and damp hot air—and naked, they kneeled and drank their fill from a quick clear stream. Where the stream pooled, they swam and bathed, tired legs barely able to carry them back onto shore. With a voice frank and earthy, Quee Lee spoke to her husband. She explained how much she had missed him. She had craved his voice and stories and his pretty mouth against her mouth, and in her dreams, she had played cruel, sordid games with his cock and fat balls. She never spoke to anyone else with those words. No other lover, not even to pretend. Perri had been gone longer than usual—several years, and without a word. "Where were you?" she finally asked. "Where did you take that lovely little dick of yours?"

Perri laughed, gently and happily. Then with a matching voice, he described his adventures. With some like-minded idiots, he had explored one of the Great Ship's engines—a moon-sized conglomeration of machines with pumps as big as cities and sentries lurking at every turn. That consumed most of his time. Then he went gambling, playing twenty-deck poker with a platoon of humans and harum scarums and Blue Passions and AI souls. In less than sixteen days and nights, Perri managed to surrender most of the allowance given him by his very generous wife. He had let himself look embarrassed and a little desperate, smiling painfully at the better gamblers, asking for one more chance. "One more hand? With a fresh twenty decks, maybe?" He charmed and begged, and of course when the cards were dealt, every suspicious eye was fixed on Perri. But his awful luck held. He had nothing. A Blue Passion at the far end of the table gathered up the enormous pot with her suckered fingers; and three days later, in an entirely different corner of the Ship, the same alien surrendered Perri's share of the profits, along with her weepy thanks.

"She was in awful trouble," Perri explained. "She absolutely needed that money."

"You're so noble," Quee Lee teased. "A woman in need—"

"Anyway," he interrupted. With his earnings, he bought a used slash-car, and in the depths of the Ship, in a looping tunnel used only for racing, he had raced. And won. And won again. He described driving the car, hands wrapped around an imaginary wheel, the stone and hyperfiber walls blurring around him. Then just as Quee Lee was about to ask to see his new toy, Perri admitted, "I crashed it. Mangled it, and myself. I was clinically dead for a full week. It took most of my winnings to rebuild my body. The autodocs asked if I wanted improvements, but I honestly couldn't think of one. Being perfect, as I am."

Both laughed.

And then, with a very slight change of tone, Perri said, "The Long River." He rolled onto his back, asking, "Do you know much about it?"

She said, "I've heard it mentioned. Yes."

"And the Dawsheen?"

She knew about them, but not much.

Perri explained the snowball world and its enduring biosphere. Quietly, slowly, he described the city perched beside the eleven-kilometer falls, and its inhabitants, and the amazing parade. A Queen had been carried past. An entire world gave Her its seed. And after the Queen was gone, safely entombed in a redoubt high above the blue ice, Perri had waited, watching the river freeze solid while the enormous snows fell, thousands of Dawsheen buried in their homes, happily falling into the eternal sleep—their bones and souls crushed beneath the newborn glacier.

It was a sad, spectacular thing to witness.

The voice that began soft and happy turned softer and awed. Perri was lying naked on the bank of the stream, on his back, staring at the illusion of stars floating inside the room's high ceiling. With her frank, practiced hands, his wife measured his mood, and when nothing happened, she admitted defeat. She curled up beside him, and tenderly asked, "What happens to the Queen?"

"She waits," he promised. "Safe and high, She waits. Everything below Her is frozen now, glaciers stretching down to the sea. But in another century or so, spring comes. The heat soars, and the ice melts, and inside that tough shell of Hers, She rides the flood down to the sea."

"And then?" she whispered.

"The Queen is a repository," Perri reminded her. "She's a living, sentient ark. But She only holds the land-dwelling species. Fishes and sea creatures . . . they rely on a second ark . . . a different sort of body that's waiting under the sea ice . . ."

"A second Queen?"

"Yes," he said. Then in his next breath, "No. It's not a Queen. It's something else entirely—"

"Her King?"

He said, "No." And then with a second thought, he allowed, "Maybe. In a certain fashion, I suppose so."

Quee Lee slid her hand across his newborn chest and belly. In countless ways, she was grateful that Perri had survived. There were moments when she wanted to beg him to remain home, giving her the same devotion that he willingly gave to his adventures. But that would never happen. Outside of a daydream, there was no way for that to happen. Rubbing the bare chest, she took a deep breath, and finally, with a quiet firm and determined voice, she surprised both of them.

"Take me," she said. Then, "The next time winter comes. Show me."

Here was a fresh twist on a very old conversation. Perri tried to smile, reminding her, "You don't normally enjoy my adventures."

"I want to meet the Dawsheen," she persisted. "I want to see their Queen."

"Maybe someone should take you," he allowed.

"Maybe I should go myself."

"It's going to be cold and uncomfortable," he promised. "Watching a world die . . . it's going to be grueling. Do you think you're strong enough to endure that sort of fun?"

"And you think you're strong?" she countered.

Then with her smallest finger, she touched the corner of a newborn eye, gathering up the glistening remains of a tear.

IX

The world was white, and damned. The snow fell in waves, burying the dead lanes and high roofs, wiping away every last trace of the city. Huddled inside their homes—inside their graves—its citizens could do nothing but wait for any good news, nursing little hopes amid wild despair. Only the river held the thinnest promise of life. Flat slabs of ice moved in a great parade, immune to fear or caution, holding their pace until their prows pushed out into the air, and dipped, each slab falling with smooth inevitability, dropping over the brink of the falls, still floating on the face of the water as it plunged into a cold, fierce maelstrom.

Lastborn took them over the brink, and down.

Eleven kilometers of air and spray and thunder lay below them. Behind the water stood the basalt cliff. Sensors began working, hunting for things that were surely trying to hide—a few bodies and probably some machinery, plus every trick of camouflage that a smuggler could drag along.

The sensors found plenty, none of it remarkable. Each vertical kilometer was examined in detail, and then the Dawsheen took them back toward the sky, flying along the waterfall's lip, peppering the current with tiny probes better suited for other, easier jobs.

Perri ignored the search, or pretended to ignore it.

"No one is here," Lastborn declared.

Perri was squinting into his elaborate map, studying an empty maze of tunnels situated on the far side of the cliff.

Again, the Dawsheen said, "There is no one." Then with an improving sense of things, he turned to Quee Lee, confessing, "My tools and patience are exhausted. I will leave you inside the jail, where you will be safe—"

"No."

Both of them said that word. Quee Lee spoke with a begging tone, while Perri nearly shouted.

Then again, he said, "No." The map dissolved and he pocketed his tiny projector. "Leave us at the base of the falls," he told Lastborn. "I've got one good place to look."

"There is, I promise, no one." But the alien relented, dashing over the little knoll where the couple had watched the Gathering, then dropping fast. Where the cliff was exposed, it formed a massive black wall decorated with that single zigzagging white line. The line was the staircase covered with snow. Now and again, little shapes came into view, crawling their way up through the snow. Half a dozen secondary parades were attempting the long, hard climb. These were the Queen's little sisters. Evolution and pragmatism demanded their existence. What if disaster struck? But no Queen had been lost during the last ten thousand Alls. They were symbols only—emergency repositories of genetic matter accompanied by smaller entourages, each encasing only a fraction of the genetic wealth held by their big sister.

The base of the cliff was bare rock, the freezing mist from the adjacent falls reducing visibility to a soggy arm's length.

"Where?" Quee Lee asked.

Perri looked at her for an instant. "Maybe you should—"

She leaped first from the craft, and again, with a half-scream, she asked, "Where?"

"We'll work our way along the base," he allowed. "Move closer to the falls."

The rocks were treacherous, slick, and jumbled. Sensing the terrain, their boots sprouted crampons. Their robes shed the freezing water, channeling it off to their downstream side. Too late, Quee Lee turned to say, "Thank you," to Lastborn. But he had already lifted off. Then to her husband, with a modest concern, she asked, "Won't the water crush us? Or the falling ice?"

"Probably," he said, stepping into the lead. "But most of the ice is slush before it reaches the bottom, and the river's down to a trickle. Compared to what it was."

"You pray," she said.

He laughed grimly, saying, "Help me pray. That just about doubles its effectiveness."

They marched. Rock litter and massive boulders quickly vanished beneath a frosting of new ice. In a sense, it was an easy walk. The cliff was always to their left, always close. A foot might plant wrong, but the boot invented some way to faultlessly hold the balance. Sometimes Perri moved ahead too quickly, and vanished. But later, as Quee Lee grew accustomed to the pace, she began to catch him, a gloved hand set firmly against his back, reminding him of her presence and urging him to hurry.

At some ill-defined moment, they moved behind the great falls.

Half a kilometer later, they were utterly blind. Their robes were pushing against their functional limits. The falling sleet sounded like an avalanche of gravel. Quee Lee refused to quit, but she was regretting her stubbornness. Never again, never, would she let herself ignore her rational instincts, following after Perri in one of his little miseries . . .

Perri stopped in the wet blackness. Crouching, he activated his holo-map. But instead of checking their position, he ordered up one of the Ship's main reactors. Then he magnified that portion of the map, peering inside the reaction chamber. The light was sudden, brilliant, and pure. This was a traveler's trick: Dial to a bright place, and let the map illuminate your surroundings.

The image couldn't be brighter. Draining the projector of its charge, it threw a white glow against the base of the cliff. They could see a cavern, or maybe some overhanging spur of rock. A glimmering light came back at them. Perri stood and walked toward the glimmer. It brightened gradually, and lifted, and, after a long while, Quee Lee looked up to see motion overhead. She was watching two figures apparently walking on their heads.

The ceiling was hyperfiber.

The bones of the Great Ship lay exposed. Tumbling waters must have chiseled away the basalt, revealing the supporting strata. She looked at herself—a sloppy, pale version of herself—and then she looked ahead again, hurrying after Perri, the air drying and the roar of the sleet falling into an angry rumble.

She didn't see the kidnappers.

Perri slowed and dimmed his map, and he kneeled, saying nothing. With a hand in the air, he asked her to drop beside him. Then he extinguished the map, letting a second light burst into view.

In the distance, the cave ended with a wall of low-grade hyper-fiber. Three men stood before it, manipulating a plasma drill, using slow measured bursts to peel away the barrier in millimeter bites. Work fast, and someone might notice the energy discharges. Work too slow, and someone might stumble into their hiding place. The men seemed perfectly attuned to their task, urgency and patience joined together. Burn, clean the new surface, and wait. Burn, clean, wait. Burn, clean, wait. The rhythm was steady and relentless, and very nearly silent. The only voice belonged to the man who had yelled at the Dawsheen waiter. "Now," he would say every minute. And the other two men would step behind opaque shields, letting the drill spit out another carefully crafted pulse.

"How did they get here—?" Quee Lee began to ask.

"We just walked past their ship," Perri interrupted, expecting the question. "It looks like a boulder. Because it is. A big hollowed out rock, reequipped and very sneaky."

She nodded, and squinted.

The drill pulsed, but she couldn't see what she wanted to see.

"The Queen—?" she began.

"I don't know," he admitted.

A minute later, the man called out, "Now."

And again, the drill pulsed. This time, Quee Lee happened to glance to her right, spotting two figures. The human was sitting on a flat slab of gray-black stone. The Queen was sitting, too. Was it Her? They weren't that far away. In the gloom, She resembled any Dawsheen. But there was a smoothness to Her features, a plainness, like a hurried sketch of something infinitely more complicated. She was wearing a plain cloak, nothing about Her distinctive. There was no hair or plumage, no flourishes. She was sitting across from Her kidnapper. Again, the drill pulsed, and the hyper-fiber continued to glow. With a voice that wasn't right for a Daw-sheen, the Queen said a few words. The man was wearing an odd wide smile, and he said a few words of his own, his voice sounding like the bleating of a child's toy.

Quee Lee tried to make sense of the scene.

And then she felt something, or heard something. For no conscious reason, she looked back over her shoulder, turning in time to see a boot perched on an adjacent rock, and the trousers tucked into the boot, the trousers lifting into a rounded body that was wearing the dark, thoroughly drenched uniform of a Dawsheen police officer.

She put her elbow into Perri's side.

He started to turn.

Lastborn aimed his weapon with a practiced touch, but his nervousness fought against an easy shot. It took another moment for him to feel sure enough to fire. The gun drained itself in one full blast, and the world turned white, the screaming ball of plasma rolling toward its target, a set of transparent diamond shields absorbing the blast, keeping the Queen from being incinerated.

Perri said, "Shit," and stood.

Lastborn unholstered his second weapon, and with that same nervous earnestness, aimed at the Queen.

Her shields had evaporated. She tried to run, and the human threw himself between Her and the attacker—a fearless, useless gesture—and Perri managed to throw a loose rock overhand, catching Lastborn on the back of his head.

The second blast hit the ceiling and faded.

In reflex, Quee Lee ran, sprinting at Lastborn.

The alien was working with his first gun, trying to find enough residual power for a second shot.

"Why?" she screamed. "Why?"

She grabbed the lead foot, and yanked, accomplishing nothing. "Why—?"

And then what felt like a great hand descended on them, and there was nothing else to see.

X

Every morning She would walk with Her instructors, and listen. The beach was made by the glaciers and living wind-reefs built from the sand. The sea was blue and warm and just a little salty. When Her instructors spoke, the tropical blue air filled with words about duty and history and honor and the great noble future. The duty was Her own, demanding and essential, while the honor was entirely theirs. Who wouldn't wish to nourish and educate the newborn Queen? Together, they shared a history reaching back into a mist of conjecture and dream; while the future lay before Her, as real as anything can be that has not yet been born.

She was an empty vessel walking beside the warm blue water—a large vessel filled with countless empty spaces, each space begging to be jammed full of important treasure.

Her powers were obvious. Every animal fell silent and still as She passed, staring at Her simple body with the purest longing. Every bush and fruited blade threw out its spores, hoping to find Her blessing. Even the tiniest microbe struggled to reach Her, crawling wildly across a dampened grain of quartz while one of Her vast and noble feet rested on the sand.

The Queen's little sisters didn't elicit such dramatic responses. One day, She looked back at them and at their own little entourages, and with a simple curiosity, She asked, "What will happen to them? What is their future?"

Her first instructor was an elderly Dawsheen woman. She answered with a dismissive tone, as if to say, "What happens to them does not matter." But then, sensing the Queen wasn't satisfied, she explained, "They will follow you, always. And hibernate in their own safe havens. And your children will eat their sleeping bodies. Except for the one or two of them that will be sent away—"

"Sent where?"

"Another world, perhaps." The face was full of indifference. The little sisters couldn't be less important to this old woman. "We roam the galaxy for a purpose," she reminded her student, gesturing to the illusion of a blue sky. "At this moment, my people are searching for suitably empty worlds."

Even at that early age, the Queen had the good sense to say nothing else.

Then there was a different walk, on an entirely different day. She sensed eyes staring and a silence. But the stare didn't come from the trees or soil this time. She looked out at the little waves, and what resembled a mossy stone bobbed in the surf, a pair of enormous black eyes watching nothing but Her.

She had never seen one of the Others.

For the briefest instant, with a mixture of curiosity and desire, She returned the gaze. And then Her instructor covered Her eyes with every hand, and a tight, sudden voice warned Her, "It should watch your sisters, not you.

"That one is not yours," the old woman cautioned.

"Your Magnificence . . . Your Other has already been chosen . . . infinitely suited for You and Your glorious duty . . . please, please, turn Your eyes away . . . that Other is sick, and peculiar, and You do not want to know anything more about it. . . !"

XI

Perri woke slowly. "There's a general alert," someone said. Then after a pause, the same voice said, "Shit."

He pried his eyes open. And breathed. His pain told him that he still had hands and feet, and an intact body. His skin was warm and bare. His arms and legs were lashed down. Someone sat beside him, similarly restrained. Quee Lee. Was she awake? Maybe. He wasn't certain. Then he looked at two figures sitting on the floor opposite him—a human hand lay hidden inside the Queen's Dawsheen-like hands, and what was meant to look like a human face betrayed a mixture of bliss and simple horror.

Suddenly, finally, Perri understood.

Again, the voice said, "Shit."

The male creature sitting before him spoke in a whisper, and a translator buried in his false throat asked, "What is wrong now?"

The smugglers sat in the front of the little cap-car, each eavesdropping on a different sliver of the security net. Loon's voice said, "Shit," a third time. And then he turned and grimaced, claiming, "We'll slip past anyway. I've got emergency routes waiting. I've beaten these general alarms plenty of times."

Quee Lee stirred.

Quietly, she called to her husband.

Perri nestled against her. "You're all right now."

"And you?"

He didn't answer. With a rapt intensity, he stared at the Queen, and after a moment, he asked Her, "Why?"

The man-figure looked at him now.

"Why?"

Neither entity answered that deceptively simple question.

Then Loon threw up his arms, saying, "This shouldn't have happened. If you'd let me kill that Dawsheen—"

The Queen bleated, and Her translator said, "No."

"No killing," said Her companion. "I explained—"

"An old, doomed Dawsheen. Good as dead already." Loon shook his head, frustrated and enraged, and helpless. "But of course we had to leave him. We had to give him the chance to get off a warning."

Again, Perri asked, "Why?"

Quee Lee was naked. Her robe, like Perri's, had been taken away, along with every link to their buried nexuses. But they were unhurt. Loon was a smuggler. In the right circumstance, he might kill an alien, but murdering another human being was an entirely different crime.

"I don't understand," Perri confessed. "Explain this to me. Why?"

Quee Lee said, "Love."

Dipping her head, she said, "Don't you see? The two of them . . . in some sense . . . they're in love with each other. . . !"

Perri shook his head, a thin laugh breaking out. "Except that's not what I'm asking them."

Now both aliens stared at him. Wary, but curious.

"I know what you want," Perri claimed. "You want each other. You're hoping to escape, to get onboard one of the little starship taxis heading somewhere else . . . another world, and freedom . . . and that's why you've gone to all this work and risk—"

"Yes," the Queen rumbled.

"And that's why they want you to die," said Perri. "You're a traitor, in their eyes. A danger. An abomination!"

"Shut up," Loon told him.

"But you're not dangerous," Perri continued, "and you're not any kind of abomination. Believe me, I understand. All you want is to be together. You want only what Queens and Others have wanted from the beginning of time. An empty world, a fresh beginning, and the chance to realize your own future . . ."

Loon started to say "Shut up" again.

But the human figure lifted a hand, in warning. And with a smooth male voice, it said, "We have a beautiful, beautiful world to build."

"I can believe that," Perri replied instantly, without any doubt.

The Queen spoke, the musical voice diluted into the inadequate words, "A new world unlike any. A lovely, elegant All!"

An alarm sounded, loud and urgent.

Loon cursed and abruptly changed course.

Quee Lee leaned forward, her lovely face smiling at them. "It must be very important to you, to sacrifice so much. It's the only thing that matters in your lives, I would think."

The Queen said, "Yes."

Despite the simple translation, Her voice held a longing and a sad desperation and the faint, dying hope that something worthy would come out of all this crazy wanting.

Again, Perri said, "I still want to know why."

They stared at him, puzzled.

"Why did you ever hire Loon Fairbanks? Why did you think he was going to be your salvation?"

No answer came.

Then Loon rose to his feet, telling everybody, "Will you just shut the hell up now!"

"That man smuggles objects, and he's not even the best at that." Perri shook his head with a growing disappointment. "You needed the finest. You deserved nothing less!"

Quietly, the Other asked, "Who is the finest?"

"Me. I am."

Silence.

"What you should do," Perri advised, "is fire Loon. Dismiss him, and do it now. This minute. Then I'll hire him and his crew as my subcontractors, and I'll try to get you what you desire, and deserve."

The Queen spoke, no translation offered.

With the tone of a sorry confession, Her partner/mate admitted, "But we have no more money to give."

"Goodness, that's no obstacle," Quee Lee blurted. Then she grinned and patted her husband on the bare knee, exclaiming, "Believe me. This darling man works for surprisingly little!"

XII

Her neighbors let her live alone for the next few years, enduring her shame. Her embarrassment. Her shocking notoriety. And then in a gradual but relentless process, they began to invent ways to cross paths with Quee Lee. She might be shopping in a market or walking in one of the local parks, and one of her human acquaintances from a nearby apartment would appear without warning, wearing a benign smile, muttering, "Hello," before mentioning in the same breath, "We haven't seen nearly enough of you lately." Even alone, they always spoke for the "We." That tiny word implied that each person stood among many, many like-minded souls. "We've worried about you," they might say. Or, "We miss you, Quee Lee. Come visit us, when you have the strength."

Strength wasn't a limiting issue. She couldn't remember when she had last felt this strong. And their worry was genuine, but only to a point. No, Quee Lee kept to herself for other fine reasons. She let her old friends speak among themselves, and gossip, and out-and-out spy. Only when it felt right did she begin walking the neighborhood again, visiting one or two of the wealthy souls who lived along her particular avenue. About her troubles, no one said a word. About her adventures . . . well, nobody could stop thinking about what had happened. She saw it in their staring faces. The wondering. The outrage. The almost comical fear that blossomed whenever they remembered that their dear friend had been involved in things illegal, violent, and strange.

About Quee Lee's husband, nobody asked. Fifty years had to pass before a woman-friend felt bold enough to say the name, "Perri," while looking at the ancient woman with a mixture of concern and simple nosiness.

"What about my husband?" Quee Lee asked.

"How is he?" the woman inquired. Then fearing that she had overstepped her bounds, she added, "Is he comfortable, where he is?"

What could she say? The truth?

Never that, no.

Instead, Quee Lee shrugged and remarked, "He's comfortable enough. And he looks reasonably contented."

"How often do you see him?"

"Every three weeks, for twenty-one minutes per visit," Quee Lee reported. "Those are the terms of his sentence. One visitor every twenty-one days, and the rest of his time is spent among the general population."

"You poor soul," the friend moaned. "We're all so sorry for you."

"Don't be," was Quee Lee's advice. "Really, it's not that awful. It's not even that unpleasant, considering."

The wicked truth was that Perri adored prison. He found himself surrounded by strange aliens and dangerous people, and the Ship's enormous brig was an entirely new wilderness open for his explorations. During Quee Lee's visits, he spoke in whispers, hinting at great new stories that would have to wait for another century to be told. In principle, they were supposed to be alone in the visitation chamber, but you could never feel sure about your solitude. The chamber was a hyperfiber balloon. A molecule-thick screen stood between them. Permeable to light and sound, but to nothing physical, the screen allowed them to undress and perform for each other, and sometimes that's what they did. Sometimes Quee Lee didn't care who might be watching them. And with an honest longing, she always told her husband, "I miss you. I want you. Make the years hurry up, would you?"

"I will," he always replied, his perpetual laugh quiet and sweet.

Perri's sentence was one hundred and one years. An excellent attorney and a surprisingly law-abiding record had helped reduce his punishment. What hadn't helped was his stubborn refusal to implicate any other player or players in that very peculiar crime.

For more than sixty years, none of the neighbors dared mention the crime.

It was another good friend who finally brought it up. He was sitting with Quee Lee, sitting in her little jungle and helping her drink some of her more exotic liquors, and when the drugs and silence got too much, he blurted out the words, "What in hell were you thinking?"

She knew what he meant. But to be stubborn, she asked, "When?"

"Because you had to know all about it," he argued. "You went off with Perri, on that little vacation of yours, and ship security claims that you were with him and those two Dawsheen—"

"They weren't Dawsheen," she interrupted. "They were sentient genetic repositories."

"According to the Dawsheen, they were criminals." Sixty years of waiting was erased. The man was too drunk and self-consumed to let this issue pass for another moment. "I saw those security digitals, Quee Lee. Everybody has."

"That isn't legal," she rumbled. "Those are confidential."

"It's a little crime," he countered. "Call the Master Captain, if you want."

She fell silent.

Again, he said, "I saw the digitals. From twenty angles, I watched your husband and that Dawsheen criminal. Sorry, I mean that sentient genetic repository criminal. Dressed up to look human, and walking with Perri and that storage trunk with the Queen stuffed inside—"

"I know what happened," she mentioned.

"Your husband was trying to slip them onboard that star-taxi. He had them past security . . . I don't know how . . . and he waved good-bye, and turned away . . . and then someone noticed something wrong, I guess . . ."

Quee Lee said nothing.

"That alien with the plasma gun. Now that was a real Dawsheen, am I right?"

"He was one of their police officers. His name was Lastborn—"

"The trunk was floating next to that human-looking repository, and then it was gone. Destroyed. The Queen was dead."

"I know."

"It was a public place, for goodness sake. Some innocent could have been hurt, or killed."

She held her tongue.

"Then the repository screamed and exposed its own weapon, and dropped to its knees, and . . ." His voice failed him. The memory of that human face—the agony, and the devastation—still bothered him after all these years. "He shot himself. I mean, it shot itself."

"I know."

"With a thousand innocent travelers running everywhere, screaming in absolute terror."

"I saw it myself," she confessed. "I know."

Eyes widened. "So you really were there?"

She didn't answer him.

"In disguise, were you?"

With a little finger, she wiped at her eyes.

"We've heard that your husband refused to implicate anyone else. He was protecting your good name, I suppose."

"Maybe."

"Protecting his sweet money tit," the man barked.

A cold moment passed. And then with a black, hard voice, Quee Lee said to her long-time friend, "Really, it would be best if you left. Now. And if you can, I think you should run. Because in another moment, or two, I'm going to find a knife, and I'm going to cut out your ugly heart."

XIII

A century and a year had passed.

Perri strolled out of the Ship's main brig, and before anything else, hugged his wife; and then together, they went on a very long journey. Like honeymooners, they stayed at various resorts and beaches and odd, out-of-the-way hotels that specialized in supplying fun to people who were accustomed to nothing else. In the middle of their travels, in full view of any watchful eyes, they rented a private suite in one of the deeper districts. For a full week, as far as any eavesdroppers could assume, they didn't leave those luxurious confines.

A hidden passageway and an unlicensed cap-car allowed two people to travel a thousand kilometers, reaching an empty corner of the Great Ship.

A second, equally anonymous cap-car carried them elsewhere.

Pressed close together, Perri and Quee Lee crawled up the narrow confines of a nameless fissure. He didn't know their precise destination. He relied on his wife to say, "Stop," and then, "There. That wall."

A hidden doorway let them pass.

The cold was abrupt, and brutal, and wonderful. The tilted floor of the cavern wore a river of blue ice. Above them, hidden in the rocks and snow, was a tiny redoubt; and fifty kilometers downstream was a brief, deep lake with just enough room for a single creature to swim in the dark, waiting for the inevitable spring.

"Another few years," Perri mentioned.

The Queen would awaken and ride the spring floods, following her own little river to its mouth.

In this relatively tiny volume, the two Dawsheen repositories would merge into one, reshuffling and reformulating their genetics, creating an entirely new lineage of species and phyla. The basis for an entirely new world would blossom inside a few dozen square kilometers; and later, when the time was ripe, another new Queen and Her Other would be born.

That's when Perri would finally slip them off the Ship.

When nobody was looking, he would send them to their own empty world.

"It'll be lovely," said Quee Lee. "Whatever they manage to make here, I'm sure it will be wonderful."

Perri looked across the rugged ice and snows, and then he turned, smiling happily at his wife.

"Let's walk around," he suggested.

She shivered under her robe, asking, "Now? What could we possibly find here now?"

"I don't know," he allowed with a boyish giggle. "That's why it's worth walking around."

The Cuckoo's Boys

1. HERE'S YOUR FIRST ASSIGNMENT:

Build a starship. And I want you to tell me all about it. Its name. How big it is. What it is made from. Tell me about its power plant and engines. How many are in the crew, and what are their names? They deserve names. Are they human, and if not, what? Draw them for me, and draw your ship, too. Do you have weapons on board? If so, what kinds? You might want to carry some little scout ships along for the ride. Anything else that you might think is useful, I'll let you take. Plus there's one piece of gear that I'm putting on board. It's a box. A box about this big. Inside is a wormhole. Open its lid, and the wormhole swallows your ship, transporting it to somewhere else. You'll travel through space and through time. Or maybe you'll leave our universe entirely.

There's no way to know what happens next.

It's all up to me.

My name's Houston Cross. Call me Mr. Cross, or Houston. I'm going to be your science mentor for the year.

John was one of the first PSs born. He is thirteen years old, and since he hasn't been skipped ahead in school, he's an eighth grader. A growth spurt and a steady lack of exercise have made him larger than many adults. His kinky black hair is short. His coffee-colored skin has a boy's smoothness, still free of whiskers on his chin and hair on the forearms. His brown eyes are active, engaged. He smiles with a nervous eagerness, and sometimes, particularly when he's excited, he talks almost too quickly to be understood.

"Thanks for taking me," he blurts.

Then he adds, "Ms. Lindstrum says you've been doing this for a long time."

Ms. Lindstrum is the school's Gifted Facilitator.

"She says I'm lucky to have you."

Houston shrugs and halfway laughs. "I wouldn't know about that."

"How long have you been a mentor?" John asks, saying it in one breath, as if the sentence were a single word.

"Five years," Houston replies. "This is my sixth."

"Have you ever worked with us?"

"Eighth graders? Sure—"

"No. I mean us. Or do you teach normals, usually?"

Houston waits for a moment, then says, "I understood the first time." He shakes his head, telling the boy, "Please don't talk that way."

"Oh. Sorry!" John is instantly angry with himself. It shows in the eyes and how the big hands wrestle with one another. "You know what I mean. Normal gifted kids."

"Sure, John."

"I'm not better than anyone else," he blurts with a robust conviction. "I don't ever let myself think that way."

"Good."

"And I try to get along. With everyone."

"That's a good policy, John. Getting along."

The boy sighs, his face suddenly very young and tired. He looks around the empty classroom, then gazes out the long window. A wide green lawn ends at a quiet street, shade pooling beneath tall pin oaks.

"Can I start?" he asks.

"Excuse me?"

"With my starship. Can I, Mr. Cross?"

"Be my guest."

The Facilitator met with Houston yesterday. She warned him that John was an only child, and he lived with his divorced mother —a common circumstance among PSs. Perhaps that's why the boy suffered from feelings of guilt and loss and powerlessness. "But in the plus column," she added, "the mother is relatively well educated, and she seems to genuinely care about him. When she finds time."

John holds his stylus in his left hand, head bent forward, using an electronic workpad for the rest of their hour. He stops only to say that his hand is sore. When the bell rings—an obnoxious, metallic clanging—he looks up in panic, exclaiming, "But I'm not done yet!"

"Work at home tonight," Houston offers. "Or tomorrow. Here. We've got plenty of time, John."

The boy scrolls through page after page of sketches and hurried labels. Shaking his head in despair, he says, "This is all shit. I'm sorry about my language, Mr. Cross. But this is all just shit."

"We'll try again tomorrow."

But the boy isn't mollified. Folding his notebook, he says, "I get these ideas. All the time. But a lot of them . . . well, they're just stupid. You know? They're *rancid. . . !*"

The mentor smiles in a thin way.

He says, "John," and pats the boy's left hand.

He says, "Believe me. Everyone chews on that shit sandwich."

Phillip Stevens was the only child of an African-American man and his German-American girlfriend. Phillip was labeled gifted before he was eight. He graduated from Princeton at eighteen, then dropped out of medical school two years later in order to form his own corporation. His first billion dollars was made before he was twenty-six, most of it coming from the rapidly growing genetics industry. His later billions came from shrewd investments and several medi-technical advances in which he played a hands-on role. Following his thirtieth birthday, Phillip began pouring his wealth into a new research facility. To visitors and the press, he boasted that he would do nothing but cutting-edge research that would alleviate human misery. But close associates grew concerned with the real direction of their work, and to those malcontents he said, "Here's six figures. Now quiet, or I'll have your nuts for lunch."

Too late, the CDC believed the warnings about the billionaire's plans.

Federal agents in bulky biosuits descended on Phillip's empire. But the criminal had already vanished, taking with him nearly fifty liters of growth media and an artificial microbe dubbed Phillip 23.

Mike was one of the last PSs born.

He has just skipped the sixth grade. No growth spurt has taken him, and judging by his wiry build, he's physically active. The face is narrower than John's, and two years younger, and something about it seems harder. He lives with parents of modest means. According to Ms. Lindstrum, the boy's genetics have little mutations. Which is normal among the lastborn. "Maybe it's his genes," she warned Houston, "or maybe it's something else. Either way, Mike has a different attitude. You'll notice it right away."

"How'd you get this job?" the boy asks. Flat out.

"With bribes," Houston replies. Instantly.

"No," says Mike, never blinking. "I bet they gave you some special tests."

Houston laughs, admitting, "They asked a lot of questions. But I don't know if I'd call it a test."

"When did this happen?"

"When I started working in the schools."

"How long have you been a teacher?"

"A mentor."

"Yeah. That." Mike has long hair—longer than any current fashion—and either through pharmaceutical tricks or the mutations, it's straighter and edging toward blond. The boy spends a lot of time pushing unruly locks out of his brown eyes. "You've been a mentor for a long time. Haven't you?"

"Several years now."

"But you didn't deal with *us* till now." He says it, then smiles with a slyness, happy to prove his special knowledge. "I've been asking about you."

"You have been."

"Shouldn't I have?"

Houston waits for a moment, then asks, "Did you talk to John about me?"

"God, no. Not that idiot."

Houston says nothing.

"No, there's some guys you used to teach. To mentor. Whatever." Mike names them—both boys are in high school now—then adds, "They thought you were pretty good. All things considered."

"All things considered, that's good news."

"They told me that you steered clear of *us*."

Houston doesn't respond.

"Why is that?"

"You weren't old enough." He speaks calmly, without doubts. "I like working with middle schoolers. Not children."

The comment makes an impact. The boy almost smiles, then remembers his next question. "What did they ask?"

"When?"

"When you became a mentor. What kinds of questions did you get?"

"The interviewer wondered what I knew about gifted students. He asked what I would do in this situation, or that one. And he checked to see if I'd ever been arrested—"

"Have you been?"

"Five times." he says. Then he asks, "Do you believe that?"

"No," the boy snorts. Then, "What about this year? Did they make you do anything special before you got us?"

"Some things," Houston admits. "I had to read various books and some very boring reports. And I went through special in-depth training for an entire afternoon. I needed to be sensitized to your circumstances and special needs."

"Oh yeah? I've got special needs?"

"Everyone does, Mike."

"What else?"

"I signed a contract. I'm never supposed to talk to the press. Ever." Houston's voice sharpens, just for that instant. Then he smiles, adding, "All questions are handled through the Special Task Office at district headquarters."

Mike seems impressed with the answers or the precautions. Or perhaps both.

Houston prods him. "Work on your starship. Okay?"

Instead of a workpad, Mike has a fat spiral notebook and a pen leaking an unearthly green ink. With his left hand, he writes *Day One* on the first page. A moment's reflection leads to a little laugh, then a sly glimpse at his mentor. "Hey, Houston," he says. "Can I have an antimatter cannon?"

"I don't know. What is an 'antimatter cannon'?"

The boy rolls his brown eyes. "It's a cannon. It shoots balls of antimatter. They explode into pure energy when they hit *anything*."

"Okay. But how would a weapon like that work?"

"What do you mean?"

"Is your ship built from antimatter?" Houston asks. "And the crew, too?"

"That would be stupid," the boy assures him. "The first time we landed on another planet—boom."

"But how do you keep your shells from destroying you?" Houston asks the question, then leans closer. "How do you manipulate something that you can't touch?"

The boy thinks hard for a moment, then says, "Magnets."

"Okay."

"We make cannonballs out of anti-iron," he says, "and we keep them in a vacuum, held there by a really powerful magnetic field."

"Good enough," says Houston.

Mike shakes his head, admitting, "Those guys I know . . . they warned me. You can really be un-fun when you want to be."

Houston says, "Good."

The boy folds himself over his notebook, working with the same fevered intensity that John showed. But he doesn't complain about a sore hand, and while the sketches are sloppier than those on a workpad, he seems infinitely more pleased with the results.

After the bell rings, Houston admits, "I'm curious. What do you want to do with that fancy cannon?"

"Blow up planets," the boy says. Instantly. Then he looks up, wearing a devilish grin.

"Is that okay with you, Houston?"

"Sure," he says. "Why not?"

The synthetic protozoan, Phillip 23, was a mild but durable pathogen carried by spit and the air. Healthy males and children rarely showed symptoms. The old and impaired developed flu-like infections, and at least a thousand died during the epidemic. But fertile women were the preferred hosts. The bug would invade the monthly egg, consume the mother's nucleus and mitochondria, then replace both with huge amounts of nuclear material.

The disease struck all races and all parts of the globe.

Victims included nuns and teenage virgins and at least one lady on death row.

During the epidemic, some 3 percent of all conceptions on the planet were baby boys carrying Phillip Stevens's genetic code.

"Your third mentee," Ms. Lindstrum began to say. Then she hesitated, contemplating her next words. They were sitting in the woman's tiny office. "The boy's name is Troy Andrew Holdenmeister. And I should warn you. His parents are utterly devoted to him."

Houston said, "Okay."

The Facilitator was scrolling through reports and memos and test results of every complexion. With a mixture of professional distance and practiced scorn, she said, "The mother has dedicated her life to the boy. She has three other children, but it's Troy who gets most of her attentions."

"I see."

"She wants to meet with you. Tomorrow, if possible."

Houston said nothing.

"And there's something else you should know: Troy isn't quite like the other PSs. His scores are lower in the usual peak areas. Math and science, and so on."

"Mutations?" Houston asked.

She shrugged, as if to say, "We can hope." But she had to admit, "He's only five months younger than John. Mutations were rare then. And the differences . . . well, it isn't likely that a few genes would change so much . . ."

Ms. Lindstrum looked like someone who had been married once or twice, and always too soon. She was tall and a little heavy around the hips, and beneath a professional veneer was a puddle of doubts and fickle emotions. Houston recognized the symptoms. They showed in the lonely eyes and the way she always would watch his eyes. He sensed that if he wanted, he could gently take hold of one of her hands, say the usual nice words, and have her. Within the week, Ms. Lindstrum would be making breakfast for him, wearing nothing but her best apron, smiling in a giddy, lovesick way.

Houston didn't reach for her hand.

"Is Troy adopted?" he asked.

Ms. Lindstrum shook her head. "I know someone who knows the family. Mrs. Holdenmeister was most definitely pregnant."

A newly standardized IQ score lay in plain sight. Houston underlined the number with his thumb, remarking, "There could have been some simple prenatal problem."

"Maybe," she agreed.

But probably not, thought Houston.

Then quietly and a little sadly, Ms. Lindstrum admitted, "It's a respectably average IQ. Enough to make any parent happy . . . if she didn't know any better . . ."

A thirteen-year-old boy sits hunched over a large, expensive workpad, focusing all of his attention on his starship.

"He loves this kind of project," says his mother. She sits at the front of the classroom, and without a gram of subtlety she stares at her son's mentor. "I'm relieved that you agreed to meet with me. Our last mentor didn't want to." The woman is small and delicate as a carpet tack, with fierce, little blue eyes that hint at a scorching temper.

Houston doesn't say what first comes to mind.

Instead, he tells her, "I want a good relationship with every parent."

"Do you have the other boys, too?" she wants to know.

He nods. "John and Mike. Yes."

"Try, if you can, to keep Mike away from my Troy." She says what she thinks, then thinks about how it sounds. To soften the moment, she adds, "John's very nice. We like him quite a bit. But the other one . . . he scares us, frankly . . ."

Houston says nothing.

He refuses to look at the woman. Instead, he stares into the blackness of the on-line screen. It covers the back wall. The teacher who uses this classroom in the morning has turned it off, which is standard policy. He makes a mental note to ask for the screen to be left ready to work, in case his students need help.

Perhaps sensing his mood, Mrs. Holdenmeister makes eye contact and tries a hard little smile. "If you need it, I can arrange for special software. And lab equipment. Anything of that sort."

"Not for now," he says. "Thank you."

"Because I'm perfectly willing—"

Houston interrupts, explaining, "What I usually do is give my students thought problems. They have to work out what's happening, and why, and what they can do about it."

"I see," she says, without conviction.

"And sometimes I'll make them face ethical dilemmas, too. What's right, what's wrong. And in the absence of either, what's best."

She opens her mouth, then hesitates.

After a long pause, she asks, "Would it be all right if I watch you at work again? With my husband. Name the day, and he'll take the afternoon off from work . . . if that wouldn't be too much trouble—"

"I don't believe so." He says it calmly, with a flat, unaffected voice.

"Excuse me?"

"I wouldn't be comfortable," he explains. "An audience isn't going to help me with what I'm doing here."

She doesn't know what to say. Sitting motionless, Mrs. Holdenmeister breathes rapidly, trying to imagine a new, more productive avenue.

She decides on pity.

"You know," she whispers, "it's been very difficult just getting him into the mentoring program. That Facilitator has fought us all the way."

"Well," Houston replies, "I agree with you on this one."

That wins a smile, cold but bright. Then she abruptly turns her head, saying, "Darling," with a big, overdone voice. "Do you have something for us?"

"Mr. Cross?" says the boy. He's nearly as old as John, but smaller. Not just thinner, but he hasn't found his growth spurt yet. Whatever the reason, he's little larger than the eleven-year-old Mike. Where the other boys have quick eyes, Troy's are simpler and slower. And while he has their voice, the words come out at their own studied pace.

"How is this, Mr. Cross?"

His mother snatches the workpad, then says, "Darling. It's wonderful!"

Houston waits.

"Isn't it just spectacular, Mr. Cross?" She hands the pad to him, then tells her son, "Great job! It's just wonderful!"

The boy and his software have drawn a starship with precise lines and in three dimensions. There are intricate details, and on the next pages, elaborate plans for the bridge and the engines. It's very thorough work, and that's all it is.

Quietly, without inflection, Houston says, "Troy." He asks, "Have you seen the movie *Starfarer*?"

"About a thousand times," the boy confesses.

"Because that's where this ship came from," Houston warns him. "You've done an exceptional job of copying it."

The brown eyes blink. Confused, suspicious.

But Mom hears an entirely different message.

"Good for you!" she sings out. "Good, good, good for you!"

2. *Your starship emerges from the wormhole.*

The first thing you see is a disk. The disk has stripes. Some dark, some candy-colored. Plus there are two blood-red swirls. And the disk itself is flattened on top and below, and it bulges out around its waist.

That's what you can see, and what else can you tell me?

"Is it Jupiter?" John asks.

"How do you know it's a planet?"

"Can I see stars?"

"Yes."

"The stripes are clouds. The swirls are hurricanes."

"All right. It's a planet," Houston concedes.

"Is it Jupiter?"

"Two red swirls," Houston repeats.

"Yeah, but that wormhole can take us through time. So it could be Jupiter. But millions of years ago."

"Good point. But it's not."

The boy nods compliantly, then grins. "Tau Ceti 5."

"Excuse me?"

"It's a planet. Haven't you heard about it?" Sensing an advantage, John explains, "They've found thousands of planets that look like Jupiter. The big telescopes spot new ones every day."

"They do," Houston agrees. "This isn't one of them."

"No?" The boy licks his lips, puzzled. "What about its sun?"

"Good question." The mentor pauses, considering his possibilities. "Two suns," he offers. "Close enough to touch each other."

"Can that happen?"

"Sometimes. But it's temporary. They'll lose momentum and fall together, then merge into one sun."

"Delicious!" he exclaims. Then, "What else can I see?"

"Moons. With your naked eyes, you count five of them."

"Big ones?"

"I don't know. How do we find out?"

John shrugs and says, "With sensors. I'll ask my sensors."

"What kinds of sensors?"

"Sensors." The boy believes in that word, and why can't Mr. Cross?

"But how do they work?" Houston asks. Then he warns him, "Not by magic, they don't. Every machine has its job and its inherent logic."

John grunts and says, "I don't know. They just work."

Houston shakes his head.

The boy compresses his mouth to a point, staring at his elaborate starship. It looks like a crystal chandelier with rockets stuck in its stem. "I don't get it," he finally confesses. "I thought we were going to explore the universe."

"So we'll start with good old universal principles," Houston tells him. "About light and energy and mass, for instance. Then later, if you really want, we can move on to those boring old moons."

*   *   *

The PS epidemic lasted thirty months. Occasionally the clones shared the womb with unrelated embryos. Sometimes they arrived as identical twins or triplets. But most were single babies, active and free of complications. In modern nations, a relatively simple test allowed expectant mothers to learn if their son was a clone. Many chose chemical or clinical abortions. And there was a deluge of orphaned babies that ended up with more forgiving or more desperate couples.

In certain backward nations, solutions wore harsher faces.

There were even places that pretended to escape the PS plague. Despite the global nature of this illness, despots and their xenophobic citizens denied ever seeing the clones, and they denied every rumor about organized infanticide. And even if babies were dying by the thousands, who could blame them?

A man and woman struggle to raise their own child. Why should they be forced to raise an abomination, too?

Which was what those babies were.

Abominations.

An opinion officially ridiculed by wealthy nations. Even while opinion polls found that a quarter to a third of their own people believed exactly that.

"The first thing I do is shoot it."

"Shoot the planet?"

"Are you going to let me?" Mike asks.

"Who am I? Part of your crew?" Houston lifts his hands, saying, "Wait. You haven't told me anything about the people on board."

"They aren't human."

"Okay."

"They're robots. Ten feet tall and built of smart metals."

Houston nods, then asks, "Do these robots have a leader?"

"Sure."

"What's his name?"

Mike dips his head, staring at his green-ink-and-paper starship. It's a bullet-shaped contraption bristling with every possible weapon.

"You'll want a good strong name," says Houston.

"Damned right!"

"How about Crocus?" he suggests.

"I like that! Crocus!" Mike nods and pushes at his hair, then asks, "Can Crocus fire his antimatter cannon?"

"Be my guest."

"All right. He lets loose a planet-busting round." Then, "What happens?"

"Nothing."

"What do you mean?"

"I mean it takes time for the round to reach its target."

Mike shakes his head, and with a disapproving tone says, "John warned me about this game of yours."

"You talked to John?"

"In the hallway. For just a second."

"I thought you didn't like him."

"I don't. He's a fat, twisted goof." Then the boy shrugs, adding, "But he always talks to me. I can't stop him."

Houston watches the narrow face, the narrowed eyes. Then, "How fast is your cannonball moving?"

"Fast."

"Make a guess."

"Half-light speed. How's that?"

"If it takes twenty seconds for the antimatter to reach the planet—"

"It's ten light seconds away." The boy dismisses the entire game, saying, "This is easy. That big planet is . . . let me think . . ." He does some quick calculations on paper. "Twenty million miles away. No, wait. . . ! Two million miles. Right?"

"Something like that."

Mike nods, happily in control. "So then. How big's the explosion?"

"Good-sized."

"Damn right!"

Houston shakes his head, saying, "The shell's moving half the velocity of light, which means it has a terrific momentum. It burrows into the atmosphere and turns to plasma and light, and the explosion comes squirting back up through the vacuum left behind it. Like out of another cannon, sort of."

"And the planet explodes—!"

"Hardly," Houston warns. "It's not nearly the explosion you want."

"That's stupid," Mike tells him.

"No," says Houston. "It's not."

The boy stares at his starship, confusion and betrayal on his face. And then a sudden little smile comes to the eyes and mouth, and he exclaims, "I get it. That world's antimatter, too. Isn't it?"

"What if it is?"

"Jesus," he says, with mock panic. Then he slams his notebook shut and says, "We've got to get the hell out of here!"

Worldwide, birth rates dropped for better than five years.

Couples delayed having children. Millions of women underwent hysterectomies, so great was their fear of conceiving a PS. The epidemic's climax was marked with incompetent news coverage sparking wild rumors. The most persistent rumor was that Phillip Stevens's genes were found inside every newborn, regardless of sex or race. And what made the rumor all the more pernicious was that it was true, in a sense: Humans were a young species. Eskimos and Pigmies shared vast amounts of genetic information. But that abstraction didn't translate well at work and home, and millions of healthy, non-PS offspring were aborted during the panic.

Even when a vaccine was available, people remained suspicious. What if it didn't work as promised?

Or worse, what if this was just the first plague? What if a hundred mad bastards were putting together their own bugs, and this mess was really just beginning?

"Maybe that planet has life," says Troy.

"Maybe so. How would you find out?"

The boy says, "I'll go there." Then he thinks to ask, "May I?"

"By all means."

Houston describes the two-million-mile voyage, and later, as the Hollywood-built starship slips into the atmosphere, Houston asks, "Who's in command?"

"The captain." Troy and his software have drawn a dozen people wearing trim blue uniforms. Everyone resembles a famous actor or actress. The captain is the tallest, oldest man, sporting a short dark beard.

"What's his name?"

"Storm. Captain Storm."

"Is he a human, or a robot?"

"Oh, he has to be human."

"Is he a good man?"

"Always." The boy looks at Houston with an imploring expression. "He wouldn't be the captain if he wasn't."

"Fair enough." Houston nods, smiles. Then he scratches his little beard, saying, "Your ship flies into a cloud and pulls in a sample."

"Of what?"

"I don't know. At room temperature and pressure, it's liquid."

"Like water?"

"Exactly."

"Maybe there's life in it."

"How would you test that?" Houston asks.

The boy inhales, then holds his breath. Thinking.

"Any ideas?"

He exhales, confessing, "I know I'm not supposed to use sensors."

"Did John tell you?"

Troy shakes his head, then catches himself.

"Don't worry," Houston says. "You can talk to Mike. I don't care." All the same, the boy seems ashamed.

Then Houston prods him, saying, "A microscope is a kind of sensor. And I'll let you use any sensor if you understand how it works."

"I do," says Troy. "I've got two microscopes at home."

"Okay. Use one of them now."

The hands assemble an imaginary slide, then the right eye squints into an imaginary eyepiece.

Watching, Houston quietly asks, "What is life?"

Then, in more concrete terms, he asks, "How do you recognize it?"

"Life is busy," the boy tells him, his voice pragmatic and pleased. "When I make a slide at home, what I look for are things that are really, really busy."

3. *You set down on a desolate world.*

A hard white plain stretches to the horizon. There's no trace of people or cities or even simple life forms. But perhaps something once lived here, and that's why you're putting on your archaeology hat.

I want you to dig into a piece of ground.

Like a scientist, you need to keep track of everything that you find. Everything. I want you to leave future generations with enough information to resurrect this dig site. Keep notes. Always. Make drawings and maps. And try to figure out what happened here.

There's a story waiting. If you can find it.

Houston has a small one-bedroom apartment that's a short drive from school. It's clean, but rarely tidy. He has lived here for a little more than five years. Prints of famous abstracts hang above the second-hand furniture. On a shelf fixed to one white wall is a pair of trophies. "Mentor of the Year," the plaques read. "Houston Cross." Both trophies show a pair of brass hands clasping—one hand large and grandfatherly, while the other is quite small and only half-formed.

He is working in the tiny kitchen.

Big old roasting pans are set in a row on the countertop. Inside each pan are pieces of shattered robots and random wires and the carefully dismantled bodies of several plastic toys. Houston bought three skeletal monsters, each with a humanlike skull and six arms rooted into a long back. He has cut them apart and thrown out the occasional piece—fossils are almost never whole—and after setting everything into a careful heap, he pours a fresh polymer-plaster into the pans, trying not to spill, and when he does, immediately cleaning up the dribbles and drops.

"Breaking news," says the television. It's an old high-density, but Houston built its AI from a kit, then trained it to find what interests him.

He glances up and says, "Show me."

"—furthermore, the study shows that once a minimally enriched environment is achieved, the boys' intellectual development plateaus—"

The pictured face could be John's. It's older than most PSs, and pudgy.

"Save it," says Houston. "I'll watch it later."

"Okay," says the machine.

He sets the three pans inside the oven, the low heat helping the plaster cure. Then he heats up last night's leftovers in the microwave and, sitting in front of the television, prepares to watch the news story.

"Breaking news," says his television.

"Show me."

"—the controversial book is the fifth most popular title in the world today. *The Cuckoo's Boys* has sold more than twenty million copies, despite being banned in much of Europe and Brazil."

The author appears. Beneath him floats a name. Dr. Paul Kaan. An ex-associate of Phillip Stevens, Kaan has a gentle face and hard, uncompromising eyes. Talking to an unseen audience, he explains, "I wrote this book because it's vital that people understand. What the PSs represent is nothing short of a debasing of our species and a debacle for our immortal souls!"

Houston watches the three-minute report.

Afterward, the screen returns to a mountain vista accompanied by a quiet dose of Grieg. More minutes pass. The oven timer goes off. Finally, almost grudgingly, Houston rises and pulls the pans out of the oven. Then he sits again, watching his dinner grow cold, and the AI asks, "Should I run the synopsis?"

"Excuse me?"

"About the intellectual development of the PS clones. Are you still interested?"

"Not really. No."

The curved tip of the butter knife bites into the plaster, and the blade itself starts to bow as John presses, working to expose a length of yellow-brown plastic bone. He's been working quickly, almost frantically, for most of the hour, taking notes only when coaxed. After two months together, Houston feels sure that the boy should be enjoying himself. But something is wrong. Is distracting him. It isn't much of a guess when Houston asks, "What's going on at home?"

"Nothing," John blurts.

"Okay."

"Nothing," he says again. Then as if caught in the lie, he adds, "Well, yeah. I got in a fight last night."

"With your mom?"

"No. Her boyfriend." He shakes his head, then shoves hard with the knife, the entire bone popping out of its hole.

"Notes," Houston urges.

"I know. I know." Abbreviated, useless observations are jotted down. Then everything comes to a halt. John drops the knife and says, "My wrist hurts. Really bad." Then he stares out the window, a dumbfounded rage in the eyes and the hard-set mouth.

After a long moment, Houston asks, "What happened last night, John?"

"I'm not *him*."

Houston waits.

"That boyfriend of hers . . . he always calls me Phillip." The boy deepens his voice, saying, "'Phillip, bring me this. Phillip, you're in my way. Phillip, get the hell lost.'"

"But you're not Phillip Stevens."

John looks at his feet now. Shaking his head.

"You're just the man's genetics."

"I told him that."

Houston says, "Good."

"PS was a different person than me. Right?"

"Absolutely."

"I mean, he was born in a different century, and in another place. Everything about his life was different than mine. Right?"

"Did you tell him that?"

"Yeah. But all he did . . . he just laughed at me. He said, 'That's just what old Phillip would say, if he was here.' "

Houston says nothing.

"Fucker," says the boy. Viciously, with a pure scalding hatred.

Then with a low, stern voice, his mentor suggests, "You shouldn't, maybe. I know you don't like your mother's friend, but calling him that name—"

"No, Mr. Cross," John interrupts. "I'm talking about the other fucker."

For four years, law enforcement agencies followed every wrong lead, interviewed millions of earnest, mistaken individuals, and through means legal and otherwise, they pulled up the bank and tax records of more than a billion suspects.

But in the end, a routine traffic accident gave them Phillip Stevens.

An unidentified man driving a dilapidated pickup truck happened to rear-end a young mother. Bumpers locked. When two uniformed officers arrived, the man was staring at a PS child riding in the back seat. Suddenly he panicked, pulling a weapon and discharging it into the air. Witnesses saw him fleeing into a nearby warehouse. There was a second, muted shot. Eventually, a SWAT team broke into the warehouse and discovered a body lying in a tiny men's room, the scene filthy with blood and bone and bits of drying brain matter.

Subsequent tests proved that the corpse belonged to the missing billionaire. His face and skin color had been altered by surgical means, but his famous DNA was instantly recognized by five reputable labs, including his own.

The young mother was labeled a hero, then lost the label when she refused ten million dollars for her role in ending the manhunt. Furthermore, she enraged many by admitting that she only wished she had known who the man was . . . she wanted to thank Phillip for giving her her wonderful son. . . !

        *   *   *

Youth is a blessing.

When Mike takes the knife to the plaster, he believes. He is *eleven*, and this is fun, and he's enthralled. Intent, absolutely focused, each slice into the whiteness is full of possibilities.

Like John and every other young boy, PS or not, scientific ritual distracts him from his fun. Notes are taken, but only under duress. Working with ink on paper, Mike jots and sketches. Then he picks up the knife with both hands, making a game of picking his next quadrant, and after a calming breath, he chisels a deep wedge of plaster.

Houston can't remember where he put which artifact, and so it's nearly a surprise to him when the boy uncovers a single golden eye gazing up at the alien sky.

Mike says, "Shit."

He giggles and says, "Neat," and goes to work with an old toothbrush, using bristles bent against Houston's teeth, sweeping away the clinging dust.

Half of the period is invested exhuming the skull. It's small and obviously plastic, yet something about it intrigues the boy. He can't stop smiling afterward, moving to the next quadrant and working his way down to a severed hand clinging to a toy weapon. With a dissecting needle, he shoves at the trigger. A weak light and muted whine come from beneath the hardened plaster.

Houston waits.

The boy looks up, grinning.

"Wal-Mart?" he says matter-of-factly.

Disappointed, Houston shrugs and says, "Maybe."

But the boy's attitude shifts. With his next breath, he's back on that other world, and with a bleak authority he says, "This is some ass-kicking monster. So something really tough must have killed it. That's what I think!"

After the bell rings, the hallway jams with students.

Houston's habit is to walk each boy to the door, then stand there and watch the kids pass by. The sixth graders are still very much children; while the eighth graders, and particularly the girls, are metamorphosing into their adult selves. By the end of the year, Houston will catch himself watching the young women. When he first began mentoring, a certain kind of girl might offer glances and winsome smiles. But five-plus years is a long time, and his wilting hair and the graying beard makes him look older than their fathers. Houston has, in effect, vanished from their hormonal radar.

Mike's locker is straight across the hall.

Still grinning about the buried skull, he fingers his lock, and when it doesn't recognize him, he slams it hard against the gray steel, then tries again.

Troy steps up behind him, saying something.

The two boys talk for a moment. Differences in age and Mike's bleached hair make them look like siblings, not twins. And it helps that Troy carries himself with a slump-shouldered shyness, while his younger brother is the cockier, self-assured one.

Houston tries to read lips. And faces. And postures.

Then he notices other students. Like him, some stare. One boy points, which triggers a second to follow his lead. Then a tall girl giggles and shouts, "Which one's real? Which one's real?"

Mike calmly flips the girl off.

Troy just dips his head, trying to ignore the taunt.

Then as Houston starts to say something to the girl—acidic and cutting and cold—she turns and skips past him, still giggling, a bony arm clipping his elbow as she passes, never noticing him.

In the end, Troy is the only boy to reassemble the entire skeleton. What's more, he uses resins and a bottomless patience to sculpt bones to replace what's missing. When the others have gone onto new missions, he continues to happily piece together and repair. In the end, both a tiny toy robot and the skeleton man look like museum displays, mounted on a new plaster landscape that he and his mother built on a rainy Saturday.

Houston hangs a dozen concepts on those toys.

Entropy. Evolution. Anatomy.

"Those extra arms wouldn't work," he explains. "No shoulders, so there's no place to anchor the muscles. Is there?"

The boy shrugs. "I guess not."

"Why would a six-armed man evolve?"

With an enduring patience, he says, "I guess he must have needed them."

"The universe tends to slide from order into disorder. Have you ever heard that before, Troy?"

"When Mom cleans my room." When he laughs, he sounds most like John. Like Mike. Like many hundreds of thousands of boys. But the grim, abstract heart of this entropy business remains out of reach. He shrugs again, and with an easygoing stubbornness, he confesses, "I don't think about that stuff much."

Trying to cushion the bad news, he shrugs and smiles, admitting, "I'm not like them, Mr. Cross. Sorry."

*   *   *

The bookstore still accepts cash.

What's more, it's large enough to keep a ready inventory of bestsellers. No need to wait around three minutes while your purchase is printed and bound. Houston can pick up a fresh copy from under a sign that reads: CONTROVERSIAL. #1 SELLER! Then he can take the copy up front and pay, asking for a sack, please.

The fear of discovery is wholly irrational.

And worse, it's laughable.

But Houston has mentored more than a dozen kids, and various parents know him, and countless teachers and administrators would recognize him on sight. Those are all exactly the kinds of people who might be browsing in a bookstore on a warm October night, which is why he takes precautions, and why he feels secretly nervous, stepping outside and strolling to his car with a forced nonchalance.

No parking slots are left in his apartment's lot. Houston's forced to leave his little car on the street. As he enters the building, he finds half a dozen neighbors and their friends on their way to a Halloween party. All are in costume, and drunk. The party must have a theme; everyone wears the same full mask, the adult Phillip Stevens reborn with rubber and fake hair.

"Out of our way!" one man shouts.

"Genetic superiority coming through!" says another.

A woman says, "Stop that," and slaps a hand off her ass. Then she slides up against Houston, beery breath telling him, "You look different. You look awfully cute!"

"He's not," says the first man.

"He's inferior," says the second man.

Then they're past him. And Houston stands on the bottom stair for a long while, doing nothing but breathing, holding tight to the rail with his free hand.

4. *You pop out of the wormhole and find yourself inside a clear thick gel. This universe is a thick transparent goo that goes on forever:*

Fire your engines, and you can move.

But barely, and your hull creaks and groans, and the instant you stop your engines, your ship comes to an abrupt halt.

Now a monster swims out of the gelatin. It dwarfs the largest whale, and it's covered with tree-sized hairs that beat like oars, carrying it straight at you.

What do you do?

No, that weapon won't work here.
And that one won't kill it.
Just pisses it off, in fact.
So what now?
You can run, but the monster is faster. It's ready to eat you and
your ship. Whole. And you've got four seconds to think this through
and tell me: Where are you?
Now three seconds.
And two.
And one.

"Mr. Cross," John blurts. "There's something new here!"

Houston fights the temptation to look for himself. Instead, he sits back and watches the boy twist at the knobs, his jaw dropping an instant before he leaps back. Dramatic, overdone. "God, it's huge!"

"Draw it," Houston coaches.

"Okay. I'll try!"

The boys and mentor have set up an aquarium at the back of the classroom—five gallons of tap water with its chlorine removed, then sweetened with straw and oxygenated with a simple airstone. Over the past five days, using Troy's donated microscope, they've watched the microbial community explode and evolve, bacteria followed by hungry parameciums—the "monsters" of the gel universe—and now the parameciums are serving as fodder for an even larger, more wondrous monster.

"It's got wheels," John reports.

"Where?"

"On this end." John commands the circles in his drawing to spin, giving his creation a liveliness. "They go around and around, then stop. And then they go again."

"How big is it?"

"Huge," the boy declares. Then he peers into the eyepiece with his right eye—none of the boys can resist pinching his left closed—and suddenly, with a quieter, more honest astonishment, he says, "Jesus, it ate one!"

"One what?"

"One of the parameciums. I saw it!"

Houston picks up the workpad, trying to remember when he first saw a rotifer swimming across a glass slide.

"You should look at it, Mr. Cross. Look!"

Anticipation makes the mouth dry. He bends over the microscope, the fine adjustment knob spinning easily between finger and thumb. As promised, the rotifer seems vast. And as if answering his wish, he watches while one of the football-shaped protozoans is caught in that intricate mouth, spinning hairs pulling the transparent carcass inside a transparent body.

Water eating water.

When you got down to it, that's what it's all about.

The woman teaches science at a different school. Their relationship is three years old, and it is convenient, and it has mostly run its course. They see each other infrequently. But as it happens, she's at Houston's apartment on that weekend evening when the television interrupts them, saying, "Breaking news."

"Not now," he tells it.

But the machine obeys its rigorous instructions. "Important, breaking news."

"Maybe the president's been shot," says the woman. Then she sits up and says, "Anyway, I probably need to get home." She pulls a heavy sweater over her head, speaking through the frizzy red wool. "I want to see this news first."

"Show us," says Houston.

"—the gunman apparently turned the weapon on himself, committing suicide. At least fourteen students died, while nine more are hospitalized, six in critical condition—"

"Where is this?" Houston asks.

"Australian Independent—"

"From the beginning. Now."

Schools always look like schools. Houston stares at a glass and brick building as the narrator reports, "Today, an unidentified male walked into the Riverview School for the Gifted, shouted inflammatory phrases, then produced a pair of handguns, killing more than a dozen boys in their early teens—"

"Shit," says the woman.

Houston is silent.

"All of the deceased, and all but two of the injured, are clones of Phillip Stevens. At this point, it's assumed that the murderer was singling them out . . ."

On screen, grim-faced paramedics are carrying dark sacks. Some of the sacks seem heavy, while others are less so.

The woman sits next to Houston, exhaling hard.

She says, "Shit," quietly. Then with a different voice, "Have you seen my rings?"

"On the kitchen counter." She always leaves her diamond and wedding band on the counter.

But she doesn't move. Instead, she places a damp hand on Houston's bare knee, telling him, "This sounds horrible. But I'm surprised that it's taken this long for this sort of tragedy to happen. You know?"

He doesn't speak.

His lover gives him a few seconds, then asks, "What are you thinking?"

He stares at those rubber sacks set in a ragged row, and he thinks that it's odd. As they are now, robbed of their faces and souls, those boys have never looked more alike.

"We'll have new security measures. Naturally." Ms. Lindstrum whispers, trying to keep her words private. It's a week after the Riverview Massacre, but there have already been three more attacks. In France. In White Russia. And two PSs killed in Boston. "Cameras in the hallway," she promises. "At least one armed guard stationed in the front office. And all of us who work directly with the boys . . . we'll naturally have to go through an extensive security check . . ."

"I've already been scrutinized," says Houston. "Six years ago."

"It's a formality," she assures.

He doesn't mention the obvious: Any determined person could kill these boys anywhere in time and space. No reasonable amount of security will protect them. And unreasonable security will just make their lives more constricted, and their murders more noteworthy.

Houston doesn't say one word, watching Troy working at the back of the room.

"You did speak with them?" Ms. Lindstrum inquires. "About what happened in Australia, I mean."

"That next day," he says.

"How were they?"

"John was shaken. 'Killing someone is always awful,' he told me." Houston closes his eyes, the voices and faces coming back to him. "Troy acted sad, and sorry. But I don't think he appreciates what happened. It's on the other end of the world, and I think his mother shields him from the news. So none of it's quite real."

"And Mike?"

"Pissed, more than anything."

"That's sounds like him," she chimes in.

But it wasn't a simple anger. The boy had made fists and drummed on the top of his desk, growling, "It won't happen to me."

"It won't, but why not?" Houston had asked.

"I'm not the same as the others. I look different." He nodded, explaining with an amoral practicality, "If some asshole comes to school firing, he's going to shoot John first. Then Troy. And finally me. Except, I'll have run away by then!"

Houston neglects to mention any of that conversation.

Misreading his grim expression, Ms. Lindstrum says, "I wouldn't worry. This is a good community, in its heart. Nothing tragic's going to happen here."

He just looks at her.

She starts to ask, "What are you thinking?"

But just then Troy spins in his chair, calling out, "Mr. Cross? I found a baby snail. Want to see?"

"Do I ever!" he blurts. "Do I ever!"

"It is an honor, Mr. Cross. Houston. May I call you Houston? And thanks for taking the trouble. I know this has to be an imposition."

"It isn't," Houston lies.

The school district's headquarters are set inside a sprawling single-story building designed on some now-defunct principle of efficiency and/or emotional warmth. The central area is one vast room. Partial walls and overly green plastic foliage divide the working areas. The ventilation system produces a constant roar, not unlike the Brownian drumming of atoms against a starship's hull. Over that roar, the man in charge of security says, "I mean it. It's an honor to cross paths, sir. We have so much trouble finding good mentors, and keeping them. Which makes you something of a legend around here."

Houston gives a little nod. "What can I do for you?"

"Very little." The man looks and sounds like a retired police officer. A military cop, perhaps. Dragging a thick hand across the hairless scalp, he says, "You used to be . . . what's the term. . . ? A professional student. At two universities. Is that right?"

"Yes."

He glances at his monitor. "Your resumé lists several impressive degrees."

"I have a trust fund," says Houston. "A little one. It gives me enough security for that kind of lifestyle."

"Good for you," says the cop. Without inflection.

Houston waits.

"Then you moved here and took up mentoring . . . six years ago. Correct?"

"Correct."

Again the hand is dragged across the scalp. "Now I couldn't help but notice. You didn't work with PSs until this year."

"I guess I didn't. No."

The cop sits motionless, clear eyes regarding Houston without suspicion.

"The boys were too young," Houston offers. "As a rule, I work with middle schoolers."

"That's what I thought." He nudges the monitor just enough to let both of them skim over a life's history.

Houston reads dates, places.

He says nothing.

"Of course there were two boys . . . older ones who skipped grades . . . and they were kicking around your current school before the others . . ."

"True enough." Then with a flat, matter-of-fact voice, Houston points out, "I had other students then. Two girls and a boy. And I felt a certain loyalty to them."

"Good for you."

Silence.

The monitor is eased aside, glare hiding whatever it shows now. The clear eyes grow a little less so, and with a pained voice, the cop says, "I'm awfully sorry. I'm required to ask these questions, sir."

"Go on," says Houston.

"Are you a member of the Defenders of the Womb?"

"No."

"Do you know anyone who you suspect could be a member?"

"No."

"How about the Birth-Righters?"

"God, no."

"Like I said, I have to ask." He pauses, considering his next words. Or not. Perhaps this is a game that he's played too many times, and he has to remind himself what comes next. "Mr. Cross," he says. "I mean Houston. Have you read any of the anti-PS literature or watched the associated digitals?"

Houston sets his jaw, and waits.

"I'm sure you know what I mean, sir. There's some awful things being published. That crazy in Australia had stacks of the stuff . . ."

"*The Cuckoo's Boys*," says Houston.

"Excuse me?"

"That book was in the crazy's stacks. As I recall."

"Perhaps. But honestly, it isn't on my list of dangerous works."

"Isn't it?" Houston leans forward, asking his interrogator, "Why not?"

"It isn't in the same category as those other works," he claims, "since it never advocates murder."

"No, it doesn't," Houston agrees.

"The boys are the blameless product of an evil man."

"Says Paul Kaan."

"Who used to work for Phillip Stevens. As I recall, they were colleagues and friends." The eyes lift and grow distant. "The moral thing to do is to give the PSs useful lives. But to protect our species, they have to be sterilized, too."

The ventilation's rumbling fades away.

"It sounds like you know the book," says Houston.

But the man won't be caught so easily. "I'm just repeating what I've seen on television, sir. That's all."

"But what if?" asks Houston. "What if Congress decides to pass laws and perform a simple clinical procedure on every boy. . . ?"

"Well what, Mr. Cross?"

"What's your feeling about that?"

"My only concern, sir, is that there is no violence inside our schools."

Houston nods, sitting back again.

The cop glances down, then asks, "Do you own a firearm, sir?"

"No."

"Do you possess bomb-making materials?"

"Yes."

The eyes lift and grow large.

An angry laugh, then Houston explains, "I've got a well-stocked kitchen, and there's a filling station at the end of the block. So in theory, yes, I can make a substantial bomb. Anytime I want."

"That's not the best answer. Sir."

"Then no, I don't have bomb-making materials."

"Good. Thank you." The eyes dip again, and quietly, speaking as much to himself as to Houston, he says, "This is what you do all day, isn't it, sir? These little mind games. . . ."

5. *You emerge from the wormhole. What you see is blackness.*
Perfect, endless blackness.
But as your eyes adapt, you begin to make out a faint curtain of light in front of you. And behind you. And above. And below.
Now, what do you do. . . ?

Mike starts to say, "Sensors," before catching his mistake.

He grimaces instead, then tells Houston, "I'll use my ther-
mometer. I put it in the airlock. What does it read?"

"About two degrees."

"Kelvin?"

"Yes."

The boy stares at his starship's newest incarnation. It's still
armored and bristling with weapons, but now bubble-like portholes
line its sides, and the robotic crew has shrunk to human proportions.

"All right," says Mike. "I use my barometer. What does it say?"

"Nothing."

"It doesn't work?"

"No. It's reading nothing. Zero."

"Pure vacuum." He nods, muttering, "I'm out in space somewhere."

Houston waits.

"Okay. I shoot my antimatter cannon. What happens?"

"Eventually, the shell strikes the curtain of light, and its surface
gets bright for as long as it's passing through. But the curtain's very
thin, and most of the shell's mass continues on its merry way."

"I get it. There's not much stuff there, is there?" He nods again,
then says, "Okay. I follow it."

"Okay."

"And I reach the curtain?"

"Eventually."

"Can I get through?"

"Eventually."

"What's 'eventually' mean?"

"A few million years, give or take."

"But my throttle's all the way open!" The boy leans back, licking his lips. "In a vacuum, I'd be going nearly light speed!"

Houston says, "Agreed."

"Okay. I stop inside the curtain. What happens?"

"It swirls around you. Like a slow, slow fog."

"I take a sample."

"How?"

Frustration builds, then collapses into resignation. "Okay. I put
a jelly jar in the airlock, then open the outer door, and some of the
fog drifts into the jar. All right?"

"Fine."

"I screw down the lid and bring the sample to the lab."

Houston says nothing.

"And I put everything in my best microscope. What do I see?"

"Lights. Tiny, bright-colored points of light."

The boy licks his lips, eyes narrowed, one hand absently sweeping the hair out of his baffled eyes.

"Most of the lights are dim and red," Houston adds. "Others are yellow. And the brightest few are blue."

"What about—?"

Houston shouts, "Wow!"

The boy halfway jumps. "What happened?"

"A big flash of light!"

"Outside somewhere?"

"No. From the jar."

"How big?" He shakes his head, asking, "Is there damage?"

"You're blind now."

"Okay. I pop in new eyes. Now what do I see?"

"One of those tiny blue lights has vanished. That's the only change."

Mike rises to his feet. Trying to concentrate, he steps up to the window, staring at the falling snow as one hand, then the other, plays with his shaggy hair.

Several minutes later, he screams, "Jesus!"

He smiles and says to the snow, "You made me huge. Didn't you?"

6. *Jungle. And a blue, blue sea.*

Swimming in the warm water are fish not too different from our fish, and creatures that resemble porpoises, and something with a round body and paddles and a tiny head stuck on the end of a long, long neck—

"A plesiosaur," John blurts.

"Exactly." A pause, then Houston adds, "Up in the sky, as close as the Moon now, is a comet. In a few hours, it's going to hit exactly where you are now. It's going to vaporize the water and the limestone below, then set fire to North America, and the world."

John winces. Then in a self-conscious way, giggles.

"What do you want to do, John?"

"I want to watch the plesiosaur. I've always liked them."

Houston knows that. Last night, his AI found a new documentary on Danish TV, and for the next thirty minutes he plays the subtitled digital on the classroom screen. Then comes lunch. The new semester has a break in the middle of the period. The mentor is expected to fend for himself. And naturally, he doesn't get paid for time not spent teaching.

When John returns, Houston outlines the situation again.

But this time he closes by saying, "In a very few hours, your plesiosaur, and almost everything else on Earth, is going to be dead."

John winces. No giggles.

"Fly up to the comet," Houston suggests. "If you want."

"I guess."

"The coma is beautiful. And the tail extends for millions of miles." He shows him photographs of last year's big comet. "Inside the coma you find a black ball of tar and buried snow. It's barely ten miles across. If you want, you can stop it now."

"I can?"

"You've got weapons," Houston points out. "What would you use if you wanted to move a mountain-sized snowball?"

"My engines. They'd melt anything."

"Do you want to use them?"

"I don't get it, Mr. Cross. What are you asking?"

"Why would you stop the comet? And why wouldn't you?"

"Well," says the boy. Then he licks the tentative hairs over his upper lip, and breathes deeply, and says, "If dinosaurs go on living, then maybe mammals wouldn't get their chance. Which would be bad for us. For human beings."

Houston leans forward, saying, "You're going to let the comet hit. Aren't you?"

The boy doesn't answer, eyes tracking from side to side.

"Would you like to see the comet's impact?" Houston offers. "I found a real good Japanese simulation. It's accurate, and it's spectacular, too."

John shakes his head.

"No, thank you," he says. "But Mike would like it, I bet."

"He loved it," Houston confides.

The boy makes fists and drums softly on his desk.

"What about the comet, John? Are you going to leave it alone?"

"No," the boy squeaks.

Houston tries to hide his surprise. Then after a few deep breaths, he asks, "Why?" with a quiet voice. "If it means there'll never be humans—"

"Good," says the boy.

Once. Softly. But with a hard-won conviction.

7. *You've decided to become a cat farmer.*
No, seriously. I mean it.
You can make a lot of money selling catskins. And since you're left with carcasses after you skin them, you start feeding that meat to the new kittens. Who grow up into your next harvest of cats. Which you feed to the next litters of kittens. And so on. And so on. Cats all the way . . .
Now, what's wrong with that plan?

Troy says, "Nothing," without hesitation. He thinks this is gross and clever.

"But," Houston warns, "you're losing energy at every stage. A cat burns calories to keep itself warm, and it's got a short gut that doesn't digest everything that it eats. That's why your dog chews on your cat's turds. They're full of energy."

"Ugh." Giggles.

The others understood the problem almost immediately. "Try it this way," says Houston. "How much meat would you have to eat every day? In order to eat enough, I mean."

"Ten pounds," the boy guesses.

"Forty quarter-pound hamburgers. Really?"

"Maybe not." Troy shakes his head, licks his lips. "How about two pounds?"

"Fine." Houston nods. "On the first day of school, you'll go to the cafeteria and eat your daily ration. Two pounds of grilled seventh grader."

"You mean like Mike?"

"Exactly."

"Neat!"

"And you'll do that for a full year. Two pounds worth of seventh graders every day. Which is more than seven hundred pounds in all."

"Mike's not that big. Not yet."

Both of them laugh. Hard. Then Houston says, "Remember. A body is bone and gruesome crap that you'd never eat. Maybe half of the carcass won't get on your plate. So how many seventh graders are you going to need?"

Troy hammers out a reasonable estimate. "Ten."

"How many eighth graders are in your class?"

"I don't know. Three hundred?"

"So we need three thousand seventh graders. And you can't just lock them in a room and pull one out whenever you're hungry. They need their food, too."

"Sixth graders!"

"How many?"

"I don't know . . . God, thirty thousand. . . !"

"Right." Houston leans forward, and smiles. "But remember, Troy. Teachers can be awfully hungry people, too."

The boy's face grows a little pale.

"Three hundred eighth graders feed how many teachers?"

"Thirty." He sickens, but just for a moment. Then the eyes quicken, and for that instant, in his face and eyes, Troy is indistinguishable from the other PSs.

"There's three principals. Right?"

"I guess there would be. Yes." Houston sits back in his chair, then asks, "Who's left standing? At the end of the year, I mean."

Troy sees it instantly.

"Only the principals. Right?"

"Right."

Then he's laughing too hard to breathe, and he gasps, and he admits to Houston, "I'm not going to tell Mom about this lesson. No, I'm not!"

8. *You give birth to a child who isn't yours. Genetically speaking.*

Phillip Stevens hijacks your reproductive system and forces you into having his clone, just as he did with millions of blameless women. Yet you feel blamed. And, of course, you're bitter. It's only reasonable to play the role of the victim here.

It's only human to want revenge.

But it's also human to be better than that. To forgive, or at least to forget. To accept and hold and cherish this gift . . .

. . . a better son, frankly, than anything you would have spawned on your own. . . .

Saturday morning, and Houston shops for next week's groceries. He spots the boy at the end of a long aisle, and for a half-instant, he isn't sure. It could be another PS, or even just a boy who happens to resemble them. But something about the don't-give-an-inch stance and the habitual pushing of hair out of the eyes tells him that it's Mike. Which means that the tiny woman next to him, lowering a blood-colored roast into the cart, must be his mother.

Two aisles later, paths cross.

The boy calls him, "Houston." Then he does a thumb-pointing gesture, telling Mom, "This is the guy."

She's holding a box of tampons. Without blinking, she throws them into the cart, then offers a tiny hand. "The famous Mr. Cross. Finally. Believe it or not, I've been meaning to get in touch."

"It's a pleasure," he replies.

"Groceries?" she inquires, gesturing at his cart.

"They are," he admits.

"What do you think of these prices?"

"They're high," Houston volunteers.

"Ridiculous," she grouses. Then just as the conversation seems doomed to canned chatter, Mom tells him, "You know, my boy hates you."

"Pardon?"

"You drive him nuts. Goofy nuts. I mean, he knows that he's smarter than his brother and sister. And his parents, of course, are perfect idiots—"

"Shut up," Mike growls. "You old lady."

Mom has a good laugh, then continues. "Anyway, Mr. Cross. Thank you. You've been getting under his skin. Which is the best thing for him, I think."

Mike says, "Jesus," and stomps in a circle.

His mother takes a step toward Houston, smiling up at him, and with a conspirator's urgent voice says, "Humble him. Please."

"I try," Houston confesses.

"Fucking Jesus!" Mike moans, squirming in every sense.

Mom turns and glares at her son, her mouth ready to reprimand. Or encourage. Houston can't guess which. But instead of speaking, she looks back at Houston and gives him an odd little smile.

Again, he says, "It's been a pleasure."

Then he takes his cart and his expensive groceries and moves on.

The field trip is the result of a lot of pleading and a slippery set of excuses. At first, John says, "You've got to eat lunch. Eat it at my house. It's just a short walk from school." But when Houston firmly refuses, the boy adds, "I've got books you'd like to see. Old ones. About science and stuff."

"What books?"

Their titles escape him. But they're about dinosaurs and flying saucers, and John adds, "I can't bring them here. They're practically antiques, and something might happen!"

Last week, there was a fight at school. Houston didn't see it, but Ms. Lindstrum reported that John was showing his starship to one of his few friends, and another boy stole his workpad. John couldn't stop himself from throwing the first punch. His only punch, it seems. He still sports an ugly maroon bruise beside his left eye.

"Mr. Cross," he pleads. "Please come over?"

The boy is sick with loneliness. But Houston has to tell him, "We need a better reason. If we're going to get permission, we'll need something special that ties directly to our work here."

The next day, John bursts into the room. "Okay. How's this? We've got a huge stump in our back yard. Hundreds of tree rings showing. Maybe we could do some sort of study, counting back in time and looking at the weather. That kind of stuff."

"Good enough," Houston tells him.

But the Facilitator has doubts. "It's not up to me anymore," Ms. Lindstrum explains. "If it involves PSs, we'll need permission from the superintendent's office."

Houston nods, then says, "The boy really wants this."

"Can you blame him?"

Houston didn't know that he was.

She promises to make the request. And for the next full week, John's first question every day is, "When are we going?"

"Never," seems like a possible answer.

But suddenly the faceless powers grant their blessing. Appropriate disclaimers are filled out. A parental signature is produced. And like explorers bound for some great adventure, the two of them pack up their equipment and make the four-block trek to an anonymous split-level on a quiet side street.

All the way there, John is giddy with excitement.

Effusive to a sickening pitch.

Five years old, at the most.

He tells silly jokes about farts and singing frogs. He boasts that he'll be a great scientist before he's thirty. With an overdone clumsiness, he trips on a crack in the sidewalk and drops in a slow-motion tumble into his own front yard. Then he suddenly grows quiet and thoughtful, saying, "By the way. Mom's boyfriend is gone. Moved out gone, I mean."

The trap is revealed.

Entering the front door, John cries out, "We're here!"

Mom can't look any less prepared for company. Bare feet. Jeans worn white against the chunky ass. A sweatshirt of some unearthly green. Physically, she bears no resemblance to her son. Chinese and European. Pretty in a fucked-over way. Sleepy, teary eyes regard this onslaught with a genuine horror. "Oh," she finally exclaims. "That's today, isn't it?"

The boy drops his workpad on the floor. "Mom!"

But the woman recovers. "Just a minute! Be right there!" She gallops out of sight, and from the back of the house screams, "Food's in the fridge, hun!"

"She forgets things," says John, shaking from anger.

"Don't worry about it," Houston tells him. His voice is angry, too. But the inflection goes unnoticed.

Lunch is egg-salad sandwiches with off-brand pop to wash them down.

Mom returns during an Oreo dessert. Her clothes have improved—newer jeans and aerobics shoes—and she's washed her face and combed her hair. But obviously, she'd rather be anywhere else. With anyone else. A condition that gives the adults common ground.

"I'm glad to meet you," she tells Houston.

"And I'm glad to meet you," he echoes.

They chat. It's polite, rigorously simple chatter. How long has Houston been a mentor? How long have they lived here? What about this warm weather? How was the sandwich, and does anyone want any more cookies?

Adults know how to be polite.

They can converse for hours, revealing nothing about their true selves.

Yet John is visibly thrilled by their prattle. He grins more and more. Mom finally asks, "Aren't you supposed to be doing a project?" And he tells her, "There's still time," without glancing at the clock.

Eventually, the kitchen grows silent.

Houston turns to the boy and says, "Maybe we should get busy. You think?"

"Oh, sure. Why not?"

They have only a few minutes to invest in the promised tree stump. Which is ample, since it's too old and weathered to teach much more than the fact that wood rots. Standing over that brown mass of fungi and carpenter ants, John looks at him expectantly and says, "Well?"

Houston imagines a dozen responses, and John's black disappointment. So he says simply, "Interesting," without defining what it is that interests him.

John hears what he wants, and for the next week, pesters Houston shamelessly.

He says, "I'm worried about my mother. She's too lonely."

He says, "You know, there's a new restaurant up on Acer. I'd take Mom, but I don't have the money."

In a pleading tone, he confesses, "You're my best friend in the world, Mr. Cross. I mean that!"

Then, the pestering stops.

And Houston discovers that he misses the boy's clumsy match-making. He misses it but doesn't say so, knowing better than to trust his own weakness. Then one day the boy arrives with a purple bruise matching the last one, and Houston asks, "Did you fight that same jerk? I hope not."

"I didn't," John mutters.

Then he looks past Houston, a cold glare matching the accusing voice. "The boyfriend's back. Again."

"I know this seems impolite. I got your address from one of last year's parents—"

"Come in, Mrs. Holdenmeister."

"You've probably got plans for tonight."

"Not really." He offers her the sofa, then sits opposite her. Looking at those hard blue eyes, he secretly thinks, You're one scary bitch.

"What can I do for you?" he inquires.

"About Troy," she mutters. Pale hands turn to fists. "About that grade—"

"The B+?"

"You're his mentor. You know how much he adores science."

"Absolutely."

"I just don't think . . . after he earned As last semester . . ."

"We had a big project this quarter. He had to do his own research and write a paper about what he learned—"

"Didn't he?"

"No, actually." He says it flat out, then sits back and asks, "Did you come here by yourself, Mrs. Holdenmeister?"

She starts to ask, "Why?" Then she shakes her head, admitting, "My husband's in the car. Waiting." With an indiscriminate rage, she admits, "He doesn't think that I should be going to this much trouble—"

"He's right."

She hesitates. Then after measuring him with those deadly eyes, she says, "I saw Troy's paper. I saw it, and it was very good."

"Because you helped him write it."

She flusters easily, nothing about it genuine. "I don't think that's true. . . !"

"I asked him. And your son has a wicked streak of honesty."

She hesitates again, not sure what to say.

"It's a quarterly grade," he reminds her, "and it's a B+. Which is very respectable, Mrs. Holdenmeister."

"Even still," she snaps, "it's on his permanent record."

"Fuck his record. Ma'am."

She swallows. Goes limp.

"We both know he's not like the others. He doesn't function as well in science. And he won't be anyone's valedictorian." Houston says it, then takes a long deep breath. Then, "Which aren't crimes. And in some ways, those are probably blessings."

"I . . . I don't know what to say here . . ."

"Let him do his own work. I'll give him a nice little A at the end of the year, and it won't mean shit in ten years. Or in another two weeks, for that matter."

Fists pull close to her belly. "You've got an ugly, awful attitude, Mr. Cross."

"Guilty as charged."

She mistakes his indifference for weakness. "I plan to complain. To the superintendent himself. A person like you shouldn't be working with impressionable young minds."

That's when Houston's rage takes hold of him.

Suddenly his mouth takes charge, asking, "What exactly did you do to your son? To make him this way, I mean."

She goes pale, except for the blazing eyes.

"Watching you . . ." he sputters. "Seeing all this damned guilt masquerading as love . . . I have to wonder if maybe, once you saw that PS baby . . . maybe you put a pillow over him and gave him a few good shoves before you got too scared to finish the job. . . !"

"Shut up!" she screams.

And rises.

Then with a tight, furious voice, she whispers, "I had *a drinking problem*. While I was pregnant. You son of a bitch."

He says nothing.

Feels nothing, he believes.

For an instant, she shivers hard enough to lose her balance. Then she puts her hand against the wall, and says again, "You're a horrible man."

"Tell me what I don't know."

She tries to murder him with her eyes.

It nearly works, it seems. But Houston makes himself stand, facing her, telling her simply, "You'd better go, Mrs. Holdenmeister. Now."

9. *I want you to invent a world, a universe, for the other boys.*

I'll send them there. In their starships, they'll explore and deci-pher the mysteries that you leave for them. And maybe they'll escape in the end, and maybe they won't. Which means, in other words, if you want to make a dangerous place, you can do that.

You've got my blessing.

Just as they have the same blessing, and that's all the fair warn-ing I'm going to give you . . . okay. . . ?

"Is it John's world, or Troy's?"

"Does that matter?"

"No," says Mike. Then, "Yes." He licks his lips, drums his fists, then tells Houston, "I bet it's Troy's."

"Why?"

"Because it's neat. You know. Not sloppy."

A map of the world covers the long screen. It has two blue seas and a brilliant dash of icecap, and its single continent is yellow except where it's brown. It is not sloppy because it's authentic. The image comes with NASA's compliments, and what Mike sees has been fitted together from a thousand fuzzy, partial images gathered by orbiting telescopes. The physical and chemical data are equally authentic.

But what waits on the world's surface belongs entirely to John.

"I'm not going to tell you who did this," Houston warns. "Just like I won't tell the others which world is yours."

"You'd better not," he growls.

"What are you going to do first, Mike? You've got a mission here."

"I'll fire my cannon. Ten times."

Houston says nothing.

"Well, can I?"

The mentor says, "If you want," and shakes his head sadly.

"Okay. I do it, and what happens?"

"The explosions melt the icecap, boil the oceans, then cause the crust to turn to magma."

"Neat!"

Houston says nothing.

"Is there anything left alive down there?"

"I don't know. You tell me."

The boy describes his flight into the hell. Crocus, the top robot, collects samples of atmosphere and liquid rock. Mentor and student agree that nothing lives there. Even if there had been a thriving biosphere, it was vaporized, leaving not so much as a fossil tooth to mark its glorious past and promise.

"Congratulations," says Houston, the word tipped in acid.

But Mike just shrugs and says, "That was easy." Then he laughs, admitting, "I don't know why I was so worried."

Half an hour later the bell rings.

Houston accompanies Mike to the door. The hallway is already jammed with scurrying bodies and sharp, overly loud voices. The boy, still proud of his carnage, grins and wades out into the current. A bigger, older boy drives an elbow into him. But it's barely felt. Mike reaches his locker and touches the lock, then slams it hard against the steel. And then John appears beside him, touching him on the arm, obviously asking him, "Which world did you get? Which world? Which world? Which?"

Houston can see their faces, can halfway read their lips.

He watches as Mike glances up at this older, fatter boy, and showing the most malicious grin the boy says, "Two oceans. And some kind of yellow land."

John can't resist. He confesses, "That's mine!"

Mike says something like, "Was it?"

Then John asks a "What'd you think, what'd you do?" sort of question.

And Mike tells him. With both hands, he creates the universal symbol of an explosion, and loud enough to be heard, he says, "Boom!"

There's no time to intercede.

Before Houston can force his way through the bystanders and into the fight, John has already slammed Mike's head into the lockers. At least three times. Maybe four. And Mike counters with a fist into the belly, leaving his attacker on his knees, gasping and pale and crying for every reason imaginable.

"It's just us for the next few days," Houston explains.

But Troy already knows the news. There's nothing bigger in a school than a bloody brawl. Unless of course it's when two PSs are doing the brawling.

Troy shakes his head, asking, "Why did they fight?"

Houston starts to offer the simple explanation, then hesitates. It occurs to him that he barely knows either boy, much less their real motivations, and thinking that he understands them is dangerous, and stupid, and very much a waste.

So instead he admits, "I really don't know why they fought, or why they seem to hate each other so much."

"I know," the boy tells him.

Anticipation makes Houston lean forward. "Why, Troy?"

"They've got to," he assures.

"But why?"

With an endearing patience, the boy shakes his head, warning him, "You can't know it, Mr. Cross.

"You might want to. But you just don't belong."

10. *Again, your starship is tiny. Microscopic. Suspended within that vast ocean, living water swimming through the dead.*

But this time the monster isn't some marauding paramecium. This time what you see has a blunt head and a long ropy tail, and it isn't feeding. Instead it's moving with a singleness of purpose, passing you and your ship without the smallest regard.

In anger, or maybe out of simple curiosity, you fire your weapons at it.

The monster wriggles and dies.

And just like that, Phillip Stevens is never born. And you, all of you, instantly and forever cease to exist.

I'm not going to ask why.

It's easy enough to see the reason.

And I won't dwell on the paradoxes inherent in this mess.

No, what I want to ask is the hardest question of all: Is this world better off without Phillip and the PSs? Or is it worse off?

That's the only question worth asking.

And you can't give me any answer. Sixty years from now, maybe. But not today. Not here. You're smart but not that smart. And even in sixty years, I doubt if you'll look me in the eye — all the thousands and thousands of you — and to the man, you will say in one indivisible voice, "The world is better off," or, "It's worse."

The best questions are always that way . . .

The Sun is plunging behind the Moon.

At its height, the eclipse will reach 80+ percent coverage. Which is a long way from a total eclipse. But since it is a warm, cloudless day, at the noon hour, the effect is dramatic. There comes a growing chill to the air. A sense of misplaced twilight. Houston twists his head and says, "Listen." But hundreds of students are scattered across the school's lawn, enjoying the cosmic event, and it's hard to hear anything but their endless roar. "Listen to the birds," he tells them.

Both boys nod in the same way, John saying, "I hear them. They're singing."

Troy points and cries out, "Look!"

Swallows have appeared, streaking back and forth.

Then a younger voice says, "Look under the trees."

Mike stands behind them. Smiling, but not. Horizontal cuts mark where his face struck the vent on his locker. And he seems taller than before. Houston noticed it yesterday—Mike's first day back from his suspension—but it's more obvious now. A growth spurt took him during his weeklong suspension, adding a goodly fraction of an inch to his gangly frame.

"The way the light is," he says. Pointing.

John sits up. "Yeah, look! What's going on, Mr. Cross?"

Crescent-shaped splashes of light dapple a sidewalk and the shady grass. Houston stands, hands on hips. "I don't know," he lies. "What do you think? Guesses?"

"It's the eclipse," Troy volunteers.

"Duh," says Mike.

Houston reprimands him with a look. Then as he starts to ask his next question, he notices a group of kids staring at them. Talking among themselves. Eighth graders. Every last one of them female.

Houston's boys are oblivious to the stares.

Mike drops to the ground. He sits as far as possible from John while still being part of their group. "It's got something to do with how the light bends," he volunteers. "It's like you can see the Sun in those little crescent things."

Troy says, "I bet so."

Then John says, "This would have been a full eclipse back in dinosaur times."

"Why?" asks Troy.

"The Moon was closer," Mike tells him.

"It covered more of the Sun back then," John adds.

Troy turns. "Is that right, Mr. Cross?"

He starts to nod, then notices one of the girls approaching them. The hesitation in her walk and the other girls' giggles implies this is a dare. Instead of speaking, Houston holds his breath, and all the boys grow silent, too. She's a tall, willowy creature with full breasts and a model's face. And in a voice that comes wrapped in a nervous, electric energy, she says, "Hi, you guys."

Then she turns, and sprints back to her friends.

"What the fuck was that?" Mike growls. "What the fuck?"

But Houston laughs out loud, saying, "That. Is a woman enamored." Saying, "I know the look. And you just better get used to it, boys."

*   *   *

"At least I can see him now," she says. "Can you?"

"Barely," says the short man.

"I've never gotten a writer's autograph. Have you?"

"I'm not much of a reader."

"Neither am I," she confesses. Then she turns to Houston, asking him, "Have you ever read anything better than this?"

He glances at the woman. Then he looks up the long line, saying, "Yes."

She doesn't seem to notice. Holding her copy of *The Cuckoo's Boys* in both hands, she tells everyone in earshot, "It had to be said. What Dr. Kaan says here."

Houston manages to keep silent.

This is a Saturday afternoon. He drove two hundred miles to stand here. The author sits in the center of a long table, flanked by thousands of copies of his phenomenal bestseller. *The New Edition*, reads the overhead banner. *New Chapters! Fresh, Innovative Proposals!!*

The short man asks, "Do you know what's in the new chapters?"

"I'm dying to find out," she confesses.

Houston waits. Then after a while, he says, "Tailored viruses."

"Excuse me?" says the woman.

"Kaan thinks we should create a virus that would target Phillip Stevens's genetics. It would destroy the clones' somatic cells. In other words, their sperm."

She says, "Good."

The line slips forward.

Houston finds himself breathing harder, fighting the urge to speak. A pretty young woman says, "Please, open your book. One copy only. To the page you want signed. And please, don't ask for any personalized inscriptions."

The author wears a three-piece suit. He looks fit and hardy, and smug.

Houston avoids looking at the man's eyes.

The line moves.

With both hands, the woman in front of Houston opens her book.

The short man in front of her leans forward and mutters something to the author, getting nothing but a signature for his trouble.

The woman takes his place, gushing, "I'm so glad to meet you. Sir!"

Kaan smiles and signs his name, then looks past her.

Houston's legs are like concrete. Suddenly, he is aware of his pounding heart and a mouth suddenly gone dry. But he steps forward, and quietly says, "You know, I have a PS son," as he hands his opened book forward. "And I took your good advice."

The author's face rises, eyes huge and round.

"I cut off his nuts. Want to see 'em?" Houston asks, reaching into a pocket.

"Help!" the author squeals.

A pair of burly men appears, grabbing Houston and dragging him outside with the rough efficiency of professionals. Then after a quick body search, they place him in his car, and one man suggests, "You should go home, sir. Now."

"All right," Houston agrees.

They leave him, but then linger at the bookstore's front door.

Houston twists the rearview mirror, looking at his own face. Tanned and narrow, and, in the brown eyes, tired. He thinks hard about everything until nothing else can be accomplished. Which takes about thirty seconds. And that's when he starts the engine and pulls out into traffic, feeling very light and free, and in the strangest ways, happy.

11. *You get an end-of-the-school-year field trip out of me.*

I always, always take my students down to our little community's renowned natural history museum. Most have already been there. According to one boy, maybe five hundred times already. But never with me. Never benefiting from my particular slant on mammoths and trilobites and the rest of those failures that they have on display down there.

Don't bring lunch money. We'll be eating at Wendy's or the Subway Barn, and I'm the one buying.

Don't bring your workpads or notebooks. You won't need them.

But if you would, please . . . remember to wear good shoes. Shoes you can walk in. And if it's at all cold outside, please, for god's sake, wear a damned coat. . . !

"It's been refused," says Ms. Lindstrum.

"Excuse me?"

"Your proposed field trip. I know the boys were looking forward to it. But what with the latest tragedy, people want to be cautious."

Which tragedy? Houston wonders. In Memphis, five PSs were found dead in a basement, each body savagely mutilated. In Nairobi, a mob killed three more. Or was it the UN's failure to condemn Singapore's new concentration camp that's masquerading as a special school.

"I'm sorry," she offers.

Over the school year, her office has shrunk. Paper files and stacks of forms have gathered, choking the available space into a stale few breaths and two uncomfortable people.

Again, she says, "I am sorry."

"It's all right." His eyes find hers. What worries him most is the way that she blinks now. Blinks and looks past him. "Is it because of that fight? Because John and Mike did fine during the eclipse, and since," he says. Then he tells her, "There won't be any incidents. I can absolutely guarantee it."

She sighs, then says, "No PS-only field trips are being authorized."

"So let me take along one or two of my old students. To beat that rule."

"No," she replies. Too urgently and with a wince cutting into the half-pretty face. Or maybe he's just being paranoid.

Houston offers a shrug of the shoulders. "Are you sure there's nothing we can do?"

"I'm certain," Ms. Lindstrum tells him. "But the four of you could throw a little party for those three periods. Safe in your classroom. In fact, I'll arrange for food and pop to be brought from the cafeteria."

"I guess that would work," Houston tells her. Then he puts on his best smile, saying, "Why don't we. A little celebratory party. Fine."

Maybe it is simple paranoia.

But a back-of-the-neck feeling has Houston peering over his shoulder. Every public place seems crowded with suspicious strangers, and his little apartment seems full of dark, secretive corners. He finds himself peeking through curtains, watching the empty parking lot below. Three times he runs diagnostic programs on his phone, searching for taps that refuse to be found. And when he finally manages to convince himself that nothing is wrong, except in his imagination, his old widescreen abruptly stops finding news about the PSs. Instead, it delivers highlights from a teaching conference in Nova Scotia. Which is a signal.

Prearranged, yet surprising.

Long ago, Houston taught the AI that if its security was breached, dump all of the old files and start chasing down a different flavor of news.

He doesn't fix the protocols now.

Instead, he pretends to watch the conferences that are being piped to him, and he runs new diagnostics on the apartment and every appliance.

That night, before the school party, someone knocks.

His lover wears nice clothes and a smile, and she says, "Hello," too quickly. She says, "I hope I'm not catching you at a bad time."

She has always, always called before visiting. But not tonight.

Houston says, "No, it's a fine time. Come on in."

She says, "For a little bit. I'm expected back home."

He hasn't seen her for a month. But he doesn't mention it. He sits opposite her and says absolutely nothing, trying to read the pretty face and nervous body, and when she can't tolerate any more silence, she blurts, "Are you all right, Houston?"

"Perfect," he says.

She swallows, as if in pain.

"How about you?" he inquires.

"They know about us." She says it, then gathers herself before admitting, "They came to me. And asked about you."

"Who asked?"

She crosses her arms, then says, "They threatened to tell my husband."

Houston speaks the woman's name, then asks, "Was it that bald security man? From district headquarters?"

"One of them was."

"Who else was there?"

She shakes her head. "He didn't give me a name."

"It's nothing," says Houston. And to an astonishing degree, he believes it. "I've had some trouble with one of the parents. I'm certain that she's filed a formal complaint. That's the culprit here."

His lover nods hopefully, staring at the floor.

He tells her, "Everyone's scared that something bad is going to happen here."

"I am," she allows.

"What did they ask?"

"About you," she mutters.

"What did you say?"

"That I know almost nothing about Houston Cross." Eyes lift, fixing squarely on him. "Which is true. All of a sudden, hearing myself say the words, I realized that you're practically a stranger to me."

He says nothing.

At this very late date, what can he say. . . ?

✳   ✳   ✳

Mentors are required to check in at the front office.

Houston arrives a few minutes earlier than normal, signing his name at the bottom of a long page and glancing sideways into Ms. Lindstrum's office, catching a glimpse of her grim face as her door swings shut, closed by someone whom he cannot see.

The school's uniformed guard sits nearby, pretending to ignore him.

Which is absolutely ordinary, Houston reminds himself.

The bell rings. Children pour into the hallway, a brink-of-summer fever infecting all of them. Houston beats the boys to the classroom, then waits in front of the door. For an instant, he fears that they're home sick, or Lindstrum has bottled them up. But no, John walks up grinning, Troy at his side. Then Mike is fighting through the bodies, making for his locker . . . and Houston tells the others, "Stay with me," and he intercepts Mike, putting a hand on the bony shoulder, saying to all of them, "Change of plans."

This spring, the school installed a security camera at one end of the hallway.

In the opposite direction, the hallway ends with lockers and a fire door. With the boys following after him, Houston hits the bar, causing the alarm to sound—a grating roar that causes a thousand giddy youngsters to run in circles and laugh wildly.

"Hey!" says Mike. "You did that!"

"No," says Houston. "It's a planned fire drill. Trust me."

Then John asks, "Where are we going? On our field trip?"

"Exactly."

"I don't have my permission slip," Troy complains.

Houston turns and says, "I took care of all that. Hurry. Please."

They climb down a short set of metal stairs, then cut across the schoolyard. Behind them, mayhem rules. Screaming bodies burst from every door, harried teachers trying to regain some semblance of control. In the distance, sirens sound. As they reach the street, a pair of fire trucks rushes past, charging toward the nonexistent blaze. Various cars are parked along the curb. Trying to smile, Houston says, "Guess which one's mine."

John says, "That one," and points at a gaudy red sports car.

Houston has to ask, "Why?"

"It's a neat car," says the boy. "And you're a neat guy!"

Now he laughs. Despite everything, he suddenly feels giddy as the kids, and nearly happy. With keys in hand, he says, "Sorry. It's the next one."

A little thing. Drab, and brown. Utterly nondescript.

But as the boys climb inside, Mike notices, "It smells new in here."

"It's a rental," Houston admits. His old heap is parked out in front of the school, as usual. He stashed this one last night. "I thought we needed something special today."

"Are we still going to the museum?" Troy asks.

He and John share the back seat.

Houston says, "No, actually. I came up with a different destination."

Mike watches him. Suspicious now.

The boys in back punch each other, and giggle, and John says, "Maybe we could eat first, Mr. Cross?"

"Not yet," Houston tells them.

He drives carefully. Not too fast, or slow. Up to the main arterial, then he heads straight out of town, knowing that Mike will be the first to notice.

"Where?" asks the boy. Not angrily, but ready to be angry, if necessary.

"There's a few acres of native prairie. Not big, but interesting." Houston looks into every mirror, watching the cars behind them.

After a minute, Mike says, "I don't know about this."

"That's right," says Houston. "Be suspicious. Of everything."

The smallest boy shrugs his shoulders and looks straight ahead now.

Houston glances over his shoulder, telling John, "There's a package under you. In brown paper. Can you get that out for me, please?"

"This it?"

"Yeah. Can you open it up, please?"

The boy never hesitates. He tears away the paper, finding a pair of hypodermic needles, each wrapped in sterile plastic. "What are these for, Mr. Cross?"

"Tear one of them open. Would you?"

"Just one?"

"Please."

It takes a few moments. The plastic is tough and designed not to be split by accident. While John works, Houston turns to Mike and says, "Be suspicious," again. "When I was your age, I was always suspicious. Suspicion is a real skill, and a blessing. If you use it right."

The boy nods, wearing a perplexed expression.

"Here it is, sir," says John, handing the hypodermic to him.

"Thank you."

"What is it?" asks Troy. "It looks medical."

"It is," Houston admits, removing the plastic cap with his teeth. "People made these things by the millions years ago. If you were poor and gave birth to a mixed-race boy, you could test his blood. Like this." He doesn't let himself flinch, punching his own shoulder with the exposed needle. Then he shakes the device for a moment, and shows everyone the dull red glow. "Now unwrap the other one. Yeah. And hand it to me."

John obeys.

In the same smooth motion, Houston jabs Mike in the shoulder. "Sorry," he offers, shaking the second device. Then he puts them together, and with a voice that can't help but break, he says, "Both showing red. See? And what do you think that means?"

12. I used to be Phillip Stevens.

He says the words, then sucks in a breath and holds it.

Not one boy makes the tiniest sound.

Finally, laughing uneasily, Houston asks, "What do you think about that? John? Troy? Mike?"

"I don't believe you," Mike growls.

"No?"

"That's a stupid shit thing to say." The boy's anger is rich and easy, bolstered by the beginnings of panic. He takes a gasping breath. Then another. Then he strikes his own thighs with both fists, telling Houston, "He died. The asshole offed himself. Everyone knows that."

Again, silence.

Houston glances in the mirror. The boys in back wear identical expressions. Lost, and desperately sad. Troy sees him watching, then looks back over his shoulder, probably hoping to find help coming to rescue them.

But there isn't another car in sight.

"You two," says Houston. "What do you think?"

"It was Dr. Stevens's body," John offers. "That's what the police said."

"The police," Houston points out, "found a body with Phillip's physical features as well as his DNA. But a body isn't the man. And if anyone could have arranged for a bunch of dead meat and organs infused with his own DNA, wouldn't it have been Phillip Stevens?"

"A full-grown clone?" says Mike.

"With a massive head wound. And what the press didn't report — except as wild rumor — were those occasional disparities between the corpse on the table and the fugitive's medical records."

"Like what?" Mike mutters.

"Like scars and stuff?" John asks.

"No, every scar matched. Exactly." Houston nods and pushes on the accelerator, telling them, "But those things would be easy enough to fake. The body was grown in a prototype womb-chamber. The brain was removed early, and intentionally. No pain, no thoughts. Phillip did that work himself. He broke the clone's big left toe, then let it heal. He gave the skin the right patterns of moles and old nicks and such. He even aged the flesh with doses of radiation. And he kept the soulless clone relatively fit through electric isometrics and other rehab tricks."

The only sound is the hum of tires on pavement.

Finally, Mike asks, "So what was wrong with that body?"

"Not enough callus. Not on its fingertips or the bottoms of its feet." Houston nods knowingly, looking across the blurring countryside, then straight ahead. "And even though the brain tissue was scrambled, the FBI found problems. Even with dehydration, there wasn't enough brain present. And what they had in jars didn't have the dendritic interconnections as you'd expect in a mature genius mind."

Again, Troy looks back the way they had come.

Houston turns right, onto a graveled road, and over the sudden rattling of loose rock he tells them, "It's not far now."

Even Mike looks sad.

"The original Houston Cross was a loner. No family, and few prospects." Houston says it, then adds, "For a few dollars and a new face, that Houston acquired a new life. And he doesn't even suspect who it is that bought his old one."

John starts to sob loudly enough to be heard.

Mike turns and glares at him. "God, stop it. You baby!"

Over the crest of the hill is a small green sign announcing NATURAL AREA. The tiny parking lot is empty. Which is typical for a weekday, Houston knows.

He pulls in and stops, turning off the engine and pocketing the key. "All right," he says. "Out."

The boys remain in their seats.

Houston opens his door and stands in the sunshine. "Out," he tells them.

From the back, Troy squeaks, "Are you going to kill us? Mr. Cross?" The words take him completely by surprise.

He shivers for a moment, then makes himself stop. And he looks in at all of them. And he tells them, "You can't begin to know how much that hurts."

13. *Why did Phillip Stevens create you?*
Any ideas?
Forget my little announcement. My name is Houston Cross, and I want you to explain to me why your father did what he did? Because I know you must have laid awake nights wondering just that . . .

The four of them walk in single file through the big bluestem prairie, following a narrow path up a hill, both hill and path vanishing in the same step.

Houston stops for a moment, watching the horizon and the rolling, windswept land, farm fields on all sides and this little patch of grass and wildflowers tucked into a spare forty acres. The nearest intelligence is a soaring red-tailed hawk. Other than the bird, no one notices them but them.

Again, he walks.

And he asks the boys, "Why did PS do it?"

"He was selfish," says John. Blurts John.

"Who told you that?" Houston responds. Then he makes himself laugh, adding, "That's right. Everyone says that he was horribly, wickedly selfish. Don't they?"

From behind, Troy asks, "Were you?"

"In a sense. Of course. Who isn't?"

At the base of the hill is a little stand of trees. Ash trees, mostly. With an enormous and stately cottonwood anchoring one end.

"But maybe there's a different answer. A harder, truer one."

"Like what?" asks Mike.

"All of you are Phillip's gift to the world." Houston slows his gait, making sure that everyone can hear. "The man had certain talents that can prosper in any time, and he decided to share those talents with his species. To enrich your generation with his genes, and when you have your own children, then enrich every generation to come."

Mike snorts, in disgust.

"What's the matter?" Houston asks. "Don't you approve?"

The boy just shakes his head, glowering at the ground.

For the last time, Troy looks over his shoulder. Then Houston places a hand on his shoulder, warning him, "Nobody knows where we are. For a little while, nobody's going to interrupt us. So don't worry. Okay?"

The eyes are wide and sorrowful, but Troy says nothing.

Then they move beneath the trees, out of the wind, their voices carrying and the mood instantly more intimate. More familiar.

Houston says, "There's a third possibility."

"What?" squeaks John.

"That Phillip Stevens remembered his childhood too well. He remembered his loneliness and how distant he felt from the other kids. A bastard, interracial child without any father . . . and maybe all of his plotting and his selfish evil was simply to make certain that the next time around . . . that he wouldn't grow up so alone . . ."

Now Houston cries.

Sobbing, practically.

Mike is unimpressed. He starts to turn away, announcing, "I don't want to do this shit anymore. I'm going back to the car."

"Please don't," Houston pleads. "I want to show you something first. Something important."

Curiosity is the richest, sweetest drug.

One after another, the boys nod in identical fashions and follow, their mentor leading them under the giant cottonwood. Head-high on the trunk is a distinctive X-shaped scar, the thick bark chopped open with a heavy blade. With his back to the scar, Houston starts to count his steps from the trunk. At a dozen, he stops. Kneels. And while tugging at the shade-starved grasses, he tells them, "Always remember. Being smart only means that you make bigger, louder mistakes."

The boys stand as close together as they have ever been.

Watching him.

"With the PS bug," explains Houston, "I assumed that only a few thousand women inside a very limited region would catch it. That's all. A minimal plague and nobody would die . . . and when it was otherwise, believe me, there wasn't anyone more surprised than me."

For an instant, Houston wonders if maybe this is the wrong place. Or perhaps he's really Houston Cross, and he is simply delusional. A pure crazy man. But then one tuft of grass gives on the first tug, then lets itself be uprooted with a hard yank. Beneath it is a pipe with a false bottom. He reaches elbow-deep and touches the bottom, the Swiss-made lock recognizing his fingertips.

"I was shocked by the disease's scope," he confesses. "And hor-rified. And very sorry."

A gentle gas-powered piston pushes up the packets of money. Hundred dollar bills create a little wall in the grass, and every boy has to step closer and gawk, Mike saying, "God, that's a lot."

"A few hundred thousand. That's all."

Troy says, "Shit," under his breath.

The others laugh, for just a moment.

"And this is twenty million dollars," Houston adds, showing them an e-card that couldn't be more nondescript. "Untraceable, in theory. Although I haven't used it in years."

"What else is there. . . ?" one of them asks. He isn't sure who. Bending low, reaching into the damp hole, he tells them, "This. This is what I wanted to show you."

Exactly the size of the piston beneath it, the disc is silvery and outdated by the latest technologies. But it's still readable, and prob-ably will be for a few more years.

John asks, "What's that?"

"When I realized the scope of my plague," says Houston, "I made a nearly full list of all the PSs. Birth dates and addresses and important government IDs. Everything that you would need to make contact with them. In this country, and everywhere else."

"But that's all old now," Mike points out.

"A lot of these boys have already died. You're right." He looks at them, one after another. Then he lets them watch as he shoves the cash back into its hiding place, leaving it unlocked, and fits the hat of sod and grass back into the pipe. "Others have moved. But if you're going to get in touch with them, you'll need to start some-where."

None of the boys can manage a word, watching him.

Houston flips the disc toward John, then says, "If you need, come get this cash. But only as you need it."

Mike bends and picks up the disk, then asks, "What are we sup-posed to do? Mr. Whoever-You-Are. . . ?"

"Dr. Stevens," Troy tells him.

"Organize your brothers. The sooner, the better." Houston stands and pockets the e-cash, then in the gravest voice he can summon, he tells them, "Things are going to get very bad, and probably before you're ready. But I know you. And I don't mean that you're just new incarnations of me. I know you as John and Mike and Troy. Together, you and the other boys are going to survive this mess that I selfishly made for you . . ."

Then, he gasps for air.

John asks, "What about you? Can't you stay and help us?"

Mike says, "I don't want him here."

Houston agrees. "I think they already suspect that I'm not Houston Cross. If they find out everything, then things will just be worse for you. Which is why you can't tell a soul about me. Ever."

Only John nods with conviction.

"But I plan to help you," he adds. "Later, when I've settled down again, I'll feed you advice, somehow. And if you need it, more money . . ."

For a long moment, no one speaks.

Then finally, with a quiet sorry voice, Houston says, "Five minutes. Give me that much time. Then walk back to the main road and wait until someone comes looking for you."

He turns, taking his first tentative step toward the car.

"What'll you do now?" asks Mike.

Houston isn't sure. Maybe he should slip into another autographing . . . this time with a copy of *The Cuckoo's Boys*, its pages laced with botulin . . .

"What you should do," Mike says, "is shoot yourself. For real this time!"

"Don't say that," John warns him.

"Why not?" the smallest boy replies. "He's just a big fuck-up."

Again, the grown man starts to cry.

Troy says, "I had fun this year, Dr. Stevens. I did!"

"Don't say awful things about our father!" John shouts.

"He's not my father, and I'll say what I goddamn want to!" Mike replies.

"Don't!"

"Oh, fuck you!"

With both hands and a hard deep grunt, John shoves Mike in the chest. The smaller boy stumbles and falls backward into the grass. Then for a moment, he does nothing. He just lays there, his face flush with blood and a wild, careless anger. Then with his own grunt, he leaps up and runs, dropping his head as he slams into that big soft body, and both boys are throwing fists and cursing, then kicking each other, ribs bruised and lips bloodied before someone throws his body between them, screaming, "Now stop! Please, please, just grow up!"

For a slippery instant, Mike wishes that it was Houston. Phillip. Whoever that prick is. Just so he can give him a few good smacks now.

But no, it's just Troy. Poor stupid Troy is sobbing, and in his own way, he's furious. Then for some bizarre, twisted reason, Mike finds himself actually sorry that it wasn't the man who stops them. Wiping the gore out of his eyes, the boy looks across the prairie and sees no one. No one. Just the tall grass waving and the empty hillside, and the shit ran away again, and there's nobody else in the world but the three of them.

That's when it starts to sink home.

For all of them.

At long last.

14. *There's no one like you in the world.*

People like to say otherwise, but they don't understand. Only people like ourselves understand. Each of us is more different than we are the same, and if you think about it, that's our best hope.

Our only hope, maybe.

For now, that's all we can tell you. But watch your mail, and watch for signs. Someday, sooner than you think, we'll talk again. We'll make our plans then.

For anything and everything, we'll have to be ready.

Sincerely,

THE CUCKOO'S BOYS.

Winemaster

THE STRANGER PULLED INTO THE QUIK SHOP
outside St. Joe. Nothing was remarkable about him, which was
why he caught Blaine's eye. Taller than average, but not by much,
he was thin in an unfit way, with black hair and a handsome,
almost pretty face, fine bones floating beneath skin that didn't
often get into the sun. Which meant nothing, of course. A lot of
people were staying indoors lately. Blaine watched him climb out
of an enormous Buick—a satin black '17 Gibraltar that had seen
better days—and after a lazy long stretch, he passed his e-card
through the proper slot and inserted the nozzle, filling the Buick's
cavernous tank with ten cold gallons of gasoline and corn alcohol.

By then, Blaine had run his plates.

The Buick was registered to a Julian Winemaster from Wichita,
Kansas; twenty-nine accompanying photographs showed pretty
much the same fellow who stood sixty feet away.

His entire bio was artfully bland, rigorously seamless. Winemaster was an accountant, divorced and forty-four years old, with O
negative blood and five neo-enamel fillings imbedded in otherwise
perfect teeth, plus a small pink birthmark somewhere on his right
buttock. Useless details, Blaine reminded himself, and with that he
lifted his gaze, watching the traveler remove the dripping nozzle,
then cradling it on the pump with the overdone delicacy of a man
ill at ease with machinery.

Behind thick fingers, Blaine was smiling.

Winemaster moved with a stiff, road-weary gait, walking into the convenience store and asking, "Ma'am? Where's your rest-room, please?"

The clerk ignored him.

It was the men's room that called out, "Over here, sir."

Sitting in one of the hard plastic booths, Blaine had a good view of everything. A pair of militia boys in their brown uniforms were the only others in the store. They'd been gawking at dirty comic books, minding their own business until they heard Wine-master's voice. Politeness had lately become a suspicious behavior. Blaine watched the boys look up and elbow each other, putting their sights on the stranger. And he watched Winemaster's walk, the expression on his pretty, frail face, and a myriad of subtleties, trying to decide what he should do, and when, and what he should avoid at all costs.

It was a bright warm summer morning, but there hadn't been twenty cars in the last hour, most of them sporting local plates.

The militia boys blanked their comics and put them on the wrong shelves, then walked out the front door, one saying, "Bye now," as he passed the clerk.

"Sure," the old woman growled, never taking her eyes off a tiny television screen.

The boys might simply be doing their job, which meant they were harmless. But the state militias were full of bullies who'd found a career in the last couple years. There was no sweeter sport than terrorizing the innocent traveler, because, of course, the gen-uine refugee was too rare of a prospect to hope for.

Winemaster vanished into the men's room.

The boys approached the black Buick, doing a little dance and showing each other their malicious smiles. Thugs, Blaine decided. Which meant that he had to do something now. Before Winemas-ter, or whoever he was, came walking out of the toilet.

Blaine climbed out of the tiny booth.

He didn't waste breath on the clerk.

Crossing the greasy pavement, he watched the boys use a police-issue lock pick. The front passenger door opened, and both of them stepped back, trying to keep a safe distance. With equip-ment that went out of date last spring, one boy probed the interior air, the cultured leather seats, the dashboard and floorboard, and even an empty pop can standing in its cradle. "Naw, it's okay," he was saying. "Get on in there."

His partner had a knife. The curled blade was intended for upholstery. Nothing could be learned by ripping apart the seats, but it was a fun game nonetheless.

"Get in there," the first boy repeated.

The second one started to say, "I'm getting in—" But he happened to glance over his shoulder, seeing Blaine coming, and he turned fast, lifting the knife, seriously thinking about slashing the interloper.

Blaine was bigger than some pairs of men.

He was fat, but in a powerful, focused way. And he was quick, grabbing the knife hand and giving a hard squeeze, then flinging the boy against the car's composite body, the knife dropping and Blaine kicking it out of reach, then giving the boy a second shove, harder this time, telling both of them, "That's enough, gentlemen."

"Who the fuck are you—?" they sputtered, in a chorus.

Blaine produced a badge and ID bracelet. "Read these," he suggested coldly. Then he told them, "You're welcome to check me out. But we do that somewhere else. Right now, this man's door is closed and locked, and the three of us are hiding. Understand?"

The boy with the surveillance equipment said, "We're within our rights."

Blaine shut and locked the door for them, saying, "This way. Stay with me."

"One of their nests got hit last night," said the other boy, walking. "We've been checking people all morning!"

"Find any?"

"Not yet—"

"With that old gear, you won't."

"We've caught them before," said the first boy, defending his equipment. His status. "A couple, three different carloads . . ."

Maybe they did, but that was months ago. Generations ago.

"Is that yours?" asked Blaine. He pointed to a battered Python, saying, "It better be. We're getting inside."

The boys climbed in front. Blaine filled the back seat, sweating from exertion and the car's brutal heat.

"What are we doing?" one of them asked.

"We're waiting. Is that all right with you?"

"I guess."

But his partner couldn't just sit. He turned and glared at Blaine, saying, "You'd better be Federal."

"And if not?" Blaine inquired, without interest.

No appropriate threat came to mind. So the boy simply

growled and repeated himself. "You'd just better be. That's all I'm saying."

A moment later, Winemaster strolled out of the store. Nothing in his stance or pace implied worry. He was carrying a can of pop and a red bag of corn nuts. Resting his purchases on the roof, he punched in his code to unlock the driver's door, then gave the area a quick glance. It was the glance of someone who never intended to return here, even for gasoline—a dismissive expression coupled with a tangible sense of relief.

That's when Blaine knew.

When he was suddenly and perfectly sure.

The boys saw nothing incriminating. But the one who'd held the knife was quick to say the obvious: A man with Blaine's credentials could get his hands on the best EM sniffers in the world. "Get them," he said, "and we'll find out what he is!"

But Blaine already felt sure.

"He's going," the other one sputtered. "Look, he's gone—!"

A cautious man was driving the black car. Winemaster braked and looked both ways twice before he pulled out onto the access road, accelerating gradually toward I-29, taking no chances even though there was precious little traffic to avoid as he drove north.

"Fuck," said the boys, in one voice.

Using a calm-stick, Blaine touched one of the thick necks; without fuss, the boy slumped forward.

"Hey!" snapped his partner. "What are you doing—?"

"What's best," Blaine whispered afterward. Then he lowered the Python's windows and destroyed its ignition system, leaving the pair asleep in the front seats. And because the moment required justice, he took one of their hands each, shoving them inside the other's pants, then he laid their heads together, in the pose of lovers.

The other refugees pampered Julian: His cabin wasn't only larger than almost anyone else's, it wore extra shielding to help protect him from malicious high-energy particles. Power and shaping rations didn't apply to him, although he rarely indulged himself, and a platoon of autodocs did nothing but watch over his health. In public, strangers applauded him. In private, he could select almost any woman as a lover. And in bed, in the afterglow of whatever passed for sex at that particular moment, Julian could tell his stories, and his lovers would listen as if enraptured, even if they already knew each story by heart.

No one on board was more ancient than Julian. Even before the attack, he was one of the few residents of the Shawnee Nest who could honestly claim to be DNA-made, his life beginning as a single wet cell inside a cavernous womb, a bloody birth followed by sloppy growth that culminated in a vast and slow and decidedly old-fashioned human being.

Julian was nearly forty when Transmutations became an expensive possibility.

Thrill seekers and the terminally ill were among the first to undergo the process, their primitive bodies and bloated minds consumed by the microchines, the sum total of their selves compressed into tiny robotic bodies meant to duplicate every normal human function.

Being pioneers, they endured heavy losses. Modest errors during the Transmutation meant instant death. Tiny errors meant a pathetic and incurable insanity. The fledging Nests were exposed to heavy nuclei and subtle EM effects, all potentially disastrous. And of course there were the early terrorist attacks, crude and disorganized, but extracting a horrible toll nonetheless.

The survivors were tiny and swift, and wiser, and they were able to streamline the Transmutation, making it more accurate and affordable, and to a degree, routine.

"I was forty-three when I left the other world." Julian told his lover of the moment. He always used those words, framing them with defiance and a hint of bittersweet longing. "It was three days and two hours before the president signed the McGrugger Bill."

That's when Transmutation became illegal in the United States.

His lover did her math, then with a genuine awe said, "That was five hundred and twelve days ago."

A day was worth years inside a Nest.

"Tell me," she whispered. "Why did you do it? Were you bored? Or sick?"

"Don't you know why?" he inquired.

"No," she squeaked.

Julian was famous, but sometimes his life wasn't. And why should the youngsters know his biography by heart?

"I don't want to force you," the woman told him. "If you'd rather not talk about it, I'll understand."

Julian didn't answer immediately.

Instead, he climbed from his bed and crossed the cabin. His kitchenette had created a drink—hydrocarbons mixed with nanochines that were nutritious, appetizing, and pleasantly narcotic. Food and drink were not necessities, but habits, and they were enjoying a renewed popularity. Like any credible Methuselah, Julian was often the model on how best to do archaic oddities.

The woman lay on top of the bed. Her current body was a hologram laid over her mechanical core. It was a traditional body, probably worn for his pleasure; no wings or fins or even more bizarre adornments. As it happened, she had selected a build and complexion not very different from Julian's first wife. A coincidence? Or had she actually done research, and already knew the answers to her prying questions?

"Sip," he advised, handing her the drink.

Their hands brushed against one another, shaped light touching its equivalent. What each felt was a synthetically generated sensation, basically human, intended to feel like warm, water-filled skin.

The girl obeyed, smiling as she sipped, an audible slurp amusing both of them.

"Here," she said, handing back the glass. "Your turn."

Julian glanced at the far wall. A universal window gave them a live view of the Quik Shop, the image supplied by one of the multitude of cameras hidden on the Buick's exterior. What held his interest was the old muscle car, a Python with smoked glass windows. When he first saw that car, three heads were visible. Now two of the heads had gradually dropped out of sight, with the remaining man still sitting in back, big eyes opened wide, making no attempt to hide his interest in the Buick's driver.

No one knew who the fat man was, or what he knew, much less what his intentions might be. His presence had been a complete surprise, and what he had done with those militia members, pulling them back as he did as well as the rest of it, had left the refugees more startled than grateful, and more scared than any time since leaving the Nest.

Julian had gone to that store with the intent of suffering a clumsy, even violent interrogation. A militia encounter was meant to give them authenticity. And more importantly, to give Julian experience—precious and sobering firsthand experience with the much-changed world around them.

A world that he hadn't visited for more than a millennium, Nest-time.

Since he last looked, nothing of substance had changed at that ugly store. And probably nothing would change for a long while.

One lesson that no refugee needed, much less craved, was that when dealing with that other realm, nothing helped as much as patience.

Taking a long, slow sip of their drink, he looked back at the woman—twenty days old, a virtual child—and without a shred of patience, she said, "You were sick, weren't you? I heard someone saying that's why you agreed to be Transmutated . . . five hundred and twelve days ago . . ."

"No." He offered a shy smile. "And it wasn't because I wanted to live this way, either. To be honest, I've always been conservative. In that world, and this one, too."

She nodded amiably, waiting.

"It was my daughter," he explained. "She was sick. An incurable leukemia." Again he offered the shy smile, adding, "She was nine years old, and terrified. I could save her life by agreeing to her Transmutation, but I couldn't just abandon her to life in the Nest . . . making her an orphan, basically . . ."

"I see," his lover whispered.

Then after a respectful silence, she asked, "Where's your daughter now?"

"Dead."

"Of course . . ." Not many people were lucky enough to live five hundred days in a Nest; despite shields, a single heavy nucleus could still find you, ravaging your mind, extinguishing your very delicate soul. "How long ago . . . did it happen. . . ?"

"This morning," he replied. "In the attack."

"Oh . . . I'm very sorry. . ."

With the illusion of shoulders, Julian shrugged. Then with his bittersweet voice, he admitted, "It already seems long ago."

Winemaster headed north into Iowa, then did the unexpected, making the sudden turn east when he reached the new tollway.

Blaine shadowed him. He liked to keep two minutes between the Buick and his little Tokamak, using the FBI's recon network to help monitor the situation. But the network had been compromised in the past, probably more often than anyone knew, which meant that he had to occasionally pay the tollway a little extra to boost his speed, the gap closing to less than fifteen seconds. Then with the optics in his windshield, he would get a good look at what might or might not be Julian Winemaster—a stiffly erect gentleman who kept one hand on the wheel, even when the AI-managed road was controlling every vehicle's speed and direction, and doing a better job of driving than any human could do.

Iowa was half-beautiful, half-bleak. Some fields looked tended, genetically tailored crops planted in fractal patterns and the occasional robot working carefully, pulling weeds and killing pests as it spider-walked back and forth. But there were long stretches where the farms had been abandoned, wild grasses and the spawn of last year's crops coming up in ragged green masses. Entire neighborhoods had pulled up and gone elsewhere. How many farmers had accepted the Transmutation, in other countries or illegally? Probably only a fraction of them, Blaine knew. Habit-bound and suspicious by nature, they'd never agree to the dismantlement of their bodies, the transplantation of their crusty souls. No, what happened was that farms were simply falling out of production, particularly where the soil was marginal. Yields were still improving in a world where the old-style population was tumbling. If patterns held, most of the arable land would soon return to prairie and forest. And eventually, the entire human species wouldn't fill so much as one of these abandoned farms . . . leaving the old world entirely empty . . . if those patterns were allowed to hold, naturally . . .

Unlike Winemaster, Blaine kept neither hand on the wheel, trusting the AIs to look after him. He spent most of his time watching the news networks, keeping tabs on moods more than facts. What had happened in Kansas was still the big story. By noon, more than twenty groups and individuals had claimed responsibility for the attack. Officially, the Emergency Federal Council deplored any senseless violence—a cliché which implied that sensible violence was an entirely different question. When asked about the government's response, the president's press secretary looked at the world with a stony face, saying, "We're investigating the regrettable incident. But the fact remains, it happened outside our borders. We are observers here. The Shawnee Nest was responsible for its own security, just as every other Nest is responsible . . ."

Questions came in a flurry. The press secretary pointed to a small, severe-looking man in the front row—a reporter for the Christian Promise organization. "Are we taking any precautions against counterattacks?" the reporter inquired. Then, not waiting for an answer, he added, "There have been reports of activity in the other Nests, inside the United States and elsewhere."

A tense smile was the first reply.

Then the stony face told everyone, "The president and the Council have taken every appropriate precaution. As for any activity in any Nest, I can only say: We have everything perfectly well in hand."

"Is anything left of the Shawnee Nest?" asked a second reporter.

"No." The press secretary was neither sad nor pleased. "Initial evidence is that the entire facility has been sterilized."

A tenacious, gray-haired woman — the perpetual symbol of the Canadian Newsweb—called out, "Mr. Secretary . . . Lennie—!"

"Yes, Cora . . ."

"How many were killed?"

"I wouldn't know how to answer that question, Cora . . ."

"Your government estimates an excess of one hundred million. If the entire Nest was sterilized, as you say, then we're talking about more than two-thirds of the current U.S. population."

"Legally," he replied, "we are talking about machines."

"Some of those machines were once your citizens," she mentioned.

The reporter from Christian Promise was standing nearby. He grimaced, then muttered bits of relevant Scripture.

"I don't think this is the time or place to debate what life is or isn't," said the press secretary, juggling things badly.

Cora persisted. "Are you aware of the Canadian position on this tragedy?"

"Like us, they're saddened."

"They've offered sanctuary to any survivors of the blast—"

"Except there are none," he replied, his face pink as granite.

"But if there were? Would you let them move to another Nest in the United States, or perhaps to Canada. . . ?"

There was a pause, brief and electric.

Then with a flat, cool voice, the press secretary reported, "The McGrugger Bill is very specific. Nests may exist only in sealed containment facilities, monitored at all times. And should any of the microchines escape, they will be treated as what they are . . . grave hazards to normal life . . . and this government will not let them roam at will. . . !"

Set inside an abandoned salt mine near Kansas City, the Shawnee Nest had been one of the most secure facilities of its kind ever built. Its power came from clean geothermal sources. Lead plates and intricate defense systems stood against natural hazards as well as more human threats. Thousands of government-loyal AIs, positioned in the surrounding salt, did nothing but watch its borders, making certain that none of the microchines could escape. That was why the thought that local terrorists could launch any attack was so ludicrous. To have that attack succeed was simply preposterous. Whoever was responsible for the bomb, it was done with the abeyance of the highest authorities. No sensible soul doubted it. That dirty little nuke had Federal fingerprints on it, and the attack was planned carefully, and its goals were instantly apparent to people large and small.

Julian had no doubts. He had enemies, vast and malicious, and nobody was more entitled to his paranoias.

Just short of Illinois, the Buick made a long-scheduled stop.

Julian took possession of his clone at the last moment. The process was supposed to be routine—a simple matter of slowing his thoughts a thousandfold, then integrating them with his body— but there were always phantom pains and a sick falling sensation. Becoming a bloated watery bag wasn't the strangest part of it. After all, the Nest was designed to mimic this kind of existence. What gnawed at Julian was the gargantuan sense of Time: A half hour in this realm was nearly a month in his realm. No matter how brief the stop, Julian would feel a little lost when he returned, a step behind the others, and far more emotionally drained than he would ever admit.

By the time the car had stopped, Julian was in full control of the body. His body, he reminded himself. Climbing out into the heat and brilliant sunshine, he felt a purposeful stiffness in his back and the familiar ache running down his right leg. In his past life, he was plagued by sciatica pains. It was one of many ailments that he hadn't missed after his Transmutation. And it was just another detail that someone had thought to include, forcing him to wince and stretch, showing the watching world that he was their flavor of mortal.

Suddenly another old pain began to call to Julian.

Hunger.

His duty was to fill the tank, then do everything expected of a road-weary driver. The rest area was surrounded by the tollway, gas pumps surrounding a fast food/playground complex. Built to handle tens of thousands of people daily, the facility had suffered with the civil chaos, the militias, and the plummeting populations. A few dozen travelers went about their business in near-solitude, and presumably a team of state or Federal agents was lurking nearby, using sensors to scan for those who weren't what they seemed to be.

Without incident, Julian managed the first part of his mission. Then he drove a tiny distance and parked, repeating his stiff climb out of the car, entering the restaurant, and steering straight for the restroom.

He was alone, thankfully.

The diagnostic urinal gently warned him to drink more fluids, then wished him a lovely day.

Taking the advice to heart, Julian ordered a bucket-sized ice tea along with a cultured guinea hen sandwich.

"For here or to go?" asked the automated clerk.

"I'm staying," he replied, believing it would look best.

"Thank you, sir. Have a lovely day."

Julian sat in the back booth, eating slowly and mannerly, scanning the pages of someone's forgotten e-paper. He made a point of lingering over the trite and trivial, concentrating on the comics with their humanized cats and cartoonish people, everyone playing out the same jokes that must have amused him in the very remote past.

"How's it going?"

The voice was slow and wet. Julian blanked the page, looking over his shoulder, betraying nothing as his eyes settled on the familiar wide face. "Fine," he replied, his own voice polite but distant. "Thank you."

"Is it me? Or is it just too damned hot to live out there. . . ?"

"It is hot," Julian conceded.

"Particularly for the likes of me." The man settled onto a plastic chair bolted into the floor with clown heads. His lunch buried his little table: three sandwiches, a greasy sack of fried cucumbers, and a tall chocolate shake. "It's murder when you're fat. Let me tell you . . . I've got to be careful in this weather. I don't move fast. I talk softly. I even have to ration my thinking. I mean it! Too many thoughts, and I break out in a killing sweat!"

Julian had prepared for this moment. Yet nothing was happening quite like he or anyone else had expected.

Saying nothing, Julian took a shy bite out of his sandwich.

"You look like a smart guy," said his companion. "Tell me. If the world's getting emptier, like everyone says, why am I still getting poorer?"

"Excuse me?"

"That's the way it feels, at least." The man was truly fat, his face smooth and youthful, every feature pressed outward by the remnants of countless lunches. "You'd think that with all the smart ones leaving for the Nests . . . you'd think guys like you and me would do pretty well for ourselves. You know?"

Using every resource, the refugees had found three identities for this man: He was a salesman from St. Joseph, Missouri. Or he was a Federal agent working for the Department of Technology, in its Enforcement division, and his salesman identity was a cover. Or he was a charter member of the Christian Promise organization, using that group's political connections to accomplish its murderous goals.

What does he want? Julian asked himself.

He took another shy bite, wiped his mouth with a napkin, then offered his own question. "Why do you say that . . . that it's the smart people who are leaving. . . ?"

"That's what studies show," said a booming, unashamed voice. "Half our people are gone, but we've lost ninety percent of our scientists. Eighty percent of our doctors. And almost every last member of Mensa . . . which between you and me is a good thing, I think. . . !"

Another bite, and wipe. Then with a genuine firmness, Julian told him, "I don't think we should be talking. We don't know each other."

A huge cackling laugh ended with an abrupt statement:

"That's why we should talk. We're strangers, so where's the harm?"

Suddenly the guinea hen sandwich seemed huge and inedible. Julian set it down and took a gulp of tea.

His companion watched him, apparently captivated.

Julian swallowed, then asked, "What do you do for a living?"

"What I'm good at." He unwrapped a hamburger, then took an enormous bite, leaving a crescent-shaped sandwich and a fine glistening stain around his smile. "Put it this way, Mr. Winemaster. I'm like anyone. I do what I hope is best."

"How do you—?"

"Your name? The same way I know your address, and your social registration number, and your bank balance, too." He took a moment to consume half of the remaining crescent, then, while chewing, he choked out the words, "Blaine. My name is. If you'd like to use it."

Each of the man's possible identities used Blaine, either as a first or last name.

Julian wrapped the rest of his sandwich in its insulated paper, watching his hands begin to tremble. He had a pianist's hands in his first life but absolutely no talent for music. When he went through the Transmutation, he'd asked for a better ear and more coordination—both of which were given to him with minimal fuss. Yet he'd never learned how to play, not even after five hundred days. It suddenly seemed like a tragic waste of talent, and, with a secret voice, he promised himself to take lessons, starting immediately.

"So, Mr. Winemaster . . . where are you heading. . . ?"

Julian managed another sip of tea, grimacing at the bitter taste. "Someplace east, judging by what I can see . . ."

"Yes," he allowed. Then he added, "Which is none of your business."

Blaine gave a hearty laugh, shoving the last of the burger deep into his gaping mouth. Then he spoke, showing off the masticated meat and tomatoes, telling his new friend, "Maybe you'll need help somewhere up ahead. Just maybe. And if that happens, I want you to think of me."

"You'll help me, will you?"

The food-stuffed grin was practically radiant. "Think of me," he repeated happily. "That's all I'm saying."

For a long while, the refugees spoke and dreamed of nothing but the mysterious Blaine. Which side did he represent? Should they trust him? Or move against him? And if they tried to stop the man, which way was best? Sabotage his car? Drug his next meal? Or would they have to do something genuinely horrible?

But there were no answers, much less a consensus. Blaine continued shadowing them, at a respectful distance; nothing substantial was learned about him; and despite the enormous stakes, the refugees found themselves gradually drifting back into the moment-by-moment business of ordinary life.

Couples and amalgamations of couples were beginning to make babies.

There was a logic: Refugees were dying every few minutes, usually from radiation exposure. The losses weren't critical, but when they reached their new home—the deep cold rock of the Canadian Shield—they would need numbers, a real demographic momentum. And logic always dances with emotion. Babies served as a tonic to the adults. They didn't demand too many resources, and they forced their parents to focus on more managable problems, like building tiny bodies and caring for needy souls.

Even Julian was swayed by fashion.

With one of his oldest women friends, he found himself hovering over a crystalline womb, watching nanochines sculpt their son out of single atoms and tiny electric breaths.

It was only Julian's second child.

As long as his daughter had been alive, he hadn't seen the point in having another. The truth was that it had always disgusted him to know that the children in the Nest were manufactured—there was no other word for it—and he didn't relish being reminded that he was nothing, more or less, than a fancy machine among millions of similar machines.

Julian often dreamed of his dead daughter. Usually she was on board their strange ark, and he would find a note from her, and a cabin number, and he would wake up smiling, feeling certain that he would find her today. Then he would suddenly remember the bomb, and he would start to cry, suffering through the wrenching, damning loss all over again.

Which was ironic, in a fashion.

During the last nineteen months, father and daughter had gradually and inexorably drifted apart. She was very much a child when they came to the Nest, as flexible as her father wasn't, and how many times had Julian lain awake in bed, wondering why he had ever bothered being Transmutated. His daughter didn't need him, plainly. He could have remained behind. Which always led to the same questions: When he was a normal human being, was he genuinely happy? Or was his daughter's illness simply an excuse . . . a spicy bit of good fortune that offered an escape route. . . ?

When the Nest was destroyed, Julian survived only through more good fortune. He was as far from the epicenter as possible, shielded by the Nest's interior walls and emergency barricades. Yet even then, most of the people near him were killed, an invisible neutron rain scrambling their minds. That same rain had knocked him unconscious just before the firestorm arrived, and if an autodoc hadn't found his limp body, then dragged him into a shelter, he would have been cremated. And, of course, if the Nest hadn't devised its elaborate escape plan, stockpiling the Buick and cloning equipment outside the Nest, Julian would have had no choice but to remain in the rubble, fighting to survive the next moment, and the next.

But those coincidences happened, making his present life feel like the culmination of some glorious Fate.

The secret truth was that Julian relished his new importance, and he enjoyed the pressures that came with each bathroom break and every stop for gas. If he died now, between missions, others could take his place, leading Winemaster's cloned body through the needed motions . . . but they wouldn't do as well, Julian could tell himself . . . a secret part of him wishing that this bizarre, slow-motion chase would never come to an end . . .

✻ ✻ ✻

The Buick stayed on the tollway through northern Illinois, slipping beneath Chicago before skipping across a sliver of Indiana. Julian was integrated with his larger self several times, going through the motions of the stiff, tired, and hungry traveler. Blaine always arrived several minutes later, never approaching his quarry, always finding gas at different pumps, standing outside the restrooms, waiting to show Julian a big smile but never uttering so much as a word in passing.

A little after midnight, the Buick's driver took his hand off the wheel, lay back, and fell asleep. Trusting the tollway's driving was out of character, but with Blaine trailing them and the border approaching, no one was eager to waste time in a motel bed.

At two in the morning, Julian was also asleep, dipping in and out of dreams. Suddenly a hand took him by the shoulder, shaking him, and several voices, urgent and close, said, "We need you, Julian. Now."

In his dreams, a thousand admiring faces were saying, "We need you."

Julian awoke.

His cabin was full of people. His mate had been ushered away, but his unborn child, nearly complete now, floated in his bubble of blackened crystal, oblivious to the nervous air and the tight, crisp voices.

"What's wrong?" Julian asked.

"Everything," they assured.

His universal window showed a live feed from a security camera on the North Dakota-Manitoba border. Department of Technology investigators, backed up by a platoon of heavily armed Marines, were dismantling a Toyota Sunrise. Even at those syrupy speeds, the lasers moved quickly, leaving the vehicle in tiny pieces that were photographed, analyzed, then fed into a state-of-the-art decontamination unit.

"What is this?" Julian sputtered.

But he already knew the answer.

"There was a second group of refugees," said the president, kneeling beside his bed. She was wearing an oversized face—a common fashion, of late—and with a very calm, very grim voice, she admitted, "We weren't the only survivors."

They had kept it a secret, at least from Julian. Which was perfectly reasonable, he reminded himself. What if he had been captured? Under torture, he could have doomed that second lifeboat, and everyone inside it . . .

"Is my daughter there?" he blurted, uncertain what to hope for. The president shook her head. "No, Julian."

Yet if two arks existed, couldn't there be a third? And wouldn't the president keep its existence secret from him, too?

"We've been monitoring events," she continued. "It's tragic, what's happening to our friends . . . but we'll be able to adjust our methods . . . for when we cross the border . . ."

He looked at the other oversized faces. "But why do you need me? We won't reach Detroit for hours."

The president looked over her shoulder. "Play the recording."

Suddenly Julian was looking back in time. He saw the Sunrise pull up to the border post, waiting in line to be searched. A pickup truck with Wyoming plates pulled up behind it, and out stepped a preposterously tall man brandishing a badge and a handgun. With an eerie sense of purpose, he strode up to the little car, took aim, and fired his full clip through the driver's window. The body behind the wheel jerked and kicked as it was ripped apart. Then the murderer reached in and pulled the corpse out through the shattered glass, shouting at the Tech investigators:

"I've got them! Here! For Christ's sake, help me!"

The image dissolved, the window returning to the real-time, real-speed scene.

To himself, Julian whispered, "No, it can't be . . ."

The president took his hands in hers, their warmth a comfortable fiction. "We would have shown you this as it was happening, but we weren't sure what it meant."

"But you're sure now?"

"That man followed our people. All the way from Nebraska." She shook her head, admitting, "We don't know everything, no. For security reasons, we rarely spoke with those other survivors—"

"What are we going to do?" Julian growled.

"The only reasonable thing left for us." She smiled in a sad fashion, then warned him, "We're pulling off the tollway now. You still have a little while to get ready . . ."

He closed his eyes, saying nothing.

"Not as long as you'd like, I'm sure . . . but with this sort of thing, maybe it's best to hurry . . ."

There were no gas pumps or restaurants in the rest area. A small, divided parking lot was surrounded by trees and fake log cabin lavatories that in turn were sandwiched between broad lanes of moonlit pavement. The parking lot was empty. The only traffic was a single truck in the westbound freighter lane, half a dozen trailers towed along in its wake. Julian watched the truck pass, then walked into the darkest shadows, and kneeled.

The security cameras were being fed false images—images that were hopefully more convincing than the ludicrous log cabins. Yet even when he knew that he was safe, Julian felt exposed. Vulnerable. The feeling worsened by the moment, becoming a black dread, and, by the time the Tokamak pulled to a stop, his newborn heart was racing, and his quick, damp breath tasted foul.

Blaine parked two slots away from the sleeping Buick. He didn't bother looking through the windows. Instead, guided by intuition or hidden sensor, he strolled toward the men's room, hesitated, then took a few half-steps toward Julian, passing into a patch of moonlight.

Using both hands, Julian lifted his weapon, letting it aim itself at the smooth broad forehead.

"Well," said Blaine, "I see you're thinking about me."

"What do you want?" Julian whispered. Then with a certain clumsiness, he added, "With me."

The man remained silent for a moment, a smile building.

"Who am I?" he asked suddenly. "Ideas? Do you have any?"

Julian gulped a breath, then said, "You work for the government." His voice was testy, pained. "And I don't know why you're following me!"

Blaine didn't offer answers. Instead he warned his audience, "The border is a lot harder to pierce than you think."

"Is it?"

"Humans aren't fools," Blaine reminded him. "After all, they designed the technologies used by the Nests, and they've had just as long as you to improve on old tricks."

"People in the world are getting dumber," said Julian. "You told me that."

"And those same people are very scared, very focused," his opponent countered. "Their borders are a priority to them. You are their top priority. And even if your thought processes are accelerated a thousandfold, they've got AIs who can blister you in any race of intellect. At least for the time being, they can."

Shoot him, an inner voice urged.

Yet Julian did nothing, waiting silently, hoping to be saved from this onerous chore.

"You can't cross into Canada without me," Blaine told him.

"I know what happened . . ." Julian felt the gun's barrel adjusting itself as his hands grew tired and dropped slightly. "Up in North Dakota . . . we know all about it . . ."

It was Blaine's turn to keep silent.

Again, Julian asked, "Who are you? Just tell me that much."

"You haven't guessed it, have you?" The round face seemed genuinely disappointed. "Not even in your wildest dreams . . ."

"And why help us?" Julian muttered, saying too much.

"Because in the long run, helping you helps me."

"How?"

Silence.

"We don't have any wealth," Julian roared. "Our homes were destroyed. By you, for all I know—"

The man laughed loudly, smirking as he began to turn away. "You've got some time left. Think about the possibilities, and we'll talk again."

Julian tugged on the trigger. Just once.

Eighteen shells pierced the back of Blaine's head, then worked down the wide back, devastating every organ even as the lifeless body crumpled. Even a huge man falls fast, Julian observed. Then he rose, walked ahead on weak legs, and with his own aim, he emptied the rest of his clip into the gore.

It was easy, pumping in those final shots.

What's more, shooting the dead carried an odd, unexpected satisfaction—which was probably the same satisfaction that the terrorists had felt when their tiny bomb destroyed a hundred million soulless machines.

With every refugee watching, Julian cut open the womb with laser shears.

Julian Jr. was born a few seconds after 2:30 A.M., and the audience, desperate for a good celebration, nearly buried the baby with gifts and sweet words. Yet nobody could spoil him like his father could. For the next few hours, Julian pestered his first son with love and praise, working with a manic energy to fill every need, every whim. And his quest to be a perfect father only grew worse. The sun was beginning to show itself; Canada was waiting over the horizon; but Julian was oblivious, hunched over the toddler with sparkling toys in both hands, his never-pretty voice trying to sing a child's song, nothing half as important in this world as making his son giggle and smile. . . !

They weren't getting past the border. Their enemies were too clever, and too paranoid. Julian could smell the inevitable, but because he didn't know what else to do, he went through the motions of smiling for the president and the public, saying the usual brave words whenever it was demanded of him.

Sometimes Julian took his boy for long rides around the lifeboat.

During one journey, a woman knelt and happily teased the baby, then looked up at the famous man, mentioning in an off-handed way, "We'll get to our new home just in time for him to grow into it."

Those words gnawed at Julian, although he was helpless to explain why.

By then the sun had risen, its brilliant light sweeping across a sleepy border town. Instead of crossing at Detroit, the refugees had abandoned the tollway, taking an old highway north to Port Huron. It would be easier here, was the logic. The prayer. Gazing out the universal window, Julian looked at the boarded up homes and abandoned businesses, cars parked and forgotten, weeds growing in every yard, every crack. The border cities had lost most of their people in the last year-plus, he recalled. It was too easy and too accepted, this business of crossing into a land where it was still legal to be remade. In another year, most of the United States would look this way, unless the government took more drastic measures such as closing its borders, or worse, invading its wrong-minded neighbors. . . !

Julian felt a deep chill, shuddering.

That's when he suddenly understood. Everything. And in the next few seconds, after much thought, he knew precisely what he had to do.

Assuming there was still time . . .

A dozen cars were lined up in front of the customs station. The Buick had slipped in behind a couple on a motorcycle. Only one examination station was open, and every traveler was required to first declare his intentions, then permanently give up his citizenship. It would be a long wait. The driver turned the engine off, watching the Marines and Tech officials at work, everything about them relentlessly professional. Three more cars pulled up behind him, including a Tokamak, and he happened to glance at the rearview screen when Blaine climbed out, walking with a genuine bounce, approaching on the right and rapping on the passenger window with one fat knuckle, then stooping down and smiling through the glass, proving that he had made a remarkable recovery since being murdered.

Julian unlocked the door for him.

With a heavy grunt, Blaine pulled himself in and shut the door, then gave his companion a quick wink.

Julian wasn't surprised. If anything, he was relieved, telling his companion, "I think I know what you are."

"Good," said Blaine. "And what do your friends think?"

"I don't know. I never told them." Julian took the steering wheel in both hands. "I was afraid that if I did, they wouldn't believe me. They'd think I was crazy, and dangerous. And they wouldn't let me come here."

The line was moving, jerking forward one car-length. Julian started the Buick and crept forward, then turned the engine off again.

With a genuine fondness, Blaine touched him on a shoulder, commenting, "Your friends might pull you back into their world now. Have you thought of that?"

"Sure," said Julian. "But for the next few seconds, they'll be too confused to make any big decisions."

Lake Huron lay on Blaine's left, vast and deeply blue, and he studied the picket boats that dotted the water, bristling with lasers that did nothing but flip back and forth, back and forth, incinerating any flying object that appeared even remotely suspicious.

"So tell me," he asked his companion, "why do you think I'm here?"

Julian turned his body, the cultured leather squeaking beneath him. Gesturing at Port Huron, he said, "If these trends continue, everything's going to look that way soon. Empty. Abandoned. Humans will have almost vanished from this world, which means that perhaps someone else could move in without too much trouble. They'll find houses, and good roads to drive on, and a communication system already in place. Ready-made lives, and practically free for the taking."

"What sort of someone?"

"That's what suddenly occurred to me." Julian took a deep breath, then said, "Humans are making themselves smaller, and faster. But what if something other than humans is doing the same thing? What if there's something in the universe that's huge, and very slow by human standards, but intelligent nonetheless. Maybe it lives in cold places between the stars. Maybe somewhere else. The point is, this other species is undergoing a similar kind of transformation. It's making itself a thousand times smaller, and a thousand times quicker, which puts it roughly equal to this." The frail face was smiling, and he lifted his hands from the wheel.

"Flesh and blood, and bone . . . these are the high-technology materials that build your version of microchines!"

Blaine winked again, saying, "You're probably right. If you'd explained it that way, your little friends would have labeled you insane."

"But am I right?"

There was no reason to answer him directly. "What about me, Mr. Winemaster? How do you look at me?"

"You want to help us." Julian suddenly winced, then shuddered. But he didn't mention what was happening, saying, "I assume that you have different abilities than we do . . . that you can get us past their sensors—"

"Is something wrong, Mr. Winemaster?"

"My friends . . . they're trying to take control of this body . . ."

"Can you deal with them?"

"For another minute. I changed all the control codes." Again, he winced. "You don't want the government aware of you, right? And you're trying to help steer us and them away from war . . . during this period of transition—"

"The way we see it," Blaine confessed, "the chance of a world-wide cataclysm is just about one in three, and worsening."

Julian nodded, his face contorting in agony. "If I accept your help. . . ?"

"Then I'll need yours." He set a broad hand on Julian's neck. "You've done a remarkable job hiding yourselves. You and your friends are in this car, but my tools can't tell me where. Not without more time, at least. And that's time we don't have . . ."

Julian stiffened, his clothes instantly soaked with perspiration.

Quietly, quickly, he said, "But if you're really a government agent . . . here to fool me into telling you . . . everything. . . ?"

"I'm not," Blaine promised.

A second examination station had just opened; people were maneuvering for position, leaving a gap in front of them.

Julian started his car, pulling forward. "If I do tell you . . . where we are . . . they'll think that I've betrayed them. . . !"

The Buick's anticollision system engaged, bringing them to an abrupt stop.

"Listen," said Blaine. "You've got only a few seconds to decide—"

"I know . . ."

"Where, Mr. Winemaster? Where?"

"Julian," he said, wincing again.

"Julian."

A glint of pride showed in the eyes. "We're not . . . in the car
. . ." Then the eyes grew enormous, and Julian tried shouting the
answer . . . his mind suddenly losing its grip on that tiny, lovely
mouth . . .

Blaine swung with his right fist, shattering a cheekbone with his
first blow, killing the body before the last blow.

By the time the Marines had surrounded the car, its interior
was painted with gore, and in horror, the soldiers watched as the
madman—he couldn't be anything but insane—calmly rolled
down the window and smiled with a blood-rimmed mouth, telling
his audience, "I had to kill him. He's Satan."

A hardened lieutenant looked in at the victim, torn open like a
sack, and she shivered, moaning aloud for the poor man.

With perfect calm, Blaine declared, "I had to eat his heart.
That's how you kill Satan. Don't you know?"

For disobeying orders, the president declared Julian a traitor, and
she oversaw his trial and conviction. The entire process took less
than a minute. His quarters were remodeled to serve as his prison
cell. In the next ten minutes, three separate attempts were made on
his life. Not everyone agreed with the court's sentence, it seemed.
Which was understandable. Contact with the outside world had
been severed the instant Winemaster died. The refugees and their
lifeboat were lost in every kind of darkness. At any moment, the
Tech specialists would throw them into a decontamination unit,
and they would evaporate without warning. And all because they'd
entrusted themselves to an old DNA-born human who never really
wanted to be Transmutated in the first place, according to at least
one of his former lovers . . .

Ostensibly for security reasons, Julian wasn't permitted visitors.

Not even his young son could be brought to him, nor was he
allowed to see so much as a picture of the boy.

Julian spent his waking moments pacing back and forth in the
dim light, trying to exhaust himself, then falling into a hard sleep,
too tired to dream at all, if he was lucky . . .

Before the first hour was finished, he had lost all track of time.

After nine full days of relentless isolation, the universe had
shriveled until nothing existed but his cell, and him, his memories
indistinguishable from fantasies.

On the tenth day, the cell door opened.

A young man stepped in, and with a stranger's voice, he said,
"Father."

"Who are you?" asked Julian.

His son didn't answer, giving him the urgent news instead. "Mr. Blaine finally made contact with us, explaining what he is and what's happened so far, and what will happen. . . !"

Confusion wrestled with a fledging sense of relief.

"He's from between the stars, just like you guessed, Father. And he's been found insane for your murder. Though obviously you're not dead. But the government believes there was a Julian Wine-master, and it's holding Blaine in a Detroit hospital, and he's holding us. His metabolism is augmenting our energy production, and when nobody's watching, he'll connect us with the outside world."

Julian couldn't imagine such a wild story: It had to be true!

"When the world is safe, in a year or two, he'll act cured or he'll escape—whatever is necessary—and he'll carry us wherever we want to go."

The old man sat on his bed, suddenly exhausted.

"Where would you like to go, Father?"

"Out that door," Julian managed. Then a wondrous thought took him by surprise, and he grinned, saying, "No, I want to be like Blaine was. I want to live between the stars, to be huge and cold, and slow . . .

"Not today, maybe . . .

"But soon . . . definitely soon. . . !"

Coelacanths

The Speaker

HE STALKS THE WIDE STAGE, A BRILLIANT BEAM of hot blue light fixed squarely upon him. "We are great! We are glorious!" the man calls out. His voice is pleasantly, effortlessly loud. With a face handsome to the brink of lovely and a collage of smooth, passionate mannerisms, he performs for an audience that sits in the surrounding darkness. Flinging long arms overhead, hands reaching for the distant light, his booming voice proclaims, "We have never been as numerous as we are today. We have never been this happy. And we have never known the prosperity that is ours at this golden moment. This golden now!" Athletic legs carry him across the stage, bare feet slapping against planks of waxed maple. "Our species is thriving," he can declare with a seamless ease. "By every conceivable measure, we are a magnificent, irresistible tide sweeping across the universe!"

Transfixed by the blue beam, his naked body is shamelessly young, rippling with hard muscles over hard bone. A long fat penis dangles and dances, accenting every sweeping gesture, every bold word. The living image of a small but potent god, he surely is a creature worthy of admiration, a soul deserving every esteem and emulation. With a laugh, he promises the darkness, "We have never been so powerful, we humans." Yet in the next breath, with a faintly

apologetic smile, he must add, "Yet still, as surely as tomorrow
comes, our glories today will seem small and quaint in the future,
and what looks golden now will turn to the yellow dust upon which
our magnificent children will tread!"

Procyon

Study your history. It tells you that travel always brings its share of
hazards; that's a basic, impatient law of the universe. Leaving the
security and familiarity of home is never easy. But every person
needs to make the occasional journey, embracing the risks to
improve his station, his worth and self-esteem. Procyon explains
why this day is a good day to wander. She refers to intelligence
reports as well as the astrological tables. Then by a dozen means,
she maps out their intricate course, describing what she hopes to
find and everything that she wants to avoid.

She has twin sons. They were born four months ago, and they
are mostly grown now. "Keep alert," she tells the man-children,
leading them out through a series of reinforced and powerfully
camouflaged doorways. "No naps, no distractions," she warns
them. Then with a backward glance, she asks again, "What do we
want?"

"Whatever we can use," the boys reply in a sloppy chorus.

"Quiet," she warns. Then she nods and shows a caring smile,
reminding them, "A lot of things can be used. But their trash is
sweetest."

Mother and sons look alike: They are short, strong people with
closely cropped hair and white-gray eyes. They wear simple clothes
and three fashions of camouflage, plus a stew of mental add-ons
and microchine helpers as well as an array of sensors that never
blink, watching what human eyes cannot see. Standing motionless,
they vanish into the convoluted, ever-shifting background. But
walking makes them into three transient blurs—dancing wisps that
are noticeably simpler than the enormous world around them.
They can creep ahead only so far before their camouflage falls
apart, and then they have to stop, waiting patiently or otherwise,
allowing the machinery to find new ways to help make them invisible.

"I'm confused," one son admits. "That thing up ahead—"

"Did you update your perception menu?"

"I thought I did."

Procyon makes no sound. Her diamond-bright glare is enough.

She remains rigidly, effortlessly still, allowing her lazy son to finish
his preparations. Dense, heavily encoded signals have to be whispered, the local net downloading the most recent topological cues,
teaching a three-dimensional creature how to navigate through this
shifting, highly intricate environment.

The universe is fat with dimensions.

Procyon knows as much theory as anyone. Yet despite a long
life rich with experience, she has to fight to decipher what her
eyes and sensors tell her. She doesn't even bother learning the
tricks that coax these extra dimensions out of hiding. Let her add-
ons guide her. That's all a person can do, slipping in close to one
of *them*. In this place, up is three things and sideways is five others.
Why bother counting? What matters is that when they walk again,
the three of them move through the best combination of dimensions, passing into a little bubble of old-fashioned up and down.
She knows this place. Rising up beside them is a trusted landmark
—a red granite bowl that cradles what looks like a forest of tall
sticks, the sticks leaking a warm light that Procyon ignores, stepping again, moving along on her tiptoes.

One son leads the way. He lacks the experience to be first, but,
in another few weeks, his flesh and sprint-grown brain will force
him into the world alone. He needs his practice, and more important, he needs confidence, learning to trust his add-ons and his
careful preparations, and his breeding, and his own good luck.

Procyon's other son lingers near the granite bowl. He's the son
who didn't update his menu. This is her dreamy child, whom she
loves dearly. Of course she adores him. But there's no escaping the
fact that he is easily distracted, and that his adult life will be, at its
very best, difficult. Study your biology. Since life began, mothers
have made hard decisions about their children, and they have
made the deadliest decisions with the tiniest of gestures.

Procyon lets her lazy son fall behind.

Her other son takes two careful steps and stops abruptly, standing before what looks like a great black cylinder set on its side. The
shape is a fiction: The cylinder is round in one fashion but incom-
prehensible in many others. Her add-ons and sensors have built
this very simple geometry to represent something far more elaborate. This is a standard disposal unit. Various openings appear as a
single slot near the rim of the cylinder, just enough room showing
for a hand and forearm to reach through, touching whatever
garbage waits inside.

Her son's thick body has more grace than any dancer of old,

more strength than a platoon of ancient athletes. His IQ is enormous. His reaction times have been enhanced by every available means. His father was a great old soul who survived into his tenth year, which is almost forever. But when the boy drifts sideways, he betrays his inexperience. His sensors attack the cylinder by every means, telling him that it's a low-grade trash receptacle secured by what looks like a standard locking device, AI-managed and obsolete for days, if not weeks. And inside the receptacle is a mangled piece of hardware worth a near-fortune on the open market.

The boy drifts sideways, and he glimmers.

Procyon says, "No," too loudly.

But he feels excited, invulnerable. Grinning over his shoulder now, he winks and lifts one hand with a smooth, blurring motion—

Instincts old as blood come bubbling up. Procyon leaps, shoving her son off his feet and saving him. And in the next horrible instant, she feels herself engulfed, a dry, cold hand grabbing her, then stuffing her inside a hole that by any geometry feels nothing but bottomless.

Able

Near the lip of the City, inside the emerald green ring of Park, waits a secret place where the moss and horsetail and tree-fern forest plunges into a deep crystalline pool of warm spring water. No public map tells of the pool, and no trail leads the casual walker near it. But the pool is exactly the sort of place that young boys always discover, and it is exactly the kind of treasure that remains unmentioned to parents or any other adult with suspicious or troublesome natures.

Able Quotient likes to believe that he was first to stumble across this tiny corner of Creation. And if he isn't first, at least no one before him has ever truly seen the water's beauty, and nobody after him will appreciate the charms of this elegant, timeless place.

Sometimes Able brings others to the pool, but only his best friends and a few boys whom he wants to impress. Not for a long time does he even consider bringing a girl, and then it takes forever to find a worthy candidate, then muster the courage to ask her to join him. Her name is Mish. She's younger than Able by a little ways, but like all girls, she acts older and much wiser than he will ever be. They been classmates from the beginning. They live three floors apart in the Tower of Gracious Good, which makes them close neighbors. Mish is pretty, and her beauty is the sort that will only grow as she becomes a woman. Her face is narrow and serious. Her eyes watch everything. She wears flowing dresses and jeweled sandals, and she goes everywhere with a clouded leopard named Mr. Stuff-and-Nonsense. "If my cat can come along," she says after hearing Able's generous offer. "Are there any birds at this pond of yours?"

Able should be horrified by the question. The life around the pool knows him and has grown to trust him. But he is so enamored by Mish that he blurts out, "Yes, hundreds of birds. Fat, slow birds. Mr. Stuff can eat himself sick."

"But that wouldn't be right," Mish replies with a disapproving smirk. "I'll lock down his appetite. And if we see any wounded birds . . . any animal that's suffering . . . we can unlock him right away. . . !"

"Oh, sure," Able replies, almost sick with nerves. "I guess that's fine, too."

People rarely travel any distance. City is thoroughly modern, every apartment supplied by conduits and meshed with every web and channel, shareline and gossip run. But even with most of its citizens happily sitting at home, the streets are jammed with millions of walking bodies. Every seat on the train is filled all the way to the last stop. Able momentarily loses track of Mish when the cabin walls evaporate. But, thankfully, he finds her waiting at Park's edge. She and her little leopard are standing in the narrow shade of a horsetail. She teases him, observing, "You look lost." Then she laughs, perhaps at him, before abruptly changing the subject. With a nod and sweeping gesture, she asks, "Have you noticed? Our towers look like these trees."

To a point, yes. The towers are tall and thin and rounded like the horsetails, and the hanging porches make them appear rough-skinned. But there are obvious and important differences between trees and towers, and if she were a boy, Able would make fun of her now. Fighting his nature, Able forces himself to smile. "Oh, my," he says as he turns, looking back over a shoulder. "They do look like horsetails, don't they?"

Now the three adventurers set off into the forest. Able takes the lead. Walking with boys is a quick business that often turns into a race. But girls are different, particularly when their fat, unhungry cats are dragging along behind them. It takes forever to reach the rim of the world. Then it takes another two forevers to follow the rim to where they can almost see the secret pool. But that's where

Mish announces, "I'm tired!" To the world, she says, "I want to stop and eat. I want to rest here."

Able nearly tells her, "No."

Instead he decides to coax her, promising, "It's just a little farther."

But she doesn't seem to hear him, leaping up on the pink polished rim, sitting where the granite is smooth and flat, legs dangling and her bony knees exposed. She opens the little pack that has floated on her back from the beginning, pulling out a hot lunch that she keeps and a cold lunch that she hands to Able. "This is all I could take," she explains, "without my parents asking questions." She is reminding Able that she never quite got permission to make this little journey. "If you don't like the cold lunch," she promises, "then we can trade. I mean, if you really don't."

He says, "I like it fine," without opening the insulated box. Then he looks inside, discovering a single wedge of spiced sap, and it takes all of his poise not to say, "Ugh!"

Mr. Stuff collapses into a puddle of towerlight, instantly falling asleep.

The two children eat quietly and slowly. Mish makes the occasional noise about favorite teachers and mutual friends. She acts serious and ordinary, and disappointment starts gnawing at Able. He isn't old enough to sense that the girl is nervous. He can't imagine that Mish wants to delay the moment when they'll reach the secret pool, or that she sees possibilities waiting there—wicked possibilities that only a wicked boy should be able to foresee.

Finished with her meal, Mish runs her hands along the hem of her dress, and she kicks at the air, and then, hunting for any distraction, she happens to glance over her shoulder.

Where the granite ends, the world ends. Normally nothing of substance can be seen out past the pink stone—nothing but a confused, ever-shifting grayness that extends on forever. Able hasn't bothered to look out there. He is much too busy trying to finish his awful meal, concentrating on his little frustrations and his depraved little daydreams.

"Oh, goodness," the young girl exclaims. "Look at that!"

Able has no expectations. What could possibly be worth the trouble of turning around? But it's an excuse to give up on his lunch, and, after setting it aside, he turns slowly, eyes jumping wide open and a surprised grunt leaking out of him as he tumbles off the granite, landing squarely on top of poor Mr. Stuff.

Escher

She has a clear, persistent memory of flesh, but the flesh isn't hers. Like manners and like knowledge, what a person remembers can be bequeathed by her ancestors. That's what is happening now. Limbs and heads; penises and vaginas. In the midst of some unrelated business, she remembers having feet and the endless need to protect those feet with sandals or boots or ostrich skin or spiked shoes that will lend a person even more height. She remembers wearing clothes that gave color and bulk to what was already bright and enormous. At this particular instant, what she sees is a distant, long-dead relative sitting on a white porcelain bowl, bare feet dangling, his orifices voiding mountains of waste and an ocean of water.

Her oldest ancestors were giants. They were built from skin and muscle, wet air, and great slabs of fat. Without question, they were an astonishing excess of matter, vast beyond all reason, yet fueled by slow, inefficient chemical fires.

Nothing about Escher is inefficient. No flesh clings to her. Not a drop of water or one glistening pearl of fat. It's always smart to be built from structure light and tested, efficient instructions. It's best to be tinier than a single cell and as swift as electricity, slipping unseen through places that won't even notice your presence.

Escher is a glimmer, a perfect and enduring whisper of light. Of life. Lovely in her own fashion, yet fierce beyond all measure.

She needs her fierceness.

When cooperation fails, as it always does, a person has to throw her rage at the world and her countless enemies.

But in this place, for this moment, cooperation holds sway.

Manners rule.

Escher is eating. Even as tiny and efficient as she is, she needs an occasional sip of raw power. Everyone does. And it seems as if half of everyone has gathered around what can only be described as a tiny, delicious wound. She can't count the citizens gathered at the feast. Millions and millions, surely. All those weak glimmers join into a soft glow. Everyone is bathed in a joyous light. It is a boastful, wasteful show, but Escher won't waste her energy with warnings. Better to sip at the wound, absorbing the free current, building up her reserves for the next breeding cycle. It is best to let others make the mistakes for you: Escher believes nothing else quite so fervently.

A pair of sisters floats past. The familial resemblance is obvious, and so are the tiny differences. Mutations as well as tailored changes have created two loud gossips who speak and giggle in a rush of words and raw data, exchanging secrets about the multitude around them.

Escher ignores their prattle, gulping down the last of what she can possibly hold, and then pausing, considering where she might hide a few nanojoules of extra juice, keeping them safe for some desperate occasion.

Escher begins to hunt for that unlikely hiding place.

And then her sisters abruptly change topics. Gossip turns to trading memories stolen from the World. Most of it is picoweight stuff, useless and boring. An astonishing fraction of His thoughts are banal. Like the giants of old, He can afford to be sloppy. To be a spendthrift. Here is a pointed example of why Escher is happy to be herself. She is smart in her own fashion, and imaginative, and almost everything about her is important, and when a problem confronts her, she can cut through the muddle, seeing the blessing wrapped up snug inside the measurable risks.

Quietly, with a puzzled tone, one sister announces, "The World is alarmed."

"About?" says the other.

"A situation," says the first. "Yes, He is alarmed now. Moral questions are begging for His attention."

"What questions?"

The first sister tells a brief, strange story.

"You know all this?" asks another. Asks Escher. "Is this daydream or hard fact?"

"I know, and it is fact." The sister feels insulted by the doubting tone, but she puts on a mannerly voice, explaining the history of this sudden crisis.

Escher listens.

And suddenly the multitude is talking about nothing else. What is happening has never happened before, not in this fashion . . . not in any genuine memory of any of the millions here, it hasn't . . . and some very dim possibilities begin to show themselves. Benefits wrapped inside some awful dangers. And one or two of these benefits wink at Escher, and smile. . . .

The multitude panics, and evaporates.

Escher remains behind, deliberating on these possibilities. The landscape beneath her is far more sophisticated than flesh, and stronger, but it has an ugly appearance that reminds her of a flesh-born memory. A lesion; a pimple. A tiny, unsightly ruin standing in what is normally seamless, and beautiful, and perfect.

She flees, but only so far.

Then she hunkers down and waits, knowing that eventually, in one fashion or another, He will scratch at this tiny irritation.

The Speaker

"You cannot count human accomplishments," he boasts to his audience, strutting and wagging his way to the edge of the stage. Bare toes curl over the sharp edge, and he grins jauntily, admitting, "And I cannot count them, either. There are simply too many successes, in too many far-flung places, to nail up a number that you can believe. But allow me, if you will, this chance to list a few important marvels."

Long hands grab bony hips, and he gazes out into the watching darkness. "The conquest of our cradle continent," he begins, "which was quickly followed by the conquest of our cradle world. Then, after a gathering pause, we swiftly and thoroughly occupied most of our neighboring worlds, too. It was during those millennia when we learned how to split flint and atoms and DNA and our own restless psyches. With these apish hands, we fashioned great machines that worked for us as our willing, eager slaves. And with our slaves' more delicate hands, we fabricated machines that could think for us." A knowing wink, a mischievous shrug. "Like any child, of course, our thinking machines eventually learned to think for themselves. Which was a dangerous, foolish business, said some. Said fools. But my list of our marvels only begins with that business. This is what I believe, and I challenge anyone to say otherwise."

There is a sound—a stern little murmur—and perhaps it implies dissent. Or perhaps the speaker made the noise himself, fostering a tension that he is building with his words and body.

His penis grows erect, drawing the eye.

Then with a wide and bright and unabashedly smug grin, he roars out, "Say this with me. Tell me what great things we have done. Boast to Creation about the wonders that we have taken part in . . . !"

Procyon

Torture is what this is: She feels her body plunging from a high place, head before feet. A frantic wind roars past. Outstretched hands refuse to slow her fall. Then Procyon makes herself spin, putting her feet beneath her body, and gravity instantly reverses itself. She screams, and screams, and the distant walls reflect her terror, needles jabbed into her wounded ears. Finally, she grows quiet, wrapping her arms around her eyes and ears, forcing herself to do nothing, hanging limp in space while her body falls in one awful direction.

A voice whimpers.

A son's worried voice says, "Mother, are you there? Mother?"

Some of her add-ons have been peeled away, but not all of them. The brave son uses a whisper-channel, saying, "I'm sorry," with a genuine anguish. He sounds sick and sorry, and exceptionally angry, too. "I was careless," he admits. He says, "Thank you for saving me." Then to someone else, he says, "She can't hear me."

"I hear you," she whispers.

"Listen," says her other son. The lazy one. "Did you hear something?"

She starts to say, "Boys," with a stern voice. But then the trap vibrates, a piercing white screech nearly deafening Procyon. Someone physically strikes the trap. Two someones. She feels the walls turning around her, the trap making perhaps a quarter-turn toward home.

Again, she calls out, "Boys."

They stop rolling her. Did they hear her? No, they found a hidden restraint, the trap secured at one or two or ten ends.

One last time, she says, "Boys."

"I hear her," her dreamy son blurts.

"Don't give up, Mother," says her brave son. "We'll get you out. I see the locks, I can beat them—"

"You can't," she promises.

He pretends not to have heard her. A shaped explosive detonates, making a cold ringing sound, faraway and useless. Then the boy growls, "Damn," and kicks the trap, accomplishing nothing at all.

"It's too tough," says her dreamy son. "We're not doing any good—"

"Shut up," his brother shouts.

Procyon tells them, "Quiet now. Be quiet."

The trap is probably tied to an alarm. Time is short, or it has run out already. Either way, there's a decision to be made, and the decision has a single, inescapable answer. With a careful and firm voice, she tells her sons, "Leave me. Now. Go!"

"I won't," the brave son declares. "Never!"

"Now," she says.

"It's my fault," says the dreamy son. "I should have been keep-ing up—"

"Both of you are to blame," Procyon calls out. "And I am, too. And there's bad luck here, but there's some good, too. You're still free. You can still get away. Now, before you get yourself seen and caught—"

"You're going to die," the brave son complains.

"One day or the next, I will," she agrees. "Absolutely."

"We'll find help," he promises.

"From where?" she asks.

"From who?" says her dreamy son in the same instant. "We aren't close to anyone—"

"Shut up," his brother snaps. "Just shut up!"

"Run away," their mother repeats.

"I won't," the brave son tells her. Or himself. Then with a serious, tight little voice, he says, "I can fight. We'll both fight."

Her dreamy son says nothing.

Procyon peels her arms away from her face, opening her eyes, focusing on the blurring cylindrical walls of the trap. It seems that she was wrong about her sons. The brave one is just a fool, and the dreamy one has the good sense. She listens to her dreamy son saying nothing, and then the other boy says, "Of course you're going to fight. Together, we can do some real damage—"

"I love you both," she declares.

That wins a silence.

Then again, one last time, she says, "Run."

"I'm not a coward," one son growls.

While her good son says nothing, running now, and he needs his breath for things more essential than pride and bluster.

Able

The face stares at them for the longest while. It is a great wide face, heavily bearded with smoke-colored eyes and a long nose perched above the cavernous mouth that hangs open, revealing teeth and things more amazing than teeth. Set between the bone-white enamel are little machines made of fancy stuff. Able can only guess what the add-on machines are doing. This is a wild man, powerful and free. People like him are scarce and strange, their bodies reengineered in countless ways. Like his eyes: Able stares into those giant gray eyes, noticing fleets of tiny machines floating on the tears. Those machines are probably delicate sensors. Then with a jolt of amazement, he realizes that those machines and sparkling eyes are staring into their world with what seems to be a genuine fascination.

"He's watching us," Able mutters.

"No, he isn't," Mish argues. "He can't see into our realm."

"We can't see into his either," the boy replies. "But just the same, I can make him out just fine."

"It must be. . . ." Her voice falls silent while she accesses City's library. Then with a dismissive shrug of her shoulders, she announces, "We're caught in his topological hardware. That's all. He has to simplify his surroundings to navigate, and we just happen to be close enough and aligned right."

Able had already assumed all that.

Mish starts to speak again, probably wanting to add to her explanation. She can sure be a know-everything sort of girl. But then the great face abruptly turns away, and they watch the man run away from their world.

"I told you," Mish sings out. "He couldn't see us."

"I think he could have," Able replies, his voice finding a distinct sharpness.

The girl straightens her back. "You're wrong," she says with an obstinate tone. Then she turns away from the edge of the world, announcing, "I'm ready to go on now."

"I'm not," says Able.

She doesn't look back at him. She seems to be talking to her leopard, asking, "Why aren't you ready?"

"I see two of them now," Able tells her.

"You can't."

"I can." The hardware trickery is keeping the outside realms sensible. A tunnel of simple space leads to two men standing beside an iron-black cylinder. The men wear camouflage, but they are moving too fast to let it work. They look small now. Distant, or tiny. Once you leave the world, size and distance are impossible to measure. How many times have teachers told him that? Able watches the tiny men kicking at the cylinder. They beat on its heavy sides with their fists and forearms, managing to roll it for almost a quarter turn. Then one of the men pulls a fist-sized device from what looks like a cloth sack, fixing it to what looks like a sealed slot, and both men hurry to the far end of the cylinder.

"What are they doing?" asks Mish with a grumpy interest.

A feeling warns Able, but too late. He starts to say, "Look away—"

The explosion is brilliant and swift, the blast reflected off the cylinder and up along the tunnel of ordinary space, a clap of thunder making the giant horsetails sway and nearly knocking the two of them onto the forest floor.

"They're criminals," Mish mutters with a nervous hatred.

"How do you know?" the boy asks.

"People like that just are," she remarks. "Living like they do. Alone like that, and wild. You know how they make their living."

"They take what they need—"

"They steal!" she interrupts.

Able doesn't even glance at her. He watches as the two men work frantically, trying to pry open the still-sealed doorway. He can't guess why they would want the doorway opened. Or rather, he can think of too many reasons. But when he looks at their anguished, helpless faces, he realizes that whatever is inside, it's driving these wild men very close to panic.

"Criminals," Mish repeats.

"I heard you," Able mutters.

Then, before she can offer another hard opinion, he turns to her and admits, "I've always liked them. They live by their wits, and mostly alone, and they have all these sweeping powers—"

"Powers that they've stolen," she whines.

"From garbage, maybe." There is no point in mentioning whose garbage. He stares at Mish's face, pretty but twisted with fury, and something sad and inevitable occurs to Able. He shakes his head and sighs, telling her, "I don't like you very much."

Mish is taken by surprise. Probably no other boy has said those awful words to her, and she doesn't know how to react, except to sputter ugly little sounds as she turns, looking back over the edge of the world.

Able does the same.

One of the wild men abruptly turns and runs. In a supersonic flash, he races past the children, vanishing into the swirling grayness, leaving his companion to stand alone beside the mysterious black cylinder. Obviously weeping, the last man wipes the tears from his whiskered face with a trembling hand, while his other hand begins to yank a string of wondrous machines from what seems to be a bottomless sack of treasures.

Escher

She consumes all of her carefully stockpiled energies, and for the first time in her life, she weaves a body for herself: A distinct physical shell composed of diamond dust and keratin and discarded rare earths and a dozen subtle glues meant to bind to every surface without being felt. To a busy eye, she is dust. She is insubstantial and useless and forgettable. To a careful eye and an inquisitive touch, she is the tiniest soul imaginable, frail beyond words, forever perched on the brink of extermination. Surely she poses no threat to any creature, least of all the great ones. Lying on the edge of the little wound, passive and vulnerable, she waits for Chance to carry her where she needs to be. Probably others are doing the same. Perhaps thousands of sisters and daughters are hiding nearby, each snug inside her own spore case. The temptation to whisper, "Hello," is easily ignored. The odds are awful as it is; any noise could turn this into a suicide. What matters is silence and watchfulness, thinking hard about the great goal while keeping ready for anything that might happen, as well as everything that will not.

The little wound begins to heal, causing a trickling pain to flow.

The World feels the irritation, and, in reflex, touches His discomfort by several means, delicate and less so.

Escher misses her first opportunity. A great swift shape presses its way across her hiding place, but she activates her glues too late. Dabs of glue cure against air, wasted. So she cuts the glue loose and watches again. A second touch is unlikely, but it comes, and she manages to heave a sticky tendril into a likely crevice, letting the irresistible force yank her into a brilliant, endless sky.

She will probably die now.

For a little while, Escher allows herself to look back across her life, counting daughters and other successes, taking warm comfort in her many accomplishments.

Someone hangs in the distance, dangling from a similar tendril. Escher recognizes the shape and intricate glint of her neighbor's spore case; she is one of Escher's daughters. There is a strong temptation to signal her, trading information, helping each other—

But a purge-ball attacks suddenly, and the daughter evaporates, nothing remaining of her but ions and a flash of incoherent light.

Escher pulls herself toward the crevice, and hesitates. Her tendril is anchored on a fleshy surface. A minor neuron—a thread of warm optical cable—lies buried inside the wet cells. She launches a second tendril at her new target. By chance, the purge-ball sweeps the wrong terrain, giving her that little instant. The tendril makes a sloppy connection with the neuron. Without time to test its integrity, all she can do is shout, "Don't kill me! Or my daughters! Don't murder us, Great World!"

Nothing changes. The purge-ball works its way across the deeply folded fleshscape, moving toward Escher again, distant flashes announcing the deaths of another two daughters or sisters.

"Great World!" she cries out.

He will not reply. Escher is like the hum of a single angry electron, and she can only hope that He notices the hum.

"I am vile," she promises. "I am loathsome and sneaky, and you should hate me. What I am is an illness lurking inside you. A disease that steals exactly what I can steal without bringing your wrath."

The purge-ball appears, following a tall, reddish ridge of flesh, bearing down on her hiding place.

She says, "Kill me, if you want. Or spare me, and I will do this for you." Then she unleashes a series of vivid images, precise and simple, meant to be compelling to any mind.

The purge-ball slows, its sterilizing lasers taking careful aim.

She repeats herself, knowing that thought travels only so quickly and the World is too vast to see her thoughts and react soon enough to save her. But if she can help . . . if she saves just a few hundred daughters. . . ?

Lasers aim, and do nothing. Nothing. And after an instant of inactivity, the machine changes its shape and nature. It hovers above Escher, sending out its own tendrils. A careless strength yanks her free of her hiding place. Her tendrils and glues are ripped from her aching body. A scaffolding of carbon is built around her, and she is shoved inside the retooled purge-ball, held in a perfect darkness, waiting alone until an identical scaffold is stacked beside her.

A hard, angry voice boasts, "I did this."

"What did you do?" asks Escher.

"I made the World listen to reason." It sounds like Escher's voice, except for the delusions of power. "I made a promise, and that's why He saved us."

With a sarcastic tone, she says, "Thank you ever so much. But now where are we going?"

"I won't tell you," her fellow prisoner responds.

"Because you don't know where," says Escher.

"I know everything I need to know."

"Then you're the first person ever," she giggles, winning a brief, delicious silence from her companion.

Other prisoners arrive, each slammed into the empty spaces between their sisters and daughters. Eventually the purge-ball is a prison-ball, swollen to vast proportions, and no one else is being captured. Nothing changes for a long while. There is nothing to be done now but wait, speaking when the urge hits and listening to whichever voice sounds less than tedious.

Gossip is the common currency. People are desperate to hear the smallest glimmer of news. Where the final rumor comes from, nobody knows. But the woman who was captured moments after Escher, claims, "It comes from the world Himself. He's going to put us where we can do the most good."

"Where?" Escher inquires.

"On a tooth," her companion says. "The right incisor, as it happens." Then with that boasting voice, she adds, "Which is exactly what I told Him to do. This is all because of me."

"What isn't?" Escher grumbles.

"Very little," the tiny prisoner promises. "Very, very little."

The Speaker

"We walk today on a thousand worlds, and I mean 'walk' in all manners of speaking." He manages a few comical steps before shifting into a graceful turn, arms held firmly around the wide waist of an invisible and equally graceful partner. *"A hundred alien suns bake us with their perfect light. And between the suns, in the cold and dark, we survive, and thrive, by every worthy means."*

Now he pauses, hands forgetting the unseen partner. A look of calculated confusion sweeps across his face. Fingers rise to his thick black hair, stabbing it and yanking backward, leaving furrows in the unruly mass.

"Our numbers," he says. *"Our population. It made us sick with worry when we were ten billion standing on the surface of one enormous world. 'Where will our children stand?' we asked ourselves. But then in the next little while, we became ten trillion people, and we had split into a thousand species of humanity, and the new complaint was that we were still too scarce and spread too far apart. 'How could we matter to the universe?' we asked ourselves. 'How could so few souls endure another day in our immeasurable, uncaring universe?' "*

His erect penis makes a little leap, a fat and vivid white drop of semen striking the wooden stage with an audible plop.

"Our numbers," he repeats. "Our legions." Then with a wide, garish smile, he confesses, "I don't know our numbers today. No authority does. You make estimates. You extrapolate off data that went stale long ago. You build a hundred models and fashion every kind of vast number. Ten raised to the twentieth power. The thirtieth power. Or more." He giggles and skips backward, and with the giddy, careless energy of a child, he dances where he stands, singing to lights overhead, "If you are as common as sand and as unique as snowflakes, how can you be anything but a wild, wonderful success?"

Able

The wild man is enormous and powerful, and surely brilliant beyond anything that Able can comprehend—as smart as City as a whole—but despite his gifts, the man is obviously terrified. That he can even manage to stand his ground astonishes Able. He says as much to Mish, and then he glances at her, adding, "He must be very devoted to whoever's inside."

"Whoever's inside what?" she asks.

"That trap." He looks straight ahead again, telling himself not to waste time with the girl. She is foolish and bad-tempered, and he couldn't be any more tired of her. "I think that's what the cylinder is," he whispers. "A trap of some kind. And someone's been caught in it."

"Well, I don't care who," she snarls.

He pretends not to notice her.

"What was that?" she blurts. "Did you hear that—?"

"No," Able replies. But then he notices a distant rumble, deep and faintly rhythmic, and with every breath, growing. When he listens carefully, it resembles nothing normal. It isn't thunder, and it can't be a voice. He feels the sound as much as he hears it, as if some great mass was being displaced. But he knows better. In school, teachers like to explain what must be happening now, employing tortuous mathematics and magical sleights of hand. Matter and energy are being rapidly and brutally manipulated. The universe's obscure dimensions are being twisted like bands of warm rubber. Able knows all this. But still, he understands none of it. Words without comprehension; froth without substance. All that he knows for certain is that behind that deep, unknowable throbbing lies something even further beyond human description.

The wild man looks up, gray eyes staring at that something.

He cries out, that tiny sound lost between his mouth and Able. Then he produces what seems to be a spear—no, an elaborate missile—that launches itself with a bolt of fire, lifting a sophisticated warhead up into a vague gray space that swallows the weapon without sound, or complaint.

Next the man aims a sturdy laser, and fires. But the weapon simply melts at its tip, collapsing into a smoldering, useless mass at his feet.

Again, the wild man cries out.

His language could be a million generations removed from City-speech, but Able hears the desperate, furious sound of his voice. He doesn't need words to know that the man is cursing. Then the swirling grayness slows itself, and parts, and stupidly, in reflex, Able turns to Mish, wanting to tell her, "Watch. You're going to see one of *Them.*"

But Mish has vanished. Sometime in the last few moments, she jumped off the world's rim and ran away, and save for the fat old leopard sleeping between the horsetails, Able is entirely alone now.

"Good," he mutters.

Almost too late, he turns and runs to the very edge of the granite rim.

The wild man stands motionless now. His bowels and bladder have emptied themselves. His handsome, godly face is twisted from every flavor of misery. Eyes as big as windows stare up into what only they can see, and to that great, unknowable something, the man says two simple words.

"Fuck you," Able hears.

And then the wild man opens his mouth, baring his white apish teeth, and, just as Able wonders what's going to happen, the man's body explodes, the dull black burst of a shaped charge sending chunks of his face skyward.

Procyon

One last time, she whispers her son's name.

She whispers it and closes her mouth and listens to the brief, sharp silence that comes after the awful explosion. What must have happened, she tells herself, is that her boy found his good sense and fled. How can a mother think anything else? And then the ominous deep rumbling begins again, begins and gradually swells until the walls of the trap are shuddering and twisting again. But this time the monster is slower. It approaches the trap more cautiously, summoning new courage. She can nearly taste its courage now, and with her intuition, she senses emotions that might be curiosity and might be a kind of reflexive admiration. Or do those eternal human emotions have any relationship for what *It* feels. . . ?

What she feels, after everything, is numbness. A terrible, deep weariness hangs on her like a new skin. Procyon seems to be falling faster now, accelerating down through the bottomless trap. But she doesn't care anymore. In place of courage, she wields a muscular apathy. Death looms, but when hasn't it been her dearest companion? And, in place of fear, she is astonished to discover an incurious little pride about what is about to happen: How many people —wild free people like herself—have ever found themselves so near one of *Them?*

Quietly, with a calm, smooth, and slow voice, Procyon says, "I feel you there, you. I can taste you."

Nothing changes.

Less quietly, she says, "Show yourself."

A wide parabolic floor appears, gleaming and black and agonizingly close. But just before she slams into the floor, a wrenching force peels it away. A brilliant violet light rises to meet her, turning into a thick, sweet syrup. What may or may not be a hand curls around her body, and squeezes. Procyon fights every urge to struggle. She wrestles with her body, wrestles with her will, forcing both to lie still while the hand tightens its grip and grows comfortable. Then using a voice that betrays nothing tentative or small, she tells what holds her, "I made you, you know."

She says, "You can do what you want to me."

Then with a natural, deep joy, she cries out, "But you're an ungrateful glory . . . and you'll always belong to me. . . !"

Escher

The prison-ball has been reengineered, slathered with camouflage and armor and the best immune-suppressors on the market, and its navigation system has been adapted from add-ons stolen from the finest trashcans. Now it is a battle-phage riding on the sharp incisor as far as it dares, then leaping free. A thousand similar phages leap and lose their way, or they are killed. Only Escher's phage reaches the target, impacting on what passes for flesh and launching its cargo with a microscopic railgun, punching her and a thousand sisters and daughters through immeasurable distances of senseless, twisted nothing.

How many survive the attack?

She can't guess how many. Can't even care. What matters is to make herself survive inside this strange new world. An enormous world, yes. Escher feels a vastness that reaches out across ten or twelve or maybe a thousand dimensions. How do I know where to go? she asks herself. And instantly, an assortment of possible routes appear in her consciousness, drawn in the simplest imaginable fashion, waiting and eager to help her find her way around.

This is a last gift from Him, she realizes. Unless there are more gifts waiting, of course.

She thanks nobody.

On the equivalent of tiptoes, Escher creeps her way into a tiny conduit that moves something stranger than any blood across five dimensions. She becomes passive, aiming for invisibility. She drifts and spins, watching her surroundings turn from a senseless glow into a landscape that occasionally seems a little bit reasonable. A little bit real. Slowly, she learns how to see in this new world. Eventually she spies a little peak that may or may not be ordinary matter. The peak is pink and flexible and sticks out into the great artery, and flinging her last tendril, Escher grabs hold and pulls in snug, knowing that the chances are lousy that she will ever find anything nourishing here, much less delicious.

But her reserves have been filled again, she notes. If she is careful—and when hasn't she been—her energies will keep her alive for centuries.

She thinks of the World, and thanks nobody.

"Watch and learn," she whispers to herself.

That was the first human thought. She remembers that odd fact suddenly. People were just a bunch of grubbing apes moving blindly through their tiny lives until one said to a companion, "Watch and learn."

An inherited memory, or another gift from Him?

Silently, she thanks Luck, and she thanks Him, and once again, she thanks Luck.

"Patience and planning," she tells herself.

Which is another wise thought of the conscious, enduring ape.

The Last Son

The locked gates and various doorways know him—recognize him at a glance—but they have to taste him anyway. They have to test him. Three people were expected, and he can't explain in words what has happened. He just says, "The others will be coming later," and leaves that lie hanging in the air. Then as he passes through the final doorway, he says, "Let no one through. Not without my permission first."

"This is your mother's house," says the door's AI.

"Not anymore," he remarks.

The machine grows quiet, and sad.

During any other age, his home would be a mansion. There are endless rooms, and each room is enormous and richly furnished and lovely and jammed full of games and art and distractions and flourishes that even the least aesthetic soul would find lovely. He sees none of that now. Alone, he walks to what has always been his room, and he sits on a leather recliner, and the house brings him a soothing drink and an intoxicating drink and an assortment of treats that sit on the platter, untouched.

For a long while, the boy stares off at the distant ceiling, replaying everything with his near-perfect memory. Everything. Then he forgets everything, stupidly calling out, "Mother," with a voice that sounds ridiculously young. Then again, he calls, "Mother." And he starts to rise from his chair, starts to ask the great empty house, "Where is she?"

And he remembers.

As if his legs have been sawed off, he collapses. His chair twists itself to catch him, and an army of AIs brings their talents to bear. They are loyal, limited machines. They are empathetic, and, on occasion, even sweet. They want to help him in any fashion, just name the way . . . but their appeals and their smart suggestions are just so much noise. The boy acts deaf, and he obviously can't see anything with his fists jabbed into his eyes like that, slouched forward in his favorite chair, begging an invisible someone for forgiveness. . . .

The Speaker

He squats and uses the tip of a forefinger to dab at the puddle of semen, and he rubs the finger against his thumb, saying, "Think of cells. Individual, self-reliant cells. For most of Earth's great history, they ruled. First as bacteria, and then as composites built from cooperative bacteria. They were everywhere and ruled everything, and then the wild cells learned how to dance together, in one enormous body, and the living world was transformed for the next seven hundred million years."

Thumb and finger wipe themselves dry against a hairy thigh, and he rises again, grinning in that relentless and smug, yet somehow charming fashion. "*Everything was changed, and nothing had changed,*" *he says. Then he says,* "*Scaling,*" *with an important tone, as if that single word should erase all confusion.* "*The bacteria and green algae and the carnivorous amoebae weren't swept away by any revolution. Honestly, I doubt if their numbers fell appreciably or for long.*" *And again, he says,* "*Scaling,*" *and sighs with a rich appreciation.* "*Life evolves. Adapts. Spreads and grows, constantly utilizing new energies and novel genetics. But wherever something large can live, a thousand small things can thrive just as well, or better. Wherever something enormous survives, a trillion bacteria hang on for the ride.*"

For a moment, the speaker hesitates.

A slippery half-instant passes where an audience might believe that he has finally lost his concentration, that he is about to stumble over his own tongue. But then he licks at the air, tasting something delicious. And three times, he clicks his tongue against the roof of his mouth.

Then he says what he has planned to say from the beginning.

"*I never know whom I'm speaking to,*" *he admits.* "*I've never actually seen my audience. But I know you're great and good. I know that however you appear, and however you make your living, you deserve to hear this:*

"*Humans have always lived in terror. Rainstorms and the eclipsing moon and earthquakes and the ominous guts of some disemboweled goat—all have preyed upon our fears and defeated our fragile optimisms. But what we fear today—what shapes and reshapes the universe around us—is a child of our own imaginations.*

"*A whirlwind that owes its very existence to glorious, endless us!*"

Able

The boy stops walking once or twice, letting the fat leopard keep pace. Then he pushes his way through a last wall of emerald ferns, stepping out into the bright, damp air above the rounded pool. A splashing takes him by surprise. He looks down at his secret pool, and he squints, watching what seems to be a woman pulling her way through the clear water with thick, strong arms. She is naked. Astonishingly, wonderfully naked. A stubby hand grabs an overhanging limb, and she stands on the rocky shore, moving as if exhausted, picking her way up the slippery slope until she finds an open patch of partially flattened earth where she can collapse, rolling onto her back, her smooth flesh glistening and her hard breasts shining up at Able, making him sick with joy.

Then she starts to cry, quietly, with a deep sadness.

Lust vanishes, replaced by simple embarrassment. Able flinches and starts to step back, and that's when he first looks at her face.

He recognizes its features.

Intrigued, the boy picks his way down to the shoreline, practically standing beside the crying woman.

She looks at him, and she sniffs.

"I saw two of them," he reports. "And I saw you, too. You were inside that cylinder, weren't you?"

She watches him, saying nothing.

"I saw something pull you out of that trap. And then I couldn't see you. *It* must have put you here, I guess. Out of Its way." Able nods, and smiles. He can't help but stare at her breasts, but at least he keeps his eyes halfway closed, pretending to look out over the water instead. "*It* took pity on you, I guess."

A good-sized fish breaks on the water.

The woman seems to watch the creature as it swims past, big, blue scales catching the light, heavy fins lazily shoving their way through the warm water. The fish eyes are huge and black, and they are stupid eyes. The mind behind them sees nothing but vague shapes and sudden motions. Able knows from experience: If he stands quite still, the creature will come close enough to touch.

"They're called coelacanths," he explains.

Maybe the woman reacts to his voice. Some sound other than crying now leaks from her.

So Able continues, explaining, "They were rare, once. I've studied them quite a bit. They're old and primitive, and they were almost extinct when we found them. But when *they* got loose, got free, and took apart the Earth . . . and took everything and everyone with them up into the sky . . ."

The woman gazes up at the towering horsetails.

Able stares at her legs and what lies between them.

"Anyway," he mutters, "there's more coelacanths now than ever. They live in a million oceans, and they've never been more successful, really." He hesitates, and then adds, "Kind of like us, I think. Like people. You know?"

The woman turns, staring at him with gray-white eyes. And with a quiet hard voice, she says, "No."

She says, "That's an idiot's opinion."

And then with a grace that belies her strong frame, she dives back into the water, kicking hard and chasing that ancient and stupid fish all the way back to the bottom.

———

Savior

GRANDPA SHOWED UP EARLY. I WAS STILL IN BED, still hard asleep. And Mom pulled at my arm, telling me, "Get up, darling." But I couldn't make myself. I was too tired. Grandpa was standing in the doorway. I'm pretty sure of that. Mom asked if this was a good thing, considering. Mom said, "Considering," more than once. But Grandpa didn't say one word. Then I was sitting up, halfway awake, and she told me, "Your clothes are laid out. Go on, honey." And they let me dress alone in the dark.

My shirts and pants were new and warm and comfortably scratchy. But my boots were leftover from last year. Even though they'd grown out as far as they could, and even though my toes felt cramped up inside them, I liked them. And I liked my hunting vest, even though it was too big and heavy. It was Grandpa's once. I liked its dirty orange color and its old smells. And whenever I put it on, before it got too heavy for me, I liked how it felt. With all those shells stuck into its little elastic pockets, I felt like a soldier. I felt dangerous and safe wrapped up inside all that ammunition.

Both of them were waiting in the kitchen. Grandpa was talking until he heard me. He looked up, and smiled and said, "Ready?"

Mom was crying. Not like last night, but she was wiping at her face and smiling at me, her eyes red and ugly. "You two have fun today," she said. As if it was an order. Then she gave Grandpa a big hug and me a wet kiss, then tried to kiss me again. But I slipped outside before she could.

Grandpa always bought himself a new truck for Opening Day.

That year's truck was parked between our houses, already running and every light burning. We climbed in, and I said, "Hi, Solomon."

Solomon was standing on the back seat, watching everything with happy yellow eyes. "Hello, Sammy," he said. "Bird day, bird day, bird day—!"

Grandpa said, "Quiet."

Solomon was a retriever-techie mix. His dog brain had a chip add-on, and there was a voice box stuck in his neck. The box made him sound like a little kid. Except he was an old dog. And I liked him, sort of. Even if we weren't friends, exactly. Dogs can be awfully jealous, and we never liked sharing Grandpa with one another.

We rolled down the long drive and past Grandpa's house, then through the first tall black gate. I waved at the night guards. There were a dozen of them, maybe more. The main road went past all those cameras and reporters. Grandpa took us out the back road to the slickway, then let the truck drive. I started to feel the warm seat under me, and I sat back and shut my eyes, and it wasn't until the dog said, "Birds," that I was awake again.

"I smell birds," said that kid's voice. "I smell birds!"

We had turned off the slickway. Grandpa was driving again, steering us down a road that looked like two paths running through the tall brown grass. I heard the grass slipping under us. The sun wasn't up. Except for a little glow past a line of trees, there wasn't anything that looked like a sunrise. I pulled myself up and coughed, then asked, "How soon?"

"Soon," said the dog. "Soon, soon."

The television was on. The news was playing with the sound turned down low. When Grandpa's face appeared on the little screen, Grandpa turned it off. Then he let the truck roll to a stop, and there was nothing to hear but warm air blowing from the vents. I felt the heat on my bare face and in my crammed-together toes. Looking out the window, I knew it was cold. Even for November. And I knew that I was comfortable here, and happy enough, and did we have to walk through these cold dark fields?

I asked the question in my head. Nowhere else.

Grandpa hadn't said one word. He usually liked to tell me our plans and ask how I was feeling, and he'd remind me how I needed to be careful all the time. Hunting wasn't a game. But when he wouldn't talk, I asked, "When does it get light?"

He said nothing.

I looked at him and saw him looking at me. Only he wasn't. Mom always told me that he had a kindly face, and maybe I knew what she meant. But something about those old eyes made me squirm. Just for that moment.

Then he patted me on the knee, saying, "Soon."

It's what the dog had said, only Grandpa's voice was old and tired and he didn't sound as if he meant it.

My gun was my grandfather's when he was a boy. He gave it to me, even though we kept it at his house where he could keep it clean for me. I always liked its weight when I first picked it up, and I loved the slick sharp sounds it made when I loaded it. The black barrel was always cold to touch. The wood parts were decorated with checkerboards where your hands held tight, and the butt was padded with thick pink rubber. Where Grandpa's guns were fancy and new, mine was simple. It didn't have any videocam or adjustable shells. I shot old-fashioned shells. Plastic and brass and nickel-iron shot. The only new trick was the strapped-on safety that kept me from accidentally shooting at people or myself.

The safety told me, "I am on the job."

Solomon whispered, "This way, hurry. This way."

"Wait," Grandpa told him.

But the dog kept going, his old hips fighting to keep up.

"He didn't hear you," I ventured.

"No, he hears," he said. "He just pretends to be deaf."

The sun was coming up, finally. But the sky in front of us was still dark, full of stars and the low stations and the big geosynchronous cities. I looked up, and maybe I was watching for the starship. And maybe Grandpa saw me looking. Because he took me by the shoulder, saying nothing. Just sort of steering me toward the field.

All sorts of crops had been growing on that ground. The harvesters had left their marks, tilling up the black ground as they passed. Here and there were masses of green leaves. Some cold-happy tailored vegetable was mixed in with the dead stalks and empty steak pods and the dried up melon vines. Just walking in that field was work. My gun and vest and boots were getting heavy. Even if I was bigger than last year, and stronger, I'd forgotten, like I always forgot, how much it hurt to pull your feet through those tangled vines.

"Slow," said Grandpa. To the dog.

The sun eased its way over the horizon. I turned and looked back at it and at the new truck, squinting hard.

Grandpa said, "Pay attention."

To me.

The dog had stopped in front of a mound of brown stalks. Sniffing hard. Was it pheasant? Or quail? Or one of the tailored species? I was hoping for something big and fancy. A screamer, or even a flashbird. Stepping closer, I lifted my gun up to my shoulder, and that's when Solomon started to growl, the black fur on his neck standing up straight, and his old body leaping inside the mound.

"Get back here!" Grandpa yelled.

Suddenly there was this wild growling.

"Come!" Grandpa screamed. "Come here!"

And the growling turned to squealing. Solomon practically flew out of there, his head down and his eyes almost shut. He went straight toward the first person that he saw. Which was me. And I smelled him exactly when Grandpa said, "Shit!"

Said, "Skunk!"

It wasn't just a smell. The stink that you smell on the slickway, that hangs around a dead skunk, is nothing compared to the juices that come out of a living animal. It's like getting hit in the nose with a hockey stick. You feel it as much as you smell it, and it makes you sick. That's why I turned and tried to run.

Grandpa was shouting, "Stop!"

He said, "Heel!"

He said, "Son-of-a-bitch!" and began firing. *Boom. Boom.* And I turned, watching him aiming square at the mound. At the skunk. *Boom. Boom.* And *boom.*

I'd never seen Grandpa that way. In the low bright light, he looked almost young, his face full of color and his eyes big and his gloved hands shoving in another five shells, every move slick and smooth. Then he aimed again, this time at the sky, and he fired off all five shots before he felt done.

Solomon was rolling in the stalks and vines, fighting to get rid of the stink.

I just stood there, feeling useless and sad.

Grandpa lowered his gun, then said, "Back to the truck, boys. Now."

Solomon was saying, "Shit, shit, shit, shit!"

I looked at the sky, up where Grandpa had been shooting, and that's when I saw the starship hanging there. Big as a big coin held at arm's length, and the same color as a coin, but square looking, with shadows filling up the nozzles of its huge, dead engines.

The farmhouse was an old house.

The farmer was an old man who didn't have any hair on his head, or anywhere. He looked at us through his storm door, then said, "Oh," with a quiet little voice. His eyes couldn't have been any bigger.

Grandpa said, "Mr. Teeson? My people talked to you this summer. About giving me permission to hunt on your land?"

"I remember that, sir. Absolutely."

Solomon was in the yard, panting. Grandpa had gotten here by driving slowly, letting the dog chase us all the way.

Mr. Teeson opened his door and stepped out, and he said, "Colonel Sattis." He said, "I can't believe this . . . Jesus. . . !"

Grandpa said, "Damned skunks."

"May I?" The farmer stuck out his hand, saying, "It's an honor."

Grandpa seemed surprised, maybe even bothered. But he managed to say, "The honor's mine." He always said those words, and he always wiped both hands against his shirt before offering one of them. Then he sort of smiled and shook the farmer's hand, asking, "Is there anyway you might help? My stupid old dog ran into a skunk."

Mr. Teeson wrinkled up his nose and said, "I kind of figured that."

Then both men laughed. And Grandpa seemed more relaxed, saying, "This is my grandson. Sam, this is Mr. Teeson."

The farmer looked at me and said, "Hello, son."

I said, "Sir."

Then he winked at me, saying, "You know, I've admired your grandfather forever. I want you to know that."

Grandpa said, "Thank you."

"I had a cousin who was in the service with you, sir."

"Perhaps I know him." Grandpa was being polite, or interested. I couldn't tell which. "In Alpha Division, perhaps?"

"No. He was a lieutenant in Beta Division."

Alpha was my grandfather's unit. Most of them lived, and all of the Betas died.

But the farmer didn't seem too sad, hunching over to explain, "Your grandpa's a great man. Did you know that?"

The man had awful breath. I swallowed and said, "I know, sir."

"I bet you do." He looked at Grandpa again. "A fine boy."

"The best."

Solomon gave a big complaining howl.

The farmer shook his head and started back into his house. "I don't have any of that new skunk-gunk, Colonel. But I keep something almost as good."

Grandpa said, "Thank you. So much."

We waited on the porch. I could hear a television. I couldn't make out what was being said, but it sounded like the news. It sounded important and angry, and I looked at Grandpa for a moment, then realized that he was deafer than his dog.

The farmer came back smiling, carrying a couple of tall cans of tomato juice. When he saw my look, he winked and said, "This is the best cure we had for a lot of years, son."

"I hate that stuff," I told him. "Do we have to drink it?"

That made both men laugh. But Grandpa's laugh was louder than normal, and the sound of it was wrong somehow.

I kept my distance, watching. Grandpa got the dog by his neck. Solomon was moaning, saying, "Shit," over and over again until Grandpa said, "That's enough!" Then the farmer led us around back, and he actually held the dog while Grandpa peeled off his shirts and boots and finally his pants. It was still very cold outside, and just seeing him made me shiver. Grandpa took the dog back and said, "Okay." The farmer opened the first can, and Grandpa poured it on the thick black fur, working it in as if it was soap. He was holding the dog by the loose skin of the neck, and Solomon twisted and kicked, and Grandpa was soon covered with the juice, and Solomon howled and complained and shook himself half-dry, little splashes of tomato juice sprinkled over both men.

I was glad not to be helping.

But I began to feel guilty, not having anything important to do.

The farmer opened the second can, laughing hard about something. Out of guilt, I asked if there was anything I should do, and he wiped his dirty face with a dirtier arm, telling me, "I don't think so, Sam." Then he said, "Colonel Sattis," with a big, crisp voice. "The boy looks sort of cold."

Just in my toes and fingers, I thought.

But I didn't say a word.

I'd never seen Grandpa look that messy. He was the kind of person who wants his hair just so, even if there wasn't much of it. He liked nice clothes, and he always tried to look younger than he was. But there he was, wearing nothing except underwear and the sticky juice. I could see his pale belly hanging forward, his arms smooth and soft. And the smooth skin of his body made his face look more wrinkly than ever, and tired, even when he tried very hard to smile.

He said, "Sam. Why don't you go sit in the car then."

"No, you don't." The farmer waved at me, saying, "We won't be much longer. Wait inside my house, if you want."

"He smells," Grandpa promised.

"Who doesn't?" Mr. Teeson was the only one laughing, telling me, "Just stay off the furniture. All right, Sam?"

I felt like a coward, and I felt relieved.

I walked back around and through the front door, sitting on the floor, Indian-style. They were showing the same digital on the old-fashioned TV. Again. And since nobody was there to tell me not to watch, I decided not to change networks.

I decided to see it through. For once.

The humongous king was wearing nothing but a thin web of black wires, and it was hanging in the air, facedown. Its body was pink and hairless, and I don't care what some people say, it looked gross. It was huge and ugly, its thick legs kicking and its hands trying to grab one another, fingers big as my forearm curling and uncurling, the thin pink blood flowing from where the wires bit tight, then dripping fast to the glass floor.

Soldiers were walking under the alien.

Someone asked, "What next?" and another person—a woman—shouted, "Delta team's still trying to dock! And Beta isn't reporting!"

"Earth status?" said a nearby voice. A voice I knew.

The woman said, "Status unchanged, sir."

Someone else said, "Colonel." Then, "Nantucket's underwater now, sir."

The colonel stepped into view. Not knowing that an alien camera was buried in the thick glass wall, he said, "Fuck," with that strong voice. He looked mostly the same, except the hair was thick and brown, and the face was smoother. He was a handsome man, and that's not me saying it. My history book called him, "The handsome colonel from the nation's heartland."

He said, "Fuck," a second time, his breath hanging in the cold air. "What about Beta?"

"No news. Sir."

Beta Division had tried to attack the weapons arrays, which was suicide. I read that in my history books, too. Most of them were cooked by the radiation before they even got to their targets.

Which was probably what happened to Mr. Teeson's poor cousin.

I felt a good little dose of anger.

"Okay," said Colonel Sattis. "Thank you."

Then he picked up a fat alien microphone, using both hands where the king would hold it with one. "No more patience," he said. "I'm too fucking tired."

What he said went into a gray box, and the box spoke to the humongous in its own rumbling language.

The humongous answered, and the box translated it as. "It is not we! We are blameless, friend!"

"Quiet," said the colonel. He sighed and said, "We've already been here. You *claim* that some faction's responsible. Some cult—"

The humongous said several words.

"Fanatics!" the box shouted. Over and over.

The colonel carried the microphone with him, walking up underneath the alien. "But there's got to be some way," he said. "Assuming that you're telling the truth. These fanatics have control of your engines and your weapons, and you really can't take those systems back. But you know things. Your ancestors built this damned ship! And you're *not* going to be stupid. Not while your people are melting our icecaps. . . !"

The colonel stopped screaming, catching his breath.

The humongous's face was straight above. As big as an elephant's face, it opened its black, black eyes, and the rubbery mouth said something.

The translation box said, "Move your people. Flee the ocean. That is the best solution."

"No!" the colonel roared.

"They only want your cold landmass. A tiny part of your world—"

"Bullshit." The colonel threw down the microphone and screamed, "Someone get me tools. And that map!"

"Which map?" asked the woman soldier.

He said, "Of their bodies. They're physiology. I want to know what I'm dealing with!" Then he started to pull off his uniform— this was where Mom sent me to bed last night—and that's when I got up off the floor and turned the television off. It wasn't that I couldn't take it. It wasn't that I wasn't curious. It's just that some- one new was walking up on the front porch.

The stranger said, "Hello."

I said, "Hi," through the storm door.

He was very tall and dark. All I remember about his face was that he looked as if he wanted to be somewhere else. Dressed in a suit, he looked strange. Maybe he was going to a wedding, I was guessing.

Staring in at me, he asked, "Is your father home?"

I said, "No."

Dad hasn't lived with us since I was three.

The stranger looked past me, squinting. Thinking to himself. He seemed halfway confused until he looked back, noticing what I was wearing. "Christ," he said. "You're the grandson, aren't you?"

I didn't say one word.

"Where is he?" the stranger asked.

Suddenly I felt sick, staring out at Grandpa's truck and the brown car parked behind it. I wanted to say something. I meant to lie, if only I could have thought of a good one.

But before I had one, a second man shouted, "I hear him! He's around back somewhere."

The tall man gave me another look, something sorry in his face.

Then he was gone.

I ran through the house, finding my way out the back door. I caught Grandpa washing his arms and bare chest with a garden hose and a lump of yellow soap. He was smiling, almost. The farmer was standing with him. Saying something. The dog was rolling himself dry in the grass. I could barely smell the skunk, and it was probably what was still sticking to me.

Grandpa said, "What is it, Sam?"

"Some men," I muttered.

Then the tall man was with us. All at once he was there, talking as if he'd done nothing all morning but practice what he was going to say now.

He said, "Sir."

With a hurried voice, he said, "I've been asked by Senator Lee to come here and warn you. In an hour, the UN issues a warrant for your arrest. And it would be best for everyone if you'll surrender yourself as soon as possible—"

"Just a minute," someone snapped.

It was Mr. Teeson. Where I thought my grandfather would cut the man off, it was the bald farmer who said, "You bastards. You stupid, stupid bastards. . . !"

The strangers in suits blinked and straightened their backs.

"This man," said the farmer. "He's a great man! Don't you

children understand that simple fact? If it wasn't for Colonel Sattis, none of you pissy little ungratefuls would have ever been born. . . !"

The tall man said, "Mr. Sattis."

Grandpa was shaking. From the cold, maybe. He turned and picked up his shirts and his pants off the ground, and with a weak hand, he tried brushing away bits of dried grass. But it was too much work, and he gave up trying. He put on his pants and shirts, one after another, and after a minute, the tall man repeated himself.

"Mr. Sattis."

"Colonel Sattis," the farmer told them.

"Colonel," said the tall man. "Your old friend's doing you a considerable favor here. If it wasn't for his personal intervention, a brigade of marshals would be coming for you . . . instead of us. . . ."

I remembered the senator. I remembered him laughing, drinking beer, and eating catfish on my grandfather's patio.

"Naturally," said the tall man, "you'll be free to retain legal council."

The farmer said, "Jesus!"

The second man growled, "This isn't your concern, sir."

Grandpa held up a hand, asking everyone to be quiet. Then he said, "I'm enjoying the day with my grandson. My grandson. And you come here under these circumstances . . . and what am I supposed to do. . . ? Go quietly. . . ?"

"We're warning you," said the second man. "We aren't here to arrest you!"

Grandpa looked at him, saying nothing. Then he looked upward as he finished buttoning his last shirt, asking, "What's going to happen? A trial?"

"Yes, sir," said the tall man. "There's got to be one now."

Grandpa said something under his breath. Then he looked in my direction, his face soft and white and very old. "So who finally filed charges against me?" he asked. "One of the humongoustarian groups?"

"Actually," said the tall man, "our own government is the plaintive."

Again, the farmer said, "Jesus."

Grandpa just nodded, saying in a sour way, "Of course they would."

Mr. Teeson took a few steps, screaming, "If you don't get off my land, boys. . . !"

"Stop," said Grandpa. To everyone. Then to the farmer, he said, "Thanks, Jim. For all your help, thank you very much."

"This is bullshit," the farmer told him.

Grandpa didn't argue. He just turned to the others, asking, "May we finish our hunt? I promised this boy a pheasant, and we haven't seen even one bird yet."

The tall man looked at his partner, then down at his shiny shoes. "We aren't here to arrest anyone, Mr. Sattis. Like we told you."

"But we could escort you home again," said the other man.

Grandpa opened his pants and stuffed in his shirttails. He didn't move quickly, but he knew what he was doing. He told them, "Thank you for the generous offer. But I don't think so."

Then he looked at me, something in his eyes scaring me.

Nobody knew that there was a camera inside the wall.

The wall and camera were destroyed along with the rest of the king's room. Melted away by the nuclear blast. My grandfather set the nuke himself. He did it because his team needed time and confusion to get where they needed to be. To do what had to be done. And for setting the bomb and killing at least a few thousand of the king's followers, Grandpa won the first of three Medals of Honor.

Grandpa never knew that he was being watched.

He set off the bomb not to hide evidence, but to help.

Everything seen by that camera—not just that day, but for the last ten thousand—ended inside a different part of the ship. Sitting, and waiting. The humongous had a thing about the past. A fat chunk of their starship was left to shrines and cemeteries and digital warehouses full of everything that had ever happened on board. Every tunnel and big room, and even their toilets, had cameras. It took our best scientists ten hard years just to learn how to pipe power into those warehouses. Then it took ten more to learn how to get anything out of them but random goop. And it's still awfully tough working inside the starship. Without a breath of air in the place, every walk means spacesuits. And without one watt of power on board, every light and every machine needs its juice from human reactors strung clear out on the outermost hull.

I've read plenty, and I've seen even more on television and in the movies. But what I knew best was what Mom told me. Not Grandpa. Nobody was supposed to ask him about the humongous. Mom always told me, "He doesn't like to dwell on the war." Then she would do it for me, telling what little she knew, telling the same handful of stories over and over again.

Last night, after watching too much of the news, Mom told me her favorite one again. As if for the first time.

She told me how she'd seen the war.

"I was about your age," she began. Which is how she always began, even when I was only five years old. "And you can't imagine how scared I was," she told me, sitting in the middle of the television with me, holding my hand with one of hers.

"The world was being attacked," she said, "which was one of the reasons I was scared. It was a totally unprovoked attack. You know what unprovoked means?"

"Unfair," I volunteered.

She nodded, saying, "It was that, too. You're right."

Then she swallowed some of her cocktail, and wiped her eyes, and she said, "But I was more scared because it was my father who was up there. Who was leading the counterattack."

I nodded, acting as if I didn't know anything.

"The aliens were talking to us with different voices," she said. "Everyone knew it. Some of the voices were halfway friendly, and others just told us to get back from the ocean. And meanwhile, the South Pole was melting, and seas were rising, and Mom and I were hiding in the basement, knowing that it was just a matter of days or hours until those awful energy guns would be pointed at us."

She shook her head, saying, "You can't imagine how it was!"

I thought I could, but I didn't say it.

She took another swallow, then said, "I got tired of the basement." As if she was afraid that I might tell someone, she said, "Against Grandma's orders, I sneaked out into the yard, in the dark, when I knew that the starship would rise up in the south. If it fired at me, I was dead anyway. Outside or in the basement, or ten miles underground, I would die . . . and before that happened, I needed to see the starship for myself. . . ."

"You saw the starship die instead," I said. I couldn't help myself.

She acted as if I'd done something wrong. Breaking a rule, maybe. But instead of saying so, she put her hands in her lap, saying, "I saw it happen. When every hatch and airlock and those . . . those dilation zones . . . when the reactors quit and they ·opened up, I saw all that air and cold water pouring out of the starship. . . !"

Mom swallowed, telling me, "That was the worst moment, Sam. I didn't know what was going on."

Then she squeezed my hand, telling me, "But I know better now. And now what I saw—what I remember so clearly—looks beautiful to me. What I remember . . . it was like some enormous comet was born right above me, milky and spreading all the way across the sky. Later I found out that the world was saved, and it was my own father who had done it. He did most of it himself. And I don't think that there's ever been a happier, prouder child than me."

She took another sip of her cocktail, and another.

Then she told me something new. Something that I never expected.

"When your grandfather came back to Earth," she confessed, "and after all the parades and interviews and the medal cere-monies, he came home. Finally. It was the middle of the night, and he walked into my bedroom and sat on the edge of my bed, and he put his face down into his hands, and he cried. That's the only time that I've ever seen your grandfather cry. When Mom died last year, there weren't two tears from him. But he sat there and wept for almost an hour. . . !"

I had to ask, "Why?"

"Because." It was obvious to Mom, but she needed a sip before she said it. "Because he was so very glad to see me, Sammy. And that's all it means!"

The farmer felt awful. Felt sick.

He said so, and he looked so, his face twisted as if he was ready to bring up his breakfast. "The bastards," he kept saying, walking us back toward the truck after the men in suits had gone. "Of all the nerve! Tracking you down, just to harass you. . . !"

Grandpa didn't say one word.

Solomon was hunting again, following a scent out of the yard and into the trees. Grandpa looked at his dog, but he didn't say anything.

I shouted for him. "Come here, boy. Come!"

But the dog had gone deaf again.

"It's not fair," the farmer sputtered. "Trying to punish you like this. Now. They feel guilty, and this is how they try to make things right."

Grandpa gave a little half-nod.

"Christ," said old Mr. Teeson, "it isn't as if you *knew*. . . ."

We'd reached the truck, and Grandpa stopped at his door. Doing nothing.

"You didn't know," said the farmer.

Grandpa turned. "What do you mean?"

"About the humongous, and what the king was telling you . . . all of that . . ."

"What was the king telling me?"

The man licked his lips, then said, "The ship was split up into factions. With the worst group trying to make a home for itself."

Grandpa didn't make one sound.

The farmer pulled a hand over his scalp, then looked at me. Talking only to me, he asked, "So what if the king was telling the truth? Nobody understood those aliens, and your grandfather had to act. He had to do *something*—"

"Shut up." The same as he said it years ago, talking to the humongous, Grandpa told Mr. Teeson, "Shut up." Then he turned and shouted, "Come on, boy! We're leaving!"

As hard as his stiff legs could manage, Solomon came back across the yard.

"I'm sorry," the farmer whispered.

Then he said, "Colonel," one last time.

Grandpa opened the back door and grumbled, "Get in."

The dog tried, but he was too sore and too tired.

He whined when his jump fell short, and Grandpa grabbed him by the neck and threw him into the back, making him squeal even worse.

I had never, ever asked him about the humongous or the starship.

I knew better.

It was so much of a rule that I couldn't remember ever being told not to do it. Although I must have been. Mom or Grandma must have said, "Don't," in an important voice. "Don't ever," they would have told me. "He doesn't like talking about it, Sammy."

I didn't ask. Even then, I didn't.

Grandpa was driving again, following a good road between the fields and little ribbons of trees, and the dog was in the back, licking his sore spots. Grandpa was the one who said, "You know what they haven't found? Those three days before. The three days we spent talking to that king. Talking to his princes or his advisors, or whatever they were. Hearing things that sounded like promises. Only nothing ever changed.

" 'We are working,' they said. 'We are trying.' They kept chanting, 'Soon, soon, soon, soon, soon.' And all that time, people were dying, and cities in every part of the world were drowning."

I stared at my grandfather, saying nothing.

"That idiot Teeson was right," he told me. "There was plenty that I didn't know. Like why it smelled inside their ship. As bad as skunk, almost. I assumed that because they were aliens, they must have liked the stink. The king didn't tell me that their ship was on its last oars, and the stink and those enormous empty rooms and all the factions and all of the rest of the bullshit were measures of how bad things had gotten."

He said, "Sam." He said, "Do anything, and there is always something you don't know. Always. Even if it comes out for the very best, there were facts and figures that you didn't consider. And that's why it's the weakest, sickest, saddest apology to say that you did it wrong because you didn't have some perfect golden knowledge at your disposal."

He seemed to be talking to me, but thinking back, I know that he was talking more to himself. His voice was steady and dry and strong, and a little bit strange because of it. Grandpa couldn't have sounded more like his old self. And for reasons that I couldn't name, that made me feel scared and a little bit sick.

All at once, he said, "Here."

We turned off the paved road, following the edge of a wide field. And that's when I remembered the place. Last year, we'd come here to hunt, and this was where I shot my first pheasant. I could still see the shot in my mind, all those feathers knocked loose and the bird dropping and me racing the dog to get to it first.

At the top of a little hill, we stopped.

But instead of hunting, we sat. Saying nothing.

Grandpa turned on the television, jumping through the channels until he found what he wanted. Then with his steady voice starting to break, he said, "Your mother hasn't let you watch it clear through. Has she?"

I looked at him, and blinked, and I managed to say, "No, sir."

"Watch it now," he told me.

He ordered me.

Even on that little screen, it was sick to see. There was my grandfather, suddenly young, standing naked underneath the alien king. He was covered with pink blood, and he was holding a long knife, and dangling beside him were two of the king's dicks. The third dick was lying at his feet, long as a man is tall, and, like a live fish, still flopping. And Grandpa was screaming, "Tell me! How do we stop them? *How?*"

"I die," the king answered, his voice huge and weak at the same time. "Please. I die. Please."

Grandpa shoved the knife up into the body itself, letting a river of blood pour over him. And he screamed, "The leads! Give 'em here!"

Someone came running, a black and a red cable in hand.

"Where is it?" Grandpa asked, looking down at some sort of biological map.

Someone said something. I couldn't hear what.

Neither could he. "That fat bunch of nerves . . . where *is* it. . . ?"

The woman came close enough to point—

And Grandpa shoved the wires up into that wide wet hole, then stepped back and said again, "How do we stop this?"

"I die," said the king.

Grandpa turned and said, "Do it!"

Someone said, "Sir—?"

"*Shit!*" he screamed. Then he moved over to a human-made box and hit a red button, and nothing happened for a half-second. Maybe longer. Then the king gave out a wail, big and deep, and he started to move, caught between those two strong nets and flopping like his own dick, only faster. Stronger. Flopping and flinging himself, and screaming right up until the nets broke free and he dropped onto the bloody floor. And he still kept moving, that whole long body arching up until Grandpa finally hit the red button again.

Again, Grandpa asked, "How can we stop this?"

The king said, "No."

Then he said, "I won't tell you."

And Grandpa, my grandpa, turned off the television. He said, "Look at me." Then he took both of his thumbs, wiping the tears off my face. And after a little while, he said, "Wait here. Stay with the truck."

I didn't feel like hunting.

Not anymore.

I was numb and sick, and sadder than I thought I could ever be. I barely heard Grandpa opening the back end, then shutting it again. Then I didn't hear anything until this sobbing started, and I forced myself to turn and look into the back. The dog was in the back end of the truck. Tied up. He was saying, "I want to go," with his little-kid voice.

I climbed out and went around back. It took me a minute or two to figure out the latch, then lift the gate high enough to unlock it. Then I saw which gun was missing, and I picked up the empty case, not really thinking. Just feeling sicker all the time. And the dog begged. Not using words, but sounding like an old-fashioned dog. So I undid the leash, and he jumped down and started off down along a line of trees.

I followed him.

I found myself starting to run, my boots heavy and getting heavier. But I kept the dog in sight, right up till he slid down, down, into a draw. And I got to the draw and stopped, spotting my shotgun's safety lying at my feet.

"I am dismantled," the machine told me.

There was a little pond in the draw. And trees. Grandpa was sitting on a downed log with the gun barrel put up into his mouth. He didn't hear me. He was too busy working at the angle of the gun, trying to get everything just so.

I tried to talk.

My voice quit working, but I managed to make a whimpering sound.

Then without pulling the barrel out of his mouth, he halfway turned and saw me, his eyes getting wider and brighter, and somehow farther away.

I stepped closer.

Talking around the barrel, he told me, "Go away."

I was thinking what he said about never knowing enough. About how a man can't just wait till he has perfect knowledge to act.

Grandpa was crying.

"Leave me alone," he said. Louder this time.

I don't know where I got the strength, but I told him, "No."

Then I told him, "They're going to find you innocent. If you explain things."

Then I sat down on the ground. Waiting.

After a little while, Grandpa managed to pull the barrel out of his mouth and put the gun at his feet, and acting more embarrassed than anything, he wiped at his tears and the rest of his face, and he pulled out a comb and ran it through his hair. Three times. I counted. Then with a tight little voice, he said, "Sam."

He said, "Do me a favor? Pick up this gun for me. Would you, please?"

She Sees My Monsters Now

"NERVOUS?" I ASK.

She lies. She says, "No," and then, "No," again. A smile emerges, faltering along its edges. Hands drop beneath the table, wrestling in her lap, and once again she lies, telling me, "I'm not particularly nervous, no."

Whatever I feel, I appear calm. I lean back, smiling a useful smile, but my expression is embarrassed with shadings of sadness. My elbows are propped on the armrests of my only chair, my hands turning, palms now turned up, emphasizing their emptiness and my own impotence. "No claws," I purr. Then I brighten my smile, adding, "And no fangs, either."

She gulps.

I laugh, gently and softly. "Hardly the image of a monster, am I?"

I have embarrassed her. A pretty enough woman, soft and small and sensitive and warm, she shrinks before me. This species of human being finds life and its pressures to be a great burden. I know her well; I have studied her peculiar ways. The occasional success always brings a stab of self-inflicted guilt. Her world is full of endless injustices and casual miseries. In response to the suffering, she wears only simple clothes derived from recycled plastics and other nonmortal sources. She embraces any ideology that promises to put things right. Because there is such a thing as right, just as some things are definitely wrong. The green copper ring on her left hand shows that she is a bride of Gaia. And at this moment, staring at me, she feels pity. Or more precisely, she pities what she envisions to be my awful life.

"You're not," she offers.

"Not what?"

"A monster," she whispers, disgusted even to say the word.

"But I *am*," I reply. "Diagnosed when I was five and placed into this program when I was nine." Then I hesitate, pretending to gather myself before I can admit, "After that first incident, they really didn't have much choice."

She flinches.

But her indigo eyes are enthralled.

"I don't blame anyone," I tell her. "I am what I am."

Women like her always hear something heroic in those words. "I am what I am." Admitting to its curse, the monster reveals its precious humanity.

She smiles again, her imagination engaged.

I nudge our conversation in a fresh direction. "Enough about me. Let's talk about you. My guess is that you've got a sweet little cat at home."

She says, "No," with relief. She is relieved to be changing subjects. "No, not a cat."

But I know that already. Brides of Gaia rarely settle for ordinary pets. When they enslave an animal, they want to accomplish something good and noble.

"Lemurs," she exclaims. "I have three of them."

"Fascinating," I exclaim.

"Genetically tweaked so they can coexist with humans. Of course." She will show me holos of her darlings. But no, she calls to them. To her children. She says, "Sally. Rhonda. Tara. Come here, dears!"

Animals disgust me. These bottom-rung primates have no more soul than a sack of bloody water. They are stupid creatures dressed in black and white pelts. Those implanted genes have rendered them obedient, and, we can hope, housebroken. They stare at me with shallow black eyes, and when I refuse to move, they look elsewhere. I'm not real. I am just an image at the far end of the table. Stupid as they are, the beasts understand that I mean nothing to them.

"They're extinct in their native Madagascar," says their owner.

I have never asked for her name.

"You're a noble soul," I purr. And then, for many fine reasons, I ask, "What do you suppose your Sally tastes like? Cooked over a hot smoky fire, say?"

Those indigo eyes are round and enormous.

She whimpers, "End link—"

I am sitting alone in my room. I have always been alone in this room. "Cold coffee and a Danish," I call out.

The room supplies both.

"And leave the line open," I command.

The room says, "She won't."

"Yes, she will," I promise.

I am allowed a single link with the world. As long as it remains open to one person, I can't speak to anyone else. The woman will understand that much. She'll watch the hours and days pass, knowing that my only portal is hers to do with as she wishes. And that's why I can say, with steely confidence, "She'll call back again. Within the week."

"How about a little wager?" the room suggests.

"Ten dollars," I offer.

"And if she doesn't return in seven days, I win."

"Except you don't think she's coming back," I remark, laughing now. "That's what you implied."

And the room laughs, reminding me, "But I know you. And if you think she can't help herself, then she can't."

She cannot.

A soft tone announces her return. It's three days later. From the gray wall before me, a cautious voice suggests, "You should close the link."

"Hello?" I call out, a perfect longing in my voice.

She hesitates. Then with a forced sturdiness, she asks, "May I see you again. Just for a moment, please."

"Wait. I need clothes." I'm dressed, but I want her to imagine me naked. Finally, with a booming voice, I tell the room, "Open the window."

My solitary table extends to the far wall. She sits with her hands folded on her tabletop, her back erect and shoulders squared. Today's wardrobe looks stiff and formal. Aiming for disdain, she tells me, "That was cruel."

"What was?"

"What you said. It was vicious and mean."

I blink, pretending confusion. "Remind me. What did I say?"

"About Sally." There isn't a lemur in sight. "I thought I should tell you. I don't appreciate that kind of talk."

"It's talk," I counter.

Her eyes narrow, betraying her own mild confusion.

"Words," I say. "Just a string of words."

But she *believes* in words. Language has a life and beauty, and, she suspects, an almost magical force. Hasn't she been deeply influenced by the right words delivered at the proper time?

I say, "Madagascar."

"Pardon?"

"What do you know about it?"

She takes a moment to wet her lips. Then, with an injured tone, she says, "It's a sad place. Deforested and eroded, and very poor."

"Yet until a few thousand years ago," I say, "it had a unique ecosystem. There were rain forests and a giant flightless bird—the likely source of the mythical roc—and there were dozens of species of lemurs, one or two of which were nearly as big as apes."

A flicker shows in the staring eyes.

"Then humans arrived," I say. "We landed on the shores and built villages, and we hunted the wild animals and chopped down their trees, and our crops grew where the forests had been, and we spread out until that little continent was jammed full of humans."

Sadly, she says, "Yes."

"I wasn't being cruel," I remark.

She turns her head, as if a sideways glance will provide a more thorough appraisal. "You weren't?"

"I was making a simple point. You see, Madagascar isn't part of Africa. It's really a very different place."

She doesn't speak.

"With the Mozambique Channel to help, its government was able to maintain its borders, and the occasional refugee who managed to slip through could be quarantined." I sighed heavily, telling her, "Africa was lucky, in one awful sense. Two-thirds of its people were killed relatively quickly. These new transcriptase viruses are brutal, but efficient. But Madagascar was spared. That's why nearly fifty-nine million people are subsisting today on a denuded landscape. That's why the next drought will bring a catastrophe. Famine and political carnage will join forces. There's going to be another Java, sad to say."

I can see her soul, injured but stubborn. "What were you accusing me of? Do you think if I was a good person, I'd send my lemurs home to help feed those starving people?"

"God, no," I exclaim.

Then I shake my head, adding, "That would be a horrific waste. The shipping costs. The care and feeding of three animals. Goodness, no. What's infinitely more productive is to send money. Make a donation to one of the local relief agencies. They know what's needed. They can buy food, or books, or even a universal window for one of the slums."

She nods, accepting my simple logic.

"In fact," I say, "I'll *give* you money. If you're going to do what I suggest, that is."

I am a monster, but what kind of person would refuse a monster's charity? Quietly, warily, she asks, "How much?"

"Ten dollars."

Perhaps she's surprised that I have cash. More likely, she's mystified that this ward of the state—a man who cannot leave his tiny home—has a firmer, broader grasp of the world than she has.

"I'll send another ten dollars," she promises.

It's a pathetically small sum. But I show my widest smile, adding quietly, "You know, when I said those hard words, I was aiming for a very different message."

She waits, holding her breath.

"What's worth more?" I ask. "Three docile lemurs, or one very difficult man?"

My room is far more than a room, and, by law, it is not mine.

Calmly but forcefully, the room cautions, "In at least three areas, you're skirting the edge of what's allowed."

"I never asked for Amy's name," I remark. "She volunteered it, and frankly, the name could be an out-and-out lie."

Silence.

I ask, "Have I solicited illegal or immoral help from that young woman?" Then I say, "No," with a genuine defiance. "And the Codes are very clear about this. An obvious breach and three federal judges are required to terminate all contact between a citizen and the individual in protective custody."

"The Codes are plain enough," the room agrees.

"Which leaves us with a third near-transgression," I continue. "What is it? Are my political views making you squirm?"

"No worse than usual," the room admits.

"But who cares?" I laugh. "Every sentient entity is free to believe whatever he or she, or it, wishes. Both the Bill of Rights and the Bill of Reason proclaim that unimpeachable freedom. For humans, and for thinking machines, too."

Silence.

"How can I live in a civilized world and not profess my personal views?"

Softly, the room reminds me, "This is an old topic."

"Does that make it taboo?"

"No." Then, with a glint of anger, the room adds, "Your third transgression lies elsewhere."

"Tell me," I urge.

"You know exactly what I mean," it says.

"I want you to say it. For the record."

"Don't worry about the record. It hears everything."

I laugh loudly.

"I like you," the room says abruptly. "I've always liked you. But the staff is worried. They've discovered some rather alarming trends in this new relationship of yours."

"What trends?" I blurt. "Did I wag my dick at her?"

That wins a disapproving silence. Then the room laughs back at me, reminding me, "I know you. Better than anyone, I know you. And dick-wagging is definitely not your style."

"Ask," I prompt.

"What?" she says.

"Anything," I beg. "Ask me anything."

Through her face, I can see her considering and then shying away from several ripe topics. Finally, Amy wonders aloud, "Why don't you ever drop our link?" She always closes her end when we're done. But even when I can't see her, I'm joined to one of her many windows—like the houseguest who refuses to leave. "You have only the one window, don't you?" she asks.

"Only this one. Yes."

Pain tightens that nearly pretty face. "Isn't there anybody else to visit with?" And then, sensing that this might be a sore subject, Amy adds, "I'll visit again. Don't I always come back?"

"There isn't anyone else," I answer. "And I know you'll return. It just took you three empty days, that first time."

She feels a poke of shame.

I backpedal, smiling when I assure, "I'm good about keeping busy. I like to exercise. I have conversations with the doctors and with my AI overseer. But mostly, I read. I know this room doesn't look like much, but these walls contain all but a handful of the world's books. Literature. History. Politics, and comedy. Which are really the same topic, I think."

She laughs weakly, and then asks, "What books are missing?"
I name some titles.

"Really? Did your doctors forbid them?"

"Oh, no. That was *my* doing." I shake my head. "They're despicable works, and I don't want them in arm's reach."

She opens her mouth, considering her response.

"Don't I have the right?" I interrupt. "Freedom to doubt, freedom to exclude. If you can't do either in your life, is it *your* life?"

Her mouth draws shut.

"And this is my life," I promise. "Everything you see here . . . is mine. . . ."

Doubt lifts her eyebrows. She braces herself with a deep, full sigh. Then, shaking her head, she says, "What happened?"

"What happened when?"

She forces herself to stare at my eyes. "When you were five. When you were first diagnosed—"

"I failed the standardized test," I confess. "On a thousand-point scale, I was two points into the red."

Amy nods soberly. Then she says, "No. I meant before that."

She's been doing research, I presume. This isn't the kind of knowledge that people like her naturally carry around with them.

"There had to be other reasons, other grounds." She embraces her fear for a moment, and, avoiding my eyes, says, "There have to be incidents of abuse. Or damage to the limbic system."

"Yes," I say, "and no."

She blinks and looks up.

"My mother was a splinter addict. Plus, there were one or two nasty events with her boyfriends. At least, there were two incidents that could be legally confirmed."

She shivers.

"But again," I say, "on the scale of what's horrible and damning, I was barely inside the red zone. Based on the best available science, I was considered marginally at risk. Thousands are, but only three or four end up being truly dangerous."

She nods, and waits.

"Yet then again," I continue, "I wasn't placed into protective custody for another four and a half years. I hadn't yet proven myself, as it were."

Her deep blue eyes are enormous. Fear and compassion stand in balance. Finally, with a weak voice, she asks, "What did you do?"

"I won't tell you."

She's disappointed, and then, on second thought, relieved.

"At least not today," I kid. Then, laughing gently, I say, "Besides, I need something to lure you back again."

Amy says, "You don't."

But really, she knows that I'm right.

"There are concerns," I am told.

Sensing that this will take time, I blank my reader. "Concerns from where? The medical minds, or legal saints?"

"From everyone," it says.

"Tell everyone to speak to me. Directly."

"That's their intention."

"Good."

But the room has been asked to lay the groundwork. "Amy has strong feelings for you," it announces. "What do you think of that?"

"They're her feelings," I remark. "She can entertain them. She can deny them. But by law and by custom, they belong to her."

"Agreed," it says.

I let the silence work. Then, "How did they acquire this deeply personal knowledge? Did she confess it to them?"

"Again," says the room. "Guess again."

I have to laugh. "We're talking about surveillance, aren't we? What? Are they eavesdropping on her windows? Prying open her little pink diary? What?"

The room reminds me, "When the woman first volunteered her time—before she selected your image from everyone in protective custody—she willingly forfeited most of the current privacy laws."

"How convenient," I purr. "Convenient, and obscene."

Silence.

"Does it bother you? A legally designated sociopath tisk-tisking the actions of health care professionals and badge-wielding law officers?"

Quietly, the room says, "Of course not."

I know the room. Sometimes better than I know myself. And when I hear those three words, I recognize that the poor AI is trying to lie to me.

With my face, I show a mild disapproval. Nothing more. I return to my book, and, after another few pages of Napoleanic intrigues, a revelation finds me. Again, I blank my reader. I sit back, clasping my hands behind my head. And the room, being infinitely observant, asks, "What's funny now?"

"She's reading them," I say.

"Reading what?" it asks.

"The books that appalled me!" I shout. And with both fists, I drum on the tabletop, laughing until I wheeze.

"Why me?"

She feigns confusion. "What do you mean?"

"I placed my name and face at that meeting nexus. The state added the warnings, for free. But you selected me anyway. Was it my age? My chiseled features? Did I look too innocent to be a monster?"

"No," she admits. "You didn't look all that innocent."

"So you *wanted* to meet a monster. Is that it?"

She hesitates.

I give her a harsh laugh that ends with a fond wink and lingering grin. "Are we back at the beginning? Shall I show you my claws and teeth?"

"Don't," she warns.

And with the next breath, she admits, "I just read Malcom's text. Parts of it, at least."

"And?"

"Sociopaths are terribly destructive. She claims. Between their criminal acts and the emotional harm they inflict, they could be the most destructive element in modern human society." Perhaps she can accept that bleak assessment, but the obvious rebuttal looms. "But when we convict them before they've become adults . . . oftentimes before they do real harm . . . well, that doesn't seem fair, or just, or even smart. . . ."

"Oh, I think it is."

I love to astonish her.

With a wave of the hand, I dismiss her objections. "Believe me, I've met enough of these people to know. They're genuine monsters. And the worst of them are far too shrewd to break any important law. To them, other people are tools. Nothing more. To feed their egos, they're drawn to politics. Or they become ministers and priests, and counselors. Any venue where they have control over other people's lives is a rich one." I have to be exceptionally cautious here. Accusing no one, I admit, "This is one area where I strongly disagree with Dr. Malcom."

"Okay," Amy mutters.

"In all, there's about a dozen areas where she blundered. Her thousand-point empathy scale, for instance. The red zone is enormous, yet her net has far too large a mesh. The smart sociopath knows what to say and how to act. With emphasis on the word 'act.' Even as a child, he or she can easily fool interviewers and the machines. At-risk people are constantly passing through—"

"I've heard that," she volunteers.

"Because the factors are badly ranked," I continue. "I have my own scale, based on observations of others and myself. I have half a dozen suggestions that could lead to a more scrupulous methodology—"

"And you wouldn't be in the red zone," she blurts. "Is that what you're saying?"

"God, no."

Her surprise is abrupt, and delicious.

"I was definitely at risk," I confess. "I haven't any doubts." I can smile at this honest appraisal, repeating myself. "At *risk*. Worthy of a good long look by the agents of public health and criminal interdiction."

Amy is at a loss for words.

"And remember," I continue. "I wasn't placed into this room for another fifty-two months. The state saw no good reason to isolate me."

She breathes.

Quietly, with a painful whisper, she asks, "What happened?"

"Before I tell you," I begin, "I want you to consider this. Dr. Malcom made the easiest mistake. She was a happy person born into comfort and means, and it never occurred to her—not once —that some people genuinely deserve to be tortured."

Amy breathes, and breathes.

"Tortured," I repeat.

"What did you do?"

"My mother had a rare gift," I mention. "Better than a thousand psychiatrists, she could find the monstrous men of the world. But instead of placing them inside secure facilities, she would simply coax them into her bed."

"You were nine," Amy whispers.

"Nearly ten," I counter. "And I was big for my age, and angry. And the latest boyfriend was drunk and high, and he'd fallen down a set of stairs, breaking his ankle . . . and I found him like that. Nobody else was home. And there I was, with a kitchen jammed full of knives. . . ."

"Congratulations."

I rise to the bait, asking, "For what?"

"She's hired a competent attorney. On your behalf, she's planning to contest your legal status."

"It won't work," is my assessment.

The room agrees with me. "And not only will she fail," it says, "but she'll spend most of her savings in the effort."

"*Her* savings," I mention. "That's her right."

"You don't care?"

"Funny," I say. Then I glance at the soft pink ceiling, pointing out, "You're always watching me. You're a high-functioning machine born and trained to do nothing else. Your life has been spent counting my heartbeats, measuring my skin conductivity and respiration rate, and, by a hundred more elaborate means, assessing my soul. Yet for some reason, you feel the need to ask me if I care."

I snort loudly, laughing at both of us.

"Why do you think that is?" I inquire.

Silence.

"What are you sensing here, old friend? Really, in your heart, what do you hope to find?"

"Thank you," I begin.

A wide bright smile starts to bubble up.

"But it's not enough," I caution. "Listen to me, Amy. You don't have the resources. You don't have nearly enough stamina. And honestly, you don't even have a legal leg beneath you."

Yet the smile completes itself, and with a practiced certainty, Amy tells me, "I can raise money. And I do have plenty of stamina. And maybe it's time for the laws to be changed. Have you thought about that possibility?"

"Once in a while," I admit.

Then I fold my hands together on the tabletop, wearing a begging expression when I tell her, "Stop this. Please. You're going to make things miserable for both of us, and nothing's going to be accomplished. I know that and I can accept it. So please, quit now."

She dismisses me with a laugh. "How do you know?" she asks. Then a paranoid thought takes hold of her. "Wait," she exclaims. "Have you been threatened? Is someone telling you to stop me?"

"Someone is," I admit. Then I lie, saying, "I want you to quit."

"I won't." She has never looked prettier. Her golden hair covers her shoulders, and those wide indigo eyes shine at me. "You're a good person. Anyone can see that. What you did when you were nine—"

"Shut up," I say.

The room and my keepers watch every portion of our conversation. One mistake on anyone's part, and I lose my link with her. Which would only make it worse, I understand. Unable to speak to me, Amy would turn into an avenging angel, impoverishing herself to save an increasingly remote memory.

"Shut up," I repeat.

But she isn't talking now. Her lower jaw is thrust out in a very unattractive way, and with her body and face, and, finally, her voice, she tells me, "I don't care. I want to help you."

"But this won't help anyone," I repeat.

"How do you know? Until you try, how can you know?"

I stare at those vivid eyes, and wait.

She manages a shallow sudden breath. "Oh, my."

"You see?" I ask.

For the last time, I have surprised her. Quietly and with a real pain, she says, "This has happened before."

"Three times," I allow.

Now she looks down at her hands, quietly wondering, "Who were they?" And then, "Women?"

"Sure."

But she isn't defeated. A pathological idealist, she needs to tell me, "This time is going to be different. I'm going to set you free—"

"You aren't going to accomplish shit. You can't, so forget it." An honest gasp rises up inside me, and years of exasperation boil out. "The system is the system. It can't be beaten. So just walk away."

Somewhere in those words, she hears a possibility. With tears on the suddenly puffy cheeks, she asks, "What would be enough?"

I say nothing.

"To end the system," she says. "What would prove that it's wrong?"

I say, "Nothing will," in a certain way.

Then I grin for a moment—a grin that I have practiced and perfected, knowing and charming and capable of transporting volumes in an instant. And I say to her, "Think," just as our link is permanently and irrevocably severed.

"You're evil," I hear.

I am awake suddenly. My table converts into a soft bed, but I have always slept on the floor, using only my arms for pillows. It must be the middle of the night. Only the faint pink glow of the nightlight illuminates a realm that never seems large. The room is always tiny. "Why am I?" I ask the room. "Evil, you say?"

"She took your advice," it tells me.

I sit up. "Took what?"

"No more games," it warns. Then with horror and sadness, it says, "One of Amy's neighbors filed an official complaint, and by law, she had to be tested."

The Malcom test, it means.

"She answered every question with the worst possible answer. And somehow, she managed to mimic some of the amoral physiological responses."

"So what?" I ask. "She's an adult without a criminal history. What's the worst that can happen? She gets labeled and put under observation for the next two or three years, and then . . . and then . . . wait, there's something else, isn't there. . . ?"

Silence.

"You wouldn't be pissed over some woman's bad diagnosis," I admit. Then after a few moments of feeling lost, I have to ask, "What else happened? What did she do?"

"Think," the room urges.

"Cruelty to animals," I realize. "What? Did she do something to her damned lemurs?"

"Something," is all it will tell me. Then with a sorrowful voice, it says, "Amy is being processed now. For the next two years, she will live in protective custody. The laws are clear, and they can't be disobeyed—"

"The laws are wrong," I say.

"And *you're* evil," it growls. "You pushed her. Trained her. Suggested what books to read, seducing her altruistic nature."

I say nothing.

"You are shit," the room tells me.

"Am I?"

"Ruining a young woman's life," it says. "And for *what?*"

With a calm, almost matter-of-fact voice, I admit, "I thought I was making a point. And I succeeded rather well, I believe."

"Did you?"

I have to laugh, bitterly and with an ocean of malice. Then I look at my own hands, asking, "Who was my audience, you stupid shit? Who was I appealing to here? A sweet, foolish girl who has absolutely no power, or the sentient and legally emancipated entity that stands guard over me . . . that comprises my walls . . . *that can open my door. . . ?*"

———

Abducted Souls

"WHAT'S THAT?"
    "What's what?"
"That guy over there. The one with the walk."
Shawn was a pretty if rather uncomplicated young woman. Gazing off in the wrong direction, she asked, "What walk? Who are you talking about?"
"No, over there," Cole growled. "See him?"
"I guess so."
Even at a distance, something was plainly wrong with the stranger's gait. He had a jerky, top-heavy style, apish arms dangling, his head sometimes rolling to one side. Not for the last time, Cole thought of a puppet being bounced along by an invisible and incompetent puppet master. Nervous or not, the stranger had a manner—a unique style—that infected anyone watching him, giving his audience a palpable unease that only grew worse as he approached.
"Know him?" asked Cole, fingertips sliding along the warm, smooth skin of a bare shoulder.
Shawn shook her head. "No."
The stranger followed the sidewalk past the Bark-Tipple Student Center, heading in their direction. A little tall and thick through the middle, he wore jeans that were tight and too short and a thin flannel shirt that looked absolutely out-of-place in the

late August swelter. His hair was black and shaggy-long and screaming for a comb. He appeared profoundly preoccupied, striding forward with a wild energy, occasionally muttering a word or two while tiny dark eyes stared in random directions. But as he passed by, he looked sideways, his gaze suddenly cutting into both of them while one of his bouncy feet caught a seam in the concrete.

The stranger began to fall, and then with a graceless lunge, the other foot managed to catch his fall. A worn basketball shoe squeaked sharply. Somehow he straightened himself and kept moving, working twice as hard just to walk just a little faster than before. When he vanished in the direction of the freshman dorm, Cole announced, "That's one weird fart of a freshman."

Shawn seemed to laugh, and then both of them fell silent again.

They began dating last spring, trading e-mails and phone calls through the summer, and Cole had even visited her hometown over the Fourth of July weekend. But their relationship had lost its momentum of late. Sitting together on the Floyd Riggins Memorial Bench, out in front of old Hawthorne Hall, each was trying to decide when and how to break up.

Not today, Cole decided, looking down the front of his girlfriend's shirt.

Because he hadn't assembled his own bed yet, much less unpacked, he asked, "So? Want to go up to your room now?"

Shawn didn't seem to hear him.

Cole stood. He was a skinny blond with fine features that some girls found attractive. "Want to?" he asked again, offering his left hand. That was when Shawn finally noticed the fresh wound on his forearm—a shiny pink gouge small enough to be hidden beneath a thumbnail.

She blinked, asking, "Is that one?"

He didn't say. Really, he didn't want to use this infirmity.

But she was intrigued, rising and taking him by the wounded arm, asking, "Did they find anything this time?"

With a little shrug, Cole said, "Not yet."

"Poor baby!"

He wrapped his unscarred arm around her very willing waist. "How about not talking about it anymore. Okay?"

The stranger had come from Colorado or Wyoming, or maybe Utah. Or maybe Illinois. What people knew for certain were his name, which was Larson Meeks, and his means, which seemed remarkably peculiar. A sophomore who worked part-time in the business office had watched while Meeks paid for his fall tuition and room and board. He had pulled a stack of hundred dollar bills from a badly worn manila envelope, casually shoving his change into one of the front pockets of his tight jeans. Mr. Oscar, in charge of all things financial at the college, oversaw the transaction with a grim astonishment. "That's a lot of money to carry," he told the new student. "If I were you, I'd put the rest in the bank."

Meeks didn't seem to hear the advice. He was busy gathering up his receipts and the official papers, folding them into a collective wad that was shoved into the other front pocket. Then he looked up abruptly, and with a wet gasp asked, "Which bank?"

Laughing self-consciously, Mr. Oscar mentioned the financial institution with which the college did most of its business.

"I guess I should," Meeks allowed. The words were amiable, but not the voice. Not the body language, either. The young man was a head taller than Mr. Oscar, and while he barked the words —"I guess I should"—he started to rock from side to side, as if his body was sick with energy, bleeding off the excess before he simply exploded. "I guess if I've got no choice—"

"I didn't say that," the little man interrupted. "I'm just suggesting—"

"Sure. Yeah." Meeks sniffed and turned, bouncing his way out of the administration building. Which would have been the end of the story, normally. But the main witness to these events was still working an hour later. An outside line rang. The student happened to pick it up. The president of First National wanted to speak to Mr. Oscar. She transferred the call, and then for no reason other than a gut feeling, she listened to one end of the conversation, absorbing enough to feel sure that the bank president was thanking his old friend for sending a fat new client bouncing through his front door.

The sophomore was named Clara. She was pretty like a doll is pretty, with fine features, a flat chest, and a shapely firm ass. Her father was an ordained Methodist minister, and like every preacher's kid, she cultivated a wild side. Her virginity hadn't lasted long in college. Her reputation as a good Christian girl had taken more than a few hits. By chance, she sat beside Cole in the cafeteria one Friday night. He had just broken up with his girlfriend; everybody knew it. On a whim, Clara asked if he wanted to see the latest *Star Wars* movie, and he said, "Sure," and their date didn't end until breakfast that next morning.

Cole couldn't entirely explain why he ended up with Clara.
Maybe because she was different from Shawn: smart and funny
and with a very different sort of body. It still bothered him that
Shawn took the breakup so well. What was it about women that
made them so confusing? But he had a good time that night. Real
aliens were nothing like the digital cartoons in the movies, but the
show was fun nonsense. Sure, he missed having breasts to play
with. But Clara was a reader, and bright, and she could tell a good
story. For instance, everybody already knew the tale about Meeks
and Mr. Oscar, but it was fun to hear it from the source.

Finishing the story, Clara smiled and shook her head. Except
for a pair of long white socks, she was naked. She had that doll-like
face, very young looking. It was like dating a fifteen-year-old, Cole
had decided. Sometimes he wished this wasn't just an occasional
thing. Yet even after four dates, Clara hadn't mentioned anything
about commitment, and, surprisingly, the absence of that kind of
talk made Cole uncomfortable. What was she thinking? What did
she want? With a peculiar horror, it occurred to Cole that she
might regard him as nothing but a convenient source of head.

Clara said nothing, fingering the scars along his left leg without
ever quite mentioning them.

A sudden grin erupted. "Did I tell you? He's showing up at
Bible study."

"Who is?"

"Who are we talking about? Larson Meeks."

"At Bible study?"

"He was there last week," she reported. Clara used to attend the
Saturday night meeting, and she still had friends among the group.
"In fact, I saw him tonight, while I was walking over here. Bounc-
ing up into the union, a little black Bible stuck in his hand."

Cole wasn't sure what to say.

"You know," continued Clara, "that Meeks is a very odd fellow."

"I kind of figured that."

Then after a pause, he asked, "Does the guy talk at the meet-
ings?"

"I guess so. Sometimes."

"About himself?"

"Everyone talks about himself," she cautioned. Then with a little-girl giggle, she added, "If not in so many words."

What did that mean?

Clara seemed to smell the question. One hand was busy playing with the newest toy in her life, and watching the toy, she quietly said, "I don't know any of this for sure. I'm getting this filtered

through Paula. But he's some kind of orphan, I guess, and there's a trust fund. He's got a ton of money. Last week he bought pizza for everybody. He said his trust was paying for it."

"Yeah?"

"Mostly, Meeks just likes to ask questions."

"Like what?"

"Big questions." She sighed quietly. "He asks the Christians how they can believe the story. Because it sounds awfully silly to him, he says. God's Son is born and does miracles, and then dies and comes back to life again, and so what? Why should that be important?"

Cole laughed appreciatively.

Clara could smile but not laugh. Not for the same reasons that Cole laughed, at least. "He wants to see miracles," she reported. "He asks for a chance to talk to God. And Christ. And who's this Holy Spirit?"

Imagining the scene, Cole asked, "What's Wallace think?"

Terry Wallace led the Bible study. He wasn't the kind of person to embrace skeptical inquiries, which made Clara's answer all the more surprising. "He lets Meeks talk," she admitted. "And then he sits there, letting other people explain Christianity to the poor guy."

Cole watched as Clara played with him.

"You like this?" she asked.

"What do you think?"

Another little-girl giggle ended with the delicious question, "What do you want me to do next?"

A multitude of possibilities ran through Cole's mind. But before he could answer, Clara mentioned in a distinctly puzzled tone, "You know, he's been asking about you."

"Who has?"

"Who are we talking about? Did you forget again?"

Cole began to sit up, genuinely startled.

With her free hand, Clara stroked the scars on his legs. "Meeks keeps asking about your story. He thinks you're interesting, I guess."

"Am I?"

"Oh, sometimes," said the preacher's kid, her gaze lifting, that pretty little mouth laughing, eyes cutting like blue-hot scalpels.

When Cole was five years old, he vanished from his bedroom. His parents were watching television in the basement. Years later, his mother would dredge up a vague memory of the family's cocker spaniel growling at nothing. She may or may not have heard a strange noise upstairs. A pop, or was it a sizzling sound? The story had a crafty way of shifting with each telling. What was certain was that Cole's father didn't share his wife's interest in the handsome young doctors on *ER*, and at some point during the evening he wandered upstairs to discover their son missing. The doors were locked, as was every window. Obviously, the boy was still inside the house. Yet the increasingly frantic search accomplished nothing, and they realized that Cole had slipped outdoors and shut the door after him, or worse, someone had sneaked into their house for no purpose other than to abduct their only child.

The police were called. Neighbors were alerted. Adults fanned out through the neighborhood, searching alleys and garages and a pair of wooded lots frequented by every small boy. But an hour's search found nothing. Two terrified parents came home to wait beside the phone. Cole's father had to pace, and passing through the kitchen, he happened to glance into the backyard, noticing a faint glimmer beneath the big Chinese elm. He had already searched the yard, twice. Neighbors and police cruisers had scoured the alley behind their house. Nobody had seen any trace of the missing boy. So what was the glow? With a numbed hope and a choking dread, he slowly walked out back, finding himself staring at the white of his son's pajamas, Cole calmly sleeping inside them.

Fear dissolved into a brief celebration, and for the next week or two, a kind of celebrity clung to the boy. But because nothing genuinely remarkable had happened, the entire incident was soon forgotten. His parents avoided mentioning his running away from home, not wishing to trigger a repeat performance. And Cole seemed to recall nothing about his tiny adventure, including why he had left or where he might have been hiding.

Almost ten years later, a small article appeared in the *New England Journal of Medicine*. Researchers at Mount Sinai Hospital had identified at least five people with these shared features: In the mid-1990s, they had vanished without explanation. When found, they showed no memory of where they were or what they might have done. Each patient had suffered one or two small puncture wounds, but no infections. And upon examination with modern imaging equipment, each was found to have one or several foreign bodies buried deep in their tissues.

The tabloids had ready explanations, but science was far less impressed. The foreign bodies had no obvious importance. Every attempt to isolate one of the mysterious bodies ended in failure. More than one frustrated researcher claimed that the little bastards simply didn't want to be found.

It wasn't until the following year, in England, that a team at Cambridge managed to isolate a BB-sized object from the kidney of a young Belfast man. They successfully removed the prize, immersing it in a liquid helium bath that succeeded in keeping it intact for almost ninety minutes. To the casual eye, the object looked like a dull gray BB. But microscopes revealed a wealth of detail. There were structures on the BB's surface—intricate features showing hints of a sluggish, supercooled motion. At a later press conference, one physicist likened it to looking down on an elaborate city . . . no, it was like gazing down on an entire world. But as for the origin and purpose of the object . . . well, that was a subject about which science could say little.

After ninety minutes, the object collapsed into an amorphous drop of calcium and nickel and magnesium and certain rare earths.

Later attempts to replicate the Cambridge work met with only partial success. Objects were seen but then retreated to some other part of the body. Or they destroyed themselves as they were lifted out of the blood and gore.

Perhaps that single successful capture was a fluke. Perhaps the object's failsafe systems had been defective, thus slow to commit suicide. Or as Freeman Dyson said in what only sounded like a joking tone:

"Maybe these little worlds talk to each other, learning from their collective mistakes."

Cole felt a tingle—that nagging if not quite alarming sense of things being a little wrong—and after a quick breath, he stopped and glanced over his shoulder. It was a moonless night, the air thick and damp. Except for the milky light on top of the occasional lamp pole, this corner of campus was dark. He saw nothing at first. There was nothing out there but a quick, sloppy scraping sound, and while his mind worked on translating what he heard, Cole's eyes continued to stare at the blackness, at the shadows, and at nothing, waiting, until a tall figure lurched out into a puddle of light three lamps from where he was standing.

Cole recognized Larson Meeks. The same short jeans and ugly flannel shirt rode on a clumsy, jerky frame. The big feet dragged across the sidewalk, making a genuine racket. His long arms seemed to lift with every stride, as if fighting to maintain a precarious balance. He was a shambles. He was pitiful. Even at a distance, he was purely weird.

Cole turned and walked on, thinking that he could remain alone. He thought about Clara for a moment, and about school, and again about Clara, and then he heard the feet closing quickly. Turning again, he found Meeks walking fifteen feet behind him. The kid must have been running, but as soon as Cole looked, he fell back into his patented walk. What may or may not have been a smile broke across the doughy face. Eyes peered out from the bottom of two deep holes. They were little eyes, dark with shadow, and nothing about them was smiling.

Cole's mouth opened, a nervous little cough leaking out.

"Glock," said a voice. And then, "You are."

"What?"

"Your name's Glock." In a moment, Meeks closed the gap completely. Then he stopped, standing too close, a grim voice saying, "Your name's Cole Glock."

"I didn't know. Thanks for telling me."

The sarcasm had no impact. The face was thick and pale, incapable of the smallest amusement. Its expression was curiosity mixed with a vigorous contempt. Or was it doubt? Either way, Meeks announced, "I know about you. You're him."

And you are one weird fuck, thought Cole.

With a sharp tone, Meeks asked, "How's it feel?"

Cole stared at the tiny eyes. "How does what feel?"

A look of undiluted disgust was followed by stubbornness, and, thinking that his point had been missed, he repeated himself. "I've heard about you. You. You're the one that got . . . you know . . . taken. . . !"

Taken. What a splendid, inadequate word.

Again, Meeks asked, "How does it feel?"

"Pretty good." Cole was joking, and this time he signaled his humor with a long laugh. "It feels good and sweet."

Lips were compressed to a painful point, and then Meeks exhaled into the closed mouth, cheeks bulging against the pressure generated by the lungs. He looked as if he was trying to blow up a giant balloon with a single breath. For an instant, it seemed as if his cheeks would rip open, his face exploding with a sloppy wet pop. But then the lips broke apart, a little wind blowing spit-spray toward Cole, causing him to step back, both hands lifting.

"Hey," he complained.

Meeks straightened abruptly. "Sorry," he blurted, nothing about the voice apologetic. Then he took a half step forward, and with a terrifying relentlessness said, "Or maybe you weren't."

"Weren't what?"

"Taken." With a snort and a superior tilt of the head, Meeks pointed out, "Others told me. Nothing's been found inside you. The doctors think maybe something's there, but they can't cut fast enough to catch it. . . !"

Cole stared at him, nodding now. And with a hard, little voice, he said, "I don't know you. You don't know me. Maybe you're right. Maybe I wasn't taken. But really, what the fuck business is it of yours?"

The question percolated its way into the churning brain.

Of all things, a smile appeared. Finally, something was humorous enough to elicit a half-chuckle and a respectful nod of the head. Then Meeks crinkled his nose, as if smelling something foul. Maybe himself. He had the muscular odor of someone who didn't approve of showers. And with a curling lip, he said, "Anyway." He shrugged with his entire upper body, saying, "I know about you."

Cole glanced at the flannel shirt. Every button was fastened, and the snug cuffs reached almost to the end of the long pale wrists.

"How about you?" Cole asked.

The tiny eyes swam inside their holes. "What about me?"

"Were you taken, too?" That would explain wearing jeans and a long-sleeved shirt in the summer. Meeks was hiding the scars left behind by surgeons who had carved and carved, trying to corral the tiny machines. "The aliens grabbed you up. Didn't they? Is that what happened?"

A look of absolute horror came into the soft white face.

Then Meeks was walking again, pushing past Cole and breaking into a shuffling run, arms flailing at nothing while a pained voice told somebody, "No, no. Not possible. No!"

At sixteen, Cole learned the world was populated with two species of girls. There were those who were terrified by what he represented, while the other species—the interesting girls—were endlessly intrigued and maybe a little spellbound by the idea of a handsome young man playing host to an alien parasite. As a rule, Cole tried to act noncommittal about his personal beliefs. With Clara and every other girlfriend, he would expose his scars and talk about the odd surgeries—metal detectors and special obsidian blades busily accomplishing nothing. "Doctors see things," he would explain, watching gentle hands dance over his battered flesh. "Dots and spots on the x-rays, mostly. But they're hard to see, and getting harder. The critters are smarter than they used to be. Or maybe they didn't exist in the first place."

"But you were abducted," the worshipful lovers would counter. "You told me the story. You vanished one night, without explanation."

"A lot of little boys slip out of their house."

"People hunted for you."

"And they found me," Cole would counter.

"Do you remember running away? Is that what happened?"

"I don't remember anything," he had to admit. "But I was a little kid. I can't remember most of the shit I pulled back then."

Cole liked to appear skeptical. It helped whenever he chose not to believe that he had been taken, and it helped even more when he did believe. He was a doubter, thus his convictions felt more real. More true. Plus, there was the tangible advantage that the girls would argue with him, practically begging for him to be remarkable, and unique, and distinctly blessed.

"What do you think they are?" Clara asked.

This was several nights after his encounter with Meeks. Since then, he had seen the odd soul only at a distance. He had yet to mention the event to anybody else. It was too silly, too weird. And for some reason, too embarrassing.

Smiling, Clara offered her opinion. "I think they're sensors. Probes. The aliens use them to watch your body, and maybe the world around you, too."

"Maybe so," Cole replied.

"What do you think?"

He was half-dressed and sprawled out on the legless little sofa that squatted beneath his head-high bed. "I know they really like seeing you naked."

She laughed.

She said, "No, really. What do you believe?"

"I like Dyson's explanation."

"Okay. What's that?"

"Suppose you wanted to visit the nearest star," Cole began. "It's not like the movies. Distances are enormous. The fuel costs are staggering. If you want to go anywhere, it's going to take centuries and trillions of dollars. Clothed or naked. Either way, you're huge and heavy, and you can't afford the ticket."

She had a pleasant laugh.

"But people build machines, and our machines keep getting smaller. Dyson argues that it's only reasonable for intelligent beings to change their own nature. To join with their machines and shrink down, becoming tiny and light, which makes it almost easy to move between the stars."

"I've heard that one before," she admitted.

"Specks of dust. Smart dust, we'll call them. It wouldn't take much energy to accelerate a bit of dust up to near-light speeds, and then the dust falls into the target solar system, slowed by the pressure of sunlight. That one mote could harvest the local dust and gas, rebuilding itself a million times over."

"A billion times, maybe."

"Or a trillion trillion times." He laughed and shrugged. "Anyway. What do I believe? It's silly, this bullshit idea that flying saucers are streaking around the globe, abducting humans so they can implant their little tracking devices. I mean, really! If the aliens are among us, they came as dust, and it they're really that tiny and prolific, then they'll spread like a virus. They'll fall from the sky, and we'll breathe them in, and without feeling a thing, they'll become part of us."

With a keen interest, Clara asked, "So what's running around inside you?"

"Worlds," he replied. "Each little BB is an alien world."

Her blue eyes grew huge and round.

"Or maybe there's nothing inside me," he allowed.

"But why'd you vanish from your bed?"

"I had a date." He gave a big laugh. "Like I said. I could have been sleepwalking. I could have been a bad little boy sneaking outside. It was dark, and nobody saw me in my hiding place, and there's nothing mysterious about it."

"But there are others," she reminded him. "People who did vanish. Who got abducted, or whatever. And the doctors and scientists . . . they have found real machines hiding inside them, right. . . ?"

"It seems so," Cole agreed.

Staring at his lover, he allowed himself a long smile. "You ever wonder?" he began. "It's the people who might have been abducted who get studied. But maybe there are good, normal reasons for their disappearances, and for the gaps in their memories, and all those ridiculous visions of aliens and flying saucers that come out of some people's brains when they find themselves hypnotized."

"What are you saying?"

"We're looking in one place, but the aliens are already every-where."

Suddenly Clara looked down at her own half-naked body, and with a nervous chuckle, she tried her best to laugh.

The freshman dorm was relatively new—a broad stack of gray bricks and gray mortar, tiny square windows peering into equally tiny rooms, each as simple and drab as the interior of a gutted eggshell. Larson Meeks lived inside one of the eggs. He lived alone. There had been a roommate—a handsome eighteen-year-old who believed that he was going to enjoy a private room. But then Meeks appeared on the eve of classes, and after four nights and a string of increasingly desperate visits to the Housing Office, the roommate finally convinced the world that he couldn't live with the man. Nobody could with Meeks. In fact, so genuine was the roommate's despair that he refused to return to the room. "I'll live anywhere else!" he screamed at the Dean. "I don't care where!" Which was a good thing, since the only available room was in the basement—a nearly windowless and perpetually damp hovel designed to serve as a storage closet, and in emergencies, as a tornado shelter.

Meeks lived upstairs, in a brightly lit room free of the tiniest embellishment. There was a narrow bed and a single set of sheets, plus a thin pillow permanently folded in half. His entire wardrobe needed three hangers and one of the room's built-in drawers. There was no phone or computer. His textbooks and a fat spiral notebook lay stacked on a simple desk pushed against the far wall. In class, he wrote extensively. Sometimes he took notes, and some-times he carefully transcribed his own relentless thoughts. Alone in his room, he tried to study, opening the notebook and whatever text was required, the intense and dark little eyes dancing across the pages. But he always ended up sitting in the middle of the room, in the plastic chair that came with the desk, legs stretched out ahead and his head flung back, eyes squinting, watching the incandescent light and the fine network of cracks that decorated the plastered ceiling.

Some nights, he never slept. Sometimes he couldn't even pre-tend to sleep, sitting in the chair while breathing hard, and then less hard. Always, the ceiling light was turned on. Even when he managed to fall asleep—a hard, exhausted slumber when he was very lucky—Meeks left the overhead light burning. Even though he never had company, he had taken the simple precaution of applying masking tape to the switch beside the door, making mistakes less likely. Also, he had purchased a considerable inventory of hundred-watt bulbs that he kept under his bed, and every day, usually around noon, he would slip a filthy sock over his right hand and stand on the chair, unscrewing yesterday's bulb. Sometimes he burned his fingertips, but he accepted that minimal cost. Changing bulbs was a precaution based on hard experience. If he slept at night, and if some defective bulb happened to fail without warning, then he would awaken to find himself swallowed up in an awful darkness, the walls and ceiling collapsing over him, doing their very best to suffocate him.

Meeks regularly visited the library. Before the end of September, he knew where to find the useful books and magazines. He had a preferred study desk among the stacks. Sometimes another student used his desk. On occasion, Meeks would wait for it in the adjacent aisle, and because his eyes had to look somewhere, he would stare at the interloper until he or she got up and left. But other times he accepted having to sit elsewhere. On a Sunday night in early October, he found himself positioned within sight of the library's front door, his attentions fixed on a bound set of old *Time* magazines. With a clear, keen intensity, he studied the colored diagrams and elaborate three-dimensional images made with scanning electron microscopes. Grimy thick fingers followed the crenulated patterns on the surface of the alien machine. Then he returned to his reading, his mouth moving as he worked hard, attempting to fix every important word into memory.

"Hello, Larson."

Did he hear something? Was that a voice? Meeks blinked, and with a slow surprise lifted his gaze, discovering four people standing before him.

Terry Wallace possessed an odd combination of discipline and undistracted intelligence, those traits allowing him to believe only what he wished to believe. He believed in medical science. Yet he also embraced the idea that illnesses could be cured through prayer and the pressure of faithful hands. With a rich voice and a natural presence, he had taken possession of the Saturday night Bible study group. Three of his flock stood behind him now. Girls, naturally. Girls gravitated toward leaders, and it didn't hurt that he was pre-med with a 4.0 grade-point average.

Smiling, Wallace asked, "How are you doing tonight, Larson?"

That was never an easy question to answer. Wishing to be truthful, Meeks took his time, dwelling on a thousand invisible factors, deciphering his health and well-being before making the simple utterance:

"Okay."

"Good, good. Glad to hear it." Everybody was smiling, aiming their smiles in Meeks's direction. Wallace said, "Good," one more time. Then with a smile and wink, he added, "You know, you don't have to study alone. We meet in the second-floor lounge in Hawthorne. Sunday to Friday, from seven o'clock to ten."

"We?" Meeks asked.

"The Christians," Wallace said with an easy pride. "The same good people you see on Saturday night."

Meeks nodded, and then he sat perfectly still, saying nothing.

Wallace glanced back at the girls, every smile becoming brighter and more false. Then he said to Meeks, "We were wondering. What is it about Christianity that interests you?"

Meeks didn't react, or even apparently notice the question.

"It seems obvious," Wallace continued. "You didn't grow up with many Christian influences. Which is fine. You can be born-again at any age, from any circumstance. Christ doesn't care when you come into His flock."

"The cross," Meeks muttered.

"Excuse me?"

"That interests me." Meeks hesitated. For a long moment, he stared at one of the smiling girls. He stared at her and let his mouth fall open, the pale tongue wandering into view and then vanishing again. "The cross, and getting nailed to it. And dying. And coming back to life again."

"That's what happened to our Savior," Wallace proclaimed.

Meeks intended to say something else. But instead, he looked down at his magazine again.

"So what are you reading?" asked the girl. Paula had bright red hair and full breasts carefully hidden behind an Econ text. "Is that for class?"

"No," Meeks allowed. "I'm just reading."

Wallace finally noticed the magazine, absorbing the head-line and one of the captions before remarking, "You know, you're wasting your time. None of that is true. Aliens and the rest of it—"

"How do you know that?" Meeks interrupted, his voice shrill and tight. "You don't think there's aliens? In this whole huge universe, you think it's only us?"

Wallace shrugged his shoulders.

"Even the closest stars are too distant to mean anything," he cautioned. "And what passes for evidence . . . these pictures and such . . . well, just because something looks strange to you and to me, it doesn't mean that extraterrestrials are the best, most reasonable answer."

A heat came into the little eyes.

Paula and the other women backed away slightly.

Unperturbed, Wallace explained, "Science is a human institution. But humans are always flawed. For almost two centuries biologists have been seeing evolution where none exists. So why should I embrace the pronouncements of a few dreamy souls?"

Meeks sucked down a deep breath, his entire body growing stiff. "Know what interests me?" he grunted.

"No," said Wallace. "What?"

Again, Meeks fingered the mysterious photograph, asking with a genuinely baffled voice, "How do you make yourself believe that crazy story?"

Then in the next instant, with a cutting logic, he added, "At least I've got pictures of my cross. See?"

"What do you mean?" Cole blurted. "Meeks is a what?"

Clara conjured up a laugh and shrugged. "An angel," she repeated. "Wallace didn't actually point and say, 'Here's an angel —a test from God—now be nice to him.' But it was pretty obvious who's on God's payroll. Everybody understood. Except for Meeks, I'm guessing."

"The two of them were actually sitting together?"

"You should have been there," she teased.

"Why were you there?" he muttered.

"It was Saturday night. My boy-toy went home for the weekend. Besides, I've still got friends in the group, okay?" Then with a nudge, Clara added, "Why don't you come join us? Pretend you're going to the zoo to study the weird animals."

"No."

"Just a joke," she promised.

He shook his head, sitting back on Clara's narrow bed. She accepted the distance with a shrug and quiet laugh. "Anything happening at the old homestead?" she asked.

"Not much," he lied. Then he thought better of it, adding, "Yeah, well. My mother found a new doctor."

Clara watched him, saying nothing.

"He's got better tools, she claims. I haven't met the man. But she made an appointment. He says he can find every Cambridge object hiding inside anybody. And in a lot of cases, he destroys them the same day."

"For a price."

"Oh, sure."

She watched Cole, and for the first time she began to appreciate how poorly she knew him. His expression was shifting constantly. He moved from anger to a hopeful grin and back again. Finally, with a visceral disgust, he admitted, "The guy's just another con artist, probably."

"Maybe. Maybe not."

"There's thousands of them, you know. If it wasn't this, they'd be selling people . . . I don't know . . . Bibles, or something . . ."

"Is your mother gullible?"

"Not really," he allowed. "But she's scared. And she feels guilty. You know, it's her fault the aliens stole me away. She should have been standing over me with a shotgun, or something."

Clara waited for inspiration, hoping the right words would occur to her. She looked across the campus—it was a nice view from the top floor of Hawthorne. But when the words didn't come, she simply suggested, "You don't have to go home again. Whenever the appointment is."

"Except Mom's driving down," he rumbled. "The doctor . . . his office is just a couple miles from here."

"Do you want to see him?"

Cole shrugged and sighed. "I really don't know."

Then he forced up a laugh, returning to easier terrain. "So tell me. How's our Mr. Meeks an angel sent from God?"

Whenever he was in public, Larson Meeks made a point of listening. In class or in the cafeteria, he would sit on the fringe of a group, waiting for them to say something interesting. In the library he would stand perfectly still behind a row of books, paying strict attention to a heartfelt conversation between friends or lovers. But the only people accepting enough to actually include him were the Christians. That was one reason to join them on Saturday night. He listened extra carefully on those occasions. Not to Wallace's sermons, which were quite long and painfully boring, and not to prayers read aloud from a two-thousand-year-old book. No, what fascinated him was what people said otherwise. What they whispered while Wallace was preaching, and what friends told one another during the quiet stretches, thinking nobody else could hear them, and how they reacted when Meeks took it upon himself to ask the very obvious questions.

"So what's an angel look like?"

"Very much like us," Wallace promised, gazing out at his audience. Then with a rare dose of humor, he added, "Their wings are kept tucked away, of course."

Everyone else broke into nervous laughter. But Meeks ignored them, his mouth pulling into a doubting smirk. "And why send His angels here?"

"To test our Christian faith," Wallace replied.

"Test it how?"

A pause. Then, "In many ways."

"And what happens if you pass the tests?"

"Your faith grows stronger," Wallace promised, smiling with a stubborn and decidedly muscular confidence. "You see, God wants His people to make themselves better. That's why he places His servants among us."

Every gaze was focused squarely on Meeks. And he noticed the stares in a dim, disinterested way. Nothing about the idea appealed to him, which is why he could so thoroughly ignore it. Of course he was no angel, and of course many in the group had doubts about what Wallace was claiming. But even the skeptical souls approached Meeks after Bible study. They would nervously ask about his life, feigning curiosity and a modicum of compassion; and with an offhand efficiency, he would mention dead parents and distant cities and a childhood that was never quite defined but always sounded as if it had been endlessly horrific.

The redhead, Paula, tried conversing with him. But it was obvious what she really wanted: Wallace. She was doing this very difficult chore to impress that soon-to-be doctor. She would smile gamely, offer a few interested words, and Meeks would stare at her chest. Then she would excuse herself, approaching Wallace with a big smile and a flirtatious attitude, making sure that he had noticed her good Christian work.

Paula had a reputation. Meeks had heard enough boys bragging about her to feel certain. But it didn't really matter. For the first weeks of school, he couldn't imagine that the busty little redhead would mean anything to him. Then one day at lunch he saw Paula eating with a blond girl. Clara. Sitting at an adjacent table, Meeks was close enough to hear them through the rumbling of louder voices and the crashing of heavy plates. Then he heard the name "Cole" mentioned, and every other sound suddenly fell away. Then Paula asked, "How many scars have you counted so far?" And he tipped his head to one side, hanging on every word.

That night Meeks arrived at the Hawthorne lounge, looking like any student ready to study among the Christians. Wallace was sitting on a long institutional sofa, decorating a Biochem text with fat yellow lines. Paula was on his right, not quite beside him but near enough to touch him, pretending to read *Moby Dick*. Meeks looked at everyone with a quick dismissive gaze and then dropped between the two of them. Wallace said, "Hello, Larson." Paula wrinkled her nose and slid up against the armrest, and quietly, with a tight little voice, she said, "Yes. Hello."

Meeks opened his spiral notebook to an empty page. Staring at the lines and white paper, he asked, "So what's he like?"

Who was Meeks talking to?

Wallace straightened his back, squared his shoulders, and with a careful tone asked, "Are you speaking to me?"

But Meeks was staring at Paula. "What's he like?"

"Who?" she sputtered.

"Cole Glock," Meeks said.

Everyone else looked up now, saying nothing.

"What's so special about Glock?" Meeks asked.

Paula laughed nervously, and shrugged, and finally muttered, "I don't know him that well."

"Oh." Meeks shook his head, dismissing the excuse. "Does he talk about it much?"

Paula blinked. Wallace was staring at her, not at Meeks. He seemed ready to judge her by how she responded to this very strange test. "What do you mean?" she asked. "Does he talk about what?"

"Being abducted."

She almost giggled. Almost shrugged.

"Is that how he gets girls in bed?" Meeks persisted. "Because the aliens took him away?"

"I didn't." She hesitated, her face coloring. "Never."

He leaned closer. "No?"

"I didn't go to bed with Cole." Then she laughed—an unhappy thin laugh that quickly died away. A weak voice asked, "Why'd you think that?"

"Because you dated him," Meeks remarked. "I heard you and his girlfriend talking. And because you're kind of a slut, sometimes."

Everyone was startled and appalled. Even Meeks noticed the

sudden chill. Looking at the others, he just laughed. "That's what I've heard. Did somebody lie to me?"

Wallace closed his text with a hard thump.

"These guys in the cafeteria were talking," Meeks explained to Paula. "You walked past and smiled. And afterward, they said you were easy. 'Money in the bank,' this one guy called you."

Paula leaped up and ran from the lounge.

Everyone was embarrassed and sorry. Wallace stared at Meeks until their eyes met. And then with a low, disapproving voice, he said, "Listen to me. Are you listening?"

"What?" Meeks grumbled.

Wallace didn't mention the insult or Paula. Instead, he told their very difficult angel, "Cole was never abducted. Never. He just pretends to have been. He uses that made-up story to manipulate people. And isn't that the most wicked, awful thing you've ever heard of?"

It should have seemed innocuous. After all, the campus was a relatively tiny world, and everyone living in the dorms ate in the same cafeteria, within narrow slots of time. Being anywhere meant being close to everybody. Why shouldn't Cole, on occasion, happen to notice Meeks walking parallel to him? Or drifting past him in the library? Or seeing him at dinner, sitting beside the Christians, those little eyes by chance staring at him for a moment or two, or ten?

For a while, Cole didn't think about being stalked. And even when it seemed as if he had a shadow, he wasn't too bothered. Indeed, he almost felt pleased. With a confident tone, he told Clara, "The guy's harmless enough. Really, it's not like he's sending me hate mail or anything."

"Or love letters either," she countered.

He shrugged off the implication. He laughed it off. He ignored it. But there was a night when he was lying awake in bed, and he heard the telltale gait of a big body moving in the hallway. Shuffling feet slid past his door, and then after a few minutes, returned again. Returned and passed again, and in that new silence, Cole rolled over and looked at the red face of his clock. It was 3:30 in the morning: that exact moment when it can't feel any later in the night or any earlier in the morning. Then it was 3:31, and the feet were approaching again, worn basketball shoes sliding along the slick, grimy floor. How many times had he walked past already? But this time was different. Lying motionless, feeling perfectly alert if not yet afraid, Cole listened to the feet move up to where they were on the far side of the hollow-cored door. Then he heard nothing. Nothing. Nothing, and he risked craning his neck to look at the bottom of the door. The gap was tall enough to shove a good-sized paperback in or out. The gap let in a ribbon of sleepless light from the hallway, and he saw the light, minus two identical splotches where legs eclipsed the bright yellowy glare.

"And he just stood there," Cole reported.

They were dressed, this time. They were sitting in Clara's room on her little bed, both dressed and neither having made any attempt to be otherwise. Clara nodded, and grimaced, and finally asked, "How long?"

"I don't know," Cole lied.

Then he admitted, "It was about eight minutes. Then I heard the prick walk away and down the stairs."

Wearing a genuine pity, she admitted, "That's spooky."

After another minute, she asked, "When did you sleep again?"

With a snorting laugh, he said, "Oh, yeah. I rolled over and went right back to sleep again. No problem."

"Did you get more sleep?"

"In Psych. A good ten-minute snooze."

She watched him, trying to weigh his worry, his despair. And then with a reasonable tone, she asked, "Did you actually see Meeks?"

"You mean, did I open the door and look at his face?"

"Because nobody's going to do anything," she warned. "If you don't actually know it was Larson Meeks—"

"Who the hell else would it be?"

"I'm just saying," she purred. "If you talk to somebody official, you're going need more than shadows under your door."

The next night Cole was trying to study at the library, fighting to make his soggy head concentrate on any safe subject. Then what felt like a feather tickled him beneath an ear, and he looked up. For a moment, he saw no one. For that instant, he could almost tell himself that his intuition was flawed and he should ignore whatever it told him. But then, from the corner of an eye, he spotted the shape moving, and he managed a glimpse of flannel passing behind the stacks, big feet dragging along as if they weighed too much to be lifted.

Cole couldn't see where Meeks went. But he heard the scream of a chair dragged across tile, and after a few minutes of distraction and building worry, he muttered, "Fuck it," and got up, walking quietly back into the same massive stacks.

Meeks had a single volume opened, nearly covering the top of

the little study desk. His back was turned to Cole. His attentions
were focused on what was before him. The stalker was now the
prey. Cole eased his way closer, momentarily entertaining ways of
scaring the bastard. Maybe he would just stare at the pasty back
of that very dirty neck, waiting for Meeks to turn around. But then
he saw the long, long scissors, and he heard the smooth cutting of
paper, and, looking over Meeks's shoulder, he watched him casually remove an entire article from an old *Physics Today*. An article
about microscopic machines, as it happened.

With a low rage, Cole said, "Don't."

Meeks wheeled around, tearing several of the remaining pages.

"You can't fucking do that," Cole barked.

His nemesis opened his mouth but said nothing, a look of pure
fear sweeping across his face.

Cole said, "Bastard," for emphasis, and then he walked away,
gathering up his own books and hurrying downstairs. With a perfect sweet pleasure, he told the head librarian what he had wit-
nessed. The librarian was appropriately horrified. With a couple
pudgy male library science majors serving as enforcers, she
marched upstairs and came down again, Meeks walking in front of
her, his head bowed, her helpers looking stern but quite grateful
that nothing ugly had happened.

Ugly required more time.

Two nights later, at three in the morning, a person or persons
unknown threw a concrete block through the library's front glass
door and carried a large gasoline can inside. The fires were set
upstairs and then down in Periodicals, but the worst of the flames
were out in five minutes. Most of the damage was done by the
sprinkler system, the water soaking thousands of volumes, leaving
them swollen and bloated and useless.

The doctor was just a doctor. Con artists and charlatans would
have glimmered with easy charm, abundant wit, and a smooth
capacity to alleviate every nebulous fear. But the man who met
with Cole and his mother was a little dour and looked as if he
was short on sleep. Summoning up all of his bedside manner, he
managed to smile—a youngish face wrapped around middle-aged
eyes, a half-muttered voice telling his newest patient, "In the seat
please. And Mrs. Glock? Would you wait out in the lobby? Thank
you."

The seat was little more than a plastic framework, just large
enough to rest upon and designed to be perfectly transparent to the

gentle breaths of x-rays. Surrounding the seat was an array of projectors and sensors and photographic plates that could be quickly twisted in any useful direction.

"How's it work?" Cole asked.

The doctor was making notes on a clipboard. With a matter-of-fact voice, he said simply, "It works quite well."

A technician adjusted the seat and a set of padded straps, and as she pulled a weblike net across his forehead, Cole looked at her, asking, "How's this thing fly?"

She was in her late twenties, maybe. Not pretty, but not unattractive either. She winked at Cole, on the sly, and as soon as the doctor retreated out of the lead-lined room, she said, "It's really a wonderful machine."

"Yeah?"

"The x-ray dose is very low, considering. The films are exceptionally sensitive. Computers play with the data, building up a very clear picture of what's inside you." Again, she winked. "You know, this machine was built to do this. When they found the first implants, there was a huge government program. Not secret, exactly. But not many people heard about it, either."

"I've read some things," Cole professed. Although as he spoke, he felt much less sure. Did he actually know about the work? Or did he just want to feel informed and involved, and his brain was playing a game with him?

As his head was immobilized, he asked, "Will you find them?"

"If they're there," she replied without hesitation.

"And pull them out?"

She was bent over in front of him, her face close as a lover's. With the smell of spearmint on her breath, she explained, "We don't have to remove anything. We just hit the target with a concentrated burst of x-rays, and it vanishes."

"Why?"

"Why what?"

"Why does the implant vanish?"

She shrugged, almost laughing. "Maybe it knows that it's trapped, so it commits suicide."

A web was pulled taut around his chin. Talking was difficult, but Cole forced himself to mutter, "How many?"

"What's that?"

"Have you found?"

"Implants?" She guessed that was what Cole was asking. With a nod and a wink, she confided, "Quite a few. A few dozen, at least."

He said nothing.

"But really," she continued, "the machine sees other things. Metal splinters from long ago. Cancers just starting out. There's talk about injecting people with new isotopes and metabolic markers, and with all of these new instruments at our disposal, we'll make the human body transparent in every way imaginable."

Cole listened, but only barely.

"Mr. Glock? Are you comfortable?"

Not particularly, but he muttered, "Yeah."

"All right. This will take about ten minutes. Whatever happens, please, sit as still as you can."

He had no choice. Lashed into place by a dozen means, he could do nothing but remain motionless as the machines whirred and changed position, humming and clattering with a desperate purposefulness. Maybe halfway through the process, he realized just how terrified he felt. For an instant, he almost believed that he was suffocating. Then he tried to decipher why he felt so awful, and something unexpected took him in its jaws and shook him hard.

Later he confided with his mother. "I won't let him," he said with a calm, sturdy voice. "I don't want the doctor to destroy them."

They were sitting in the tiny, overheated lounge, twenty minutes into what was proving to be a very long wait. Two patients sat on the opposite side of the room. They seemed more interested in his words than his mother did. Not meaning to stare, they stared nonetheless, watching the sixtyish woman set down the dog-eared copy of *Good Housekeeping*, and then with a mild, humorless voice, ask her son, "What does that mean? You won't let him destroy what?"

"My implant. Or implants."

She was appalled, but her voice tried to remain civil. "What do you mean? Why would you ever—?"

"We don't know what they are," Cole argued. "What do they actually do? What do they represent? Should we destroy them, just because they might have been given to us by aliens?"

Mother shuddered, trying to gather her thoughts.

"I mean," Cole continued. Then his voice faltered, and he had to try again. "I mean, what if they are worlds? Miniature planets where billions of sentient organisms live out their lives. Do we have the right to murder them?"

"Stop," she growled.

She picked up the magazine again, rolling it into a tight cylinder. Then she hit herself on the knee, asking, "Why am I paying for this? Do you think insurance covers these games?"

"It doesn't. I know."

Then she smacked him on the knee. "Darling," she snarled. "If I have to cut it out myself, while you're sleeping . . . don't think for a second that I won't. . . !"

But in the end, there was no decision to be made. The dour, young-faced doctor led his newest patient into his office and showed him a sampling of freshly developed images. "The Cambridge objects resemble bright little stars," he explained. Then he stepped back and let both Cole and his mother stare at tissues and bones rendered as bright and dark shadows. After a few moments of silence, he added, "I don't see any stars. Not one."

"So where'd they go?" his mother barked.

"Perhaps the earlier surgeries took them," the doctor replied. "Unless of course—"

"They were never there," Cole interrupted.

"That's another possibility, yes."

"But what if. . . ?" His mother found herself with a well-practiced paranoia, but no easy place to use it. "What if the implant's just hiding?"

"It can't be," the doctor promised.

"Are you sure?"

He couldn't feel more certain.

"Or it's changed its nature somehow." Mother couldn't drop the possibility. She had spent years and a small fortune to rid her son of a unique disease, and she couldn't stand the notion that she had wasted time and money as well as her precious fear. "The implants adapt. Maybe they're adapting to your machine."

The doctor forced himself to smile, pretending empathy.

"I'm very sorry," he told them with a flat, unsympathetic voice. "There are so many reasons why that simply isn't possible."

What Clara believed—the guiding principle that was gradually emerging in her slick, sharp mind—was that people built their own gods. But not in the same way craftsmen built a seaworthy boat, investing ample time, using only the best timber and rope and brass, every tool appropriate and held only by competent hands. No, human gods were always built in bad times. Souls adrift in some figurative ocean would gather up the available wreckage and flotsam, cobbling together a crude, artless raft full of inconsistencies and outright fabrications. Then every new believer would cling to this minimal salvation until the winds finally abated, and still they would cling tight, waiting for the next storm. Unless they lost their faith, and then they would let go and swim by themselves, paddling across the warm, deceptively blue seas.

But what if somebody built a religion in the good times? What would a genuinely seaworthy god look like, and sound like, and give back to its true believers?

She was contemplating those questions, and now and again she listened to Cole. But really, she didn't have to pay strict attention. Cole had been repeating himself for a long while. "Arrogant bastard," he said with a numbing regularity. "Does he really think that he can see everything inside me? That's crazy. I mean, I can think of ways . . . tricks . . . that would let them hide. For instance, the probes . . . the worlds . . . could split up into little pieces, then reassemble later . . . right. . . ?"

She nodded automatically. "I guess so."

"If they know what's happening outside me . . . if they watch the world at all . . . they'd have plenty of time to get ready for the doctor . . ."

Clara watched her boyfriend. Fully clothed and lying on her bed, Cole stared up at the ceiling, his expression weary and angry, but more than anything, lost. He ran his hands through his blond hair. His eyes were damp enough to glisten. His mouth opened, ready to repeat another endless complaint. But she'd had enough, and with a suddenness that took both of them by surprise, Clara said, "Except that doesn't make very much sense. Does it?"

For the first time in an hour, Cole looked at her.

"The technician told you they've been finding genuine probes," Clara pointed out. "Which implies that whatever these things are, they really can't escape from that stupid machine."

"What are you saying?"

"You were never, ever abducted."

A moment later, with a firm, unsorry voice, she added, "The x-rays didn't find anything because there's never been anything to find."

Cole's eyes dried up.

"Okay," he muttered.

"But remember? It doesn't matter to you. That's what you told me." More than her rationality was at play now. Emotion caused her voice to lift, gaining momentum. "You don't know where you were that night. All those little surgeries were unnecessary. Nobody knows what the aliens want or can do, but you're right about one thing: They probably have the technologies to easily infect every last one of us. If that's what they wanted to do."

His surprise evaporated, replaced by a tangible resentment and a sense of betrayal.

But Clara didn't let herself stop talking. "Why does it bother you so much?" she kept asking. "You claimed you didn't really believe. So why is it so important now, Cole? I don't understand. Explain that to me."

Yet her boyfriend seemed as perplexed as anyone. Sitting up in bed, he said, "I don't want to talk about it."

"You've been talking about it since our first date," she countered.

He grimaced and said, "Not true—"

"Or maybe I can explain it," she interrupted. "Your entire life is wrapped around that one night, and you don't have any choice. It's a religion. Did you know that? You were brought up to believe that superintelligent aliens took you into their mothership and gave you something wondrous, or something horrible. Whatever they gave you, it made you a special person."

Cole stared at her, his mouth clamped shut.

"Except today, you found out that you're not special. And maybe you've never been."

"Hey," he muttered.

He was such a frail boy, and not in a pleasing, sweet way. Hopelessly unaware of his own mind, he regarded her with a mixture of horror and simple rage. "Don't," he warned.

"I'm trying to help," she replied.

"Don't try."

A hard question posed itself, and in an instant, with an astonishing ease, Clara answered the question to her own satisfaction. Then with a careful distance and a very firm voice, she told him, "You should go home. Now."

And when Cole stood, she added, "And we shouldn't see each other anymore. Sorry, but I think we're pretty much done."

A Canadian front had pushed through during the day. Cole wasn't wearing a heavy coat, so after slipping out of Hawthorne Hall, he walked quickly, hands tucked in his pockets, his breath rising toward a clear star-rich sky. The only other person was a youngish man riding a mountain bike. Pumping the pedals as he approached Cole on the sidewalk, the rider gave him a hard glare before heading toward the girl's dormitory. Cole saw him once again, on the far side of campus, just as he was entering the back-door of his dorm. In the last week, the cyclist had become a local fixture: a sentinel positioned by the local police; a plainclothes officer who couldn't have been more obvious if his stocking cap caught fire.

Eventually it was midnight, and then it was one o'clock in the morning. By two, Cole had given up all hope of sleep. By three, lying in the dark, he had gotten himself into a state of mind where he felt almost relieved to hear the big feet sliding down the hall-way. For whatever reason, Meeks didn't walk past his room half a dozen times. Tonight he stopped in front of Cole's room on his first pass, those telltale blotches of shadow showing beneath the door. Another three minutes passed. Cole watched the clock and listened to the quick wet sound of breathing. When he finally sat up, he moved slowly, working not to make any noticeable sound. On bare feet, he climbed down to the sofa and the floor, and for another minute or two he studied his surroundings, finally pulling a half-melted candle from an empty wine bottle and, turning the bottle in his hand, holding it by the narrow, cool neck as he crept toward the door.

Cole took one deep breath, and a quick shallow breath.

In a single motion, he flung open the door and lifted his weapon. The door crashed against the wall, and a brilliant light flooded over him, and swimming backward through the glare was Meeks—a big clumsy figure too startled to do anything but retreat, too clumsy to keep his feet under him, the old shoes leaving the slick industrial Formica, his ass hitting with a hard jarring thud.

Then, silence.

Cole seriously entertained the image of breaking the bottle against the door jam and chasing Meeks out of the building with it. But when Cole saw the panicked face, watched the pale thick hands lift, fending off a thousand imaginary blows, he discovered that he didn't want to chase Meeks at all. With his free hand, Cole turned on his room's ceiling light, and he said, "Get in here. I want to talk to you."

The two men remained standing. One rocked, shifting his weight from leg to leg. The other stood with his back to the window, one hand still clinging to the bottle. After a minute, Cole said, "I want to know." He watched his visitor with a mixture of fascination and scorn. "What's your story?"

Meeks licked his lips, twice. Gasped and licked them a third time.

"And why do you fucking care about me?"

"I know," Meeks said. The long arms lifted, wrapping around his own waist. "How it feels."

"Yeah?"

"Inside you. Moving, being part of you . . . little machines like worlds . . . I know all about it . . ."

"You got abducted, did you?"

But Meeks astonished him. With a defiant, almost offended shake of the head, he said, "No. Never, no."

"Fine. So how do you know?"

Silence.

"I don't believe you," Cole warned. "If you aren't going to tell me—"

"It's a secret," Meeks whispered, a profound fear making his eyes burn. "A project . . . government project . . . very secret . . ."

"What project?"

"Harvesting," Meeks said. "From people like you . . . abducted people . . . they harvest the alien machines, probes, worlds . . . with liquid helium and special tools, they collect them and store them, and inject them . . ."

"What?" Cole sputtered.

"Into somebody else." Meeks looked up, as if startled to find that he wasn't alone. "Implants. To study their effects. Hundreds and thousands of harvested machines are put inside special people—"

"Like you?"

Meeks dropped his gaze again. It was safer to talk to the rug on the floor between them. He could trust his voice better when he didn't have another face distracting him. "They paid me," he muttered. "A fortune, they paid. And they studied me. My reactions. How I feel them inside me. Thousands and thousands of them swimming through me. Reading my thoughts. Giving me new thoughts. Making me see things, do things . . . you know? With you, do they. . . ?"

"What? Make me do things?"

"I have so many of them," Meeks complained. "The doctors tried pulling them out again, but they couldn't find all of them. Cut, cut, cut! And cut again. But they couldn't get them—not enough—and they finally let me go."

"Our government did that?"

"It's a secret special project," Meeks said with a shake of the head. "But I'm gone from it now."

Cole stared at the pitiful figure. He studied the tight long-sleeved flannel shirt and the odd gyrations that only grew worse as they stood there. It was nearly 3:40 in the morning, and the only sound was the rambling urgent voice that spoke with authority about white rooms and cloaked doctors and machines that dwarfed the x-ray contraption that Cole had seen today. He listened to an elaborate and horrible story about possession and cruelty, long incisions that were opened again and again, allowing the faceless doctors to hunt their tiny quarry; and there were little moments when Meeks would look up at him, something less than a smile breaking across the soft, cold face, and someone's voice would say out of that mouth, "I don't know who's talking. Me, or the worlds inside me."

Gradually, Cole heard the sound of distant sirens bellowing.

"You know how I feel," Meeks said with a desperate hope. "Don't you know what it's like?"

The sirens came from a fleet of fire trucks. With red lights spinning, they drove past Cole's dormitory, each braking with a dragon's hiss and turning onto the campus's main road. Then with a massive urgency, they began accelerating again, racing off toward the Ethel P. Hawthorne Dormitory.

Oblivious to the wailing sirens, Meeks said again, "You've got to know how it feels."

With a grim delight, Cole replied, "Not even a little bit."

Gasoline bombs had been hidden in the janitor's closets at the bottom of both stairwells. Egg timers and a crude detonator gave the arsonist time to escape. The obvious goal was to trap the residents in the upper floors. But a senior living on the garden level heard the first thunderous *woosh* of flame, and, stepping out into the smoke and vapors, she managed to pull the fire alarm and then drain two fire extinguishers, stunting the blaze before it could run wild. The other bomb failed to ignite for another four minutes. The dormitory was quickly engulfed in filthy black flames, but there was enough time for almost every student to escape to the surrounding grounds, in the bitter cold—the half-dressed residents of Hawthorne joined by hundreds of gawking males.

Cole was one of the last to arrive. He listened to Meeks until someone pounded on his door, shouting, "Hawthorne's burning down!" Then he threw on a coat and forced Meeks into the hallway, leaving him there, hurrying downstairs, though not appreciating the magnitude of the blaze until he was outside, watching a whirlwind of light and smoke, arching water, and diffused screams.

Into that mayhem, he screamed, "Clara!"

Girls wearing next to nothing huddled together. Faces offered themselves and were found lacking. He pushed between groups, shouting in horror. Someone talked about gasoline, and someone else said, "Arson." Then he turned and worked his way back through the crowd again. As part of the roof collapsed, he felt the heat play against his face, and he kept screaming the name, and a familiar face emerged from the confusion to tell him, "She didn't, Cole. I can't find her, either. Clara. I can't—"

What? Who was talking?

The face stared up at him. It felt like an age before he finally recognized the features through a patina of black soot and his own runaway panic. Paula. She had a hand on his arm. Paula was crying, and screaming, hysterical in her own right. "Clara was going down the hall, trying to wake everybody up . . . I ran . . . she told me to hurry, so I ran down the stairs . . . just in time, I got out . . ."

Another long portion of the roof collapsed, sparks raining down as someone armed with a loudspeaker told the crowds to step back, to stay clear.

Days later and for the rest of his life, what horrified and sickened Cole was the reason why he did what he did next. The fire was a tragedy, yes, and Clara was dead, and some little lump of clarity told him who was responsible for this nightmare. But when he spotted Meeks standing at the back of the crowd, Cole didn't react for any of those reasons. Instead, he thought about nothing but that here was a man who claimed to possess hundreds of the sorry little things upon which Cole had based his entire life.

Meeks stood with his face pointed in the direction of the fire but his attention was plainly divided. Whatever he was thinking, it preoccupied him so much that he couldn't react when he saw Cole running toward him. As if puzzled, his eyes blinked and stared at the oncoming figure. Too late, he took a grudging step backward. Then came the impact, and for the second time that night, he was knocked on his ass. But the ground was softer than tile. He started to get up, still halfway indifferent to everything around him, and that's when Cole kicked him, just behind the tip of his chin.

The blow put him on his back.

Cole grabbed him and tried to lift him up, screaming. Cursing. Forcing him back to his feet again, and aiming at the doughy face with his clenched right fist. But Meeks found just enough balance to pull away, and fear gave him enough speed to carry him almost a hundred yards.

Cole tackled him from behind. Tackled him and kicked him, then shoved him under the nearest street lamp. He fully intended to kill the man. He used his fists until his right hand was broken in two places, then he lifted the ugly face by its hair and drove it into the concrete walk, and then a hand grabbed at him, and he had to waste precious time slapping the hand away. Again he kicked, aiming for the groin, and then various hands and arms pulled him off Meeks, the stern voice of the bike-riding police officer telling him, "Stop. Now. Just stop."

Bloodied but still distracted, Meeks managed to sit up. His shirt was torn, every button scattered across the pavement and grass. A chest paler even than his face shone in the lamplight. And on that chest, and the belly below, and everywhere else on that long, clumsy body, was not one mark. Not even the tiniest scar. There was no trace that anyone had ever cut into him, because the simple, boring truth was that nobody ever had.

The arsonist was arrested a few minutes later. One of the coeds had seen him emerging from a closet a few minutes before the fires began. She not only pointed him out of the crowd, she walked up to him and gave him a hard shove. Later, armed with a search warrant and worthwhile caution, the authorities opened the freshman's basement room, discovering a Dear John note from a female library science major, plus an assortment of half-made detonators and at least ten cans of high-octane gasoline.

Meeks's former roommate was charged and tried, and he served most of a fifteen-year sentence before being released on parole.

The fire was spectacular, and the national news played video clips, but nobody actually died in the disaster. Suffering from smoke inhalation, Clara had been ushered to a waiting ambulance where she sucked at the oxygen while various rescue workers treated her rightfully as a hero. She dated one of those young firemen for a few fun months. Eventually she graduated with honors, and after several short-lived careers, she ended up in Nevada, devising software for the suddenly burgeoning microchine industry.

Arrested for assault, Cole was booked and then bailed out of jail by his thoroughly embarrassed mother. But the case never reached trial. A misdemeanor plea was accepted, in part because witnesses attested to a difficult relationship between the assailant and his victim. But mostly because Meeks's guilt-ridden parents had approached the police, explaining what they thought was best for their own son.

A few days after the fire, there was a surprise knock at Cole's door.

By then, he had a roommate. With an entire dormitory lost, there'd been wide-scale reshufflings of room assignments. But it was early Saturday evening, and the little sophomore was chasing some rumored party. Alone, Cole rose and opened his door with his good left hand, discovering an elderly couple looking in at him with sorrowful eyes. Their son stood in the hallway behind them. Meeks was bruised but not as badly as Cole had feared. "We just wanted to say that we're very sorry," the mother reported. She was short and fat and looked about a thousand years old. "If we had known how he was acting, that he wasn't taking his medicine . . . well, we wouldn't have let him come here. You can be sure of that, Mr. Glock."

Nothing about Meeks resembled the rumors. He had parents who loved him. He was from Gary, Indiana. And he was already in his early twenties. Mental institutions and other distractions had slowed his progress through school. But with the newest medications and his adult status, this leap from home had seemed inevitable.

Quietly, with his own keen embarrassment, Cole told him, "No, *I'm* sorry."

The battered face blinked slowly, and from beneath a stew of chemicals and pure exhaustion, a voice said, "Okay. Not bad. Been worse."

"Get well," Cole urged.

"No," the fat, little mother said emphatically. "For now, we're going to set our sights lower."

They left.

Alone again, Cole felt nervous, and sad. Worthless, and worse than worthless. After too much silence, he picked himself up and went outside, and with a sureness that couldn't help but surprise, he strode into the Bark-Tipple Student Center. Terry Wallace was just finishing his sermon. Nobody was paying close attention to what he was saying, but he seemed perfectly pleased with his performance. Then Cole stepped into the lounge, and, to a face, everyone was startled. Startled, but then a wary pleasure began to emerge, and smiles, and some of the people relaxed as Cole settled on a chair next to Paula.

"I'm just going to sit and listen," he told them.

"We're thrilled to have you," said a somewhat dubious spiritual leader. "If you want, ask questions of us. Please."

Cole wished he had a question at the ready.

Instead, all he managed was a quick shrug of his shoulders, a little smile in Paula's direction, and then he sat back, beginning to work on a simple, durable faith that would carry him at least through this one night.

One Last Game

Saturday

PATIENCE WAS ONE OF MOM'S WORDS.
Tolerance and *cooperation* were two more fat favorites.

Of course she didn't say those words by their lonesome. It was more like, "Be patient with people. Be tolerant of people. Cooperate, even when it hurts." Then after a big pause, she'd say, "No, you need to cooperate particularly when it hurts. Promise me that. Please, would you, Neil?"

He pretended not to be listening.

Then she looked back at him. She made certain that he saw her stern face, and for the trillionth time, she said, "I know you'll be the oldest one there. But that's just the way it is, and you're going to have to make the best of things."

The best of things—that was pure, undiluted Mom.

Neil treated her to a little nod and shrugged as if his shoulders ached. Then just to shut her up, he said, "All right. I'll try."

"Do more than try," she countered.

Which was a pretty stupid way to talk, if you thought about it. What could any person do besides try? Yet Neil made himself nod as if agreeing, and that bought him another twenty minutes of being unpestered. He was sitting in the back of the van, alone with their luggage and groceries and the old croquet set, listening to his music while playing a few rounds of Nuke the Fools. It helped him concentrate, the game did. He barely noticed the ugly-ass country sliding past their shit-for-guts van. But then he stopped playing, giving his eyes a rest, and he found himself staring out over the flat fields of corn and things that weren't corn, and he was thinking about the lake again. Neil didn't quite believe in this lake. Maybe his folks believed that it existed. And maybe the Hawthornes honestly thought they owned a cabin beside the water. And sure, people had been talking about Okoboji since Neil could remember, telling stories about the boating and the swimming and shit like that. A few friends even came home with bad sunburns. But that didn't prove anything. This semi-famous lake was just a little drop of blue in their Rand McNally, and it was so many words spoken by others, and Neil was fourteen years old—a huge and important and extremely wise age—and he didn't believe in anything just because everyone said that it had to be true.

Dad was driving; Mom was using their Rand McNally to navigate. She seemed to be telling him where to turn next, and Dad said something, pointing at the dash, and Mom did a good job of looking out the window, pretending not to notice. Their van was a genuine pile of crap. Red lights came on every time they took it out on the road. Usually the lights didn't mean anything, and they got home fine. But this was a long-haul trip, and Neil could taste the worry in the air. And the worry got worse when they pulled off the interstate, nothing but little two-lane state highways between them and this mythical lake.

They stopped in some little-ass town. "For lunch," Dad claimed. But mostly it was to give the engine a chance to breathe.

They had burgers at Hardees, then, while they were walking back to the crap-van, Mom said, "Why don't you sit in the middle seat? Would you do that for me?"

"Why?" Neil asked.

Mom didn't have a good excuse. So instead, she told the truth. Looking straight at him, she said, "It doesn't look right. Us up in front and you way in the back."

It looked just fine to Neil.

But he moved his gear to the middle seat and settled behind Dad as the old man wrestled with the van, trying to get it running again. *Grind-grind-grind.* Pause. Then another *grind,* followed by the sputtering roar of an overheated, under-oiled, and basically spent engine. Then Neil had his music going nice and loud, and he was nuking cities filled with nothing but fools . . . right up until Mom yanked off his headphones and covered the game screen with an angry hand, repeating what she's said only a million times before.

"Be patient with these kids. I know you'll be the oldest, so I expect you to take some responsibility for the others."

Neil looked out at the ugly-ass fields.

"What did I just say?" Mom asked.

"That I'm a child," he grumbled.

She could have said anything. But instead of talking, she decided to look sad and frustrated, throwing that sad look toward Dad. And maybe the old man felt her eyes. Whatever, he gave a half-glance over his shoulder, telling Neil, "Yeah, that's what you are. A child."

Then he looked forward again, eyes jumping from the temperature gauge to the oil-pressure gauge and back again. And talking to someone—Neil or Mom, or maybe to himself—he said, "But you're not the oldest kid. Not in this bunch, you're not."

The game group was five couples. The Hawthornes. The Shepherds. The Millers. The Jensens. And Neil's folks. Most everyone had graduated together from the same high school, and if you listened to them, you'd think that it was the best time of their lives. Neil couldn't count how many times he'd heard those same stupid stories about the same long-ago people. It was as if everything had happened just yesterday. Not twenty years ago, or whatever it was. Mom openly claimed that she'd loved her school days, and she missed them. But Neil had noticed how all these happy schoolmates went to the same junior high too, yet nobody seemed to talk about those days—a fact that proved what Neil could sense for himself. That junior high sucked, and nobody, even if they had the power, would ever make themselves fourteen again.

Dad wasn't like those other adults. He came from the far end of the state, from entirely different circumstances. He was a Marine for a couple stints, and he met Mom when he finally got to college. A few years later, they were married and living half a mile from the house where Mom grew up, and they began hanging out with her old school buddies. That's how the game group got rolling. Once a month, everyone would show up at someone's house or apartment, and they'd pick a game that everybody could play together. Back then, only Neil's folks were married. A face or two changed during those earliest days. But eventually everybody settled down and got married, and those were the people that Neil knew today. Except for a few teachers, Neil knew them better than any other adults. Which wasn't to say he knew them all that well, or that he felt warm and gushy toward them.

Neil was the first kid born in the group, and, for a little while, he was important. There was a bunch of old videos that his folks brought out whenever he needed to be embarrassed. They showed him as a toddler performing tricks for a room full of laughing, drunken adults. Walking was a trick back then, and he was the center of the universe. But then he suddenly got to be five years old, and the Hawthornes and Shepherds had their first babies on the same day. After that, everyone was having kids. Triplets, in the Jensens' case. Everyone had their own, and Neil was forgotten, and today there were eleven kids, counting Neil, with him being the only only-child in the bunch.

That wasn't the plan. He'd heard it a billion times from Mom, and maybe twice from Dad. Neil was an accident. "A nice accident," Mom would always add. "A lovely one." But definitely, he was a big surprise.

There was supposed to have been a baby sister or brother. That was the plan when they moved into their current house. Money had been saved, and Dad was doing well enough at work, and they were trying. "Trying." It was the word they'd offer to the game group, halfway laughing but smiling in a serious way. Sometimes, Neil could hear them trying. Once, after the group had gone home, his folks were too drunk or just assumed that he was sleeping, leaving their bedroom door open and trying their damnedest. But judging by the noises, someone was too drunk, and things weren't working as they should. Which made for a pretty strange set of sounds to be hearing when you're ten years old, lying in the dark and unable to sleep.

There was a bedroom next to his folks' room just waiting for the baby. But Mom was having troubles. That was one bit of news Neil had to pick up without being told. Mom had gained weight when she had him, and that was a problem. Maybe. So she took up this brutal diet and started to exercise. Then her doctor told her to stop running, because that didn't help either. And then it wasn't a matter of what she weighed or how much she rode the stationary bike. It was something about Mom's plumbing, and that's when things got real serious. There were trips to special doctors and weird whispering about eggs and wriggly sperm and tricks done in someone's fancy kitchen. And there were the bills that came in thick white envelopes that Dad would open as if expecting to find bombs.

Finally, there came a day when nobody mentioned baby sisters and brothers. Something big and final had been decided. The next thing Neil knew, his father was punching out the wall of the nursery, joining it with the master bedroom. Dad was doing the work by himself because, as he put it with a grim satisfaction, "I don't know what I'm doing, so I can do it cheap."

Everything about their lives was cheap these days. It was because of the doctor bills and because Dad got passed over at work, two or three times at last count, and because Mom had decided to quit her office job, thinking that she'd make more money and have more fun if she worked at a desk in their big, damp basement.

Sometimes his folks were nothing but fools. They were a burden for Neil, and an embarrassment. It was bad enough they had trouble making house payments, while at the same time the rest of their gang had trouble spending all of their money. Every game night, someone had to boast about what they were buying or building or making in the stock market. Nobody was rich-rich. But some of those people could see real wealth from where they were standing, while Neil's parents were fighting just to keep their old friends in sight.

After every party, there was the complaining.

There was the wishing.

There was Mom saying, "I'm glad Matt's doing well, but why does Becky have to keep bringing up his promotion."

Then Dad would say, "The Shepherds are going to France again. Did you hear?"

"And the Millers are heading for Tahiti," Mom would growl. "For two long weeks after Christmas, Sarah told me."

Which made Dad wince and feel sad about himself. He was a plain man with a narrow mouth and sorry eyes, and Mom was pretty but fat again, fatter than ever, and when she was feeling sad, her eyes got big and bright, and her wide mouth clamped down until there was nothing but an angry little line. They fed off each other, which couldn't be good. It was something that Neil was beginning to see for himself. And that was why he tried to butt in, just one time, clearing his throat in a big way and telling them with his best reasonable voice, "I know what you should do. Stop going to the damned game nights, if they're so awful."

It was a smart suggestion. It was smart when he said it, and it was still smart today.

But his folks hit him with hard, hurt looks, and Mom told him, "Don't be absurd. These are our friends."

More her friends than Dad's. But Neil didn't say the obvious.

"We just have to blow off steam every now and then," Mom told him. Or maybe she was talking to herself. "It's okay, in private," she added. In public, of course, everyone would have to be tolerant, and patient, and cooperate with the windbags.

Yeah, Neil knew the speech.

Mom looked at Dad, telling him something with her eyes.

Then Dad cleared his throat, agreeing with Mom. "We've invested a lot of years with this group, and they're our friends." Then after a little pause, he added, "And I'm not going to be the first one to drop out."

Which was a pretty stupid reason to do anything, Neil knew. But he didn't say it, or anything. Sometimes you can try all you want, but people just won't listen to the things that are true.

There was a real lake, as it turned out. Rolling corn fields gave way to a few wind-beaten trees and a busy little town filled with summer traffic, plus little prairie ponds set beside the highway, and coming up over the crest of a sudden hill, Neil caught a glimpse of bluish-green water surrounded by an army of cabins and houses. The Hawthornes had just built their cabin, and the group had been invited up for the weekend. That word—"cabin"—brought to mind things like outdoor johns and beaver pelts nailed to pine walls. But Neil remained skeptical, and it was smart of him. Following the directions on the printed invitation, Dad pulled into a long driveway of clean new concrete. A big swing set and sandpile were set in the newly sodded lawn. Two minivans and someone's fat-ass Expedition were parked where the driveway widened. There was a two-car garage, and sprouting off the back of the garage was a long building that would have looked like a house anywhere else in the world. And a big house, at that. Just how big wasn't apparent from the driveway. They had to climb out and take the long walk up a fancy flagstone path to the first door. The doorbell sounded like real bells. One of the kids opened the door. Neil remembered the face but not the warpaint or the plastic sword.

"What's the password?" the kid barked.

"Hello, Collin," said Mom, her and Dad stepping past the kid.

"What's the password?" he asked Neil, poking him in the belly with the point of the sword.

"I'll let you live," Neil rumbled. "How's that?"

Collin swallowed those words and shrank down a little bit. But then he smiled and lifted his sword, an important voice saying, "You can pass."

The house went on and on. There was a hallway and stairs leading up and a kitchen and some kind of playroom on the ground floor, and, after that, a dining room and living room that were visible from a distance. The living room was more windows than walls, and the early afternoon sun was making the air conditioning work. "If this is a cabin," Neil thought out loud, "then our house is a damned shack."

"Enough," barked Dad.

But the old man was thinking the same thing.

"Where's everyone?" asked Mom.

Collin was following them. "In the front yard," he reported.

Didn't they come from the front yard? Apparently not. The door leading outside had been left open, which had to piss the air conditioning off. Neil could hear the machine running. He was following his folks out across a narrow green lawn, climbing a last little rise before the world fell away. A smaller second building was perched on the steep slope, zigzagging stairs leading to it and then past, reaching a wooden dock that stretched out into the water. Kids were running on the dock and bobbing in the greenish water, and they were shouting. A girl's voice was shouting, "Help, I'm drowning. Help!"

Nobody seemed to notice. She was just making noise apparently. But even if it was noise, Neil wished that she'd shut up.

A pontoon boat was tied against the dock, and a little sailboat and about a thousand inflated doughnuts and styrofoam kickboards were scattered across the dock and on the water and taking breathers on the muddy sand of the beach. A square platform was moored farther out on the lake. Two grown men were on top of it, wrestling. They looked silly in those long swimsuits. They were a little fat, and pink, and very slow. It was Mr. Hawthorne and Mr. Miller. A couple million bucks were pushing hard at each other, and, after a moment, they collapsed from exhaustion, laughing and flopping down on their backs.

Most of the kids were in the water. They wore life jackets. Even Claudia Hawthorne wore a big orange jacket, splashing in the shallowest water, shouting, "Help me!" at the top of her lungs.

The adults were sitting at the end of the dock, waving hard at the newcomers. Mom and Dad practically broke into a run, needing to get to them. To say their hellos and show off their smiles. Everything was very social and very loud, and Neil wanted to be anywhere else. He was thinking about his games in the van, thinking that maybe he could take them and vanish inside that big house. But when he turned to look back up the stairs, he noticed Mrs. Miller swimming hard from somewhere up the beach. It was a long way to the next dock, but he had the impression that she had come that far. She did a mean freestyle, steady and strong and lifting her head high every now and then, checking on her position. When she reached the dock, she stood on the lake bottom and wiped her face a couple times. Squinting, she said, "Neil?" with a friendly voice.

He said, "Hi."

Then she grabbed a little ladder and started to climb out, tired arms lifting her only so far before she had to pause, her feet feeling for the lowest rung. The warm green water was sliding off her swimsuit and off her body. It was a one-piece suit. Mostly, it was solid and thick, and nothing showed. Except that it wasn't meant for real swimming, and when she finished her climb, she happened to bend forward, the soaked fabric pulled down by its own weight, letting her tits halfway pour out into the sunshine. They were big and soft-looking and white as could be, and Neil couldn't do anything but stand there, staring hard, thinking that there was something dangerous in this. In this staring. But he could practically see Mrs. Miller's nipples, and there wasn't anything else in the world.

A few seconds later, he was asking Dad for the car keys.

"Leave your games alone," Mom growled at him.

But with perfect honesty Neil could tell her, "No, I'm going to get my suit and change. I want to go for a swim."

To his folks, that sounded like welcome news.

"If you can, bring in some of our luggage—" Dad started.

"Maybe," was the best that Neil could promise. Mrs. Miller was bending over again, toweling herself dry, and it was all that he could to keep his eyes in his skull.

In that little while it took Neil to put on his suit and run back to the dock, everything had changed. Most of the adults had moved to the pontoon boat, and the outboard was growling, making the air stink. Still in street clothes, his folks were flanking Mrs. Miller, as if keeping her safe, and Mr. Hawthorne gave Neil a big wave, asking, "What do you want? A trip around the lake, or stay here and help kid-sit?"

Dad said something too soft to be heard.

"I'll come along," Neil volunteered.

Which gave the adults an excuse for a good little laugh.

After two minutes of chugging across the open water, Neil was wishing that he'd stayed behind. Everyone was talking, and the only subject was the cabins. Who owned what? Which were the prettiest? The fanciest? The best to buy? Neil ended up watching the water and the other boats, and he gave Mrs. Miller a good glance when he didn't think anyone would notice. But she was wearing a shirt now, and there was nothing to see but her strong smooth legs—except once when she moved on the padded seat, a few curly dark hairs sneaking out through the elastic of her suit, hinting at everything that was hidden.

The lake was filled with fast boats pulling water skiers and flocks of roaring, graceful jet skis. The big pontoon boat plodded its way through that delicious mayhem. People had to slow or steer wide of them, and it was embarrassing. Out of simple frustration, Neil asked Mrs. Hawthorne, "Why don't you have any jet skis?"

"We'll get some toys like that," she replied. "When Claudia and Collin are your age, and ready."

Jet skis weren't toys; they were serious, important machines. But Neil didn't bother correcting the woman. Instead, he sat quietly and let his mind wander along with his eyes. Time grew slow and heavy as their boat made its circuit of the lake. There was a novelty with the sun on the water and the occasional tickle of spray against his upwind cheek, but the fun wore down after a while. In some ways, it was neat to sit among happy adults, listening to their quick patter, wondering at what point in his life he would find such a confident, almost brazen voice. But by mid-voyage, he was completely bored and more than a little uncomfortable. Mrs. Miller had thrown a towel over her legs, protecting them from the sun. Mr. Hawthorne was letting the other men take the wheel, but nobody thought to offer that responsibility to the boy. Neil moved back beside the rumbling motor, letting himself broil in the sun, ignoring his mother when she said, "You're going to burn." He wouldn't. Not this late in the summer, he wouldn't. Then with the adults huddling under the canopy, Neil was free to stare at the water and think about anything, including how much he wanted to be anywhere but here.

Finally Mr. Hawthorne took back the wheel and pulled up next to his dock. But Neil wasn't happy here, either. The triplets were screaming on the beach. Claudia was still shouting, "I'm drowning. Help me, help me." Collin and the two Shepherd boys were running on the hard planks, beating each other with Roman swords and styrofoam noodles. It would be a fun game, for about two seconds. Neil resisted the temptation. Mrs. Jensen was sitting nearby, pretending to be a lifeguard when she wasn't reading her fat novel.

When Claudia yelled for help again, the woman looked up. But it was Neil that she was watching. "How was your trip?" she asked, showing a sly little smile.

Mrs. Jensen wasn't as pretty as Mrs. Miller. Or as built. But Neil had always liked talking to the woman.

"Did you have fun?" she pressed.

He said, "Yes," because that seemed like the polite thing to say.

Mrs. Jensen's sunglasses had slipped down her whitened nose. She pushed them back up, and her smile changed, and shaking her head, she said, "Really? I'd have a hard time buying that."

Despite his doubts, the rest of the afternoon had its fun. Neil began by swimming out to the floating platform and back again, then diving into the weedy depths with a leaky mask strapped to his face. When those adventures got old, there were chicken fights in the bath-warm shallows. Neil was too long and lanky to ride anyone. Not that he wanted to ride, of course. But he didn't weigh much more than a hundred pounds, and some of these kids were real chunks. Fat or solid, they were hard to lift, and moving with them on his shoulders was about the toughest work he'd ever done. It was the little kids who made the best partners. Like the Jensen triplets. They were wiry and strong for five-year-olds. Barbie Jensen would wrap her legs around Neil's neck and shoulders, and an adult man carrying some beefy kid would charge and knock the girl backward. But she'd pop right up again. And if they got behind the man while he was fighting someone else, they could knock him off his feet, and that's how you sometimes won this very simple game.

Between rounds, Claudia swam up to him. She was turning ten in another month, and her parents had already bought her a pony as a birthday gift. She explained all of this in a breathless rush, floating high in the water because she was fat and because of her big, orange life jacket. Then she said, "Let's be partners. Okay?"

She had to be as heavy as Neil. That's why he asked, "If I say yes, what'll you give me?"

Not missing a beat, Claudia said, "You can ride my pony."

"Oh, wow," he said sarcastically. "Gosh, jeez."

Claudia heard what she wanted to hear. She assumed they had a deal, and when Neil turned to leave, she grabbed hold of his head and flung her thick legs over his shoulders. Neil was trapped, at least for the moment. He sank into the warm water, letting the girl scramble into position above him. Then he rose up to where he was holding most of her weight and too much of his own. He sagged and moaned under the waves, then lifted his mouth high enough to take a pained gulp of air, moving them into deeper water to let himself stand taller, bracing for the first assault.

Neil's plan was to lose. Someone would give them a little shove, and he would pitch to one side as if shot, dive deep, and slip free of the fat girl.

But their opponents were Hannah Miller riding high on her mother's strong shoulders. Mrs. Miller was in shallower water, her suit filling with water as she lifted her eight-year-old into the air, those big breasts threatening to spill free. Then she adjusted her straps and started her charge, laughing as she pushed her way through the lake. Neil watched how the water lifted and broke over the pale smooth flesh, and he stared as the breasts dove beneath the surface, bearing down on him. Then something obvious occurred to him, and he grunted to Claudia, "Hold on. Tight!"

It was a short, forever sort of battle. The four of them collided along with their foam and shouts, and the high arms were grasping while the lower arms held tight to the clinging legs. Neil and Claudia had momentum, and Mrs. Miller was laughing too hard to fight back. For an instant, it looked as if she might lose. Claudia gave Hannah a yank, and their opponents started to fall. But the fat girl didn't have a killer instinct. She let them recover, which was fine with Neil. Then everyone was close and pushing hard, and Neil felt a small strong hand against his ribs, then tugging at Claudia's foot. It was a woman's hand. It was touching him, pretty much. So Neil reached out and yanked at Hannah's foot, and his quick fingers brushed against one of Mrs. Miller's breasts—her left breast—the wet fabric barely obscuring the living swell of flesh that seemed to Neil, for that wondrous instant, to be the genuine center of the universe.

Then Claudia confused him for her six-hundred-pound pony. She threw her weight to one side, their center of gravity suddenly outside Neil's body, and he was falling sideways, his bare feet dancing across the muddy sand of the lake floor. He wanted to remain standing. He desperately wanted a second chance to touch the breast. Another quick feel; that would be perfect. But the fat girl kept fighting him, twisting her legs and hips, and Neil was underwater and sinking fast when a pain attached itself to his badly twisted neck, causing him to scream and drop deeper, shoving at the girl's fat ass in order to free himself, at last.

Neil's neck had broken.

That was his first horrific impression. But then he realized that he could move his limbs and even swim, buoyed up by the water and a white-hot misery. He surfaced weakly and made no sound for a moment or two. Where was Mrs. Miller? Nowhere close, he realized. She and her daughter had wandered off, looking for fresh victims. Meanwhile Claudia splashed behind him, telling the world, "I'm drowning, help!" She screamed, "Neil! Look at me!" So he turned, his neck burning somewhere near its mangled base. Then she giggled and said, "Save me, Neil! Save me!"

It was easy to say those next words.

"You're as big as a fucking pony!" Neil snapped.

For the first time today, Claudia fell silent.

"You broke my neck, you goddamn horse—!"

His belongings were in the house, set in a heap in the room where his parents were planning to spend the night. The unair-conditioned boathouse was reserved for the children and whichever parents drew the long straw. But for now, Neil could use his parents' bed. He was under strict orders to sleep and also to keep a big ice pack pressed against his aching neck, which was a ridiculous pair of assignments. Between the pain and the cold, sleep was impossible. So what Neil did instead was play a few rounds of Time's Arrow, pretending that he was Agent Nano searching through Roman times, trying to stop Count Kliss and his minions before they forever altered history.

"How are you feeling, dear?"

He froze the game and folded up the screen. Without moving his head, Neil told his mother, "The same."

The pack was more water than ice now. Mom took it from under him and sat on the edge of the bed, starting to rub his neck and then thinking better of it. She bit her lower lip for a moment, then said, "You know, she has a crush on you."

A sudden impossible hope pounced on him.

But Mom had to ruin everything, saying, "Claudia practically adores you."

"Oh," Neil whispered. "Her."

"She's awfully sorry for this. I don't think she's stopped crying yet." Mom was telling him this for a reason, but she wouldn't just come out and say it. She didn't know what Neil had said to the fat girl, or she was pretending not to know. Either way, she decided to change the subject, smiling when she said, "Dinner's almost ready. If you want, come down and eat with the rest of us."

His neck ached, but Neil was famished, too.

"Laura says it's just a muscle strain."

Laura Shepherd was a dermatologist, which made her opinions a little suspect.

"Are you coming?" Mom pressed.

Neil unfolded the screen again, but only to clear the game. He wasn't doing that well anyway. Obviously, what he needed was food.

Dinner was loud and busy and extraordinarily boring. Mr. Shepherd had cooked spaghetti in big pots, and it came out clumped together and raw in the middle. Yet the adults had to tell each other how delicious everything was. Neil ate with them in the big living room. The kids and Dr. Shepherd used the dining room. Spills would be less of a problem there, and there were spills. The new carpet was stained at least twice before the kids were banished outside with popsicles. Plastic plates and empty bottles of wine were thrown into bulging trash sacks. More wine was opened, plus some tall cans of beer. Then the kids were brought back inside and stuffed into the playroom, along with maybe twenty million toys, six of which being interesting enough to play with.

There were fights over those six good toys.

If Neil was healthy, he would have helped referee. But he wasn't well. He sat in the living room with his neck ridiculously straight, making a show of his misery. It was Dad, of all people, who vanished into that mayhem; and that left Neil in the equally unwelcome position of taking Dad's place in the evening's first game.

He had never played charades before and never would again. It was acting in public, which was something that he wouldn't do. So Mom did double-duty, standing in front of their team and making a fool of herself. And Neil did try to contribute to his team's efforts, but the books and movies and songs were from a world that he barely knew. Sometimes he'd blurt out a wrong answer, but mostly he just stayed quiet. And when his team lost, he pretended that it didn't bother him. That it was just a stupid game, which it was. One of several stupid games that were played in rapid succession.

Neil watched the adults, listening to what they said when they weren't playing. Everyone looked tired and sounded happy and maybe they were a little drunk. Mrs. Miller was wearing summer clothes. Shorts and a light blouse and sandals. Neil kept remembering that her name was Sarah, and he would wonder how it would sound to say Sarah when he was alone again, in the dark. Her face was red from the sun and pretty in a grown-up way. He was watching her face when she noticed his gaze, and with a sudden little wink, she asked, "What should we play next?"

She was talking to the room, but the room was too busy to notice.

"My mother just turned seventy," Mom was shouting, apparently responding to some distant conversation. "And she doesn't even look sixty, which I'm taking to be a very good sign for my future."

In Neil's eyes, Grandma was nothing but a sputtering old seventy. Yet he decided to sit there, conspicuously saying nothing.

"And do you know her life expectancy?" Mom continued. "I mean what those charts . . . the actuarial charts . . . do you know what they're predicting for her. . . ?"

"Ninety-plus years," Mr. Jensen replied. "It's something like that, I would think."

Mom nodded. "Another twenty-three and a half years. Yes!"

Mr. Jensen was a lawyer and a genius. He was a small man, a little pudgy around the middle, and he looked like a genius should look, wearing thick glasses, and his thick black hair going twenty ways at once. When the group played Trivial Pursuit, Mr. Jensen played alone. It was the group's special rule. He had no partner and no help, but more often than not, he'd still win their stupid game.

"If our parents reach old age," he explained, "then they've escaped the hazards of risky behavior and bad genetics. And if they have healthy habits after that, most of them are going to be around for a long time. One or two of them will make it to a hundred, easy."

The adults reacted to this news with a horrified cackle.

"God!" Dr. Shepherd called out. "I'm going to have to keep my house clean for another thirty years . . . just in case his mother shows for a snap inspection—!"

The laughter rose, then collapsed when it ran out of breath.

Mr. Hawthorne said, "Bullshit! Are you telling me that I've got to listen to my old man complain about politics until the middle of this century?"

"Maybe so," said Mr. Jensen. "Maybe so."

Mrs. Hawthorne grabbed her husband by the knee. "Maybe we should give our folks sky diving lessons. What do you think? For their anniversaries?"

Everyone howled with laughter.

Mrs. Miller said, "Or a float trip through the Grand Canyon, maybe?"

Which made Mom blurt, "Perfect! My mother can't swim a stroke!"

Neil couldn't believe what he was hearing. Sure, his parents liked to complain about their parents. But to say that you want them dead . . . to say it in public, even if it was just a joke . . . well, it made Neil uncomfortable and sad. Watching them bend over with laughter, he caught a glimpse of frustrations that were deep and private, and ancient . . . frustrations that he'd always assumed were peculiar to fourteen-year-old boys. . . .

Mr. Jensen cleared his throat. "Life spans are growing," he told Mom, and everyone. "If a woman in our generation can reach seventy, then she'll almost certainly live well past the century mark."

Mom got a look. She halfway shuddered, then made herself laugh. And turning to Neil, she blurted, "Just think, honey. I'm going to be your mother for another hundred years!"

Neil didn't know what to make of that threat. The adults had to be drunk. Whatever this was, this was a disgusting and fascinating business, and Neil could only just sit on the brand new couch, sipping his fifth or sixth Coke of the day, wondering where things would lead next.

"Imagine," said Mrs. Hawthorne. "We're only a third of the way there!"

"If we make it to old age," Mr. Jensen cautioned. "Which is less likely for men than for women."

"As it should be!" Mrs. Miller trumpeted.

Again, Mom looked at her son. But she was asking Mr. Jensen her question. "And how long will our children live? Can you guess?"

"I can always guess," he replied, laughing softly.

Everyone seemed to be enjoying themselves, laughing and bending close to hear whatever he might say next.

"One hundred and fifty years," Mr. Jensen offered.

"That much?" Mom cried out.

"Or a thousand years, maybe."

There was laughter, but it had a different color now. It was a bright, uncomfortable sound that evaporated into an abrupt and very nervous silence.

"Look at the last hundred years," Mr. Jensen continued.

"Antibiotics. Transplants. Genetic engineering. Hell, how much of that was predicted?"

A genuine interest grabbed hold of Neil. "You really think so?" he sputtered.

"You'll live to walk on other worlds, my boy. I guarantee it."

Neil had always liked the man.

"Who knows what you might accomplish, given a thousand years?"

It was an idea that made Neil happy and warm, wiping away most of the pain in his poor neck. And that's when the idea hit him. It came from an obvious source, but he didn't mention his computer game. "Maybe when I'm done traveling to the planets," he began. "I don't know, but maybe I could travel back in time. . . ."

"To where?" blurted Mrs. Miller. Then she added, "To when, I mean. And where also, I guess. Wouldn't it be?"

Neil thought of Rome and the Dark Ages and the other popular haunts of his computer self. But instead of those possibilities, he heard himself say, "Here. Maybe I'd come back to now, and here, just to tell you how things turn out and . . . I don't know . . . maybe let you know about the future, in little ways. . . ."

That brought giggles and winces and every other uncomfortable expression.

For a moment, Neil felt foolish. He hoped this topic would pass. Collapse, and vanish. But then Mr. Jensen found something worthy in the possibility. Even intriguing. He jumped to his feet, swayed for a moment, then said, "Let's get the kids in here. Right now."

Mom asked, "What for?"

"We've got another game. A new game." Then he promised everyone, "It won't take two minutes. Or it'll take forever, depending on how you look at things."

People exchanged big-eyed looks, then agreed to play along. Mrs. Hawthorne went to get Dad and the kids. At Mr. Jensen's insistence, three video cameras were set up and left running. The kids were herded back into the room and told to sit together, as if posing for a group picture, and when Mr. Jensen finished his glass of dark wine, he stood in front of his audience, saying in a big, half-drunken way, "Listen to me. This is the night! We want to ask you a favor. A huge favor. When you've learned how to travel in time . . . maybe a thousand years from now . . . we want you to come back here. If it's possible. Please. Will you promise us that? Will you?"

These were little kids. They looked fried from too much fight-ing and too much fun, and whatever Mr. Jensen was saying, it was too strange and large for them to understand. But he sensed their limits. He made a stabbing gesture at a camera, adding, "We're going to talk to you about tonight. That's our promise. For years and years, your parents are going to remind you about the big commitment that you're making to us now."

But they hadn't said anything. Mostly, the kids sat motionless, looking ready to fall over into exhausted heaps.

"Promise us," said Mrs. Miller, getting into the mood of the moment. "Hannah? Say that you promise."

Her oldest squirmed, then said, "Okay. I guess."

Then Mrs. Miller turned to Neil. "You should promise for all of them. Would you do that for us?"

If anyone else had asked. But it was Sarah Miller, and he whis-pered, "Sure," and gave the cameras a little glance.

"What are you sure about?" Mom pressed.

Without too much life in his voice, he told them, "We'll come back. If it's possible, we'll visit you."

There was a strange, long pause. The adults acted as if they were waiting for some flash of light and the miraculous appearance of travelers from the far future. But then it was obvious that noth-ing would happen, and it was embarrassingly obvious that some people needed to stop drinking, at least for the time being. Over the next half hour, most of the kids were successfully installed in the boathouse. The Hawthornes volunteered to stay with them, and that left the master bedroom free for Neil's parents, which left him with a real bed instead of a hard cot in the hot boathouse.

Being an invalid wasn't too awful, Neil decided. He undressed slowly and climbed under the new white sheets, and Mom came in to check on him and collect her belongings. She said, "Here," and produced a little white pill. "Sarah gave this to me. It's a pain pill, and it'll help you sleep."

Neil wasn't too old to stop his mother from feeding him medi-cine.

"Sleep," she said again, rising and making certain that the lights were off in her wake.

Then the party started up again. The adults had found their second wind, more beers were opened, and there was a loud, gun-shot-like bang as a cork flew. That's when the pill started to work on him. Suddenly Neil felt himself tumbling down a long dark hole, feeling warm and weak, and his eyes were pulled shut by their own considerable weight, and even his heart seemed to grow stiller as something that wasn't true sleep took hold of him.

His room was directly above the front door.

He halfway remembered that.

And when he heard the ringing of a bell, close and insistent, some dim, still-conscious part of him was able to think, "That's someone. Someone outdoors. Someone who really wants to come inside. . . ."

Sunday

The dreamless sleep ended with the abrupt closing of a door. Neil's eyes found themselves open again, revealing a strange room filled with a staggering light. Where was he? Then he remembered this room and his borrowed bed, and in his codeine-inspired confusion, he decided that Mom must have left a light burning after all. It felt as if only a minute had passed, at most. Someone had finally answered the doorbell. That's what he'd just heard, he decided. And that brilliant light was coming from . . . where. . . ? From the bedroom window, apparently. How ridiculous was that? But after several deep breaths, the obvious burrowed its way into his consciousness. Night was finished; somehow it had become morning. Entire hours had passed in what felt like a heartbeat. And once he accepted that improbability, Neil could let his eyes close again, trying to will himself back into that timeless place.

The air conditioning was running. He heard the steady hum of chilled air shoved through a vent, and in the distance, the constant complaining efforts of a compressor. But then it was cool enough indoors, and the machinery shut itself off with a solid *thunk*. He heard the *thunk*, followed by an imperfect silence. Birds were singing. A man at the far end of the cabin spoke a few words, then a few more. Then Neil heard the sharp aching sound of a person crying, and his natural first thought was to assume that a kid was pissed or sad or just too tired to do anything but cry. Except it sounded like a woman crying. Like his mother, sort of. And that sound finally made him sit up, dressing slowly, taking frequent breaks to rub at the stiff center of his neck.

The crying came from the master bedroom; hadn't his folks spent the night there? Except when Neil looked in through the open door, he found Mrs. Hawthorne sitting on the edge of the giant bed, wearing last night's clothes, mopping at her face with a soggy Kleenex.

Neil was embarrassed, and he was fascinated.

The woman looked into the hallway, but nothing registered in her sad, red eyes. She had a puffy old face, and the hair that she always kept just so had become frazzled and dirty. Quietly, she took a deep breath. Then she dropped her head and sniffed hard once and unwadded the Kleenex before giving her nose a hard, long blow.

Neil retreated, finding the stairs and the kitchen. But the other adults were missing. Probably sleeping off their night. Serves them right, he thought with an easy piety. He snagged a cold pop, then drifted into the living room. Mrs. Miller was stretched out on the longest sofa, a brown afghan covering everything but her face and the small bare feet, eyes closed tight and a stillness embracing her entire body, making it appear as if she wasn't really breathing.

Neil hovered, watching her sleep.

Then she opened her eyes and looked straight at him. She was awake, alert. In her pretty face were hints of something that wasn't quite surprise, and the eyes were huge and red, blinking to make themselves wet.

"I'm sorry," Neil sputtered. "I woke you—"

"No." She shook her head. "No, I wasn't. You didn't."

He sipped his pop, trying to find something worth saying.

Mrs. Miller began to sit up, then remembered something. With the afghan still covering her body, she reached behind herself and deftly refastened her bra. Then she straightened the shirt that she'd worn last night, and she let the afghan fall to the floor and blinked her eyes hard a few times, rubbed at them, and with her face pointed at her toes, she asked, "What did you hear?"

"When?"

"Never mind." She looked at Neil. She was genuinely staring at him, as if he was an object deserving her fascination. Or was it fear? Then she asked the question again, but with different words. "How did you sleep?"

"Hard," he admitted.

"Codeine does that," she allowed. And she smiled at him. Then she thought to ask, "And how's your neck today?"

"Better."

She started to say, "Good." But another thought intruded, and she sat up straight and nodded toward the door, saying, "They're outside. On the patio. Go on."

His folks, she meant. They were sitting on the iron furniture, watching the sunrise. Neil preferred to be here, talking to this woman about sleep and body parts. But she was urging him to go see them, and that's what he did. Neil closed the door behind him, thinking of the air conditioning. He could feel his folks' eyes cutting into him. Even before Neil looked at them, he knew they were staring. A feeling of deep shame took hold of him. Obviously, he had done something wrong. Something horrible. Then he remembered that ugliness with Claudia, and the shame made him shiver. Honestly, he deserved at least a few hard words. That's what he told himself. But when he looked up, they were smiling. They weren't his parents; his parents never smiled so much. At him. Grinning like idiots. At him.

Neil settled on the first iron chair, set his pop between his feet, and asked, "What?"

Dad said, "What?"

Mom just sighed and said, "Nothing. It's nothing."

"It got pretty wild last night," Dad offered. "Did we bother you?"

"Maybe," Neil began.

Both of them squared their shoulders and waited.

Then Neil said, "No," and gave a big shrug. "The last thing I heard . . . I'm pretty sure . . . was someone at the door. . . ."

Dad started to say something, then caught himself.

Mom made herself look up at the trees, and to nobody in particular, she said, "Listen to the birds."

These weren't his parents; they were sloppy imposters.

A nearby door flew open. Everyone gave a little jump. Then came the wild screams of a boy charging out of the boathouse, little feet slapping against the plank stairs. Neil saw one of the triplets pop into view, followed by his brother and Collin and the three Shepherd kids. A little race was being run. They were followed by the Miller girls, Hannah holding tight to her young sister's hand. Claudia, accompanied by her father, was talking in a rapid, almost breathless voice about a dream involving her stupid-ass pony. And after them came the rest of the missing adults, the Jensens holding tight to their daughter who, grouchy from a lack of sleep, kept slapping at their clinging hands, screaming and squirming, complaining with a shrill and defiant little voice.

For no good reason, Neil's parents started to laugh now.

"Listen to her," Dad said, lacing his hands behind his head and leaning back in his chair. "Doesn't she sound good?"

"Great," Mom exclaimed.

Neil just had to stare at them. Did they have any idea how stupid they sounded? And how embarrassed they were making him feel?

*   *   *

An explanation drifted at the edge of sanity.

Clues and hints and the very odd expressions from these very odd parents could be pieced together, giving Neil an idea that made him snort and shake his head defiantly. No, he wouldn't believe that. No, no, no!

"What's the matter?" Mom asked, dropping a third piece of French toast onto his syrup-encrusted plate.

"Nothing's wrong," he told her.

"You're right," she sang out, giving her son a fond pat on the back.

Which made it all the harder to say nothing. Neil glanced at her, then realized that he was sneering. So he looked down the dining room table, pleased to see that he wasn't the only one noticing this bullshit. Hannah fidgeted as her dad insisted on giving her another big hug. Jake Shepherd told his mom to please stop staring at him, please. Only the Hawthorne kids seemed comfortable with this crazy mood. They asked the adults for more French toast and more milk, even though they hadn't finished their first helpings. Then Claudia saw her mother staggering downstairs, and with a bullying voice, she said, "Mommy, my syrup's cold. Can you warm it up for me?"

Makeup was plastered thick on the woman's face. Mrs. Hawthorne walked over to her daughter and yanked her plate away, never looking at her or saying a word.

"In an hour," Collin announced, "I'm going swimming." He was already wearing his swimsuit. "I'm going out to the float and back again. Twenty times."

The adults became quiet and watchful.

Hannah pointed out, "That's a lot of times."

Neil didn't feel hungry anymore. He was sorry for accepting more toast, because now it was destined for the disposal.

The microwave beeped. Then Mrs. Hawthorne returned, carrying Claudia's plate with a dishrag.

The girl took a bite, then said, "Ugh! It's too hot now."

Her mother stared at the plate. Only at the plate.

"This isn't what I wanted," Claudia complained. "I can't even put it in my mouth."

Her brother said, "Chicken fights. I want to chicken fight."

The Jensens finally stopped tickling their daughter. They glanced at the other parents, meaningful looks exchanged in rapid succession.

"And a boat ride," Collin proposed. "Dad? Dad? Can you pull an innertube with our boat? And can I ride it, maybe?"

For a flickering moment, that sounded like fun to Neil.

"Not today, son. No." Mr. Hawthorne had cooked their breakfast, and he'd just wandered into the dining room to measure the remaining hunger. He was wearing an apron and a hard face, keeping his emotions in control. He looked sad and angry, but he wouldn't show anyone why or at whom. Yet the anger was in his voice, every word stiff and slow as he told Collin, "We aren't doing anything like that today."

"Anything like what?" Neil muttered.

Mr. Hawthorne rubbed his hands in the apron. Then to everyone at the table, he said, "We aren't going into the water today. We can do anything but that."

Mrs. Miller said, "Anything," with emphasis. "Like, maybe we can go see a movie. Isn't there a theater down in—?"

"Absolutely," said Dr. Shepherd. "Or we can rent a stack of movies."

Neil was picturing himself straddling an innertube being towed by the pontoon boat. It wasn't a jet ski, but it could be fun. For a little while. Plus it would happen outdoors, and wasn't that why people came to places like this? To be out on the water?

"No swimming at all?" asked one of the Shepherd boys.

"Not for us," said Mrs. Jensen, ignoring the frowns building on her triplets' faces. "Not today, we won't. No, thank you."

"You've all had too much sun," Mr. Miller blurted.

Nobody was burned. Neil could see that for himself.

"But you can have anything else," Mr. Hawthorne repeated. "What do you kids want? Name it. Anything!"

"A horse," Claudia called out.

That brought a sudden, unnerved silence.

The girl didn't care. She stared at her mother, and with a gushing, hopeful voice, she said, "A real horse. A thoroughbred. Can we go get one? There's a stable just down—"

"No horses," her father warned her. "We've told you."

"But you just said, 'Anything'. . . !"

Neil's father stepped forward, waving his arms to get everyone's attention. Then he almost shouted, "Guys? We decided last night." His voice was a mixture of conviction and desperation. "For today," he told them, "and for a lot of good reasons, we're not going anywhere near the lake."

Someone had to ask the question.

"What reasons?" Neil pressed.

Dad seemed disappointed to hear those words. But before he could summon up a lame excuse, Claudia interrupted, her shrill and cutting voice saying, "I'm tired of my pony. I want a real horse!"

Her mother descended on her, pulling away the French toast and shouting, "No. We're not going to spoil you anymore. No!"

A perplexed and embarrassed look swept across the girl's face. Then anger flickered, found its heat, and she gathered herself, letting loose a rain of tears.

"And no more tantrums, young lady! Do you hear me?"

Which made Claudia even louder, the wail rising like a tornado siren before it finally collapsed into gut-born sobs.

Mr. Hawthorne stared at his wife, saying, "Darling, I don't know—"

"What? What?" Mrs. Hawthorne was crying and screaming, using the plate as a prop, flinging it back and forth as she asked everyone, "Am I being unreasonable here?" Then she dropped the plate in front of Claudia, buying the girl's silence with its crash. "Oh, things are changing now. Are you listening to me, young lady? I don't want a spoiled, self-centered daughter who can't say two nice words to her mother when she's an adult—!"

Incredibly, Dr. Shepherd told her children, "You didn't hear that."

Neil looked at his own parents; they struggled to avoid his gaze.

Claudia shrank down, sobbed lightly, then halfway fell out of her chair, doing a fat-girl sprint into the living room and dropping onto the sofa, letting everyone watch as she kicked and wept into the brown afghan.

Finally, Dad gave Neil a halfhearted glance.

"What happened last night?" Neil asked him. Asked everyone. Then before anyone could hammer together a lie, he added, "And don't tell me we came back through time to visit you! Because that's not possible. And even if it was possible . . . I wouldn't do it, not in trillion damned years. . . !"

The only sound was Claudia weeping, and even that had lost its vigor.

Then Mr. Jensen asked, "But what if, Neil? What if coming here was the decent, right thing to do?" He pulled a hand through his matted hair, then to underscore his question, he gave his daughter a little kiss on her embarrassed forehead, adding, "What if by doing that you were accomplishing one enormous and very good thing?"

*   *   *

Neil was angry in too many ways to count, and for reasons he couldn't even name. He sat on a toy bench inside the playroom, pretending to watch over the kids. But nobody seemed to be doing much of anything, not even quarreling. Like Neil, the kids were keeping quiet, listening carefully, little snatches of their parents' conversations managing to find their way in from the living room.

"What did you think? First, I mean."

"Quiet."

"First," he said again. Mr. Miller asked the question. "When you saw them?"

"I didn't believe it," Dr. Shepherd muttered.

"I didn't believe them," said Mom, with conviction.

"They can't hear us," someone promised. Mrs. Miller?

Then Dad said, "What I guessed? It was you, Bill." Bill was Mr. Jensen. "I mean, since it was your game. You invented it. So I just assumed that you'd hired actors, probably weeks ago. Coached them and made them wait for a signal, and it was all just—"

"A practical joke," Mom interrupted.

"A setup," said a man. Which man?

Then Mrs. Jensen whispered a name, then started to ask, "When you heard about her, did you still think—?"

"Exactly," Mom blurted. "Not a joke, no."

Several voices chanted, "No," in the same moment.

Then a man said, "Keep it down," and the conversation evaporated into a hushed murmur.

Hannah left the kids to sit beside Neil and hear better. But there was nothing to be heard, and finally she whispered, "What do you think?" She stared at Neil, her legs crossed hard and both hands on her high knee, her body slumped forward as if she was trying to make herself tiny. "What?"

"It didn't happen," he told her.

"What didn't?" She was a smart girl. It showed in her face and particularly in her bright eyes, and she was older than eight in her voice. But she was still just a kid, and she hadn't put things together. "I don't understand," she admitted without shame. "Who came to see them last night?"

"Nobody did," Neil told her.

The other kids were sitting on the floor, toys scattered around them or held by indifferent hands, every eye focused squarely on Neil.

"They got drunk," he growled. "They don't know what they saw."

But his audience couldn't embrace that answer either. They sighed and returned to their lazy playing, and Hannah moved closer to Neil, trying to listen again. They were sitting in the same twisted position, heads as close to the doorway as possible, both hearing Hannah's mother ask someone, "Now whose moon is that?"

Dad said, "Saturn's."

But then Mr. Jensen said, "No. It's Neptune's."

"Which one lives there?" asked a man. Mr. Shepherd, was it?

Someone whispered an answer. But it was said so softly that Neil couldn't decipher the name, or if it was a name. Although didn't it sound a lot like his father's quietest voice? And maybe he hadn't said a name, but instead simply offered, "Mine."

Mr. Miller said, "Oh, I'd never live out there. I don't suffer the cold well."

The adults laughed for a moment, then fell silent.

Neil could hear Hannah breathing. He wished that she wasn't sitting this close, but he didn't say anything, and glancing at her, he noticed that she had her mother's face. In a kid sort of way, she was pretty.

Someone mumbled a question.

And Dad repeated it. "Yeah. Why aren't they worried about changing the big stuff? Like history. Did anyone ask them?"

"I asked," Mr. Jensen volunteered.

"And?" someone prompted him.

"It has to do with quantum mechanics," the man replied.

Hannah asked, "What's that? Want-um mechanics?"

Neil placed his finger to his lips, listening hard now. But he couldn't hear half of the words—not near enough to make sense of things—which was why he stood and crept into the doorway, careful to keep just out of sight.

"Move through time," Mr. Jensen was explaining, "and you cause the universe to divide. To split. It's something that happens regardless of the direction you happen to be traveling. Whether it's backward in time, or, like us, moving ahead at our snail's pace."

"What does all that mean?" Mrs. Miller asked with a tight, frustrated tone.

"I turn right, or I turn left," Mr. Jensen explained. "Or I walk straight ahead. These are the sorts of decisions that each of us makes every day. Easily and effortlessly. But when I turn right, there's another version of me who turns left. And a third that keeps walking straight ahead, bumping into the wall. You see? The quantum universe is vast in ways we can't perceive. Everything that can happen, does. It's just that in our particular version of the universe, a single string of events is the story."

That brought a puzzled, perfect silence.

Mr. Jensen continued. "The universe has an infinite number of Earths, each with its own unique history. And it's possible—from what they said, it's even easy—to move backward in time. So when you arrive at some past Earth, what you're doing is causing that Earth to split again. I turn left. I turn right. I walk straight. Or—I come to a halt because suddenly I've got a time traveler standing in my path. . . ."

"I still don't get it," Mrs. Hawthorne growled. She was still angry and sad, using the loudest voice of any adult. "You don't make much sense, Bill."

"It's hard to grasp," Mr. Jensen agreed. "And I'm pretty much exhausted, too."

There was more whispering, in the living room and behind Neil.

Then Mr. Jensen continued, saying, "What would have happened is still happening. But not in this universe. Not to us." Then after a brief pause, he said, "And not to my daughter, thankfully."

A murmur of approval fell into silence.

Then Mom asked, "So why aren't these visitors everywhere? If traveling is so easy, and all—?"

"It's easy," Mr. Jensen agreed, "but it's also unlikely. I mean, well . . . what are the odds that one of us will visit a certain tropical beach during our lifetimes? Vanishingly small. And besides, when a traveler arrives somewhere—somewhen—he doesn't erase the old timeline. It's still there. He's just adding a new complication. One complication among trillions of complications."

"Complications," growled Mrs. Hawthorne.

"Anyway," said Dad.

Then the adults were talking at the same time, quietly and quickly, their words smeared together into a tired but excited tangle of sounds.

Neil started to step back, kicking Hannah in the shin.

She was directly behind him. And almost every other kid was crowded behind her, standing and kneeling, listening hard to words that couldn't make any sense. But isn't that how it was when you're a kid? Nothing makes sense, yet you can't help yourself. You listen to the adults, waiting for anything that you can remember and use.

Neil looked at their faces, at the eyes staring up at him, and he wished they would just go away. But then a thought hit him. He took a little breath and smiled, and he whispered, "Okay. Tell me, guys. What do you want to do today?"

Claudia answered first. She was sitting alone in the middle of the playroom, dressing soldiers in doll clothes. Without looking up, she snapped, "I want to swim."

"Shush," Hannah told her.

Neil herded everyone far back into the room. "Is that what you want? To go down to the water?"

They nodded and said, "Yes," with loud, impatient whispers.

Then he said, "Okay," and looked at the bare white wall for a moment, deciding how it could be done. "Okay," he said again, louder this time. And he kneeled down low, making sure that everyone was listening when he said, "This is how we're going to do it."

The adults sat limp in the chairs and sofas, looking sick and exhausted. But most were smiling like people whose faces were stuck in that position. The Hawthornes were the exception. They couldn't stop being angry about whatever had happened last night. Which had never happened, Neil reminded himself. He still didn't believe any of this crap, and he wouldn't ever, and that thought helped him find a voice that was strong and certain, and believeable.

"They want to go out front and play," Neil reported. "I'll watch them. If you want."

"Out front?" Mrs. Hawthorne snapped.

Then he remembered. "In the back yard, I mean." The front yard was beside the deep, dangerous lake. "They want to play on the swings and in the sandbox. If that's okay with you guys."

"It's all right with me," said Dad, laughing to himself.

Mom was half-asleep. Every adult seemed ready to drift away, except for Mr. Jensen and Mrs. Miller. He was probably still explaining time travel to her, and she was waiting eagerly for the boy to leave them alone again.

"Just keep them in the back yard," Mr. Hawthorne barked.

Neil looked at him, saying, "I will. Sir."

"If you get in trouble—" Dad began.

But Neil was already leaving, slipping back into the playroom and giving the kids a big nod and wink. "Like we talked about," he said. "Be quiet, and quick."

They went out the main door, out onto the hot, new driveway, then slipped through the split-rail fence into the adjacent yards. Neil led the way while Hannah stayed at the back. A private sidewalk ran between the next two overgrown cabins. The kids kept a trespasser's silence as they slipped between the buildings. Then they used a narrow path running back along the high ground between the cabins and the big lake, everyone shrinking down low for the last little ways, reaching the boathouse stairs without being noticed.

Their swimsuits were still damp and sandy from yesterday's fun. They dressed in shifts, then ran down the last long stretch of stairs. The lake was vast and brilliant, stirred by a thousand fast boats. An infectious fun erased the last traces of guilt. It was easy to jump into the water and paddle where you wanted, forgetting about parents and their odd commands. But first Neil barked at the others, telling them to put on their life jackets. "Keep together, and stay in the shallows," he demanded. Then looking straight at Claudia, he added, "And unless you're dying, don't scream for help!"

Neil didn't bother with a life jacket. He plunged in feet first, letting the warm water pull him under, and he popped up kicking and laughing, half a dozen hands grabbing him from behind, half a dozen kids trying to climb on his back at once.

"Chicken fights!" Collin called out.

But Neil was the only one big enough to carry anyone, and what was the point? No chicken fights for now, he argued. Which was how the grabbing became a game in its own right. Suddenly every kid was chasing him around the shallows, little hands clinging to his shoulders and elbows and around his waist. Sharp nails left him cut and bleeding. But nothing hurt too badly. It was fun, everyone laughing as he slowly, laboriously pulled them along. Then Neil would take a big gulp of air and dive, twisting to shake off his pursuers, and after a good long swim above the weedy bottoms, he would surface again, his lungs burning for the next few breaths, barely having enough time to recover before the kids again descended on him.

One time he came up too close to the others. The Jensen girl —wiry little Barbie—instantly threw her arms around his neck. The others grabbed her and held tight. Yesterday's pain returned, but Neil mostly ignored it, bending forward and pumping with his legs, towing five or six kids into deeper water. Then he dove, and Barbie almost let go. Almost. But she managed to put her second arm around his neck, squeezing and locking her hands together, forcing Neil back up to the surface, forcing him to take a quick breath before diving deeper than before, kicking and twisting and the girl still holding onto him, a frantic strength making her arms feel like bands of warm iron.

Neil finally used his hands. It was like cheating, taking hold of her little arms and giving them a jerk, then another. Then he twisted and tugged a third time, and Barbie was gone, and he swam another few yards underwater, coming up in water too deep to stand in, using the last of his strength to stay afloat while he breathed in quick, useless gasps.

Someone swam up to him, and he ducked instinctively.

Then the kid was past, and he came up to find several kids happily swimming toward the end of the dock, their little orange jackets keeping them high in the bright chopping water. Where were they going? Toward the floating platform, he realized. Everyone was breaking his first rule. "You're supposed to stay in the shallows!" he cried out. "Hey, guys! Guys! Listen to me!"

Nobody heard him over their own laughing and the whine of outboard motors. Or maybe they heard him fine and didn't care.

Either way, Neil was furious. He broke into a steady freestyle, trying to catch them before they got past the end of the dock. But he was tired, and he kept swimming crooked, and all those idiot kids were at the float when he finally reached them. "Hey!" he barked. "Who said you could come out here?"

"I said so," Claudia reported. Then she made a show of climbing the little ladder and dropping onto the platform's green carpet.

Neil was too tired to scream.

The other kids climbed the ladder or held onto the algae-painted sides, and, desperate to rest, Neil used the ladder, almost staggering when his full weight was out of the water. There was no place to sit, much less lie down. So he stood in the middle of their little square island, and after a minute of panting, he thought to count heads.

They were one short, he realized.

"Who's missing?" he asked, looking at Hannah first. But he already knew who wasn't here, and right away, he told the eight-year-old, "You were supposed to watch her!"

"Who?" the eight-year-old asked.

"Barbie. Where is she?"

The stubborn happiness refused to give way to serious thoughts. Instead, the kids giggled, and Collin pointed out, "She was riding you when I saw her."

A chill took hold of Neil. Standing tall, he looked toward the shoreline, finally asking himself how that little girl had stayed with him underwater. She'd removed her life jacket or it had come loose. And that's when he remembered what the jacket looked like. It was an old-fashioned pillowy kind, orange but stained by years of hard use. And then he saw the jacket sitting against the beach, the wakes of the passing boats pushing it a little higher with each sloppy wave.

"Stay here!" he roared.

Some little turd happily said, "We will," and broke into a big laugh.

Neil hit the water swimming. He was trying to remember where he was when he was wrestling with the girl, and when he was halfway certain that he was in the right place, he dove and started hunting for anything like limbs and a body. But he couldn't see far in that green water. Not without a face mask, he couldn't. So after a couple useless dives, he surfaced and climbed up onto the dock, feeling exhausted and terrified and sad and miserable. Where were the goggles? In the pontoon boat, he decided. And he found them under a pile of wet towels, but it took forever, and suddenly he was thinking that maybe he should run up to the cabin now and tell them what had happened. He should find help. Which was the first thing that he should have done, he realized, taking the wooden steps two at a time.

Voices descended on him.

Someone muttered something harsh, and there was crying, and Neil stopped and looked up the long staircase, watching as his parents came down fast now, followed by the Jensens, and between them, sobbing hard, their little daughter.

Neil sagged against the railing, relieved.

Then Dad said, "Mister," to him. Which was what he always said when Neil was in the deepest shit. "Mister." What you usually call an adult who's worthy of your respect.

"You had no right," his folks told him. "None."

Probably not. But Neil had to clamp his mouth shut, putting on a brave face before muttering, "Everyone's fine."

"Not because of you," Mr. Hawthorne pointed out.

Dad said, "Matt," to Mr. Hawthorne. There was a warning in the name. Then he turned back to Neil, saying, "We gave you orders, and you disobeyed them."

Neil was standing at the end of the dock. The kids had been

herded back out of the water, and now they were climbing the stairs with the best sluggish gait they could manage. Neil was the danger here. The spark plug to the rebellion. That much had been decided, and, before things got worse, the adults had to put a stop to his evil ways.

"Neil," said Mr. Jensen, his voice more forced then friendly. "This is the situation. I know I'm not supposed to tell you this, but you see, we had some very odd visitors last night, and they stayed the night, and they said . . . well, quite a bit. More than they intended to say, I'd guess."

Neil showed them a glowering face.

"My daughter would have drowned today," Mrs. Jensen blurted. "But these visitors came back to warn us—"

"I didn't warn you," Neil growled.

Mom took him by an elbow, ready to tell him otherwise.

So he said, "I did not warn you," with a slow, precise voice. Could they understand what he was telling them? "I was asleep. In bed, and asleep."

"You're right," Mrs. Miller agreed, trying to smile at him. "It wasn't you. But it was you, and them, from a very distant future—"

"No," he snapped.

Mom said, "Honey," and tried to take the elbow again.

But he shook her off, telling her, "Don't do that."

"You have a wondrous future," Mr. Jensen told him. "If you're careful and can live long enough, Neil . . . well, there's just nothing that you can't achieve in your very long life. . . ."

"Think of it," Dad told him.

Why was this so awful? Neil was almost shaking because he felt so sick and nervous. So deeply and enormously scared of everything.

"You aren't supposed to know that much," Mrs. Miller admitted. Then she touched him on the shoulder, and again, she made herself smile. "But you deserve to know. You're old enough." The smile seemed to grow warmer. Fonder, and genuine. "Ask us anything. If you promise to keep what you hear a secret, we'll tell you what they told us."

"You deserve to know," Mom assured him.

"To understand," Dad added.

"Anything," Mrs. Miller repeated, now moving up beside him, giving the boy a rough little hug around the shoulders.

With an astonishing ease, Neil pushed her away.

Then he turned, and with the adults calling out his name, he dove off the end of the dock, hitting the lake with a good flat *slap* and breaking into a strong freestyle, his head down except when he breathed, arms working and his tired legs kicking, carrying him past the floating platform and out into the open lake itself.

He swam until he felt breathless, then after a few deep gasps, he swam out even farther. A chill reached up from the deep water. The air around him was being torn by the high, angry whine of motors. The knifelike prows and keels crossed in front of him and behind. A flock of jet skis was somewhere nearby, hitting the high waves with a delicious wet *thud*. He couldn't see anyone chasing after him, nor did he bother to look. All that mattered was the swirling bright water, chaotic and vast. All that Neil wanted was to keep his limbs moving, keep himself swimming alone, working his way across this enormous lake that still, even now, he couldn't quite believe in.

First Tuesday

AFTER A LOT OF PESTERING, MOM TOLD STEFAN, "Fine, you can pick the view." Only it wasn't an easy job, and Stefan enjoyed it even more than he'd hoped. Standing on the foam-rock patio, he spoke to the house computer, asking for the Grand Canyon, then Hawaii's coast, then Denali. He saw each from many vantage points, never satisfied and never sure why not. Then he tried Mount Rushmore, which was better. Except Yancy saw the six stone heads, and he stuck his head out long enough to say, "Change it. Now." No debate; no place for compromise. Stefan settled on the Grand Canyon, on a popular view from the North Rim, telling himself that it was lovely and appropriate, and he hoped their guest would approve, and how soon would he be here. . . ? In another couple seconds, Stefan realized. *Jesus, now. . . !*

A figure appeared on the little lawn. He was tall, wearing a fancy suit, that famous face smiling straight at Stefan. And the boy jumped into the house, shouting with glee:

"The president's here!"

His stepfather muttered something.

Mom whined, "Oh, but I'm not ready."

Stefan was ready. He ran across the patio, leaping where it ended. His habit was to roll down the worn grassy slope. But he was wearing good clothes, and this evening was full of civic responsibilities. Landing with both feet solidly under him, he tried very hard to look like the most perfect citizen possible.

The president appeared solid. Not real, but nearly so.

The face was a mixture of Latin and African genes. The dreadlocks were long enough to kiss his broad shoulders. Halfway through his second term, Perez was the only president that Stefan could remember, and even though this was just a projection—an interactive holo generated by machines—it was still an honor to have him here, and Stefan felt special, and for more reasons than he could count, he was nervous. In good ways, and in bad ways, too.

"Hello?" chirped the eleven-year-old boy. "Mr. President?"

The projection hadn't moved. The house computer was wrestling with its instructions, fashioning a personality within its finite capacity. There was a sound, a sudden "Sssss" generated by speakers hidden in the squidskin fence and sky. The projection opened its mouth; a friendly, reedy voice managed, "Sssstefan." Then the president moved, offering both hands while saying, "Hello, young man. I'm so very glad to meet you."

Of course he knew Stefan's name. The personality could read the boy's public files. Yet the simple trick impressed him, and in response he shouted, "I'm glad to meet you, Mr. President!"

The brown hands had no substance, yet they couldn't have acted more real. Gripping Stefan's pale little hand, they matched every motion, the warmth carried by the bright eyes and his words. "This is a historic moment, Stefan. But then you already know that, I'm sure."

The first nationwide press conference, yes. Democracy and science joined in a perfect marriage. President Perez was invited here for a symbolic dinner, and he was everywhere else at the same time. It was a wondrous evening . . . magical. . . !

"A lovely yard," said the president. The eyes were blind, but the personality had access to the security cameras, building appropriate images as the face moved. With a faraway gaze, he announced, "I do like your choice of view."

"Thank you, Mr. President."

"Very nice indeed. . . !"

Holo projectors and squidskin fabrics created the illusion of blue skies and rugged geology. Although nothing was quite as bright as it would appear in the real outdoors, of course. And the squidskin rocks and the occasional bird had a vagueness, a dreamy

imprecision, that was the mark of a less-than-good system. Sometimes, like now, the antinoise generators failed to hide unwanted
sounds. Somewhere beyond the president, neighbors were ap-
plauding, and cheering, making it seem as if ghosts inhabited the
ghostly canyon.

President Perez seemed oblivious to the imperfections. Gesturing at their garden, he said, "Oh, I see you're doing your part. How
close are you to self-sufficiency?"

Not close at all, really.

"Beautiful eggplants," said the guest, not waiting for a response.
"And a fishpond, too!"

Without fish. A problem with the filter, but the boy said nothing, hoping nothing would be noticed.

The president was turning in a circle, hunting for something
else to compliment. For some reason, the house wasn't wearing its
usual coat of projected paints and architectural flourishes. Their
guest was too complicated, no doubt. Too many calculations, plus
the computer had to show the Grand Canyon . . . and the real
house lay exposed in all its drabness. Glass foams and cardboard
looked gray and simple, and insubstantial, three walls inside the
yard and the fourth wall pointed toward the outdoors, the brown
stains on the sky showing where rainwater had damaged the squidskin.

To break the silence, Stefan blurted out a question. "Mr. President, where do you stand on the economy?"

That's how reporters asked questions.

But the great man didn't respond in the expected way. His
smile changed, remaining a smile but encompassing some new,
subtly different flavor of light. "I'll stand on the economy's head,"
he replied. "With my feet apart, ready for anything."

Was that a genuine answer?

Stefan wasn't sure.

Then the president knelt, lowering his head below the boy's,
saying with a happy, self-assured voice, "Thank you for the question. And remember, what happens tonight goes both ways. You
can learn what I'm thinking, and in a different way I'll learn what's
on your mind."

Stefan nodded, well aware of the principles.

"When I wake," said the handsome brown face, "I'll read that
this many people asked about the economy, and how they asked it,
and what they think we should be doing. All that in an abbreviated
form, of course. A person in my position needs a lot of abbrevia-
tions, I'm afraid."

"Yes, sir." Stefan waited for a moment, then blurted, "I think you're doing a good job with the economy, sir. I really do."

"Well," said the guest, "I'm very, very glad to hear it. I am."

At that moment, the genuine President Perez was inside a government hospital, in a fetal position, suspended within a gelatin bath. Masses of bright new optical cable were attached to his brain and fingers, mouth and anus, linking him directly with the Net. Everything that he knew and believed was being blended with his physical self, all elements reduced to a series of numbers, then enlarged into a nationwide presence. Every household with an adequate projection system and memory was being visited, as were public buildings and parks, stadiums and VA facilities. If it was a success, press conferences would become a monthly event. Political opponents were upset, complaining that this was like one enormous commercial for Perez; but this was the president's last term, and it was an experiment, and even Stefan understood that these tricks were becoming cheaper and more widespread every day.

In the future, perhaps by the next election, each political party would be able to send its candidates to the voters' homes.

What could be more fair? thought the boy.

Stefan's stepfather had just stepped from the drab house, carrying a plate full of raw pink burgers.

In an instant, the air seemed close and thick.

"Mr. Thatcher," said the projection, "thank you for inviting me. I hope you're having a pleasant evening. . . !"

"Hey, I hope you like meat," Yancy called out. "In this family, we're carnivores!"

Stefan felt a sudden and precise terror.

But the president didn't hesitate, gesturing at the buffalo-augmented soy patties. "I hope you saved one for me."

"Sure, Mr. President. Sure."

For as long as Stefan could remember, his stepfather had never missed a chance to say something ugly about President Perez. But Mom had made him promise to be on his best behavior. Not once, but on several occasions. "I don't want to be embarrassed," she had told him, using the same tone she'd use when trying to make Stefan behave. "I want him to enjoy himself, at least this once. Will you please just help me?"

Yancy Thatcher was even paler than his stepson. Blonde hair worn in a short, manly ponytail; a round face wearing a perpetually sour expression. He wasn't large, but he acted large. He spoke with a deep, booming voice, and he carried himself as if endowed with a dangerous strength. Like now. Coming down the slope, he was walking straight toward their guest. The president was offering both hands, in his trademark fashion. But no hand was offered to him, and the projection retreated, saying, "Excuse me," while deftly stepping out of the way.

"You're excused," Yancy replied, laughing in a low, unamused fashion. Never breaking stride.

Mom wasn't watching; that's why he was acting this way.

Things worsened when Yancy looked over his shoulder, announcing, "I didn't want you coming tonight, frankly. But the kid's supposed to do an assignment for school, and besides, I figured this was my chance to show you my mind. If you know what I mean. . . ."

President Perez nodded, dreadlocks bouncing. "Feedback is the idea. As I was just telling Stefan—"

"I'm an old-fashioned white man, Mr. President."

The boy looked at the drab house, willing Mom to appear.

But she didn't, and Yancy flung open the grill and let the biogas run too long before he made a spark, a soft blue explosion causing Stefan to back away. Nobody spoke. Every eye, seeing or blind, watched the patties hit the warming rack, sizzling quietly but with anger, Yancy mashing them flat with the grimy spatula that he'd gotten for Christmas last year.

Then the president spoke, ignoring that last comment.

"It's a shame this technology won't let me help you," he declared, with a ring of honesty.

Yancy grimaced.

The patties grew louder, the flames turning yellow.

Obstinately ignoring the tensions, the president looked at his own hands. "A poverty of physicality," he declared, laughing to himself.

That was it. Something snapped, and Yancy barked, "Know what I like, Mr. President? About tonight, I mean."

"What do you like?"

"Thinking that the real you is buried in goo, a big, fat glass rope stuck up your ass."

Stefan prayed for a systems failure, or better, a war. Anything that would stop events here. His fear of fears was that the president would awaken to learn that Yancy Thatcher of Fort Wayne, Indiana, had insulted him. Because the boy couldn't imagine anyone else in the country having the stupid courage to say such an awful thing.

Yet their guest wasn't visibly angry. He actually laughed, quietly and calmly. And all he said was, "Thank you for your honesty, sir."

Yancy flipped burgers, then looked at Stefan. "Tell your mom it'll be a few minutes. And take him with you."

It was such a strange, wondrous moment.

The boy looked at his president, at his smile, hearing the conjured voice saying, "Yes. That's a fine idea." Built of light and thought, he seemed invulnerable to every slight, every unkind word.

Stefan had never envied anyone so much in his life.

Mom was a blizzard of activity, hands blurring as they tried to assemble a fancy salad from ingredients grown in the garden, then cleaned and cut into delicate, artful shapes. She loved salads, planning each with an artist's sensibilities, which to Mom meant that she could never predict preparation times, always something to be done too fast at the end. When she saw Stefan step inside, she whined, "I'm still not ready." When she saw President Perez fluttering for that instant when he passed from the outside to the kitchen projectors, she gave a little squeal and threw spinach in every direction. Then she spoke, not leaving enough time to think of proper words. "You've lost weight," she blurted. "Since the election, haven't you. . . ?"

Embarrassed again, Stefan said, "The President of the United States," with a stern voice. In warning. Didn't Mom remember how to address him?

But the president seemed amused, if anything. "I've lost a couple kilos, yes. Job pressures. And the First Lady's anti-equatorial campaign, too."

The joke puzzled Stefan until he stopped thinking about it.

"A drink, Mr. President? I'm having a drop for myself. . . ."

"Wine, please. If that's not too much trouble."

Both adults giggled. Touching a control, Mom ordered an elegant glass to appear on the countertop, already filled with sparkling white wine, and their guest went through the motions of sipping it, his personality given every flavor along with an ethanol kick. "Lovely," he declared. "Thanks."

"And how is the First Lady?"

It was a trivial question, Stefan within his rights to groan.

Mom glared at him. "Go find Candace, why don't you?" Then she turned back to their guest, again inquiring about his dear wife.

"Quite well, thank you. But tired of Washington."

Mom's drink was large and colorful, projected swirls of red and green never mixing together. "I wish she could have come. I *adore* her. And oh, I love what she's done with your house."

The president glanced at his surroundings. "And I'm sure she'd approve of your tastes, Mrs. Thatcher."

"Helen."

"Helen, then."

The kitchen walls and ceiling were covered with an indoor squidskin, and they built the illusion of a tall room . . . except that voices and any sharp sound echoed off the genuine ceiling, flat and close, unadorned by the arching oak beams that only appeared to be high overhead.

Mom absorbed the compliment and the sound of her own name, then noticed Stefan still standing nearby. "Where's Candace? Will you *please* go find your sister, darling?"

Candace's room was in the basement. It seemed like a long run to a boy who would rather be elsewhere, and worse, her door was locked. Stefan shook the knob, feeling the throb of music that seeped past the noise barriers. "He's here! Come on!" Kicking the door down low, he managed to punch a new hole that joined half a dozen earlier kickholes. "Aren't you coming up to meet him—?"

"Open," his sister shouted.

The knob turned itself. Candace was standing before a mirrored portion of squidskin, examining her reflection. Every other surface showed a fantastic woodland, lush red trees interspersed with a thousand Candaces who danced with unicorns, played saxophones, and rode bareback on leaping black tigers.

The images were designed to jar nerves and exhaust eyes. But what Stefan noticed was the way his sister was dressed, her outfit too small and tight, her boobs twice their normal size. She was ready for a date, and he warned her, "They won't let you go. It's only Tuesday."

Candace gave her little brother a cutting, worldly look. "Go lose yourself."

Stefan began to retreat, gladly.

"Wait. What do you think of these shoes?"

"They're fine."

She kicked them off, without a word, then opened the door behind the mirror, mining her closet for a better pair.

Stefan shot upstairs.

Their honored guest and Mom remained in the kitchen. She was freshening her drink, and talking.

"I mean I really don't *care*," she told him. "I *know* I deserve the promotion, that's what matters." She gave her son a quick, troubled glance. "But Yankee says I should quit if they don't give it to me—"

"Yankee?"

"Yancy, I mean. I'm sorry, it's my husband's nickname."

The president was sitting on a projected stool, watching Mom sip her swirling drink once, then again.

"What do *you* think I should do? Quit, or stay."

"Wait and see," was the president's advice. "Perhaps you'll get what you deserve."

Mom offered a thin, dissatisfied smile.

Stefan thought of his comppad and his list of important questions. Where was it? He wheeled and ran to his room, finding the pad on his unmade bed, its patient voice repeating the same math problem over and over again. Changing functions, he returned to the kitchen. There'd been enough noise about decorating and Mom's job, he felt. "Mr. President? Are we doing enough about the space program?"

"Never," was the reply. "I wish we could do more."

Was the comppad recording? Stefan fiddled with the controls, feeling a sudden dull worry.

"In my tenure," the voice continued, "I've been able to double our Martian budget. Space-born industries have increased 12 percent. We're building two new observatories on the moon. And we just found life on Triton—"

"Titan," the boy corrected, by reflex.

"Don't talk to him that way!" Mom glowered, thoroughly outraged.

"Oh, but the fellow's right, Helen. I misspoke."

The amiable laugh washed over Stefan, leaving him warm and confident. This wasn't just an assignment for school, it was a mission, and he quickly scrolled to the next question. "What about the oceans, Mr. President?"

A momentary pause, then their guest asked, "What do you mean?"

Stefan wasn't sure.

"There are many issues," said the president. "Mineral rights. Power production. Fishing and farming. And the floating cities—"

"The cities."

"Fine. What do you think, Stefan? Do they belong to us, or are they free political entities?"

Stefan wasn't sure. He glanced at his pad, thinking of the

islands, manmade and covered with trim, modern communities. They grew their own food in the ocean, moved where they wanted, and seemed like wonderful places to live. "They should be free."

"Why?"

Who was interviewing whom?

The president seemed to enjoy this reversal in roles. "If taxes pay for their construction—your tax money, and mine—then by what right can they leave the United States?" A pleasant little laugh, then he added, "Imagine if the First Lady and I tried to claim the White House as an independent nation. Would that be right?"

Stefan was at a loss for words.

Then Mom sat up straight, giving a sudden low moan.

Yancy was coming across the patio. Stefan saw him, and an instant later, Mom jumped to her feet, telling her son and guest, "No more politics. It's dinnertime."

Yancy entered the kitchen, approaching the projection from behind.

The president couldn't react in time. Flesh-and-bone merged with him; a distorted brown face lay over Yancy's face, which was funny.

"Why are you laughing?" snapped Yancy.

"No reason," the boy lied.

His stepfather's temper was close to the surface now. He dropped the plate of cooked burgers on the countertop, took an enormous breath, then said, "Show your guest to the dining room. Now."

Taking his comppad, Stefan obeyed.

The president flickered twice, changing projectors. His voice flickered too, telling the boy the story of some unnamed senator who threw a tantrum whenever rational discourse failed him. "Which is to say," he added, "I have quite a lot of practice dealing with difficult souls." And with that he gave a little wink and grin, trying to bolster the boy's ragged mood.

Stefan barely heard him; he was thinking of floating cities.

It occurred to him that he'd answered, "Yes, they should be free," for no other reason than that was his stepfather's opinion, voiced many times. The cities were uncrowded. Some allowed only the best kinds of people. And Stefan had spoken without thinking, Yancy's ideas worming their way inside him. Embarrassed and confused, he wondered what he believed that was really his own. And did it ever truly matter?

Even if Stefan could think what he wanted, how important could his opinions ever be?

The table was set for five, one place setting built from light. The president took his seat, Stefan across from him, scrolling through the comppad in search of new questions. Most of these came from his social studies teacher—a small, handsome Nigerian woman who didn't know Yancy. *Why do we maintain our open border policy?* He didn't dare ask it. Instead he coughed, then inquired, "How are your cats, Mr. President?"

Both of them seemed happy with the new topic. "Fine, thank you." Another wink and grin. "The jaguars are fat, and the cheetah is going to have triplets."

Miniature breeds. Declawed and conditioned to be pets.

They spoke for a couple minutes about preserving rare species, Stefan mentioning his hope to someday work in that field. Then Mom burst into the room with her completed salad, and Yancy followed with some bean concoction, making a second trip for the burgers. Somewhere en route he shouted, "Candace!" and she appeared an instant later, making her entrance with a giggle and a bounce.

If anything, her boobs were even bigger. And the room's holo projectors changed her skin, making it coffee-colored.

Mom saw the clothes and her color, then gave a shocked little groan. But she didn't dare say anything with the president here. Yancy entered the little room, paused and grimaced . . . then almost smiled, glancing at their guest with the oddest expression.

Why wasn't he saying anything?

The president glanced at Candace for half a second. Then he looked straight ahead, eyes locked on Stefan. Big, worried eyes. And his projection feigned a slow sigh.

With her brown boobs spilling out, Candace sat beside President Perez. Mom glared at her, then at Yancy. But Yancy just shook his head, as if warning her to say nothing.

Seven burgers were on the plate. The real ones were juicy; the one built from light resembled a hard lump of charcoal.

Stefan realized that he was growing accustomed to being ashamed.

Candace took nothing but a small helping of salad, giggling and looking at their guest with the same goofy flirtatious face that she used on her infinite boyfriends. "Hey, are you having a good time?"

"Mr. President," Stefan added.

His sister glared at him, snapping, "I know *that.*"

"I'm having a fine time." The apparition never quite looked at her, using his spoon to build a mound of phantom beans on the phantom plate. "You have a lovely home."

Mom said, "Thank you."

Candace giggled, like an idiot.

But she wasn't stupid, her brother wanted to say. To shout.

Yancy was preparing two burgers, slipping them into their pouches of bread and adding pickles, mustard, and sugar corn. Then after a first oversized bite, he grinned, telling the house computer to give them scenery. "Mount Rushmore," he demanded. "The original."

Squidskin re-created the four-headed landmark. Presidents Barker and Yarbarro were notably absent.

The current president was staring at his plate. For the first time, he acted remote. Detached. A bite of his charred burger revealed its raw red interior, blood flowing as if from an open wound. After a long pause, he looked at Stefan again, and with a certain hopefulness asked, "What's your next question, please?"

Candace squealed, "Let me ask it!"

She shot to her feet, reaching over the table, her boobs fighting for the privilege of bursting out of her shirt. Before Stefan could react, she'd stolen his comppad, reading the first question aloud.

" 'Why do we maintain our open border policy?' "

The pause was enormous, silence coming from every direction at once. Mom stared at Yancy, pleading with her eyes. Everyone else studied the president, wondering how he would respond. Except he didn't. It was Yancy who spoke first, in a voice almost mild. Almost.

"I don't think it matters," he replied. "I think if we want to do some good, we've got to turn the flow back the other direction. If you know what I mean."

"I think we do," said President Perez.

"Fifty years of inviting strangers into our house. Fifty idiotic years of making room, making jobs, making allowances . . . and always making due with less and less. That's what the great Barker gave us. Her and her damned open border bullshit!"

Stefan felt sick. Chilled.

Mom began, "Now Yancy—"

"My grandfather owned an acreage, Mr. President. He ate meat three times a day, lived in a big house, and worked hard until he was told to go half-time, some know-nothing refugee given the other half of his job, and his paycheck . . . !"

"Employment readjustments." Their guest nodded, shrugged. "That's a euphemism, I know. There were problems. Injustices. But think of the times, Mr. Thatcher. Our government was under enormous pressures, yet we managed to carry things off—"

"Some know-nothing refugee!" Yancy repeated, his face red as uncooked meat. "And *your* party took his home, his land, to build a stack of apartment buildings."

Stefan tried not to listen. He was building a careful daydream where he had a different family, and he was sitting with the president, everyone working to make his visit productive, and fun.

Yancy pointed at the old Rushmore. "A great nation built it—"

"An individual built it," the president interrupted. "Then his grateful nation embraced it."

"A free nation!"

"And underpopulated, speaking relatively."

Pursing his heavy pink lips, Yancy declared, "We should have let you people starve. That's what I think." He took a huge breath, held it, then added, "You weren't our responsibility, and we should have shut our borders. Nothing in. Not you. Not a rat. Not so much as a goddamn fly . . . that's my opinion. . . !"

President Perez stared at his own clean plate. Eyes narrowed. The contemplative face showed a tiny grin, then he looked up at Yancy, eyes carved from cold black stone.

With a razored voice, he said, "First of all, sir, I'm a third-generation U.S. citizen. And second of all, I believe that you're an extraordinarily frightened man." A pause, a quiet sigh. "To speak that way, your entire life must be torn with uncertainty. And probably some deep, deep sense of failure, I would guess."

Stefan sat motionless, in shock.

"As for your opinions on national policy, Mr. Thatcher . . . well, let me just say this. These are the reasons why I believe you're full of shit."

The rebuke was steady, determined, and very nearly irresistible.

President Perez spoke calmly about war and famine, a desperate United Nations, and the obligations of wealthy people. He named treaties, reciting key passages word for word. Then he attacked the very idea of closing the borders, listing the physical difficulties and the economic costs. "Of course it might have worked. We could have survived. An enclave of privilege and waste, and eventually there would have been plagues and a lot of quiet hunger on the outside. We'd be left with our big, strong fences, and beyond them . . . a dead world, spent and useless to us, and to the dead." A brief pause, then he spoke with a delicate, sorrowful voice, asking, "Are you really the kind of man who could live lightly with himself, knowing that billions perished . . . in part because you deserved a larger dining room. . . ?"

Yancy had never looked so tired. Of those at the table, he seemed to be the one composed of light and illusion.

The president smiled at everyone, then focused on Stefan. "Let's move on, I think. What's your next question?"

The boy tried to read his comppad, but his brain wouldn't work.

"Perhaps you can ask me, 'What do you think about this hallmark evening?' "

"What do you think?" Stefan muttered.

"It should revolutionize our government, which isn't any surprise. Our government was born from a string of revolutions." He waited for the boy's eyes, then continued. "I love this nation. If you want me angry, say otherwise. But the truth is that we are diverse and too often divided. My hope is that tonight's revolution will strengthen us. Judging by these events, I'd guess that it will make us at least more honest."

Yancy gave a low sound. Not an angry sound, not anything.

"Perhaps I should leave." The president rose to his feet. "I know we've got another half hour scheduled—"

"No, please stay!" Mom blurted.

"Don't go," begged Candace, reaching for his dreadlocks.

Mom turned on her. At last. "Young lady, I want you out of those clothes—!"

"Why?"

"—and drain those breasts. You're not fooling anyone here!"

Candace did her ritual pout, complete with the mournful groan and the teary run to the basement.

Mom apologized to their guest, more than once. Then she told Yancy, "You can help Stefan clear the table, please. *I* will show our president the rest of *my* house."

Stefan worked fast. Scraps went into the recyke system; dishes were loaded in the sonic washer. Through the kitchen window, he saw the Grand Canyon passing into night, its blurry, imperfect edges more appropriate in the ruddy half-light. And it occurred to him that he was happy with this view, even if it wasn't real. Happier than he'd feel on any ordinary plot of real ground, surely.

His stepfather did no work. He just stood in the middle of the room, his face impossible to read.

Stefan left him to set the controls. Mom and the president were in the front room, looking outside. Or at least their eyes were pointed at the lone window. With a soft, vaguely conspiring tone, the president said, "It's not my place to give advice. Friends can. Counselors and ministers should. But not someone like me, I'm sorry."

"I know," his mother whispered. "It's just . . . I don't know . . . I just wish he would do something awful. To me, of course. Just to make the choice simple."

What choice? And who was she talking about?

"But really, he only sounds heartless." She tried to touch their guest, then thought better of it. "In five years, Yankee hasn't lifted his hand once in anger. Not to the kids, or me. And you're right, I think. About him being scared, I mean. . . ."

Stefan listened to every word.

"When you come next month," Mom inquired, "will you remember what's happened here?"

President Perez shook his head. His face was in profile, like on a coin. "No, I won't. Your computer has to erase my personality, by law. And you really don't have room enough to store me. Sorry."

"I guess not," Mom allowed.

They looked outside, watching an airtaxi riding its cable past the window. The building across the street mirrored theirs, houses stacked on houses, each one small and efficient, and lightweight, each house possessing its own yard and the same solitary window facing the maelstrom that was a city of barely five million.

Several presidents were visible.

They waved at each other, laughing with a gentle, comfortable humor.

Then their president turned, spotting the boy at the other end of the little room, and he smiled at Stefan with all of his original charm and warmth, nothing else seeming to matter.

Mom turned and shouted, "Are you spying on us?"

"I wasn't," he lied. "No, ma'am."

The president said, "I think he just came looking for us." Then he added, "Dessert. I feel like a little dessert, if I might be so bold."

Mom wasn't sure what to say, if anything.

"Perhaps something that *looks* delicious, please. In the kitchen. I very much liked your kitchen."

They gathered again, a truce called.

Candace was dressed as if ready for school, looking younger

and flatter, and embarrassed. Yancy had reacquired a portion of his old certainty, but not enough to offer any opinions. Mom seemed wary, particularly of Stefan. What had he heard while eavesdropping? Then the president asked for more questions, looking straight at Yancy, nothing angry or malicious in his dark face.

Crossing his arms, Yancy said nothing.

But Stefan thought of a question. "What about the future?" It wasn't from his comppad's list; it was an inspiration. "Mr. President? How will the world change?"

"Ah! You want a prediction!"

Stefan made sure that the comppad was recording.

President Perez took a playful stab at the layered sundae, then spoke casually, with an easy authority.

"What I'm going to tell you is a secret," he said. "But not a big one, as secrets go."

Everyone was listening. Even Yancy leaned closer.

"Since the century began, every president has had an advisory council, a team of gifted thinkers. They know the sciences. They see trends. They're experts in new technologies, history, and human nature. We pay them substantial fees to build intelligent, coherent visions of tomorrow. And do you know what? In eighty years, without exception, none of their futures have come true." He shook his head, laughing quietly. "Predicted inventions usually appear, but never on schedule. And the more important changes come without warning, ruining every one of their assessments." A pause, then he added, "My presence here, for instance. Not one expert predicted today. I know because I checked the records myself. No one ever thought that a president could sit in half a billion kitchens at once, eating luscious desserts that will never put a gram on his waist."

Yancy growled, asking, "Then why do you pay the bastards?"

"Habit?" The president shrugged his shoulders. "Or maybe because nothing they predict comes true, and I find that instructive. All these possible futures are defined, and I don't need to worry about any of them."

A long, puzzled silence.

"Anyway, my point is this: Now that we've got this technology, every prediction seems to include it. In fact, my experts are claiming that in fifty years, give or take, all of us will spend our days floating in warm goo, wired into the swollen Net. Minimal food. No need for houses or transportation. Maximum efficiency for a world suddenly much less crowded." The president gazed at Stefan, asking, "Now does that sound like an appealing future?"

The boy shook his head. "No, sir."

"It sounds *awful*," Mom barked.

Candace said, "Ugh."

Then Yancy said, "It'll never happen. No."

"Exactly," said their guest. "It's almost guaranteed not to come true, if the pattern holds." He took a last little bite of his sundae, then rose. "You asked for a prediction, son. Well, here it is. Your life will be an unending surprise. If you're lucky, the surprises will be sweet and come daily, and that's the best any of us can hope for. I think."

The silence was relaxed. Contemplative.

Then the president gestured at the projected clock high above their stove. "Time to leave, I'm afraid. Walk me out?"

He was speaking to Stefan.

Hopping off his stool, the boy hugged himself and nodded. "Sure, Mr. President. Sure."

The Grand Canyon was dark, the desert sky clear and dry. But the genuine air was humid, more like Indiana than Arizona. There were always little clues to tell you where you were. Stefan knew that even the best systems fell short of being *real*.

In a low, hopeful voice, he said, "You'll come back in a month. Won't you, sir?"

"Undoubtedly." Another smile. "And thank you very much. You were a wonderful host."

What else? "I hope you had a good time, sir."

A pause, then he said, "It was perfect. Perfect."

Stefan nodded, trying to match that smile.

Then the image gave a faint, "Good-bye," and vanished. He suddenly just wasn't there.

Stefan stared at the horizon for a long moment, then turned and saw that the house was whole again. Their computer had enough power to add color and all the fancy touches. Under the desert sky, it looked tall and noble, and he could see the people sitting inside, talking now. Just talking. Nobody too angry or too sad, or anything. And it occurred to Stefan, as he walked toward them, that people were just like the house, small inside all their clothes and words and big thoughts.

People were never what they appeared to be, and it had always been that way. And always would be.

Afterword

MY WIFE AND I AWOKE DESPERATELY EARLY ONE morning to catch the shuttle to Chicago, then crawled aboard a packed flight to Boston and the 2004 WorldCon. Somewhere above Lake Michigan, jangled by coffee and having exhausted the considerable pleasures afforded by the in-flight magazine and repackaged television shows, I decided to do some serious reading. On WorldCon trips, my habit is to drag along one of the *Year's Best* anthologies. After shopping through the table of contents—I never attack anthologies or collections from front to back—my eyes settled on the one story I genuinely needed to read. Sitting beside me was a fellow who was also WorldCon-bound. He happened to know who I was, and when he saw what I was doing, he asked, "Why are you reading that one? Don't you know how it ends?"

A fair question, since I was picking my way through "Night of Time." Which means that a person with a strong mathematical similarity to me happened to write these words more than three and a half years ago, and slightly different versions of me checked over the editing and galley proofs, and cashed the check that paid for the work. But I have written quite a few stories over the last decade—ten or twelve each year—and some months had passed since my last look at "Night." Yes, I remembered how my story ended, pretty much, but some of the critical details had slipped from my grasp.

"I'm having dinner with my editor tonight," I explained, using the simplest, easiest excuse. "Maybe he'll ask about my next book, and I was wondering if there's a novel hiding inside this critter."

The fellow seemed to accept my logic.

But as I continued to read, I couldn't see any lurking novels. Sad to say, at least during that particular plane ride, I was thoroughly stuck.

Normally I won't bother with a story unless it offers me two qualities: a voice or tone that lends the work its personality, and the clear promise of a genuine destination. Often the destination changes along the way. Many times my endings are written with the final draft, when my head is full of the work and everything feels obvious. But when I am finished with a story, I am finished. Once the story is printed out and shipped away, I try hard to forget it. I'll work with other voices and push toward fresh destinations, and only when two or three or maybe ten editors reject the old story will I consider looking at it again, with fresh eyes.

By some measures, the oldest story in this collection is "On the Brink of That Bright New World." It was written on an electronic typewriter. Every draft had to be cranked back through the rollers, one piece of parchment at a time. And I doubt if any story of mine has ever gone through as many drafts as "Brink." According to my records—a piece of notebook paper jammed full of scribbles and check marks—the story existed first under a different title, "After the Spectacle." About that version, I remember little. But I sent it to one of those vanished markets that wasn't on my A-list, which implies that I didn't have much confidence in the story. And the editor sent it back soon afterward, without comments or encouragement.

My next version used the present title but not the final plot line or science fictional speculations. As I recall, I had the Earth's sky change without warning—an event I used with much greater success in *Beyond the Veil of Stars* (Tor, 1994). I must have been pleased with the outcome because I submitted the manuscript to one of Robert Silverberg's anthologies. Unfortunately he had a different estimate of its worth, and Mr. Silverberg is not one to tell you, "Nice try," when he means to say, "I didn't much like this."

After that, I cut the story in half and sent it to *Full Spectrum*. But that didn't seem to help much either.

I might have given up on the whole project, except I'm a stubborn ape and I rather liked my new title. So I scrapped the first plot line and came up with a story much like the present one. Ellen Datlow said it was ambitious but not right for *Omni*. Ed Ferman said thanks, but it didn't work for *F&SF*. Then I rewrote it again and earned a nice long letter from Gardner Dozois, full of useful suggestions that I conscientiously ignored. I sent "Brink" back to Ellen, and then back to *Full Spectrum*. Then I rewrote it for what I hoped was the very last time and shipped this tiresome collection of words—by now I was quite sick of the damned thing —to my best hope, which was Gardner again.

According to my minimal records, Gardner sent the story back with another letter attached.

Good suggestions, I wrote to myself.

Then I rewrote it again, trimming portions of the story and gaining far too much confidence. I don't remember details, but I can read the implications in my synopsis of Gardner's next letter:

Bad suggestions.

In those days, I recorded only the month and day, but not the year, when I sent off a manuscript. I have no way of being sure, but either I mailed Gardner my next version of "Brink" ten days before the previous version was returned to me—an interesting experiment in time travel—or the story sat in my file cabinet for most of a year before I finally realized that my editor's bad suggestions were actually rather inspired.

Again, I rewrote it and sent the new "Brink" to Gardner.

But traditions die hard, and he rejected my best version yet. On the increasingly crowded page, I wrote, *Good, modest suggestions* and *Close to sale.*

I carved off another five hundred words, then mailed away the version that sits in this volume, or at least something very much like it.

Which leads me to this point: When some wise soul tells you that writing sounds like fun and easy work, hit him in the teeth. Go on. You have my permission.

Most of my professional life has been spent on the brink of poverty. To make my rent, I occasionally find other lines of work. In general, I've gravitated toward either thoughtless brute labor or brief, demanding stints of relatively well-paid fun.

"The Cuckoo's Boys" is the direct result of thoughtful labor applied to something other than storytelling. Our local public schools used to have well-funded programs for gifted students. Mentors were hired to entertain and occasionally educate kids who were deemed bright and bored. To get the job, I had to endure an interview full of what-would-you-do-ifs, along with a background check, too. (I'm wanted in four states, but under the name "Lucky Morris.") Then came a prolonged dance with administrators and prospective students and their various family members. Because I wasn't a woman, the parents of one girl turned me down. Other potential students went to schools on the far side of town. Driving thirty minutes for fifty minutes of work and then driving home again . . . well, that seemed like an expensive way to make a buck. But finally the gifted facilitator at a nearby middle school found my resumé in the slush pile. She had a kid with a high IQ and a genuine fondness for science. I was hired without meeting the lad beforehand. ("I scare my teachers," the boy confided to me later, for good reasons.) I soon received two more boys, tutoring the three of them individually over a block of three well-paid hours. Then for the next year and a half I worked to keep them interested and challenged, or at least not too awfully bored.

I wrote "Boys" several years later. The teaching lessons used in the story were yanked directly from the games I played with my guys. And my tone with them remains in the story: accept nothing at its face value. Having no budget or special facilities, I concentrated on thought problems and ad hoc competitions. Then at the end of our first year, I got permission to take all three boys to the university museum and out to lunch. Fossils and cold sandwiches are always fun, but for me, the day's highlight was early on: We were walking past the cars parked in front of the school, and as an experiment, I asked the boys which of these cars was mine. Any guesses? At the time, I was driving a silver four-door Corolla. But one boy pointed at a muscle car with its rear end jacked up high and its body painted some obnoxious orange or red.

"Why do you think that's mine?" I asked, genuinely puzzled.

"Because that's a happening car," he declared happily. "And Mr. Reed, you're a happening guy!"

If only.

To write "The Cuckoo's Boys," I borrowed pieces of my students and invented the other characteristics—family problems as well as an atmosphere of suspicion and implied danger. In other words, whatever I felt was necessary for the fiction. My conception of the three clones was that they differed from one another for many good reasons. But the central difference wasn't their adoptive parents or the occasional mutations that would naturally creep into a mass cloning. To me, the difference was that they were functioning as identical twins multiplied over and over again. Twins raised in the same household tend to find separate interests, and one will typically be more outgoing and confident. (I went to junior high with twin boys who were equally funny, but in very different ways; none of us ever confused Dan for Dave or vice versa.) My working assumption was that genetically identical boys numbering in the thousands would feel an enormous pressure to diverge—particularly when none of them wants to be who they are. At least that was my logic for drawing three separate personalities attached to the same basic face.

Johnny Carson used to joke about the most obscure incidents in his childhood, and afterward he'd explain that if you were in his business long enough, you used everything. The old Nebraskan was ruthlessly mining his past for anything that might earn a laugh.

I know how he felt.

I mined my students for one story, and I've done the same with friends and family. For instance, my wife and I used to belong to a group of similar-aged couples that got together every month, playing games and eating too much while having a drink or two. (There was one weenie nondrinker in the group. Me.) Yet the casual reader shouldn't assume that I used those particular friends as templates for the characters in "One Last Game." Perhaps that's what I intended to do. Perhaps traces of them are there. But when I began the story—from the very first sentence—I found a voice that I liked quite a lot. Neil, the glowering and suspicious young teenager, is one of my favorite inventions. He was built from nothing, it seemed, and he was a perfect fit for what I was trying to accomplish—mature enough to see what was happening, bold enough to make his caustic views known, but thoroughly excluded from the adults' final game.

In the end, Neil's parents and the other grown-ups came from a different source. Decades ago, my parents belonged to a flock of upper-middle-class people who gathered at each other's big house in order to drink too much and then drink some more. Though far from impoverished, we were the poorest family in the group—a fact that led to some considerable discomfort. Whenever it was our turn to host, I would get shoved off into my folks' bedroom, on the questionable theory that it was a quiet refuge. Then I would lay awake half the night, listening to the scotch-fueled chatter and bawdy jokes. Neil's parents are mutations of my parents, and I can only hope that the suspicious, ill-tempered boy at the story's center is a sharper, braver version of me at that particular moment in life.

My wife and I were out for an evening with friends—a childless couple: vegetarians and devoted liberals with too many cats and every good intention. We were sitting in a coffee house near the University of Nebraska campus, and the topic drifted to the effect spouses have on each other's psyche. What he fears becomes what she fears, for instance. Suddenly one of us uttered the sentence, "She sees my monsters now." Honestly, I can't remember if I said it or if it was the other husband. Either way, I immediately saw significance in the words. "That would make a sweet title for a story," I announced. "I'm going to use it someday."

Our friends looked at each other, laughing nervously.

And that's when I knew I was going to use a character who was liberal and vegetarian and who kept too many cats. No, make that too many lemurs. After that, I let the story percolate through me for a few months, and I probably made a few false starts before finding the logic that would carry me along—a prisoner locked away in a tiny room, slowly and patiently manipulating the only soul that can help him win his freedom.

I was happy enough with the story, but Gardner had reservations about the final few lines.

There was a minor rewrite accomplished via e-mail.

Eventually "Monsters" was published and won a Reader's Choice Award from *Asimov's*. By then, our friends had moved out of state, and I've never gotten up enough steam to call them and confess what I did with that inspiration.

Whenever I begin a new project, I have a sense of just how good the story should be. Oftentimes I fall short of my goal. But if I am careful and smart, bold at the right moments and cowardly when it serves my needs, the finished project finds a home, and maybe it will become an honored guest.

"First Tuesday" was one of those sweet times when I had modest goals, but somewhere in the writing I surrendered myself to my characters. Of course I liked the young boy, Stefan. I feel comfortable drawing immature males. And speaking of which, his stepfather, Yancy, acquired a shadow-casting reality for me—a quality that science fiction neither chases nor often applauds. The president is pure wish fulfillment—someone I might like to see pacing in the Oval Office. Mom is a neurotic goof perfectly suited to her family. And the sister . . . well, I didn't know what I was doing with her. I felt more like a reader than the writer when Stefan ran to his older sister's room. When her door opened, I wasn't sure what we would find. But there was Candace, standing in front of the squid-skin with inflated boobs, fully realized and waiting for me.

Much of my work is instinctive, unconscious, and very nearly invisible. But that's true with all of us, whether we write fiction or insurance policies or compose the legend of our own lives. Most human activity is internalized. Awake or asleep, the brain is always doing a fantastic amount of work. I recently read that when an adult mammal closes his eyes, the visual centers of the brain continue firing at eighty percent capacity. But that isn't true of infants. Why not? The best guess is that babies haven't built a sophisticated model of their universe. To them, reality is a chaotic and senseless jumble that vanishes whenever they blink. Only later, as they mature, can they acquire their own peculiar vision of what is real and what might be. Then when their eyes close, their mind remains absorbed, playing with images and possibilities too swift and subtle to be noticed by the conscious self.

What I like best about "First Tuesday" is something that I see very little of in science fiction. My story is wrapped around a dysfunctional and peculiar but genuinely ordinary family. None of the four flesh-and-bone people will ever save the Earth from aliens or ride a starship to another world. (Maybe Stefan becomes famous, but I think the odds are long.) The boy and his relations are not building the future, they are merely riding on it, and only through illusions and self-deception can they maintain any sense of control.

Science fiction has made a comfortable life for itself by telling stories with a different cast of characters: brave explorers who have no families, brilliant scientists who decipher the most elaborate puzzles in twenty crisp pages, political leaders with a hawk-clear vision of the future, and those other plucky souls drawn from the same little stockroom. None of these characters are human. I certainly don't know them, not in my life or any honest history. Our explorers have often been lousy fathers fueled by vanity, luck, and a staggering ignorance of the dangers awaiting them. Scientists work best in swarms, and the toughest problems require generations to solve. Leaders with the clearest vision of the future are most likely to fail, inflicting lasting damage along the way. And meanwhile, the real future is being pulled from places never imagined, and it has been written by more souls and far odder circumstances than anything you will ever find in any one-hundred-thousand-word novel.

*   *   *

James Patrick Kelly has read "Coelacanths" several times, and whenever he sees me at a convention, he mentions the story, shrugs, and makes some soft, baffled sounds.

That rather pleases me.

Not that being obtuse was my goal. What I wanted was a story based on a minor incident in my own life, lending it as much strangeness as possible, while always keeping the characters as close to human as possible.

My backyard is decorated with little ponds filled with lazy fish, and beyond the fence is an acreage where raccoons live, coming out at night to eat trash and dog food and sometimes other treats. Years ago, one of those ring-tailed bastards grabbed one of my favorite fish, leaving nothing but a tidy pile of scales. I'll show him, I thought. I happen to know the director of our local Humane Society—a scrappy, little runner named Bob Downey. Bob loaned me a live trap and promised that the murderer would be released in a park miles outside the city limits. But raccoons are smarter than some people, I had always believed. How easy would it be to catch the culprit? Bob laughed gently while explaining, "But raccoons are a lot greedier than they are smart. If he's hungry, believe me, you won't be able to keep him out of a baited trap."

Maybe so. But over the next few weeks, I caught every local cat and opossum, but no raccoons. With winter bearing down, I just about gave up on the hunt. Then one morning I looked out the bathroom window and saw something huge and brown stuffed inside the wire cage. My first thought was that two massive house-cats had been trapped together. But when I went outside, I discovered a masked face staring at me with pale, sun-washed eyes. Then I noticed how the sand and stones of the patio had been disturbed under the trap, how little paws had clawed at the cage's doorway— from outside — in a desperate bid to free the prisoner.

The beast was massive in a never-missed-a-meal fashion. When I picked up the trap, using both hands, the nearby bushes began to shake. I saw two or maybe three raccoons drop out of their hiding places and sprint away. Which was when I realized, finally, that I had trapped somebody's brother and son, or maybe a family's care-less mother.

But I'm built of stubborn stuff. I drove my catch to the Humane Society—a three-mile trip, at the most. The women behind the desk promised they would care for my fat fish-killer. But they wouldn't take him to any distant park, since that would involve work. Instead, they planned to release the raccoon in the woods adjacent to the Humane Society—where almost every wild critter from Lincoln was released at one time or another. And I realized then that if my enemy had any sense of direction, and if I didn't hit the green lights on the drive home, he would probably beat me back to the patio.

After that adventure, I stopped caring about individual fish. To the best of my ability, I ignore the raccoons, and they remain fat and sassy on trash and dog food and the occasional golden pet that doesn't know better.

A year or two later, I began a story tentatively titled "Horsetails." In my backyard, beside the main pond, I keep a plastic pot filled with that very ancient plant—a short emerald-green forest that resembles a city of skyscrapers meant for very tiny souls. I intended to write about the people living in a great city that just happens to be set in some god's backyard pot. Then the story grew with added vantage points, including a human character named Procyon—the genus name for a raccoon, by the way.

In a sense, the science behind my story is inescapable. Evolution on Earth has produced a long parade of increasingly complicated organisms. I see no reason to believe that the parade now ends with human beings. (Or the crew with shovels who have to clean up our crap.) But we shouldn't feel too paranoid about our own future: If the tradition from every past stage in life continues, the appearance of superintelligent organisms will simply add species to the top of the heap, and the heap will grow wider. Bacteria once ruled our world, and, to a great extent, they still do. Insects were first to fly, but the appearance of birds and 747s hasn't chased them out of the skies. Gods will probably have an easier time than us spreading into the universe, but why shouldn't we ride with them? Cockroaches will, and bacteria. In that context, the universe of "Coelacanths" seems inevitable to me, and probably halfway bearable.

Not that I wish to live there, mind you.

For several reasons, the title became "Coelacanths." The horsetail image was too obscure, even for me. Keeping to my backyard setting, I decided to honor my fish, and since coelacanths are among the most famous of the world's unsuccessful vertebrates, I decided to put them in the final scene: My raccoon woman goes for a little swim in their water, but I don't allow her to eat any of the ignorant, fat, and prosperous creatures.

Humans losing control. Out of that same purplish vein, I bled "The Children's Crusade."

The title was on my to-do list for years and years. In college, my World Civilizations teacher spoke briefly about one of the more bizarre crusades—the marshalling of children throughout Europe who marched off in the direction of the Holy Land, most of them ending up dead or enslaved. The lecture had a lasting effect. What would bring modern kids into that sort of fix? I asked myself. After my daughter was born, I saw possibilities. I used her difficult birth and what I guessed could be trouble for her in the near-future, and the rest of the story followed naturally from those emotions and assumptions. Where "Crusade" changed, at least for me, was in the final scene: The daughter, Very, calmly voices an opinion that I hadn't consciously considered. She was attempting a dangerous, even foolhardy adventure, but it was her life and her soul to risk, and shouldn't she be allowed the choice?

As a side note, I'll make a small confession: Some years ago, I was a guest of honor at a wonderful science fiction convention in Nancy, France. Serious people asked what I thought about a manned mission to Mars. It's one of the standard questions in the SF field, and I guess my audience expected a standard answer. But instead of demanding a much-enlarged space program, I argued that a manned mission would be a mistake. First of all, there is the expense. If the interest is science, then robots will learn more than people can and for a fraction of the cost. Secondly, there are the technical limits, at least for the present. I can imagine NASA placing living bodies on the other world, but bringing them home again will be a much more difficult trick—an element that I used in "Crusade." My ultimate doubt though comes from the demands of moral behavior. There are good and growing reasons to believe that life exists on Mars—the present whiff of methane in the atmosphere is the best evidence—but if there is life, it exists in small, possibly fragile populations. Studying these bugs with clean robots will be difficult enough, but it would be impossible to keep a crew of farting, skin-sloughing humans from leaving behind a forest of alien bacteria.

In my mind, Mars should be allowed its solitude, at least until we have half an understanding about what it is that we will modify/destroy beyond all recognition.

My father fought in World War II—a sailor onboard the small escort carrier *Bismarck Sea*. On the night of February 21, 1945, a suicide pilot hit and sank his ship, killing more than half the crew, and my father spent his most memorable birthday floating in the dark waters off Iwo Jima.

Years later, while I was suffering through eighth grade, a class-mate invited his own father to come to school and speak to our honors class. A career officer in the military, the man spoke in clear, unsentimental terms about the ongoing war in Southeast Asia. He had fought in the Tet Offensive, and, despite the carnage, he was very much pro-war. But his matter-of-fact tales of torture and carnage made a lasting impression on at least one spellbound eighth grader.

When the stakes are exceptionally high, what rules govern a soldier's conduct?

"Savior" mixes elements of these two fathers, and, because it felt right, I borrowed an incident from a youthful hunting trip. The skunk is genuine, and the tomato juice, and a dog terribly sad-dened by his horrible circumstances.

For years, "Winemaster" was a working title, plus a few rough pages that led nowhere.

In its first incarnation, the story put a quiet and very nervous man by the same name inside a sealed bus traveling across a poi-soned, unpopulated landscape. Sharing the ride was a fat, obnox-ious armed guard—a rent-a-cop based loosely on a fellow I knew back in college. Some undisclosed danger lay over the horizon, and the two men had an unpleasant conversation ending in silence. At that point, I lost interest in the story. But the two men continued their ride inside my head, and a story that was rather dif-ferent and much more workable eventually found its way to me.

I drove Winemaster on a route that I have traveled once or twice. The fat man followed after him, but until the final pages, I had no clear idea what he wanted from the timid refugee. Then I reached the end, and I discovered a logic that felt nothing but inevitable.

"Abducted Souls" steals heavily from my college experience. I went to Nebraska Wesleyan with a group of high school friends, most of whom were subsequently converted to Christianity. I never joined the faithful. But since it was a small college, and because I didn't belong to any fraternity or other quasi-religious organization, I still socialized with my old buddies. In the cafeteria, I would eat with the Christians, and I could talk with most of them, and, believe me, I could happily date their women. And I studied them like a scientist who sits in a jungle clearing, watching some tribe of polite, magic-worshipping apes.

My junior year was especially painful—adolescent unhappiness and sleepless nights—and later, when I was emerging from my slump, one of the Christian women admitted that her group had thought I was very close to converting. In reality, I was closer to suicide than accepting Christ in my life. But of course a lot of Christians are here today because their ancestors were trapped in some awful corner, physical or emotional, and there was no way out but to fling oneself on the first raft that drifted past.

In these times, I asked myself, what would it take for someone with my temperament and beliefs to be tempted, even for a single night, to become a True Believer?

I don't remember where I read this story: A bride was selected for the Russian tsar, or was it one of the Mongol conquerors? Either way, she was a beautiful young maiden who lived in the far reaches of Siberia, and, accompanied by guards and her family, she began the enormous journey to Moscow. Several years later and with thousands of miles of wilderness crossed, she had one or two children. She may well have been pregnant again when she arrived at her fiancé's door. A guard was the father, and there might have been retribution against him. But according to my soggy memory, the wedding went off without a hitch.

This is an illustration of how my head works, and how it doesn't.

I don't know the source of this historical tidbit, or even if it's genuine. Maybe I dreamed it up on my own. Whatever the truth, I thought it could be the basis for a pretty good story, perhaps involving aliens or long-lived people. Years passed, but nothing happened to the idea. Finally, I decided to work another story into the *Marrow* universe. I wrenched the idea out of my to-do file and forced my queen into a vital role that she really didn't want to fulfill. Which is perhaps why, in the end, she found the means to escape her fate in "River of the Queen."

Good for her.

And finally, again, "Night of Time."

Perhaps "On the Brink of That Bright New World" is the oldest published story in this collection, but, by a rather different measure, "Time" is its senior by several years. I wrote the first version in college for a short-story class. It's been twenty years since I last looked at that particular manuscript. But what always lingered in my mind was the brilliant historian and his seemingly simple-minded sidekick, the two mismatched souls wandering across an ancient and exceptionally complex landscape.

My audience for the original "Night of Time" was a poet/professor and less than a dozen undergraduates. I wrote five stories for the class, and this one was easily my best effort. But my alien duo wasn't well received by my peers. Few forces in nature are more conservative than twenty-year-old English majors. Most of the students said nothing favorable and nothing unfavorable either. They had absolutely no interest in science fiction. But that didn't stop the others from generating comments. Our best writer put on a very sour expression, complaining that nothing about my work was real. Science fiction wasn't real, which was why she couldn't enjoy any of it. Then our second-best writer—a scrawny, glowering fellow with a perpetually depressed air—tried to give me some concrete advice. My story was laced with a numbing mishmash of history lessons; wouldn't it be better to give the reader more coherent information about all these dead civilizations and extinct aliens?

Thirty years later, the easy response would be to point out that nobody at that table was named Joy Williams or T. Coraghessan Boyle. To my knowledge, none of my fellow students ever managed careers for themselves in mainstream fiction. But they were smart people and better writers than I was at the time, and their criticism had value. The original "Night" had only two nonhuman characters. Science fiction loves the idea of aliens, but most SF stories keep human beings placed squarely in the middle of the action. By adding Ash, I made "Night" into a more approachable work. And instead of letting my Vozzen historian lecture about every subject, I kept him squarely focused on the themes that mattered.

In a sense, this is a belated thanks.

As a rule, I find most adolescents to be a rigid and rather cranky lot who work hard to fit into small groups. But if the group decides to be adaptable and imaginative, then governments will fall and art forms will be reinvented.

By contrast, middle age can bring a more tolerant attitude.

My poet/professor, William Kloefkorn, didn't normally read science fiction. He admitted that weakness on several occasions. But he was always open-minded about what I was trying to accomplish, and before the semester ended, he gave me two extremely helpful bits of advice. In his comments about "Night of Time," he wrote that I had a considerable imagination, but I needed to learn how to keep it under control. And he told everybody in the class everything he knew about writing novels. "Type like hell," he suggested, "and number your pages."

Both of those suggestions have helped me enormously over the years.

Meanwhile Bill Kloefkorn has become Nebraska's official state poet. Since Lincoln is a small city, we cross paths on occasion, and he has remained interested and enthusiastic about my work. For that and for the help he gave me long ago, I think it's fair to dedicate this collection to him, with much thanks.

A final note:

Since that plane flight to Boston, I again reread "Night of Time." Then, one Saturday afternoon, my daughter went down for a long nap and I used the time to stretch out on my own bed and close my eyes. When I woke, I had a new novel in my head. I would tell the enormous life story of Ash, and I would give him a conundrum that no mortal should face, and in the process, the Great Ship itself would be explained.

But the rest of that story needs to wait, at least for a little while.

Robert Reed
Lincoln, Nebraska
December 2004

Two thousand copies of this book have been printed by the Maple-Vail Book Manufacturing Group, Binghamton, NY, for Golden Gryphon Press, Urbana, IL. The typeset is Electra with Equinox display, printed on 55# Sebago. Typesetting by The Composing Room, Inc., Kimberly, WI.

The Dragons of Springplace

ISBN 0-9655901-6-X

Cloth, 312pp, $23.95

Robert Reed's
First Short Fiction Collection

"Reed has one of the truly original imaginations among
the newer generation of SF writers, and his unique vision
is often expressed more powerfully in his short fiction . . .
What is rapidly becoming a trademark setting for Reed's
best short fiction is the planet-sized, ancient, multicultural
generation starship that shows up in stories like 'The
Remoras,' 'Chrysalis,' and 'Aeon's Child,' and very nearly
steals the show every time."
— Gary K. Wolfe, *Locus*

Golden Gryphon Press
www.goldengryphon.com